"A technically ambitious performance. . . . Clifford and Janice are wonderfully realized."
—Stuart Dybek, *Chicago Tribune*

"One of those novels bound to be beloved simply because it rings so true."
—*The Advocate*

"Startling. . . . A must-read novel from a very talented writer." —*Out*

"Sweeps through the sexual revolution and into the age of AIDS with all its powers of revelation intact. . . . An impressive, insightful novel."
—*Library Journal*

"Greg Johnson has proved himself a writer whose best work penetrates the hearts and minds of his characters with enviable clarity and ease. . . . As an observer of the urban South, he's on to something new. No folksiness here—instead, there is life in a city outside the New York-Los Angeles axis with a flavor of its own."
—*San Francisco Chronicle*

"Memorable . . . a thoughtful novel . . . Mr. Johnson has a gift."
—*New York Times Book Review*

"Johnson is an excellent writer." —*Atlanta Journal-Constitution*

"Despite its sexual frankness, *Pagan Babies* is more about love than sexual expression. Johnson explores the complexity of desire between gays and straights."
—*Asheville Citizen-Times*

"Bold and strong and strikingly original . . . I liked *Pagan Babies* very much indeed."
—Alice Adams, author of *Almost Perfect*

"Radiant . . . characters rich with life." —Frederick Busch, author of *Closing Arguments*

GREG JOHNSON's fiction has appeared in a variety of magazines and in such anthologies as *Prize Stories: The O. Henry Awards* and *New Stories from the South: The Year's Best.* His first collection of critically acclaimed short stories, *Distant Friends*, won him the Georgia Author of the Year Award in 1990. He lives in Atlanta.

OTHER BOOKS BY GREG JOHNSON

SHORT STORIES
A Friendly Deceit (1992)
Distant Friends (1990)

POETRY
Aid and Comfort (1993)

CRITICISM
Understanding Joyce Carol Oates (1987)
Emily Dickinson: Perception and the Poet's Quest (1985)

Greg Johnson

*PAGAN
BABIES*

A PLUME BOOK

PLUME
Published by the Penguin Group
Penguin Books USA Inc., 375 Hudson Street, New York, New York 10014, U.S.A.
Penguin Books Ltd, 27 Wrights Lane, London W8 5TZ, England
Penguin Books Australia Ltd, Ringwood, Victoria, Australia
Penguin Books Canada Ltd, 10 Alcorn Avenue, Toronto, Ontario, Canada M4V 3B2
Penguin Books (N.Z.) Ltd, 182–190 Wairau Road, Auckland 10, New Zealand

Penguin Books Ltd, Registered Offices: Harmondsworth, Middlesex, England

Published by Plume, an imprint of Dutton Signet, a division of Penguin Books USA Inc.
Previously published in a Dutton edition.

First Plume Printing, March, 1994
10 9 8 7 6 5 4 3 2

REGISTERED TRADEMARK—MARCA REGISTRADA

LIBRARY OF CONGRESS CATALOGING - IN - PUBLICATION DATA
Johnson, Greg, 1953–
    Pagan babies / Greg Johnson.
        p.   cm.
    ISBN 0-452-27132-0
    1. Man-woman relationships—United States—Fiction.
2. Friendship—United States—Fiction.   3. Catholics—United States—
Fiction.   4. Gay men—United States—Fiction.   5. Women—United
States—Fiction.   I. Title.   II. Series.
[PS3560.037775P34   1994]
813'.54—dc20   93–27532
                                                                      CIP

Printed in the United States of America
Set in Perpetua
Designed by Steven N. Stathakis

—for my parents,
Jo Ann and Raymond,
and for my grandmothers,
Loretta Johnson (b. 1903)
and Johanna Untersee (b. 1892)

I was still my own unhappy prisoner,
unable to live in such a state yet pow-
erless to escape from it. Where could
my heart find refuge from itself?
Where could I go, yet leave myself
behind? Was there any place where I
should not be a prey to myself?

—ST. AUGUSTINE, *The Confessions*

Wherefore receive now from my lip
Peripatetic scholarship. . . .
Ruling one's life by commonsense
How can one fail to be intense?

—JAMES JOYCE, "The Holy Office"

Part

ONE

J a n i c e

Children approach the altar, hands folded as in prayer. Boys to the left, girls to the right, white jackets and white dresses in two immaculate lines down the aisle, every movement practiced and memorized, perfected. A boy approaches Father Culhane with his small pink tongue pushed out, quivering. Hands folded. Eyes that close briefly, the lids trembling. The church packed with family and friends and well-wishers gives an audible *Aah* as the host enters the child's mouth. One sigh. In unison. Then a girl approaches, black ringlets and pale cheeks. Wobbly knees. Tongue quivering again. Hands folded again. *Aah* says the well-dressed congregation, attentive and eager, ready for the next child, never tiring of this.

And so on. Janice Rungren is the eighth child, the fourth girl, to approach Father Culhane in his glittering white vestments, the chalice raised in his hand like a bright beacon she must follow, not letting her eyes dart away. Her blond hair shining, brushed lovingly down her back by her mother and her cousin Ruthie, her scapular scratching her chest just where her heart lies pounding, frantically pounding, she approaches anxiously like all the others, her trembling hands folded so that they almost touch her chin. She closes her eyes, feels the papery host on her tongue, but the pounding of her heart distracts her and she doesn't turn to leave quite quickly enough, Father Culhane has to touch her shoulder and frown and nod toward the pews. Then she understands: it is over. Then she gets moving, turning away from Father Culhane, her legs brittle as matchsticks.

Now she is facing the congregation, the smiling faces, a bobbing sea of faces, but she can't pick out her parents or her Uncle Jake and Aunt Lila or Ruthie her cousin and best friend, who will make her First Holy Communion next year and is surely watching Janice's every move. Janice's heart pounds, skitters, she feels paralyzed before the congregation, but now she gets moving, her hands are folded beneath her chin exactly as Sister Mary Immaculata had instructed and she has reached the girls' pew and nothing is wrong. She can now turn her back to the smiling staring bobbing faces—hundreds, thousands of faces!—and take her place beside the other girls and all will be well. Yet Janice is hurrying, she isn't remembering Sister's patient careful instructions and so it happens, inevitably it happens, that one of her white-patent shoe straps catches against a corner of the kneeler and the church tilts crazily and Janice is falling, she bangs her bare knee against the wooden bench, she cries *Ow!* involuntarily but not as loud (so her mother and Ruthie will later whisper, consolingly) as Janice believes at the moment, in her extreme embarrassment and fear. The other white-veiled little girls can hardly contain themselves, their heads are bowed, fingers over their mouths, giggling, shoulders shaking, as scarlet-faced Janice sits down at last, her eyes stinging, her heart an anguished lump in her chest, for she knows everyone saw her stumble and fall, they heard her cry *Ow!* like a little idiot, unable to practice self-control at the critical moment, unable to do anything right.

Her face throbs and glows, her hot eyes look straight ahead as Father Culhane continues distributing the host as though nothing had happened.

Minutes later the pew is filled, the right front pew with its row of little girls, and it might have been that nothing *had* happened, that Janice Rungren had not fallen, had not become upset, had done nothing wrong at all!—for now she sits quietly, looking no different from the other little girls, her veil in place, hands resting in her lap. Her cheeks pale, her heart perfectly still. Like all the others.

April, that had been; a brilliant April morning when she'd stumbled and fallen during the First Holy Communion service at Sacred Heart Church, had fallen and made a commotion and ruined the ceremony, as Mary Frances Dennehy and Lucia Gonzalez informed her at recess the next morning, sticking out their tongues and flouncing away from Janice. Never mind that her mother had said not to worry about it, receiving the body of Christ in her own little body was what counted, not some tiny stumble that hardly anyone had noticed; never mind that her cousin Ruthie gave her long doleful looks at the "celebration" dinner that night at Uncle Jake and Aunt Lila's, looks of commiseration, looks of deep sorrow; never mind the expensive crystal rosary her Grandma Rungren had sent special delivery from California as a Holy Communion gift, with a note saying how "proud" she was, what a "good little girl" Janice was—never mind all that, Janice knew that Mary Frances and Lucia were right, she could interpret the smug looks of the other little girls who had not stumbled and fallen, she understood the just-perceptible coolness in Sister Mary Immaculata's behavior during arithmetic class that next week, her pale blue eyes not quite meeting Janice's.

How they had practiced, after all! How tirelessly Sister had drilled the boys and girls, showing them how to walk, how to fold their hands, exactly how to put out their tongues when the big moment came! Once reentering the pew the children should walk sideways, Sister said, they should keep facing the altar and let their feet move sideways, methodically, slowly. "Crabwise," Sister Immaculata said. "This is how crabs walk," she said, not smiling, moving herself with great skill down the pew so that all the children could see. Some of them poked each other and whispered jokes, saying that Sister Immaculata was so tiny and frail that she looked more like a miniature penguin than a crab, but Janice hadn't misbehaved during the rehearsals; she had watched closely, hungrily. Though she could not see Sister's legs or feet underneath her floor-length black habit, nonetheless she understood, the toes were to stay pointed forward, you were to make your legs into a pair of scissors opening and closing, as Sister said, but *sideways*, so that you would always be facing the altar, *crabwise*, so that your continued earnest adoration of the Host of Hosts would seem to be your most pressing concern, not finding your own seat. Did everyone understand? *Yes, Sister*, the class had said in unison, day after day. Were there any more questions? *No, Sister*, the class had intoned, in one practice session after another, until even Sister Immaculata, not known as one of the more relaxed and trusting nuns, had believed that nothing could go wrong.

And nothing would have, of course—except for Janice. All the children, boys and girls, had lived up to Sister's expectations—except for Janice. Guiltily, Janice spent much of her time remembering the pre-Holy Communion meeting that Sister Immaculata had held in the church basement, at 8:00 that fateful Sunday morning; it wasn't another rehearsal, Sister had told the children, but she did want to "inspect the troops," as she said, she did need to check veils, shoes, fingernails, she always felt better if she had the children to herself, during that last nerve-racking hour. And besides, she had something to give them. As their homeroom teacher and as First Holy Communion coordinator she had some gifts to distribute, gifts of little monetary but great spiritual value which she hoped the children would treasure all their lives. (Of course, there were also gifts for Sister Immaculata, purchased by a group of the children's parents and presented by Mary Frances Dennehy's father, Sacred Heart's wealthiest parishioner, after the ceremony: a bouquet of pink roses, a plain but handsome stopwatch inside a chamois pouch and drawstring, and as a "gag" gift a shiny new silver whistle ["Mary Frances says you've just about worn out your old one," Mr. Dennehy joked after Sister opened the gift] of the kind all the nuns employed to get the attention of their students, and as punctuation during lineups and marching drills, and as a symbolic bleep of authority whenever that might be needed.) And what lovely gifts Sister Immaculata distributed to the children!—holy cards of the Sacred Heart, of the Assumption of the Virgin Mary, and of the "Little Flower," St. Thérèse of Lisieux; a new missal covered in white leatherette with a tiny crucifix embedded inside the front cover, and on the facing page an elaborate gold inscription that read *My First Holy Communion* and separate lines for

"Name" and "Date"; a white pearlized rosary for the girls, a hand-some black rosary for the boys; and most important of all—as Sister informed them—a box containing their Holy Communion flower. Janice saw the excitement in Sister's eyes as she passed out the plain wooden boxes, she saw the rapturous pinkish glow in her cheeks as the children opened the boxes and exclaimed over the perfect white flower and its garland of succulent green leaves that lay nestled inside. But Sister told them, clearing her throat, getting down to business: "The leaves of this flower represent your earthly lives, your bodies which eventually will grow and age and wither and die. The white flower, however, represents your soul, which will triumph in eternity. If you look in that box a month from now, or in a year, or in ten years, the leaves will be withered and corrupted. They will *die*. But the flower will never die. It will stay white and beautiful forever, just as your souls will be white and beautiful after your First Holy Communion. The flower will not die, just as your souls will not die."

Sister paused dramatically to let this sink in, then said she would answer any questions.

"Why did the flower come in such a plain box?—it's like a big matchbox," the plump and freckled Mary Frances Dennehy asked.

"Aah," Sister said, lifting her forefinger, "the box holding the flower represents your coffin, the container of your bodily corruption."

The children looked again at the box.

"But if the flower represents the soul," said Annie Shelton, the only other blond little girl in the class besides Janice, and the pupil who had maintained the highest grade average both last year and this year, "then why would it be in the box? Doesn't the soul rise out of the body after death? Doesn't it go to heaven?"

"Well, yes," Sister said, fumbling, "but once the leaves die, you see, the box no longer represents the coffin. Then it's just a nice little wooden box that holds the flower, which represents your im-mortal soul."

Annie Shelton was frowning; tiny creases along her forehead were visible despite the white netting of her veil. She said, "But *before* the leaves wither, while the box *still* represents a coffin, wouldn't the soul, which is represented by the flower, have already risen up to heaven? I mean, the soul wouldn't *still* be contained—"

"Well now," Sister interrupted, with her little mocking laugh, her deadly *harrumph,* "let's leave all that to the theologians, Annie. Are there any more questions?"

"What if the flower does die, just like the leaves?" asked Brian McGreevy, a dark-haired studious boy who already, in second grade, had begun showing an aptitude for arithmetic and science. Although Sister Immaculata taught arithmetic, Janice knew that she wasn't all that fond of Brian: he asked too many questions. Occasionally Sister would ignore Brian when he raised his hand in class.

"It won't," Sister said. "It can't die."

"But what if it does?" Brian asked. "What if *mine* does?"

"It won't, it *can't,*" Sister repeated, a bit more sharply. "It's impossible."

"But what if—"

Sister blew her whistle, loud.

The look of gentle rapture had left her face, Janice saw, reluctantly obeying Sister's orders to close the little wooden box, put all the gifts away, and begin to contemplate the momentous occasion of Christ's body and blood entering their own bodies less than an hour from now. ("The Host is *not* a symbol," Father Culhane and Sister Immaculata had both insisted, during the weeks and months of preparation, "it is the actual body and blood of Christ," and one day Janice turned in her seat toward Billy Henson, the profusely freckled but really cute boy she had liked all during first and second grade, and cried, "Yecch!"—which made Billy and several other children giggle uncontrollably and earned Janice a rap on the knuckles and a black cross next to her name for that day.) Clearly, Sister was excited and nervous, and in those last minutes of waiting before they proceeded upstairs to the vestibule for the communion procession she got even more nervous, glancing repeatedly at the ancient wall clock above the main basement doors, taking deep breaths, sighing, once or twice blowing her whistle for no discernible reason; and naturally Sister's jittery behavior communicated itself to the children. Often in the long ensuing weeks Janice had tried telling herself that she was nervous because Sister was nervous, that she wouldn't have stumbled and fallen if everyone—priest and nuns, parishioners, family members, the children themselves!—hadn't made such a big deal of this, and occasionally she went to her bottom dresser drawer and took out the little wooden box as if to reassure herself that the flower was still pure and unsullied and beautiful, and of course it was (though the leaves had turned brown and icky, just as Sister had predicted), and then she would look at the little box that symbolized a coffin and try to imagine her own coffin and herself inside it. Would that be so terrible? she thought gloomily. Lying in her coffin forever, having no troubles at all?

So went those awful weeks between First Holy Communion and the end of school, Janice bothered by her friends' teasing at school and bad dreams almost every night and that vague lumpish sorrow that lay stubbornly inside her chest, just about where she imagined her lily-white soul should have been, though Janice had begun to believe she'd been "standing behind the door," as the schoolyard joke went, when God passed out the souls. Nor was her father any help, saying things like *Don't worry, you livened things up a bit—nobody likes a little Miss Perfect, anyway,* and another night, while having a few beers and looking through a photo album crammed with Holy Communion pictures (her mother was up in her room, that evening: had not come down for dinner), his murmuring yes, yes, she'd screwed up but didn't we all, his eyes glassy and faraway as he tousled Janice's fine blond hair, rubbing his knuckles along her scalp in a way that Janice, technically speaking, hated, though she loved to hear her father talk and so she didn't complain. And her mother, what of Janice's mother? At least her father was tall, hawk-nosed, handsome; at least her little friends in the neighborhood and at school and even her cousin Ruthie thought he was "cute" and giggled whenever he teased them or played the Big Bad Wolf and said he'd like to eat them up, at least he came home from the office where he sold insurance, sold lots and lots of insurance and won plaques and free vacations to Puerto Rico, came home and bounced Janice on his knee and said she was his sweet little blond-haired girl, and she wouldn't ever forget that, would she? "But what about Mommy?" Janice asked, trying not to sound cranky (though it was Mommy, not Daddy, who complained often about Janice being "cranky," or "fidgeting" too much, or behaving "like a little brat"; it was Mommy, not Daddy). "Why does Mommy stay in her room so much," she asked, "why won't she take me anywhere, why doesn't she get dressed in the morning like other mommies instead of staying in her housecoat till after lunch, why does she"—but her father put one finger to his lip and winked.

"Ssh," he said. "Mommy's tired, very tired."

"Tired from what? She doesn't do any—"

Then her father grabbed Janice's sides and threw her on the bed and tickled her like crazy, and yes Janice laughed and laughed, and no she could not stop.

At other times Janice didn't laugh, though she tried to keep her parents' stepped-up arguing at the fringes of her awareness; only much later did she know how much she had heard and comprehended. But yes they argued, Mr. Rungren wanting Janice to have a baby brother or sister, Mrs. Rungren *not* wanting Janice to have a baby brother or sister, Janice overheard the arguments from the TV room or from her dainty four-poster bed with the white canopy and big flouncy pillows, her mother and father shouting in their own bedroom about something called "the pill," Mr. Rungren saying they should listen to the Pope, Mrs. Rungren saying he'd never listened to the Pope before, so why now, could he please answer that? He wouldn't want another baby so badly if *he* had to suffer that kind of pain, said Janice's mother, in her whining resentful voice, and anyway her doctor had said another baby might not be a good idea, might be risky, and Mr. Rungren shouted that he'd said no such thing, those were lies, lies, why couldn't Janice's mother try to be a normal healthy woman, do her duty as a wife and mother, was it so much to ask, really, a man wanting more children in his house? And soon they were moving to another house, after all, a much bigger house; why did Janice's mother think he worked so hard, didn't she think he wanted a son, a boy in his own image, didn't he have normal fatherly wishes and emotions?

And Janice's mother had wept, wept. "You don't understand, you don't care about *me,* about the pain and anguish, about having another child nagging after me, wanting this, wanting that, it's too much, it's too *much*," but then Janice's father had lost his temper, and as Janice turned a page in her illustrated copy of *Jungle Book* he shouted, "So you're afraid of a little pain, are you, well how about this?"—and there was a slapping sound, he must have been slapping her a little—"how's this for pain, how's this," and then the bedroom door slammed and her father thudded down the stairs and out into his workroom and from behind the master bedroom door Janice could hear her mother's soft weeping, a kind of weak and ragged weeping, helpless, babyish, and Janice had reached aside for her Chatty Cathy doll and slapped its dimpled cheeks and whispered, "Well, how about this, how's this? Well?"

Thank God, the summer intervened. Her birthday came in mid-June, her eighth birthday; there were heaps of presents from Mom and Dad and from Ruthie, of course, since the girls were so close, and Grandma sent money from Los Angeles so Janice could "pick out a little something" for herself. These days her parents bickered rather than fought, they didn't talk about babies anymore, and Janice's mother spent more and more time at home, even arranging to have groceries delivered because she didn't like driving, didn't like going out by herself. And anyway she liked being home with Janice, as she told Aunt Lila over the phone, though Janice had gotten so moody this summer—kids did go through the phases didn't they, her mother laughed, as Janice listened from the top of the stairs or from a little-used extension out in the hallway near the garage. Janice with her lips parted, her eyes narrowed. Janice with her heart like a fist in her chest, beating, stubbornly beating.

It was late June, it was July, for a while Janice had dreaded going back to school but now she longed for it; she didn't like staying home all day with her mother, who spent hours getting up and dressing, daubing her face with powder and reddish-orange lipstick and heavy purplish eye makeup that made her look like either a raccoon or a bandit, Janice couldn't decide which, and all for nothing because she wouldn't leave the house. Her mother puzzled over mail order catalogs when it was time to buy Janice's school clothes and talked on the phone to Aunt Lila and every few hours did a load of laundry or dusted a shelf, and spent the rest of her time criticizing Janice for keeping her room so messy, for playing too noisily, for fidgeting, for wanting to go outside where almost anything could happen. But when Janice did go outside she no longer enjoyed herself; she felt bored by the neighborhood kids she had once liked. After all, they hadn't witnessed Janice's humiliating stumble and fall during First Holy Communion last spring, and she couldn't have explained to them about the dreams in which the entire ordeal replayed itself, and Janice stumbled again, and fell, and said *Ow!* in that single painfully drawn-out syllable to which she would often wake, her legs twitching under the covers. In short, the neighborhood kids were non-Catholic—they didn't count. In their stupidity and innocence they angered her, too, so she would slap her Chatty Cathy doll or make a ferociously sour face when she heard her mother calling or pinch her cousin Ruthie during their frequent weekend visits for no reason, knowing Ruthie would whimper quietly for a while, her eyes big and blue and stunned behind her glasses, but knowing also that Ruthie adored her pretty blond cousin no matter what, so Ruthie would never tell and Janice would never be punished.

So when September does arrive Janice is actually looking forward to school, she knows this is where she belongs. She no longer cares what the nuns think, she doesn't care if she gets into trouble, she doesn't mind if kids like Mary Frances Dennehy and Lucia Gonzalez shove her during recess or write "Janice is a stupid baby" on their book covers; even when she learns that Sister Immaculata has been reassigned from second to third grade and will be her homeroom teacher again this year, Janice takes the news in stride. Over the summer Sister has gotten thinner and tinier if that were possible, but still her eyes roll and dance as she talks about all the fun they'll have this year, then turn bright and hawklike as she lays down the rules and describes the penalties for miscreant behavior. On that first morning she also introduces a new boy in the class, a boy Janice is startled and intrigued to find sitting directly in front of her, so that she can see only the back of his head—dark hair cut so short that his scalp shows through, bony but strong-looking shoulders, a profile (Janice stretches out into the aisle, trying to see him better) that looks a bit prideful, with a high forehead and a narrow, hard-set chin. Sister Immaculata asks the boy to stand up and turn around so that the class can see him, and Janice notices his eyes, which look both scared and detached from all this, if not better than all this, and a thin mouth that is turned down on one side in what seems to be a smile, a grudging and self-conscious half-smile, and when he sits down again Janice feels a little chill run down her back.

Cute, she thinks.

She begins kicking the back of the new boy's desk.

For the rest of September she kicks at his desk occasionally, when she thinks of it, but he never turns around; at recess she stands near him and giggles, one hand over her mouth, but he always glances in another direction, that one side of his mouth turned down, looking bored as he waits for the bell to ring. (As a new boy, he isn't accepted into the other boys' games those first few months, but spends recess time just walking around the playground, hands in his pockets, as if he's here by some mistake and is patiently waiting for that mistake to be rectified.) Once, when he's straddling one end of a seesaw by himself, she comes over and sits down on the other end; but he won't put his weight down, won't start the seesaw going, and finally gets off and lets Janice's end fall to the ground. *That* hurts Janice's feelings, and that afternoon she kicks at his desk during arithmetic class with a special ferocity and Sister Immaculata notices and cries out, "Janice! Get yourself up here—at once!"

So Janice drags her feet up the aisle, not glancing at the new boy, and when she reaches Sister's desk the nun harangues her for five minutes, ten minutes, asks her what has gotten into her this year, why can't she be still, why is she always whispering and kicking at the other students who are trying to learn something and be good boys and girls, how can Janice live with herself knowing that she has more black crosses for conduct beside her name than any other student, girl or boy? And what *is* she giggling about, anyway, doesn't she know enough to be ashamed, isn't she embarrassed to be criticized in front of the whole class, or has she gone beyond that?

Sister pauses.

Janice shrugs her shoulders, reddening, but she isn't embarrassed or angry, she's used to this by now. Throwing her eyes to the ceiling, she holds out her hands.

"You're like an accident," Sister Immaculata says sternly, using one of her favorite expressions as she strikes Janice's knuckles with her ruler not one but three times, "like an accident waiting to happen. Do you hear that? You remember who told you that, Janice Rungren. *I* did."

(Janice remembers something her mother had shouted at her father, last summer, as Janice listened from her room: "I'm going to use something, I'm *not* risking another accident!—not again, not ever again!")

"Yes, Sister," Janice says, giggling. On her way back to the seat she glances at the new boy, who is watching one corner of the ceiling, pointedly ignoring Janice. But later, much later, he comes up to her and asks for her two hands, asks if the ruler hurt very much, and she decides to lie and says yes, yes it hurt a lot, and he takes the two hands and he isn't smiling that little smart-alecky smile, he's very serious, very solemn, and he lifts the two hands and kisses them one by one. Janice's heart fills. Janice's eyes fill. When she wakes up and understands that she was dreaming, her heart stays full for a minute or two, she doesn't feel cheated that it was only a dream; instead she feels elated and hopeful, she feels that she was transported to heaven for a moment, just a moment, and despite everything she's going to get that feeling back. She lies there for a long time, very still, staring at the blank white underside of her canopy, and solemnly she makes a vow: she'll make that moment happen, make it real, if it's the last thing Janice Rungren ever does.

Clifford

Sister Mary Immaculata stands before the class, her head tilted, her smile a bit rakish and self-absorbed—her usual demeanor when speaking of sacred things. She is diminutive, sharp-faced, spry, her competence and energy only highlighted by the voluminous black folds of her habit, the big wooden rosary beads clicking at her waist, the stiff squarish white wimple that gives Sister her uncanny resemblance to Anne of Cleves. A nun's near-total concealment draws her pupils' eyes ineluctably to her face, and Sister Immaculata's is particularly animated, capable of startling shifts. For eight hours daily each pupil may chart his worth in the sight of God by Sister's expressions (especially those in her steely-blue eyes, behind her rimless spectacles) and the children are familiar with her dazzling repertoire: the looks of deep-browed scorn, the sidelong glances full of mischief and fun, the grimaces of utter exasperation as Sister flings her eyes toward Heaven. When religious matters are involved, however, Sister becomes something of a child herself. Today she is excited, her eyes moist, her very smile tilted, a bit drunken, as she speaks in her rushing melodic voice here on this ordinary Wednesday, at just after nine in the morning. She is telling her third-grade class about pagan babies.

Behind Sister's head is a chalkboard of deep green, spanning the front of the room, and lining the wall above are illustrations of the more important fractions—½, ¼, ⅛—cut from construction paper and decorated with crayoned borders, with tiny stars of red, green, royal blue, with sequins of gold and silver. Sister Immaculata teaches arithmetic to grades one through six here at St. John Bosco, but third grade is her homeroom, she has thirty-five students, she is known as one of the stricter, more pious nuns. She is nothing like Sister Mary Catherine, who plays basketball at recess with the girls and sometimes the boys, her mannish frame and grinning ruddy face barely constrained by her habit; she is certainly nothing like Sister Mary Ignatius, the youngest and prettiest nun, who is often late for her English classes and even for mass in the chapel, and who sometimes giggles behind her fingers when the stentorian voice of Sister Mary Joseph, the school's no-nonsense principal, comes over the loudspeaker at 3:15 for end-of-day announcements. No, Sister Immaculata is competent but unremarkable, she goes by the book, she takes equal pleasure in dispensing holy cards with a benevolent smile and in despotically wielding her ruler. Perhaps because of her mathematical background, she has an above-average love of regimentation: her rows of students are neatly arranged as in a geometrical design. There are five rows, seven students each. The fourth student in the second row is the new boy, Clifford Bannon, and he alone is not paying strict attention to Sister's discussion of pagan babies, of the

grinding poverty in Pakistan and Honduras, of the Christlike mission-
ary work of the Maryknoll fathers for which the children, several
times each year, are asked to shell out their nickels and dimes.

. Even now in November, three months into the year, Clifford
looks a bit out of place; he hasn't developed the look of a parochial
school student, the navy or khaki trousers and the preferably starched
white shirt and the vapid, glazed-over facial expression. He looks
more like the public-school student he was for his first two years,
making the kind of picture—crew cut, baby-faced, "cute" in his
school clothes—that people laugh over when they come across the
snapshot decades later, in their sophisticated twenties or thirties.
This morning Clifford wears wrinkled new gold corduroys that make
a swishing noise when he walks, a red-checked shirt coming untucked
on one side, a loudly ticking Timex given Clifford by his father (to
his mother's angry dismay) as a First Holy Communion gift. On that
drizzling Sunday morning last May, his father had met them for
brunch at the Adolphus Hotel in Dallas, turning aside his mother's
complaints about his missing the communion service, joking that he
definitely "had time" for Clifford and then pulling the Timex out of
his pocket. "Now he can clock that three-hour fast before communion," his father had said, winking at Clifford. Then he'd cleared his
throat, and begun speaking to Clifford's mother in a calm, businesslike voice. When he finished, he asked Mrs. Bannon and Clifford if
they had any questions. Neither did.

A few weeks later, during that boiling hot summer of 1961,
mother and son left their big white-columned house in Highland
Park, heading southeast into this ordinary smallish city where Clifford, according to his mother, can enjoy a normal childhood. While
his mother drove, chattering busily, Clifford had stared at the passing
countryside: they had entered the "Piney Woods" of eastern Texas,
his mother informed him, weren't the trees and hills lovely, wasn't
Clifford glad to be leaving that big awful city? But Clifford didn't
reply. About every half hour they'd passed through some bleak little
gray-toned town, virtually identical to the previous one—a collection
of sooty redbricked buildings near the town square, a railroad crossing, a few sad-looking factories, some prim white-framed houses that
must be the "good" part of town, an irregular scattering of colorless

shacks that must be the "bad" part of town, and in fact Clifford saw black children staring dolefully back at him from the sagging porches of these shacks—and as his mother went on, *Isn't everything lovely, aren't you glad?* occasionally Clifford shot her a quick glance, but he didn't feel puzzled, really, or even irritated; already he knew better. Then he turned back, stared indifferently out the window once again, and they were back in the country: in the near distance were cotton fields, occasional pastures in which spotted cows stood motionless except for their ceaseless chewing, and every few miles an oil derrick or two ... *did Clifford know that there was lots of oil in eastern Texas, maybe your mom'll find herself some rich oilman one of these days, some big fella in boots and a Stetson, how's that for an idea?* and his mother gave her jangling laugh but Clifford did not reply. He'd been noticing how the movement of the oil wells seemed as monotonous as the cows chewing their cud, that relentless movement up and down, up and down, so that Clifford had been relieved when, at last, they'd reached the smallish city of Vyler, though he'd come to hate the word during those months before they left Dallas, since it represented both the terrifying future and the loss of everything he'd known—his father, their family, the past itself.

His mother picked this city for their new life, *our new life*—a phrase she uses often, and how Clifford hates it!—because one of her old school friends lives here, though they don't see much of Mrs. McCord, who has five children and a part-time job clerking at a ladies' clothing store. Now that Clifford is in school and she has gotten their house in shape—it's a modest two-bedroom brick, with a carport—Clifford's mother spends half of her time looking for a job and the other half trying to stay "active" in their new parish. After all, as she told Father Culhane after mass on that first Sunday, clutching his forearm out on the church steps, she didn't know anyone yet and she wanted to get involved, she wanted to be helpful, she felt a real sense of community here, almost a small-town atmosphere ... and how refreshing that was! Why, Dallas might be a thousand miles away, for all you could tell down here! Even Clifford had known that she was trying too hard, speaking too loudly; he saw how the priest, a virile red-haired Irishman, became more guarded as his mother spoke, his eyes squinting as against a bright light, his smile forced and brittle. Anyway, Clifford's mother told him, as a widow she knew she'd have to try harder, *as a widow* she didn't want to sit around feeling sorry for herself, she wanted to keep busy, and Father Culhane agreed that was important, didn't he? Embarrassed, Clifford had tugged at his mother's free hand, trying to pull her away. Yes, very important, Father Culhane had said carefully, and he'd extricated himself from Mrs. Bannon's grasp by reaching out to pat Clifford's head (very skillful, Clifford thought) and then stepped aside and was gone, absorbed into the crowd of other parishioners flooding out of church that morning.

"I'm not sure he liked me," said Clifford's mother, in the car. "What do you think, honey? Did he like me?"

"He liked you," Clifford said, in the same automatic voice—a soft buzz, a monotone—he used to give the Latin responses during mass.

"I'm not sure," his mother said, lighting a cigarette as she drove, her hand trembling a little. "I thought he seemed anxious, sort of, like he wanted to get away. Did he seem friendly to you, honey? Did you like him?"

"I liked him," Clifford responded.

But now, this morning, Clifford isn't thinking about his mother or Father Culhane or the pagan babies; instead he's locked in a daydream. Even when he feels something, from behind him, he doesn't pay attention: it's that talkative blond-haired girl, the one who's always getting in trouble, kicking at the back of his desk. Janice Rungren, her name is. Later he will understand that she was trying to warn him, for Sister Immaculata in her shrewd way has started down the aisle toward Clifford without a single break in her discussion of pagan babies.

But Clifford keeps thinking about the boy who lives next door to Clifford and his mother, whom Clifford had watched and day-dreamed about ever since they moved here last July. The boy's name is Ted Vernon; he's taller and older than Clifford, tanned and well-muscled in his arms and legs, and he spends a lot of time riding his bike and on scout hiking trips and swimming down at the YMCA. Clifford knows all this despite having met Ted only a couple of times, and even then only to say "hi" while loitering out in the driveway just for that purpose, hoping Ted would come along. Both times Ted was on his bike, said "hi" back and waved, but for some reason no conversation had developed. Because Ted is twelve and heroically handsome and popular throughout the neighborhood, while Clifford is only nine and nondescript and still plagued by the aura, he knows, of a new and probably weird kid living with his "wid-owed" mother, the two boys haven't hit it off. Ted isn't snobbish and Clifford isn't shy, but nonetheless something has held him back; and so far he's had to content himself with spying out the living room's picture window as Ted comes and goes, on his way to scout meetings (his father, a skyscraper version of Ted with a grin that would melt steel, drives his son to these meetings in the family Buick), on his way to the Y in his cinnamon-red suit that has a Y-member pin affixed to the right leg and bulges impossibly at the crotch (his mother, a pleasant-faced blonde who resembles June Cleaver, chauffeurs these after-school trips), or just cruising around the neighborhood on his ten-speed, stopping to talk with little kids in their driveways or adults working in their gardens or anyone at all. Ted is always friendly, blond and tanned and grinning, while Clifford stares out the picture window with a wistful expression, hoping Ted will glance toward the window and lift his hand in a friendly wave. When this happens Clifford feels a tingling at his scalp, or at the back of his neck, though he knows that Ted forgets about the gesture—forgets about *him*—in the very next instant.

At such times Clifford gulps in frustration. At such times even as Clifford waves back he knows he is jinxed, for he hasn't found a way into Ted's deeper awareness, he can't seem to crack the byzan-tine code of politics and decorum that regulates every neighborhood society of kids. Yet Clifford still believes the moment will come, someday, when Ted will realize that Clifford is next door to stay and will call out to Clifford, who will be loitering cooperatively in his driveway once again, *Hey, come on over, you like to climb trees?* (From his bedroom window Clifford has watched Ted shimmy up the towering pecan tree in his backyard, invariably reaching the dizzying topmost branches.) Or Ted will say, *Hey, bring your bike over, I'll show you around the neighborhood!* (Ted knows everyone, of course, for blocks in all directions: whereas Clifford seldom gets to leave the house, his mother doesn't want him "gallivanting around"—and besides, she'll add, what if "someone stops and carries you away," one side of her mouth downturned, a knowing emphasis on the "someone.") Or, as Clifford's most luscious, most abandoned daydreams would have it, Ted might say: *Hey Clifford, come on over and spend the night, why dontcha? We'll tell ghost stories or something. We'll talk all night!*

Clifford's hands are sweating, his knees are twitching, but not because Sister Immaculata has now paused beside his desk, her arms crossed and hands vanished inside those roomy sleeves, clearing her throat mockingly.

"Clifford, we certainly don't want to interrupt your wool-gathering," Sister says smartly. "But you've probably collected enough to make winter coats for everyone—wouldn't you say so, class?"

This is an old joke and the class barely titters. Behind him, Janice Rungren is still kicking at his desk but now rather idly, mechanically.

"Janice, stop that!" Sister says, not bothering to glance at her.

Sister Immaculata pauses. The room is still.

"Well, Clifford?" she says at last.

Clifford knows better than to show his irritation; he tries to copy the bland, glazed-over expression he sees often in the faces of his classmates.

"Sorry, Sister," he mumbles.

"And have you heard a word I've said?" Sister snaps. "About the pagan babies?"

"No, Sister," Clifford says quietly.

He wipes his sweaty hands on his shirt cuffs and then refolds them.

"Class," Sister says, not taking her reproving gaze from Clifford, "how do we save the pagan babies?"

"With our prayers, Sister," the class recites. "And with our money."

"Why do they need our prayers?" Sister asks, her voice managing to express both delight in the class and grave disappointment in Clifford.

"To save their souls, Sister," the class intones.

"And why do they need our money, class?" she asks.

"To nourish their bodies, Sister," says the class.

"Very good," Sister says, taking her arms out of her sleeves. Clifford is always amazed by how much the nuns' sleeves will hold, for he sees that she still clutches the bulky envelope from the Maryknoll mission in her left hand. The envelope includes an "adoption certificate" for each pupil, on which they can mark the deprived country of their choice, and indicate whether they're adopting a boy or a girl. They also get to name the pagan babies they adopt, and during the last go-round Clifford had named his baby "Dennis," after his younger brother who had died of brain fever as an infant. This had been the second week of the term and Sister Immaculata had seemed very moved when she asked about the name and heard about Clifford's brother. She had put a gold star beside his name in her record book; she'd told the class what a "welcome addition" a boy like Clifford was to St. John Bosco, and hoped that some of the other pupils who named their pagan babies "Buster" after a cocker spaniel or "Lizzie" after Elizabeth Taylor would have learned a valuable lesson. But that was then, and this is now. Sister Immaculata informs Clifford that when the recess bell rings, he will proceed to Sister's desk for a rap on the knuckles with her ruler, followed by a session of writing *I will not daydream* over and over on the blackboard while the rest of the class goes outside and enjoys themselves. Does Clifford understand?

"Yes, Sister," Clifford says, unable to keep from sounding bored. He has started thinking about Ted Vernon again, deciding cynically that there is some kind of plot, in this new world he and his mother have entered, to keep him from being happy for a single moment.

Now Sister is holding up two photographs. "These are some little Brazilian children," she says, "who live so far in the country's interior that Christ's message hasn't yet reached them."

Sister revolves in place so that all the pupils can see the two pictures. The girl is only four or five, wearing a ragged little dress. She has very dark skin, a sly gap-toothed smile.

"Her name is Maria," Sister says.

The boy is a few years older, shirtless and dirty-looking, but his smile is bold, even impudent, the teeth white and sharp. His eyes shine with mischief.

"See what a handsome boy he is?" Sister says. "His name is Eduardo. These children, you see, were photographed by the missionaries, who gave them Christian names. So we can't name them again."

Now Sister turns back to Clifford.

"Just to make sure you never forget this day, Clifford Bannon," she says very slowly, deliberately, "maybe you'd like to adopt one of these children."

She holds the two photographs only inches from his eyes.

"You did bring your money, didn't you?"

"Yes, Sister," Clifford says.

He looks from one picture to the other, the homely dark-skinned girl, the handsome dark-skinned boy, and feels a familiar sensation at the pit of his stomach. An ache. A hollowness. It's this feeling, these past few months, that has cast him into a world of his own, as though an invisible wall had risen to separate him not only from Ted Vernon but from the memory of his father and from the kids in this new school, who snicker behind his back, who give him stray kicks or insults in the playground, who don't seem to know or care who Clifford Bannon is. Such a feeling does weigh heavily on a nine-year-old and gives rise to something very like cynicism, a notion that perhaps nothing matters, after all, and he may as well please himself. This thought now seizes him as the class waits, as Sister holds up the pictures, as Clifford moves his eyes mechanically back and forth.

"Clifford . . . ?" Sister Immaculata prompts him.

"I'll take Eduardo," Clifford says.

2

Clifford

Clifford and Janice, Janice and Clifford—by the time they reach sixth grade and their last year at St. John Bosco Elementary School their names have long been linked, no one remembers how it started or seems to care, least of all Clifford Bannon himself. He doesn't mind Janice: that's what he tells his mother all that September and most of October, when Mrs. Bannon remarks upon Janice's friendly but "aggressive" behavior. He doesn't mind, she's just outgoing and doesn't mean any harm: that's what he says as they're driving away from the school, Janice having delayed them by following Clifford to his mother's shiny new pink-and-white Chrysler, talking and chattering even after Clifford climbs into the backseat and turns away rudely to stare out the opposite window. At such times Janice hangs onto the opened door, plays with the electric windows, lets the air conditioning out of the car, and when he still won't look around she pushes her head inside and talks to Clifford's mother, smiling, undaunted: Hello Mrs. Bannon, how are you, what a pretty dress, what a pretty new car! So it goes for five minutes, ten minutes, until Janice finally backs away and Clifford's mother pulls the Chrysler out of the lot.

"Clifford, who *is* that little girl?" she asks, and then quizzes him about Janice's parents, where did they live, what did Janice's father do, and was Janice a nice little girl? Or——?

"She's okay," Clifford says glumly, slump-shouldered in his usual after-school posture; his mother often complains that he won't tell her anything, he's so secretive, so grumpy, why don't they ever *talk* anymore——you know, like they used to. (When? When did we ever talk? Clifford thinks but doesn't say.) He stares out the window so his eyes won't snag on the rearview, where he knows his mother's eyes await him, dark and quick-moving, frantically wanting something, something; he doesn't know what, except that he doesn't have it. Though he did say, one afternoon: "Her father's a big shot in some insurance company, they just moved out into that fancy subdivision, Lazy Acres. So I'm sure you'd like them."

She hadn't caught the sarcasm.

"Really? Lazy Acres?" she said, her fingers flexing on the wheel. "Well," she said quickly, "I'm sure Janice is a nice girl——she's a pretty little thing, isn't she?"

His mother gave a hoarse laugh, a conspirator's laugh of the kind Clifford never acknowledged.

"She's okay," he repeated, hoping the "Clifford and Janice" business hadn't reached his mother's ears. The talk would displease her, of course; unlike the mothers of other boys at school and around the neighborhood, Mrs. Bannon never made reference to Clifford's having a "girlfriend" someday, her intently focused tunnel vision of the future had aborted that possibility just as her blurred recollection of the past had ignored the failure of her marriage. Her thoughts were mostly occupied, it would appear, with her renewed interest in the Catholic church and its "exalted idealism," as she called it, its immense power to comfort and console. Ever since last spring, when Father Culhane had handed out booklets entitled *The Religious Vocation——Do YOU Have the Calling?* in theology class, Clifford's mother had talked often of Clifford's becoming a priest, had even sent off to several seminaries in San Antonio and Houston for brochures and application forms. Because her endless talk of Clifford as a seminarian, then a priest——her laughing delighted talk of Clifford as a bishop or even a cardinal, why the heck not?——seemed to make her so happy,

Clifford hadn't contradicted her, much less said (though he often thought) that he wouldn't enter the priesthood if God sent an engraved invitation.

His mother was seldom happy, he reasoned; let her think what she wanted to think.

This was the same technique he'd used on Janice, after all, ever since his first year at St. John Bosco, when she'd informed him that they would get married one day. When Clifford said he didn't plan to get married, not ever, Janice had laughed her shrill eight-year-old laugh, as at the delightful ignorance of a much younger child. Only last year, after Mary Frances Dennehy had commandeered the thin-armed Edwin Brewster and proclaimed that they were "boyfriend and girlfriend," Janice had said abruptly to Clifford one day that *they* were boyfriend and girlfriend, and he hadn't exactly denied it; nor did he bother to respond when he heard the taunting refrain of "Clifford and Janice, Janice and Clifford" out on the playground, knowing that no one cared one way or another, not really, since no one paid much attention to *them*.

Only his mother would care, and that's why Clifford became tense and sullen whenever Janice followed him out to the car, insisting that she should "get to know" Mrs. Bannon. If his mother had thought for a minute that Janice was his girlfriend, Clifford mused, then she would hate her automatically, criticize her up and down—never mind Lazy Acres, never mind the Rungrens' sprawling trilevel home and their two-toned Coupe de Ville in the garage. Out of some perverse fondness for her energy, her rebellion, Clifford wanted everyone to like Janice and thus the question kept arising: *Was* Janice Rungren his girlfriend?

One Friday morning in late October, Janice herself asked the question, though not in so many words; and Clifford responded clumsily, of course, and accidentally hurt her feelings, setting off the first in a series of long embittered silences that were to punctuate their relationship always, no matter how careful Clifford might become in later years, how cautious and guarded. Even on that sunny October morning he'd wondered if anyone saw them sneaking away from the playground—Clifford and Janice, Janice and Clifford—or if they did, said anything about it; probably not, Clifford reasoned.

For even when their names were linked in the school's gossip mills, Clifford and Janice were hardly the "romantic" couple of the sixth-grade class, though Janice with her mane of long silky blond hair was allowed to be pretty (for such a "spoiled brat," anyway), and Clifford by the lights of certain fifth- and sixth-grade girls, cocking their heads in a moment of thoughtful assessment, was considered "cute, sort of," with his close-cropped dark hair and precise, bony profile, his neat clothes and good manners. No, when the kids gossiped it was usually about Jimmy Bridges, a tall good-natured boy said to be the best hope for Pius XII's junior high football team next year, and tiny raven-haired Jeanette O'Malley, easily the prettiest girl at St. John Bosco and a shoo-in for the junior high cheerleading squad. About these two the gossip was near-constant but reverent, a matter of hushed speculation—were they "going steady" even though Father Culhane had forbidden going steady, even for sixth-graders, in a stinging spring assembly address last year; had they met for a Saturday afternoon movie downtown and sat way in the back, snuggling and kissing, Clark McElroy *swears* he saw them, Tina Bird says he definitely did *not*, since Jeanette spent that whole weekend with *her;* had Jimmy really developed a crush on a girl from his neighborhood (a little simpering dark-haired thing who went to public school and not only wasn't Catholic but was rumored to be Jewish), thus breaking Jeanette's sweet little heart in two?

Or there was the amusing romance of Mary Frances Dennehy, who had unfortunately gained a few pounds each year and was now almost the school's fattest girl (but not *the* fattest, thanks to Belinda Janeway in the fifth grade—that slob) and still the richest girl, roly-poly Mary Frances with her wispy red hair and scattering of freckles and her loud braying laugh, now the girlfriend of spider-thin Edwin Brewster—what a funny, strange-looking couple they made!—whom Mary Frances dragged hither and yon all during the school day, sitting him down beside her at lunch, holding fast to his wrist all during recess while she chattered with Lucia Hernandez and her other girlfriends, then pecking his cheek at odd, stray moments, when the nuns weren't looking—how amusing, how cute they were! And where did Mrs. Dennehy find those frilly expensive school dresses (*too* dressy for school, some whispered) in Mary Frances's size? (She drives up to Dallas to do Mary Frances's shopping, rumor has it; no, she takes the train to New Orleans; no, she flies to New York where the clothes are custom-made. It had been Mrs. Dennehy, after all, who'd put her foot down when the nuns had suggested to Father Culhane that uniforms be required of the students, as was the case in larger parishes like Dallas or Houston. What about the poor Mexican children? Mrs. Dennehy had asked Father Culhane, during the parent-teacher meeting when uniforms were discussed. They couldn't afford tuition, most of them, so how could we expect them to buy *uniforms,* too? And some of them have eight or ten children! Father Culhane had to agree that Mrs. Dennehy had a point; and he didn't care to offend his wealthiest and most outspoken parishioner, who enjoyed sending Mary Frances to school in those costly dresses.)

Or there was the contemptible romance, if you wanted to call it that, between creepy stuck-up Annie Shelton, the smartest girl in school, who read books during recess and wouldn't let anyone copy off her tests, and the even creepier Brian McGreevy, who wasn't even twelve yet but already had pimples, and stuttered if you asked him anything, and wore a slide rule attached to his belt (a canvas belt left over from Cub Scouts—what a shithead) and every year won the academic achievement award in math and science. They'd walk through the schoolyard, Annie and Brian, hand in hand, whispering together, oblivious of any commotion around them, while girls like Mary Frances Dennehy and her eternal sidekick Lucia Hernandez and flocks of bland faceless girls like Virginia Bailey and Jennifer Jenks and Trudy Cravens would cry out, *Yecch!* or *Help me, Mother Mary, I'm losing my lunch,* and during P.E. class the boys would "unintentionally" shove Brian into the mud during touch football or one of the boys' knees would "accidentally" ram itself into Brian's crotch in the gym during basketball, leaving him writhing in pain next to the bleachers, his face empurpled with agony, his slide rule clacking uselessly against the gleaming wood floor. . . . But what did they expect, anyway, kids like Annie and Brian, so smart but so out of it, inspiring such universal scorn? Even the nuns disliked them.

So there was little time to bother with Clifford and Janice, Janice and Clifford, they were on the social fringes, they didn't belong to any particular clique but they weren't unreasonably hated; their behavior was erratic and the nuns alternately liked and disliked them (for they *could* be well-behaved and charming when they tried, and both did well in their schoolwork), and besides, wasn't there something a little *weird* about those two, something you couldn't put your finger on, exactly, so you might as well ignore?

And so, Clifford hopes, maybe no one did see them; or if they did, would immediately forget. Something had possessed Janice, the kind of wild random impulse, Clifford guessed, that caused her to giggle in theology class or participate in boys-only pranks like throwing spitballs or mimicking the nuns behind their backs or inking obscene words on the backs of her hands and then displaying them to the class—the sort of behavior that Clifford disdained but somehow admired in Janice. So he hadn't really resisted when, a few minutes ago, she seized his wrist abruptly out by the swings—the other kids were playing volleyball, a game both Clifford and Janice hated—and dragged him back into the unfenced wooded area that was "off limits" to the kids from St. John Bosco, had pulled him into the shade of stolid pines and enormous gnarled elms, saying *Ssh* and giggling as she led and he followed and they ran for the deep woods, finally reaching a footpath that led to a scattering of weathered old sheds owned by the school. They were mostly storage sheds, plus a big smelly garden shed where the school handyman, Gus Ramirez, kept his supplies and spent much of his time. The dense woods surround and hide the sheds, so the clearing is eerie, dim, hushed; as they crunch through the brittle gold-and-crimson leaves toward the garden shed Clifford can no longer hear the noises from the playground, can scarcely imagine the sun-filled air, the hectic motion. Here except for their own quick bodies and voices the world is still.

"Look, isn't this neat?" Janice says, pulling Clifford inside. She shoves the slatted wooden door closed, then latches it.

What's "neat" about it? Clifford wants to say, but doesn't. His nostrils twitch at the heavy close odors—potting soil, peat moss, damp. A half-pleasant dreamy stench but also stifling, somehow threatening. The shed is crammed with garden tools—hoes and rakes and clippers. A couple of wheelbarrows, a pile of wooden crates.

Hoses in snakelike coils. Against one wall are sacks of peat moss, metal containers of insecticide, a short stack of boxed seedlings. The only signs of Gus Ramirez are a scarred pine table in one corner, covered with newspapers; a coffee mug; an ashtray with a cigar butt inside; and beside the table an old army cot overlaid with a soiled-looking quilt. Now Janice pulls Clifford toward the cot and his nostrils twitch again: the cigar smell rises through the moist clayey air, rank and rotten and foul.

"We'd better get back," Clifford says.

"What for?" says Janice, and she plops herself down on the cot, begins idly fraying one corner of the quilt with her busy white fingers.

"That looks dirty," Clifford says. "You'd better put it down."

"Ooh, this looks dirty," Janice mimics him, "greasy old Ramirez has touched it, ooh, poor Clifford with his clean little hands."

Grudgingly, he smiles. He likes it when she teases him.

"C'mon, sit down," she says, patting the cot beside her. "It's not *that* dirty."

So he sits, hands in his lap. He says, "What if Ramirez comes back?"

Janice pokes him in the stomach, lightly.

"Today's Friday, dumbbell. He's not here on Friday."

She laughs brightly and he's afraid someone will hear, so he covers her mouth with one hand but then tickles her side with the other hand—what is he doing?—and of course she screams, alternately giggles and screams, and before he can pull his hand away she has gotten one finger in her mouth, her sharp white front teeth bite down for a second, hard; but he doesn't cry out, doesn't even flinch. The pain is pleasant somehow, and now he turns the finger sideways, staring. Where her teeth made their neat indentations the skin is broken and blood rises to the surface slowly, dreamily. He stares at the blood.

"Did I do that?" Janice says, bending toward him.

They watch as the blood rises, thickens.

"Here, let's play doctor," Janice says, and before he can react she has stood and pulled her underpants from beneath her wool plaid skirt and is gently patting his finger. The white cotton panties absorb the blood, and though Clifford tries to jerk his hand away Janice holds his other wrist firmly. In a moment she stops patting him and they both bend to look. The bleeding has stopped.

"There you go! Cured!" Janice cries. She tosses the panties in a trash can next to the cot and laughs, inclining her blond head against Clifford's shoulder.

"Now it's your turn," she says.

Clifford feels dazed, addleheaded; he doesn't know why they're here but at the same time he'd rather stay with Janice than go back to the schoolyard and stand around waiting for the bell. He looks at his Timex: it's 12:40, there are twenty more minutes until the end of after-lunch recess.

"What do you mean," he says vaguely. "My turn to what."

"To play doctor," she says, crooking her arm through Clifford's. "Haven't you ever played doctor?"

"That's for little kids," he says hoarsely, not looking at Janice. "A game for little kids."

"For little kids and for big kids," Janice says.

Her voice is bright, her words are quick, whereas Clifford's own brain has gone dim, befuddled. The heavy damp smell of the soil and moss has made him drowsy. She planned this, he thinks with a vague sense of alarm, it might have seemed that she grabbed his arm impulsively but she knew it was Friday and the shed would be empty and she waited until the playground monitor, Sister Mary Ignatius, went into the cafeteria for her tuna sandwich and carton of milk; he always assumed he was smarter than Janice but maybe it isn't true.

"Well, I guess I haven't," he says. "Why don't you teach me how."

Janice stands next to him, giggling, and starts to unzip her skirt.

"I've never played doctor with a boy before, have you?" she says, and now her giggling sounds uneasy. "I mean, have you played it with a girl? Clifford?"

"Not yet," Clifford says.

*   *   *

Lately the sixth-grade class at St. John Bosco has heard a great deal about *impure thoughts,* and *occasions of sin,* and *bad companions,* and sundry other means by which the devil achieves his ends. Whenever Clifford hears these phrases he thinks instantly of Ted Vernon, not Janice Rungren, and he remembers Father Culhane's warning that the devil often assumes *a pleasant guise.* Though Clifford tries to make light of it, joking to himself that Ted *is* a pleasant guy, isn't he, nonetheless he'd begun feeling confused and troubled as early as last summer, several months before Janice Rungren dragged him into the woods.

Three years older than Clifford, half a foot taller, big strapping blond-haired Ted Vernon had once seemed so glamorous, so unattainable, but it happened that gradually they'd become friends, and by now it appeared that among the neighborhood kids Clifford was Ted's best friend and that his daydreams of those first months in the neighborhood—so long ago!—had come true. As time passed, however, it also happened that Clifford endured a few disillusionments about Ted, figuring out that Ted was so popular and well-liked because he was the type who didn't demand much, didn't offer much, and maybe wasn't even very bright; but Ted did like Clifford and in the past six months had begun to seek *him* out, instead of vice versa. Which Clifford found pleasant. Which Clifford found gratifying. So they went on aimless lazy bike rides through the neighborhood, they stopped for chocolate malts or a game of pinball at the Dairy Queen, sometimes on weekend nights they "camped out" in Ted's backyard, in the orange canvas pup tent left over from his scouting days. Several times that summer and autumn they'd slept in the tent and eaten bologna sandwiches and fried pies supplied by Mrs. Vernon and smoked an illicit Marlboro or two and talked till the wee hours, although it was mostly Ted who talked and Clifford who listened. Listened, in recent weeks, with mingled fascination and alarm, because suddenly Ted had become interested in girls, in sex, in various myths and theories and suppositions about sex, and he wondered what did Clifford think, what did Clifford know? His questions were frantic but hushed, oddly reverent. Had he ever seen a girl naked, had he ever read *True* magazine, or *Playboy* magazine, did he know there were actually magazines (Ted didn't know the titles, but one of the senior boys had brought a few to school) that showed people having sex, completely naked and having sex in glossy color pictures? Did Clifford get a hard-on when he saw pictures like that, did he wake up with a hard-on in the morning, did he ever beat off, could he come yet, did he have wet dreams, did he really *like* wet dreams and could he remember much about them, could he remember them at all?

No, Clifford said. *No,* or *I don't know,* or *Maybe,* or *I guess*—just enough to keep Ted talking, he knew that Ted only needed a sounding board, he wasn't really interested in *him;* or so Clifford thought until lately, specifically one late-summer night when Ted had propped his official Explorer Scout searchlight against the tent pole at their feet and flicked the switch and suddenly their tiny shared space glowed with light, a pale warm orange-yellow light that Clifford all his life would associate with delicious comfort and privacy. Then Ted pushed back a corner of his sleeping bag to show that he'd kicked off his underwear and had taken hold of himself and was stroking idly, rather expertly Clifford thought, and Ted said, "C'mon, don't you ever beat off?"—and before Clifford could react Ted reached across and unzipped his bag, laughing, flicking one finger against the crotch of Clifford's white Jockey shorts, which had stiffened, which had bulged, so Clifford watched and did what Ted did, though now he couldn't avoid one of Ted's questions—he had to tell the truth.

"I've heard about wet dreams at school," Clifford said, "but I guess I haven't had one. I guess I can't—can't come. Not really."

"Yeah, but you're only twelve," Ted said, looking down at himself and stroking harder now, his fist slapping loud against his belly. "When I was twelve I couldn't, either, I'd just get that tingly feeling when I beat off, but then one day it happened—it just happened."

"Oh," Clifford said.

"But you get the feeling, don't you?" Ted asked. "That tingly feeling?"

"Yeah," Clifford said, "yeah, I guess so," but in watching Ted he'd lost his concentration, his own hand had slowed and he'd even started to get soft. The more energetic Ted became—twisting his legs one way and then another, his fist moving so fast it seemed to blur, his mouth tensed with effort and his shoulders raised as he worked and watched himself and grimaced and panted—the more intense he became the quieter Clifford got, his own belly hot with excitement, his own breath coming fast. At first he'd felt embarrassed that Ted was so huge and he was so—well, so ordinary—but there was no point in being embarrassed, he thought, Ted hadn't noticed or didn't care, and anyway he was older and much bigger in general; very much bigger, in fact. The searchlight's pure strong beam reflected off the orange canvas of the tent, glowed along Ted's smooth hairless muscular chest and arms, his flat belly, his bent legs and the fist working busily between them, pumping, twisting, pulling, and Clifford realized he *was* hard again just at the moment Ted threw his head back, saying *Oh, oh*—and when he whispered, "I'm going to shoot, watch this," Clifford's eyes widened at the amazing milky spurt that flew like a slender rope into the air. It fell across Ted's tensed thighs, his forearm, his fist which still gripped but had slowed, had relaxed a bit, and when Ted whooped and pointed and said, "Look!" Clifford saw that he'd hit the canvas roof, there was a milky white spot just above Ted's legs and abruptly Ted had laughed and wiped himself with a corner of the sleeping bag and reached his sticky hand across to grab hold of Clifford.

"Now you," he said.

Clifford hadn't resisted, and for the first time Clifford *did* come—Ted let out an even louder whoop when Clifford's own head went back for a moment, his own legs tensed. He looked down to see the bit of liquid hovering like a bead, like a pearl, at the tip of that red pulsing flesh he scarcely recognized as part of himself—it hovered for a moment, then rolled down the side of Ted's fist.

"You did it, Cliff!" Ted cried, and they both laughed and Ted wiped his hand again and flicked off the searchlight and within thirty seconds fell asleep.

August, that had been; and though they never talked about that night or any of the others, Clifford knew what to expect when they camped in Ted's backyard, as they did nearly every weekend now, to Ted it seemed ordinary and matter-of-fact and he continued talking about girls and asking questions, speculating and wondering and dreaming. For his part, Clifford was alternately bored and entranced, he wanted Ted to keep talking, keep talking, even when Ted asked questions that Clifford couldn't answer. While Ted rambled on about sex Clifford would sometimes think about the "health" lecture that Father Culhane had given one September morning, in place of P.E. class. He supposed that some of Ted's questions had been answered during that lecture—in a manner of speaking—but he hadn't told Ted or anyone outside the school about it. He'd found the whole ordeal embarrassing, somehow. Shuffling their feet, snickering, the sixth-grade boys had filed into one room while Sister Mary Joseph took the girls into another room, and the vigorous red-haired priest had lectured tirelessly on impure thoughts and occasions of sin and self-abuse, especially self-abuse which did not cause insanity or blindness, he admitted, but which could definitely cause a hernia, or a pulled muscle in the groin, or chronic spasms of the sexual organ not unlike epileptic seizures. Painful as these maladies were, they barely suggested the torments of hell lying in wait if you died after self-abuse but before going to confession, self-abuse being a mortal sin, so Father Culhane offered some practical tips on avoiding this particular snare of the devil.

For instance: boys should not dawdle in the bathroom, they should do their business and get out fast.

For instance: boys should take brisk five-minute showers but *not* tub baths, which allowed time for physical languor and admiration of the body and a dangerous idleness of mind.

For instance: boys should not get into bed at night until they were extremely tired. They might try wearing themselves out with pushups and jumping jacks beforehand, and if they didn't fall asleep within five minutes they should determinedly count sheep until they did, or say the Apostles' Creed over and over, but under no circumstances should they simply lie there, let the mind wander, create an opening for carnal thoughts.

All the sixth-grade boys, Clifford included, sat open-mouthed as Father Culhane discussed these occasions of sin, pacing the front of the room, his athletic figure conveying an outraged, bristling virility as he described the devil's cowardly tricks, his use of various means—bad companions, books and movies, even our own day-dreams!—to encourage impure thoughts. Father Culhane had thrilled the boys by saying frankly that even *he,* an ordained priest, sometimes fell prey to lustful reveries, sometimes found that the most innocent situations could be transformed (in an instant!—for such was the wily quickness of the devil) into occasions of sin, moments of blended fascination and disgust, sudden urges, lurid promptings. . . .

Several times Father Culhane had stopped his pacing; had taken a handkerchief from the folds of his cassock and wiped his sweating brow. Then, clearing his throat, the priest had gone on to talk about venereal disease, which could rot a certain part of your body, he was sure the boys knew which part that was; and about perverted older men—he'd spoken the word *homosexual* just once, quick and disgusted out the side of his mouth—who preyed on young boys if they weren't careful, and whom Father Culhane imitated, in the lecture's single humorous moment, by dangling one wrist and batting his eyelids; and about the sanctity of marriage and the function of sex as a means to make babies, which was its only allowable function and they'd best remember that. Afterward the boys had filed out of the room sniggering and poking at one another, some looking discomforted, some looking rather pale, and that day at lunch Janice Rungren had rushed up to Clifford and asked what Father Culhane had said, Clifford wasn't going to believe what Sister Mary Joseph had told *them,* but Clifford had curled his lip and turned away. Yes, the entire ordeal of the "health" lecture embarrassed him, and it seemed unfair that he should feel, despite himself, envious of Janice Rungren, who talked of such matters so frankly; or of blue-eyed Ted Vernon with his eager curiosity, good healthy innocent Ted, who would probably never feel an ounce of guilt in his life, who would grow up to become an ordinary smiling Methodist just like his parents.

And one evening, out in the pup tent, the question had suddenly overwhelmed Clifford: which of them was the "bad companion," he or Ted? Father Culhane had explained what to do if you encountered a bad companion, but what if you suspected—no matter how vaguely, uncertainly—that you *were* one?

* * *

So Clifford is not eager, not smiling as he stands above Janice, shifting his weight back and forth. For some reason he looks at his finger, which is no longer bleeding. Briefly he considers picking at the crust that has formed along Janice's toothmarks—get the finger bleeding again, create a distraction.

He's amazed by Janice. She lies on the cot gazing up at him, one arm behind her head, her shoulders and legs still tanned from the summer, her toes twitching; helplessly Clifford's eyes graze her midsection, so tender and white—the just-perceptible swelling beneath her nipples; the belly long and flat and unmarked; and between her legs the twin plump mounds, also like swellings, with their downy thatch of scarcely visible pale blond hair. He looks, he looks away. He looks back. Clifford's heart pounds as Janice adjusts herself, fidgeting, glancing down at herself and then back at him, her smile provocative, almost taunting as she cries, "C'mon, doctor! Do your stuff!"

He steps closer. Not knowing what else to do, he takes hold of her jaw.

"You're not sick," he tells her.

Janice rolls her eyes. "You're the doctor and I'm the patient," she says. "You're supposed to examine me, dumbbell."

From a distance, an incalculable distance, he hears the end-of-recess bell.

What does everyone want from him? Clifford wonders. His mother, Janice Rungren, even Ted Vernon—they're always pulling at him, asking questions. He can't believe how insistent they are, he can't believe anything matters so much. And anyway, he reasons, he's eventually going to lose them. Already he avoids his mother because he must avoid her to stay sane, and next year Ted will start high school and he'll have a girlfriend and no more time for childish games with Clifford Bannon, and of course he knows where Janice is headed. Already she's one of the prettiest girls in their class, blond and slender, her eyes widely spaced, her nose small, pert, dusted with freckles; she's one of the taller girls, too, last year she was taller than any of the boys. Some combination of circumstance and fate and mutual unspoken recognition has brought them together these past few years in the lunchroom and playground of St. John

Bosco, but that will change soon enough, he knows that she'll keep getting prettier each year and that she will aid and abet the process any way she can, and when they transfer out to Pius XII next fall she'll start getting the attention of the high school boys and he'll lose her, there'll be no more Clifford and Janice, Janice and Clifford—yes, he thinks, he's going to lose her, he's quite certain of that.

He's going to lose them all.

"Hey Cliffie," Janice says, using a nickname she knows Clifford hates. "Hey, I need some medical attention, I'm getting goosebumps down here!"

The words are jaunty but he hears how the mischief and humor have left her voice; he sees her blond-lashed eyes darken to tiny points as she takes his hand, the wounded hand, and puts it across one of her tiny budlike nipples.

"Here, examine my heart first—like *this,*" she says, pressing the back of his hand. And despite himself he feels something in his groin, that unmistakable stirring and hardening. But the rest of him has also hardened—his mind and heart, his tight prim smile. He retrieves his hand and starts to back away.

"Better get dressed," he says. Then he mumbles a few more words.

"What?" Janice cries. "What did you say?"

Shamefaced, he mumbles the words again: ". . . a priest, didn't you know, didn't I tell you? I'm going to be a priest."

"Clifford?" she says, a look of puzzled hurt in her eyes.

She's still a little girl, he sees: she has a child's body, white and defenseless. Her thin naked shoulders are trembling.

"Better get dressed," Clifford says again. He smiles coldly, he turns and walks away.

On Friday evenings they have a simple dinner—a "working-class" dinner, as his mother often jokes—of fish sticks and mashed potatoes with butter, and maybe Jello for dessert, and while they eat they review the week together. This evening is no different, and for a while his mother talks in her hoarse rapid murmur of her accomplishments, ticking them off her fingers one by one. At the store where she works, The Fashion Plate, she'd canvassed the other salespeople and even the Jewish owner about the Christmas drive, seeking volunteers to visit poor families in the area, asking them to put aside old toys and clothes; she called Father Culhane to volunteer for the drive committee again this year, though he hasn't yet returned the call; she went around the neighborhood one day after work and spoke with six—or was it seven—of the women on their street, including that blond-haired Mrs. Vernon, whom Clifford's mother considers too reserved, too standoffish, and she tried to organize a coffee-klatsch for Saturday mornings ... though none of the women had committed themselves, exactly. "It's so hard," she says to Clifford, who has already finished his fish sticks and is well into the potatoes, "so *hard* meeting people, getting to know people. Sometimes I think they don't like me, honey. I really do."

"They like you," Clifford says, reaching for his milk.

"I'm not sure, honey," his mother replies, "I'm really *not*," and this time Clifford just nods. After more than three years of their living alone together, just the two of them, Clifford knows exactly what responses are best, how to calm her down if she's overexcited, how to stimulate her thinking if she's depressed. Lately his favorite tactic is simply to let her talk, especially when she's complaining about her job or about Father Culhane not appreciating her service to the parish or about the other women at work or in the neighborhood, none of whom are friendly enough, none of whom ever calls on the phone. She always has to call *them,* and she's getting tired of that.

"Even Rita McCord," she says now, wistfully. "She got me her old job at that tawdry little store—The Fashion Plate, what a joke that is—and now it's like she's gone away, washed her hands of me. We'll probably never see her again."

"Don't be silly, Mom," Clifford says, trying to keep the irritation from his voice. "She's got five kids. She's *busy*."

"That's why I haven't heard from Father Culhane about the Christmas drive, I'm sure," his mother says, lighting a cigarette though she has scarcely touched her plate. "Rita's the type the priests go for, they always like the baby-makers, don't they?—whereas if you're a widow, forget it. They don't even see you. You're invisible."

His mother lifts her hand before Clifford can get out a word.

"No, it's not my imagination," she says. "You know better than that, Clifford, sometimes I think you just ignore things, you deliberately ignore them—your father was that way, you know. When anything wasn't convenient for him to see, why he just didn't see it. It just wasn't *there*."

Clifford is startled by the mention of his father, though his mother had announced recently that they might as well be "open" about discussing him, to deliberately not discuss him was giving the man a significance he didn't deserve, and anyway he *was* dead, his mother had whispered—Clifford believed that, didn't he, she asked, that she really was a widow, he really *was* without a father? Not only for practical purposes, but in reality? In essence?

A stray unbidden smile had come to Clifford's lips and he'd said, "Sure, that's right," quick and low and ironic—as though speaking to himself.

"Anyway, Cliff," his mother says now, "you saw Father Culhane last Sunday, out on the church steps after mass. He said hello, I guess, but wouldn't even smile, then turned away like he wanted us out of sight. Turned his *back* on us."

Clifford says, "You take it the wrong way, Mom, he has hundreds of people to greet after church, you don't understand that people are busy, he and Aunt Rita and—"

"I was right in the middle of a sentence, and he turned his back—just like that!"

His mother snaps her fingers.

Though Clifford allows himself a brief exasperated roll of his eyes, he knows from past experience that his mother is relatively happy when she's either complaining about her present life or chattering brightly about the future, spinning fantasies about all the "church work" she wants to accomplish, about their "strategy" for getting Clifford into the best possible seminary.... Though years will pass before Clifford Bannon comes across the term "manic-depressive" in a college psychology text, he knows already that his mother's "happy" times, despite all the constant chattering turmoil, are far preferable to her spells of black depression when she dwells on the past instead of the future, moping around the house in an old nylon bathrobe, her dark short hair unwashed and greasy, her face pale and coarse without makeup, the pores so large and oily-looking that Clifford can hardly bear to look at her; at such times he has caught himself thinking, guiltily, that she deserves her fate, that her sorrow is far more determined than whatever bonds of love or familiarity hold the two of them together. When depressed his mother indulges in long rambling monologues about Dennis, about her lost baby Dennis and how sweet he'd been, how blond and soft and perfect, she knows he is in limbo not in hell, no God could be cruel enough to send such a little angel to hell—but then He'd been cruel enough to take him, hadn't He, to let the little darling die, knowing his mother wouldn't survive it, really, would never be the same?—yes He'd been cruel enough to do that, hadn't He?

And there were other occasions when his mother plunged into grief: last fall, on the weekend after the president's assassination, she had declined into such a deadly blank-eyed torpor that Clifford on his own initiative had telephoned Mrs. McCord—"Aunt Rita," as he'd always called her—and begged her to come over. Though he'd been aware of his mother's infatuation with the president and his family—she'd said more than once that they were the "ideal family," the "perfect family," surely they were going to lead this country to a pinnacle of greatness that could scarcely be imagined—even Clifford had been surprised by her reaction to the events up in Dallas, he hadn't supposed that any event out there, out in the world, could make her descend into such a state. (Clifford remembered in horror that in the days before the assassination his mother, reading about the planned visit, had talked idly about their driving up to Dallas on that day and trying "to get a glimpse" of the president and his wife—if only it weren't a school day, she'd said wistfully. Yes, in succeeding days he'd recalled his mother's words in outright horror: the thought of him and his mother standing there, on the motorcade route, made Clifford feel physically ill.) And so Clifford had panicked, hadn't known what to do—but fortunately Aunt Rita had interceded.

Bright-voiced and efficient, despite her own grief over the president's death, Rita had vacuumed and done laundry and stocked the pantry in a single evening, all the while scolding Clifford for not having called sooner, and then she led his mother—who'd sat at the

kitchen table all the while, chain-smoking, bewildered—back down
the hallway for a bath and a change into fresh pajamas, and an hour
later had reported to Clifford, sighing, that she'd finally drifted off.
Then Aunt Rita had phoned his mother's boss (her own former boss)
at home, and had explained why Irene hadn't shown up for work
on Saturday, yes she knew the Christmas rush had already started
but female troubles didn't operate according to any sort of timetable,
and did Mr. Cohn want her to be more specific? He didn't, evidently.
Rita hung up the phone, expelling her breath in relief, and turned
toward Clifford, who'd been slouched in front of the TV, watching
"My Three Sons" as though oblivious to everything that was happening. Aunt Rita had stalked over to the set and snapped it off. She'd
run a hand through her short reddish hair, and with her arm raised
Clifford could see the fabric of her housedress pulled tight against
her plump breasts, against the slight bulge at her abdomen—and
Clifford thought, helplessly, Another baby? *Another* baby?

"Now listen here," Aunt Rita had said. "We've got to have a
little talk, you and I."

And talk they did, for an hour or more, Aunt Rita saying that
Irene was her oldest and dearest friend and that she was glad to
help, *glad* to help, but that she couldn't do everything. She had a
husband, she had a large family, she couldn't come running over
here every evening. . . . "Your mother's okay, she's just a little depressed," Rita said. "You know how she felt about the Kennedys,
and also I expect she's still not recovered from—she's still trying to
cope with—"

And she'd broken off, as she'd done in the past when on the
verge of mentioning Clifford's father.

"Anyhow," she resumed, "you're the man of the house now"—
she gave him a friendly poke in the shoulder, she touched his cheek
but he reddened and turned away—"and look," she said, "I know
it's tough, I really can imagine what it's like, being around someone
who—"

Again she broke off. Clifford knew that Rita McCord wasn't a
naturally tactful person, and that was one of the things he liked
about her, along with her selfless energy and quick thinking; but

he'd known, too, that they weren't going to see much more of her, that in the midst of all her activity that evening she'd given some thought to what she could and could not do.

"The house is clean," she'd said finally, tying a scarf around her head as she stood by the door. "And I want you to keep it clean—let that be one of the things you and your mother do together. That's important, doing things together—and don't forget it. Now, I've set her alarm for seven, so in the morning just pretend it's an ordinary Monday. I've got her an outfit hanging in the bathroom—do everything you can to get her off to work, out of the house. . . . Work is the best cure for the blues, believe me—I know." She laughed, patting her belly. "Why, I've never been depressed a day in my life!"

Rita left before he could thank her, and though it had taken several days Clifford had finally coaxed his mother back to work, and soon enough she was coming home laden with Christmas packages—after her shift at The Fashion Plate ended she would spend hours shopping for him and herself, and for all the McCords, for Father Culhane, even for her one surviving relative, her brother Pete over in Atlanta, whom she hadn't contacted in months. . . . As Christmas approached, he'd recognized all the signs of his mother's "recovery": the quick breathless monologues in which she recounted all she'd accomplished that week and all the people she'd met, the conquests she'd made; the ceaseless activity around the house, cleaning and straightening, putting up the Christmas tree, and stockings above the fireplace, and everywhere mistletoe, angels' hair, sprigs of holly; her plans for redecorating after New Year's, going through magazines and swatch books, calling local decorators on the phone for bubbly one-sided conversations; and finally, once the holidays were over and the house had been redone and her job had gotten "boring, just a little," her growing absorption in Clifford, his school life and his spiritual life, his religious vocation, his plans for the future. . . . Thinking back over the past year, Clifford can never pinpoint the moment she actually began referring to the seminary and the priesthood, or exactly how she had elided past Clifford's silence into the presumption that he *did* have a vocation, that he had ambitions not merely to become a parish priest but eventually to "work his way up the ladder"—as his mother said laughingly, draw-

ing hard on her cigarette—and someday become a monsignor or a
bishop, why not, who knew how far he could go?

At about this time, Janice had developed her sudden bizarre
interest in Clifford's mother, asking what was his mother like at
home, why wouldn't Clifford talk about her, why did she seem so
angry on some days and so happy on other days, did she want to
get married again, did she ever have dates with anybody, and what
had Clifford's father died of, exactly?—and although Clifford put her
off, usually, with one of the little phrases they used, like "Mind your
own beeswax," or "What's it to *you*, kiddo," Janice never gave up.
Just the other day she had asked how Mrs. Bannon could own such
a pretty new car and such pretty clothes if she's just a store clerk,
and why is she always talking to Father Culhane after church, and
why does she smoke so many cigarettes, is it because she's nervous
or does she like the taste? Sometimes she'd break off, as if perplexed
by her own insistence. "I really *like* your mother," she would say,
and Clifford wouldn't reply; or he'd say, "Yeah, she's okay," and try
to change the subject. He didn't like Janice praising her, she didn't
even know his mother so how could she *praise* her—but he didn't
want anyone to criticize her, either. One day last year a tall sneering
kid named Jack Snyder had said something about the way Mrs.
Bannon laughed, said she "croaked like a frog in heat," and Clifford
had come across the lunch table like something shot from a catapult
and choked Jack Snyder's thick neck until he turned purple and kept
choking until Sister Mary Catherine pried away Clifford's fingers,
one by one. That was Clifford's first three-day suspension from school
and when he got back Janice had said, "Welcome to the club."

To escape the din of other people's voices Clifford had lately
begun spending more time on his schoolwork—especially his assignments for art class, which had absorbed him more than anything else
this year. In his other classes he daydreamed a lot, he was lackadaisi-
cal, he could get a B + or even an A without paying much attention,
but his attitude changed when St. John Bosco's newest lay teacher,
an energetic and exotic-looking woman named Miss Ramsay, arrived
on the scene—a teacher with "superior credentials," according to
Sister Mary Joseph's introduction during the first school assembly
that September; and, according to the schoolyard gossip, a woman

who had sacrificed her home in El Paso and a handsome Mexican fiancé and a university teaching job in order to tend her dying mother, who lived alone in a small frame house not far from St. John Bosco. But interest in Miss Ramsay's past was quickly displaced by her startling appearance, for she was a stunning woman in her forties who wore her silver-streaked black hair pulled flat against her skull, fastened in back with a clasp of turquoise or gold. She wore dresses with full skirts (bought in Mexico, the girls whispered) in dramatic reds and royal blues, often with a black cape slung carelessly over one shoulder, like an elegant serape; she wore necklaces of turquoise or jade or glossy black enamel, and matching long earrings that swung delicately when she tilted her oval-shaped head, mesmerizing the more impressionable of her students. Soon enough the boys fell in love with her, though the girls tried making fun of her for a while—offering tentative jabs at the prepossessing way she swept into the classroom ("Who does she think she is," Trudy Cravens whispered, "Loretta Young?") or the way, once she started talking in her low-pitched whispery voice, her coral-red lipstick would rub onto her teeth. But the girls had to admire her confident manner, her beautiful clothes and rather daring makeup, so that soon enough Miss Ramsay had won everyone over (even the nuns, some of whom allowed themselves, those first few weeks, a knowing smirk or lifted eyebrow whenever Miss Ramsay rustled past them in the hall). Clifford knew that Miss Ramsay hadn't even been conscious that she'd waged, and quickly won, a battle for the school's collective heart, since it was clear that the woman thought about nothing but her work.

Miss Ramsay's eye, Clifford noticed, would focus not on the individual student but on the piece of paper laying on each desk, with its unique arrangement of lines and squiggles and shadings. "Ooh, that's interesting," she would say as she went around the room, intoxicating the students with her heavy musk perfumes, and with the precise flicks of her red-painted finger onto the parts of a drawing that especially troubled or intrigued her. "Keep working, keep trying," she would say to the less talented students, their mouths twisted with effort as they labored to please her, the sides of their hands smeared with charcoal and perspiration. One day during the second week of school Clifford had experienced a rush of pleasure so intense he thought he might faint, simply because Miss Ramsay had paused beside him, had stared long and hard at his half-completed still life—a porcelain vase with chrysanthemums that Miss Ramsay had placed on her desk at the beginning of class—and had whispered, so low he could scarcely hear, "Aah, I have *one* genuine talent, I see—which is enough, which is quite enough!"

No one else had heard, and when Clifford swung his head around Miss Ramsay had moved to the next student. Clifford felt his blood tingling along his arms and fingers, his nostrils flaring at the scent of her perfume and in the glory of her unexpected praise. All during childhood he had sketched idly, dreamily, filling numberless Indian Chief tablets with his own peculiar renderings—skyscapes filled with ragged, drifting clouds, rooms dominated by hulking, over-sized furniture, faces or nude figures that he drew not from life but from his imagination, most of them never quite "finished" (or so his mother complained, her brows drawn together as she flipped through the pads) and all with a blank, anonymous look that somehow pleased him. Evidently they pleased Miss Ramsay, too, and during this fall term, inspired by her praise, he had done more drawings than in his previous twelve years put together: he would sit in a lounge chair by the living room window, his feet perched on the sill, or lie sideways in bed with one hand supporting his head, the other moving with quick, effortless skill along the page, with a power and sense of rightness that seemed not quite his own.

He was happy, at such times.

But on this Friday evening he isn't thinking about art or the compensations of his life, he's too frustrated and vulnerable, he has been finished with his meal for half an hour and sits listening help-lessly to his mother rambling on about other people, the quirks and deficiencies and general heartlessness of other people. Yes, Rita McCord was just jealous, probably, because Irene had "advantages" that Rita didn't; even in college Rita had part-time jobs while Irene just went shopping in the afternoons, or read for hours in some quiet corner of the library, and it was the same, of course, with Clifford's father, because he couldn't bear the fact that she had some money of her own, that she could get by without him if need be, his big heartless male ego couldn't stand for *that*. . . . Yes, she said, lighting another cigarette, nodding, she knew how men were, and naturally it was the same with Father Culhane, priests were only men after all, so of course he perceived her as an enemy, a natural enemy, though he probably wasn't conscious of it. But that's how people reacted, she said, to a self-sufficient woman, they felt there was something wrong with her, they shunned her out of envy and sheer hatefulness. . . .

So his mother goes on, talking endlessly, shuffling through her handful of obsessive topics, pausing only to gaze off into the distance and draw on her cigarette and narrow her dark blurry eyes as though staring down some invisible adversary. All at once Clifford feels that he cannot escape, that he will never move beyond this immediate constricted circle of his mother's fears and obsessions. Tonight he has plans to meet Ted at 8:30 for a camp out, perhaps their last together for this year since the weather will soon turn cold, but even this thought does not console him. In fact, he has that same sense of loss he often suffers with Ted out in the tent, when Ted has zipped himself back into his sleeping bag and gone instantly to sleep, leaving Clifford alone and bewildered, and rather hurt, his excitement and pleasure shrunk almost to nothing.

No, he thinks, he cannot escape the ordinary thin depressing reality of his life at school, his life with his mother, for he had glimpsed the flash of pain and resentment in Janice Rungren's eyes this morning as he backed away from her, his limbs and face tightened, a cold light issuing from his own eyes, just as he'd seen his mother's sudden grimace last night when she came upon him from behind, surprising him, while he sat drawing by the window. He'd been sketching one of those anonymous female heads, this one with mussed dark hair as though she'd just arisen from sleep, and a face that looked perplexed and half-formed, and his mother had startled him, laughing hoarsely, saying as she turned away, "My God, I don't look quite *that* bad, do I?" Clifford saw his mother's ugly grimace of self-recognition and had looked back at the drawing, alarmed. For the first time he saw that the head—a three-quarter profile, the face only vaguely sketched in—did suggest weariness and melancholy combined with preternatural excitement, the hair shapeless and un-tended, a mad gleam of mingled dissatisfaction and hopelessness in the half-closed eyes. . . . Recognizing his mother in the drawing, he'd felt a sharp resentment at her intrusion, a stifling hopelessness of his own. He'd felt constricted by the power wielded by his mother, and even by Janice Rungren—some great energy they possessed that was formed out of madness and love and that demanded a response he could never imagine, much less give. So that now, unable to bear his mother's voice, her predictable litany of complaints and hopes and fears, he responds at last when she repeats her absurd claim that Father Culhane is an enemy—a "natural enemy"—and this time adds that she hopes Clifford will be a different sort of priest, much more compassionate, much more understanding of women and their needs.

"No," Clifford says, when she pauses to get her breath. The word tolls distinct as a bell.

Slowly, her blurry dark eyes focus and rise to meet his. Yes, he thinks, she's the woman from his drawing: her dark hair cut brutally short in back and fluffed carelessly at her ears and forehead, her skin grainy and sallow from too many cigarettes, too much brandy to stave off her loneliness at night, and her eyes dark, damp as if with grief or mucous, so that it's difficult to tell if she's gazing inward or directly at Clifford. .

"What?" she says, an uncertain half-smile on her lips as she touches a finger to her earlobe, not sure if she heard correctly. "What did you say, honey? Did you—"

"No," Clifford says, in a blunt hard-edged voice. "*He's* not your enemy, Father Culhane's not, and neither is Aunt Rita. And—and neither is Dad."

His mother draws a quick breath, like a small hiccough, at the foreign sound of "Dad." She can't remember the last time he used that word, probably—and neither can Clifford.

"You're the enemy," he says, his hands fiddling with the silverware as he speaks, aware now that his heart is pounding. "You're *your own* enemy," he says very slowly, distinctly.

Frowning, she stabs out the cigarette in her helping of mashed potatoes.

"Cliff," she says, "I don't know who you've been talking to—"

"Nobody," Clifford says. "Not Aunt Rita, not Dad, not anyone at school. Nobody. Quit trying to shove the blame onto somebody else."

He hardly knows what he's saying—he's listening to himself as he goes along, wondering if the words are true.

His mother gives an odd strangled laugh. She says, "I don't know what's gotten into you, Cliff, maybe it's puberty or something, I don't know, but obviously there's something *wrong*. . . ." Her fingers trembling, she reaches for another cigarette but discovers the pack is empty; she crumples the cellophane quickly.

"Yes, something is very wrong with—"

"Nothing's wrong with me," Clifford says, "don't try to blame *me*, either," and he hears the sudden whine in his voice. Only a moment before he'd felt so grown-up, so sure of himself.

Surreptitiously he lowers his eyes, glancing at the Timex: it's 8:45, Ted is already waiting.

His mother's skin has turned a ghastly white. She has begun pulling at her lower lip, a gesture he remembers from last fall, when she'd sat around for days in that soiled bathrobe, not speaking, until Rita McCord finally rescued them.

He might as well finish, he thinks.

"As for this priesthood crap," he says roughly, "that's just a daydream of yours, you know. I never wanted to be a priest."

She reaches out her hand. She says, "Clifford—"

"I'd make a lousy priest!" he cries, jumping up from the chair. Sudden tears sting his eyes. "I don't even believe that stuff, it's a crazy religion, you'd have to be crazy to believe—I don't even think *you* believe—"

"Clifford," his mother says, also rising, "please don't worry, we'll go down and talk to Father Culhane tomorrow, something has come over you, I really think the devil has wormed his way into— but don't worry, honey, I know you don't mean any of this, I know you aren't one of *them*—"

Suddenly she is frantic and shivering—suddenly, he's quite sure, she is all right. She's a mother, once again; she has found herself.

"Anyway," she says, shaking a finger at him, "I think you'd better stay home this evening—you've been spending too much time with that Vernon boy, I think, and besides I'd like you to stay here, stay here with me, and in the morning I'll call Father Culhane and set up an appointment and we'll—"

"No!" Clifford shouts, backing away from the table, kicking a chair to one side in his awkward fury, his painful self-consciousness—for he doesn't want to throw a childish tantrum, that would be playing right into her hands. Yet he feels his stomach constricting, coldly, his chest and throat feel so tight he can scarcely breathe, his sensation of claustrophobia is so strong that he feels he has to escape, say anything or do anything, just so he can get out the door and away from his mother.

He tries to breathe. He tries, oddly, to smile. Where is that ironic Clifford Bannon from the classrooms of St. John Bosco, where is that half-mocking little grin he uses to respond to both praise and blame?

"I'm leaving," he says hoarsely. "You can't stop me."

"Clifford, I insist that you— Clifford, stop right there, don't you dare defy your own—"

"And yes," Clifford says, smiling coldly, ignoring her words but giving her an almost affectionate look before turning away, before running out the back door to meet Ted Vernon—"Yes, Mom," he says, stifling a sudden urge to laugh, "I'm definitely one of *them*."

Out in the tent he feels jumpy, not quite himself, even though several hours have passed, and when Ted asks an unexpected question Clifford wants desperately, for a perilous quicksilver moment, to blurt out the truth. They've just gotten into their sleeping bags and of course Ted is talking about sex, asking if the girls in Clifford's class have started bleeding yet, have their tits started growing yet, what about that girl he mentioned sometimes, that Janice Rungren, have *her* tits started growing, does he know what time of the month women can get pregnant, has he ever seen a grown-up woman naked, except for his mother, has he ever spied on his parents in their bedroom, late at night, has he ever seen them both naked together and what were they doing, were they—

Ted stops himself.

"Gee, I'm sorry," he says. "I forgot."

"Don't worry," Clifford says.

"When was it your father died?" Ted asks. "You must have said before, but I don't remember."

"My mother has been a widow," Clifford says slowly, "for the past three years. Since before we moved here—right before."

"Gee, that's tough," Ted says kindly, rising on one elbow. Ted has the big searchlight propped against the tent poles at their feet but now Clifford wishes Ted couldn't see his face, he desperately wishes their conversation hadn't taken this turn. When Ted asked about seeing grown-ups naked, Clifford had remembered standing at the bathroom door—he must have been four or five—one morning as his father came out of the shower, swathed in steam, his body big and hairy and pink-skinned. He had seemed like a great smiling god rising out of the sea, arms raised as he toweled his blond head, skin glowing, genitals swinging loose and free. He'd been smiling, humming a tune; he turned to the sink and reached for his shaving things without noticing Clifford, and Clifford had backed away, remembering an argument his parents had had earlier that week, his father shouting, "Oh, so you wish you were dead? Well where does that leave me, anyway? How am I supposed to live on *that*?"

Yes, he almost blurts out the truth to Ted Vernon, but he stops himself at the last moment; at the last possible moment.

"Bet you miss him, huh," Ted says.

But Clifford doesn't reply.

Janice

Janice and Clifford, Clifford and Janice, the rumors scatter like wildfire through St. John Bosco Elementary School, beginning that Tuesday morning during recess when Henry Ramirez, son of the school's gardener, whispers something into the ear of Jack Snyder, who tells his girlfriend, Trudy Cravens, who tells all the fifth- and sixth-grade girls, and one of *them* says she definitely saw Janice and Clifford the previous Friday after lunch, sneaking away, sneaking hand-in-hand back through the woods. Mary Frances Dennehy says importantly that *she's* not surprised, she always knew there was something fishy about Janice Rungren; and that Clifford Bannon is downright *strange,* making all A's the way he does but never saying much, looking angry all the time—she won't be surprised if they both get expelled when Father Culhane finds out; and maybe they'll be excommunicated, too, and doesn't that mean you're going straight to hell? But Henry Ramirez isn't sure about Father Culhane, he overheard his parents talking late last night about what to do, and Mrs. Ramirez had said that maybe Gus should tell Sister Mary Joseph, or one of the lay teachers?—everyone knows what a fiery temper Father Culhane has, and what if Gus himself were somehow blamed? Or maybe he shouldn't tell anyone at all, just mind his own business and pretend that nothing had happened?

"That's just like old Ramirez," one of the boys says when Henry is out of earshot. "Stupid lazy greaser, he just wants to save his own hide."

"Well, he doesn't have to pay tuition for Henry or Lupe, not like *our* parents do," says one of the girls. "So he's scared to death of Father Culhane. I mean, Gus Ramirez could lose his *job.*"

"Knowing Janice," says another, "she probably *would* blame Gus. She's so crazy about that stupid Clifford."

"Yeah, no telling what they've been up to—I wouldn't put anything past them."

"C'mon, you guys, Janice isn't that bad, is she? *Is she?*"

Rumors spread, theories evolve, all day Tuesday and Wednesday there is whispering between bells, pointing in the hallways, staring and giggling at recess; suddenly there is a magical space around both Janice and Clifford that no one violates. The whispering groups fall silent whenever one of them walks by, Clifford who's always gazing into the distance—strange kid!—while Janice gives everyone her slit-eyed glare, as if taunting them, daring them; but what's really newsworthy, what everyone notices by late Wednesday is that Clifford and Janice aren't talking to *each other.* Quickly the word spreads that Janice took a seat at the opposite corner of the cafeteria from Clifford on Tuesday and Wednesday both, they didn't talk before homeroom on either morning as usual, they didn't amble around the playground together during recess as usual, talking and laughing, as if pretending that no one else existed. Instead Janice has started hanging around with that dopey fifth-grade cousin of hers, Ruthie what's-her-name, Ruthie *Dawes*, that moon-faced little idiot with the thick glasses, and Clifford just sits out by the swing with his nose in a book or else watches the boys play touch football, though you can never tell if he's really watching or not. He's got that thin-lipped angry smirk on his face like he's mocking the other boys and their game or else is a million miles away, thinking of something else altogether.

It's not until that afternoon's theology class that everything comes apart, unravels. Except on Fridays, when Father Culhane visits the school, the sixth-graders have Sister Mary Joseph for theology, the only class taught by the smiling stern-voiced principal except for an occasional "health" lecture or special assembly address; she has been away from regular teaching for a long while, so her classroom disciplinary skills have eroded a bit. She doesn't have "eyes behind her head" like Sister Mary Immaculata and Sister Mary Catherine, so she ignores minor whispering and note passing, and handles even the bolder miscreants with only a mild rebuke, or a twitch of her pale bony finger. Lecturing, she has an airy insouciant manner, as though she's pleased to escape her office for a while, and on that Wednesday she doesn't seem to notice that Janice Rungren sits with her shoulders tensed and lower lip protruding, staring a hole into the back of Clifford Bannon one row over and two seats up, or that Clifford himself is aimlessly sketching in his notebook, head bent low, ink-stained fingers crimped tightly at the base of his pen.

Bet he's doing a picture of his girlfriend—you know who goes a note passed from Mary Frances Dennehy through Trudy Cravens's small perspiring hands to Lucia Gonzalez, who sits directly behind Janice.

Yeah, with no clothes on goes the note from Lucia back to Mary Frances, and Trudy has glanced at both notes en route and for several minutes the three girls try hard to stifle their giggling.

Sister Mary Joseph doesn't seem to notice. For the past half hour she has been discussing a topic dear to her heart—the stigmata. Sister Mary Joseph is a plain, blunt-faced woman with coarse skin and a prominent nose, but when she speaks of her pet subjects—the miracle at Fatima, the bodily assumption of Mary—her expression is childlike, otherworldly, and her students often giggle and exchange glances out of discomfiture more than amusement. Is *this* Sister Mary Joseph, the cool-headed principal who spends her days handling a stream of obstreperous students and disgruntled parents and administrative crises of every description? Is *this* the pragmatic, even-tempered woman who issues school orders and announcements over the loudspeakers each day without a moment's pause or hesitation? Yet here she is, blunt-fingered hands gesturing broadly, cheeks flushed and eyes damp as she discusses the handful of saints who have been blessed with the miraculous appearance on their bodies of Christ's wounds: who actually suffer, during the three-hour Passion on Good Friday, the spontaneous flowing of blood at their palms and feet, the sudden gash in their sides, the droplets of blood circling their foreheads like a crown. When Sister speaks the word *blood,* her voice has the same hushed and reverent tone used by the sixth-grade girls when they talk about love and marriage, and it is clear especially when she speaks of reputed modern-day bearers of the stigmata— Padre Pio in Rome, or the Bavarian peasant Theresa Neumann, who died only a couple of years ago—that she would welcome the stigmata herself. She remarks that being children, being young and unsullied still, the class ought to pray for such a gift in their lives, pray that it might happen to them or to someone close to them. What joy, what indescribable rapture to be the first American blessed with the stigmata!—and it was hardly impossible, after all. Christ had loved children, the Blessed Virgin had always favored peasants and students, ordinary young students—so yes, it could certainly happen!

By now, even Janice and Clifford are paying attention; some of the children are squirming in their desks; a few have glanced surreptitiously at their palms. Sister Mary Joseph, her face damp, her gray eyes alight, doesn't seem to notice her pupils' discomfort. She glances around, smiling, and nods happily when Brian McGreevy raises his hand.

"But what about afterward?" he asks. "Don't they need a doctor, after all that bleeding? Don't they need a transfusion?"

A scattering of giggles and snickers.

"No, not at all," Sister says, obviously pleased by the question.

"Doctors have no part in this. The wounds are miraculous in origin—they're a manifestation of Christ's passion. They appear and disappear, or they may remain for months, even years—but the person doesn't bleed to death. No one has ever died of the stigmata."

"But doesn't it hurt?" Mary Frances Dennehy asks, smiling sideways at Lucia and Trudy and Jennifer. "I mean, doesn't the bleeding hurt?"

"Yes indeed," Sister says, unfazed. After pacing about the room during her lecture she has now returned to her desk, hands folded as if providing an example to the class; she's the archetypal principal, abrupt and confident. Provider of answers. Dispeller of doubts.

"Yes," she says, ardently, "it hurts a great deal, since it duplicates the suffering of Christ's three-hour ordeal on the cross."

"Well, then *I* wouldn't want it," says another of the girls, and there's a sudden intake of breath from the class. The kids near the front of the room—all except Clifford Bannon, that is—twist their heads around, though of course they know who has spoken, they're quite familiar with Janice Rungren's trembling but petulant voice.

Sister Mary Joseph, being Sister Mary Joseph, expresses no shock or displeasure, but only leans her bulky frame a bit further across the desk.

"Excuse me?" she says, cupping her hand at one side of her veil (where her ear is well concealed but scarcely disabled; her ability to hear from any distance a whispered remark, especially an impious or disrespectful remark, is legendary at St. John Bosco). "Would you please repeat that, Janice?"

Janice's face has reddened; she kicks at the chair in front of her (Annie Shelton's chair, and Annie has turned halfway around with her nose wrinkled viciously at Janice) and looks miserably out the sides of her eyes toward Clifford, quiet well-behaved Clifford Bannon whose dark neat head still hasn't turned around. She says, taking a deep breath, trying to sound pert and offhand, "I said, I don't think I'd want it, Sister. The stigmata, I mean."

"Oh, you wouldn't, would you?' Sister Mary Joseph asks, and now most of the students turn back to her, attuned to the good humor and contempt mingled oddly in her voice. Some of them notice, maybe, that her fingers are no longer interlaced but have begun tapping lightly on the desk. Some of them notice, maybe, that her cheeks have visibly paled.

As the class waits, Annie Shelton begins swinging her arm wildly in the air.

"What is it, Annie?" Sister says evenly, her eyes still on Janice.

"Sister, is that where the word 'stigmatize' comes from? Like if someone is stigmatized, like Hester in *The Scarlet Letter,* or—"

"Never mind, Annie," Sister says abruptly. "This isn't English class, you know."

Annie Shelton slumps a little in her chair.

"Janice, would you stand up, please?" Sister asks.

The classroom is still.

She hesitates, she glances around, but after a few seconds, Janice gets awkwardly to her feet. Even now she keeps looking at Clifford, whom she blames for everything bad that has ever happened in her life, and mentally commands him to turn around (for she read in an advertisement in one of her mother's astrology magazines that you could use mental telepathy to make others do your bidding, following a manual that cost only $7.95—she had coaxed her mother into sending off for the book but it hasn't yet arrived); but of course Clifford won't budge and has even returned to his sketch as though nothing is happening. Little *Father Bannon,* as she has begun to think of him, derisively, little *Father Cliffie Bannon,* little *Pope Cliffie I*—of course he's preoccupied with priestly thoughts, of course he's much too good to glance around.

"Now," Sister Mary Joseph says, with an amused but unsmiling gaze that everyone knows is her most dangerous expression (the eyes filled with a humorous cold light, the lips a tight thin line), "would you care to repeat that, Janice? One more time?"

Rolling her eyes, Janice spits out the words: "I said, I wouldn't want the stigmata. I wouldn't *want* it."

"Is that right?" Sister says. "Well, I don't think it would want *you,* either."

So it's all a setup, a joke she has concocted in that shrewd quick-thinking way of parochial school nuns; and the class knows instinctively that it is permitted to laugh; and it does laugh, raucously.

Likewise Janice knows instinctively that she cannot sit down until given permission and so she remains standing, laughter washing around her—around her and Clifford, the only other student who isn't laughing—and as the laughter subsides one of the bolder kids, Jack Snyder, says loudly, "Yeah, but Rungren already had the stigmata—she had it last Friday. Ask Gus Ramirez!"

So it's out in the open, finally. Shockingly. Even the "class clown" Phil Witherspoon, even the sixth-grade girls' ringleader Mary Frances Dennehy wouldn't have dared such a comment, they're too smart for that. (Whereas Jack Snyder, besides being a bully and having grime-stained fingers from working in his father's auto-repair shop, has maintained the lowest average in the class since first grade: the last time he bloodied a smaller kid's nose Sister Mary Catherine screamed that he'd end up in the state penitentiary one day, which will turn out to be an accurate prediction.) Despite Sister's ashy-pale face and Janice's trembling shoulders, though, a few of the pupils can't control themselves. There are stray glances, titters. For two days now the class has been gossiping about nothing but Janice and Clifford, about Gus Ramirez and the garden shed and the blood-stained panties, and now the tension is nearly unbearable; everything is breaking open, unraveling; and of course Sister Mary Joseph must act quickly.

"Janice, go to my office," she says in a brisk voice, less angry than businesslike.

Janice leaves the room with her lower lip either trembling or sneering—it's difficult to tell.

"Class, write a two-page essay on the stigmata by the end of the period," Sister says.

Heavy black skirts swishing, she hurries after Janice, not bothering to quell the chattering and shrieking that begin the instant she steps out into the hall.

Sister begins by giving an outline—a "thumbnail sketch," she says, as if this were a classroom lecture—of Janice's reputation here at St. John Bosco. Its ups and downs, its wild fluctuations; the splendid peaks, the woeful valleys; the misleading calm plateaus.

Does Janice understand what that word means, "reputation"?—

a very important word for a young lady to know, she adds, arching her famous left eyebrow. *Very* important.

A long pause, while Sister gathers her thoughts.

Gazing across at Janice.

"Do you understand me? Janice?"

Mechanically Janice nods, not meeting Sister's eyes. She sits in the big overstuffed black Naugahyde chair where so many have sat, her hands clutching the worn cracking arms so many have clutched; focusing on the opposite wall, a spot roughly six inches above and to the left of Sister's veil, she assumes the blank unreadable gaze of the parochial student in trouble, an expression that Janice has mastered very well. She gives away nothing; she does not even move except to let her scuffed cordovan saddle shoes kick and fidget idly beneath the chair, just out of Sister's eyeline.

It's the same posture she assumed last night during those two phone calls that came so close together—Father Culhane, wanting to speak to Janice's father; that crazy Mrs. Bannon, wanting to speak to Janice's mother—while Janice had simply sat beside the telephone table in the dining room as her father had ordered, waited as her father and mother paced about and questioned her, and questioned each other, and argued and exclaimed and threw disbelieving looks at Janice.

All her mother's fault, Mr. Rungren had said, soon after hanging up with Father Culhane, though Janice had just told him in a bored faraway voice exactly what had happened—how Clifford had cut himself, he'd been fooling around with one of the garden tools, one of those sharp-bladed hedge clippers Gus Ramirez had left lying out; how the blood had gushed from Clifford's hand and Janice had nothing else to use, but he hadn't seen anything, *of course* she'd made him turn his head, and soon enough the bleeding stopped, and they went back inside the school without telling anyone what had happened; for nothing *had* happened, really.

So Janice told her father in a logical, faintly resentful voice, as though enduring some pointless formality.

That's right, it's *your* fault, Mr. Rungren had told his wife, rampaging through the downstairs rooms, going to the kitchen for a beer but then returning, going out to the game room and kicking the Ping-Pong table, kicking the beanbag chair against the wall but then returning, the *only* thing she had to do in her miserable existence was to look after Janice, see to Janice, while he spent fourteen hours a day trying to earn money for this oversized house and Mrs. Rungren's finned monstrosity of a car and the ungodly tuition for that fancy parochial school, and now he comes home to hear *this*, to hear that his eleven-year-old daughter had already gotten involved in— had already started experimenting with—had wandered off into the woods with some degenerate kid and ruined her reputation and made a *fool* out of Arthur Rungren. Did she know how many families in this stinking parish were customers of his—very big, important customers? Did she know how they'd be able to show their faces at mass on Sunday, didn't she have any pride, any *female* pride in her duties as a mother? Or was there such a thing—here he looked from Mrs. Rungren, who stood with her arms folded and lips trembling in the corner, to Janice who had fixed her gaze on the wall, and then back to Mrs. Rungren again—*was* there such a thing, anyway, did females *have* any pride?

"I guess not," Mr. Rungren spat out. "Judging by the two of you."

That's when the phone had rung a second time and Janice's mother had stalked over to the little table at Janice's elbow, but then could only listen helplessly to Clifford's mother—her shrieking was audible even to Janice, Mrs. Rungren had to hold the receiver several inches from her ear—and had occasionally interjected a *But* or a *Why are you* or a *Listen here*. But when Mrs. Bannon finished she just hung up and Janice's mother stared at the receiver in her hand, her blue-shadowed eyes wrinkled in disbelief, in histrionic rage and disgust, and finally she threw the receiver down and crossed her arms again and puckered her lips as though she'd just bitten down on a lemon.

"Bitch," she said. "That miserable croaking bitch, how dare she—"

Soon enough her parents had worn themselves out; they were more interested in fighting with each other than in punishing Janice, and after having her repeat the story a fourth or fifth time her father said, "Oh, the hell with it," and sent her up to bed. So that now, staring at the wall behind Sister Mary Joseph's head, Janice knows she must manipulate the nun into a similar response, into her own version of "Oh, the hell with it," and then Janice will be able to leave this stuffy cell-like office with its pale green walls and gruesome pictures of the Sacred Heart, the punctured and bleeding Sacred Heart, she can simply leave and no grown-up will ever mention the incident again and she can resume her career of hating Clifford Bannon.

So she says *Yes, Sister* at the appropriate times, *No, Sister* at the appropriate times, she hears the ticking of Sister's loud cheap alarm clock on her desktop, right next to the brass JFK bookends that keep Sister's favorite volumes—by C. S. Lewis, by Thomas Merton, by St. Thérèse, "The Little Flower"—in a neat and tidy row. Sister has droned for some minutes now about her perception that a small number of students here at St. John Bosco are specially gifted, that there is only a handful of students, really, who have both the brains and vitality—what one might call the "passion," Sister says, hurrying past the word—to excel at anything they try, to achieve any goal they set for themselves.

"But mere intelligence isn't enough, you know," Sister is saying. "Good grades aren't enough. It takes courage and spunk to succeed in the world out there—it takes a certain amount of stubbornness and pride."

Janice waits. Even her feet are still, her toes curled around the chair's two front legs.

"It also takes," Sister says, spacing the words for emphasis, "a spirit of—of adventure, you might say. Doesn't it, Janice? Don't you think that life requires our curiosity, our desire to try new things?"

If Sister means what she seems to mean, then Janice has entered a new world; this must be some kind of trick. Now Sister is opening her drawer and Janice looks quickly while the nun's head is bent and sees the bulky manila envelope Sister places before her on the desk.

"Janice?" Sister says. "Look at me."

Reluctantly, Janice looks. The half-pleasant musicality has left the nun's voice; she's getting down to business. "I'd hoped your classmates wouldn't gossip about this"——she flicks at the envelope with the back of her hand——"but one of the girls saw you, evidently. You and Clifford Bannon."

"Saw us?" Janice says.

"Saw you," Sister repeats, her eyes hardening as the moments slowly pass. "And Mr. Ramirez, of course, found these"——this time, she doesn't bother to flick the envelope——"and he informed Father Culhane, who spoke to your father and asked me to speak to you."

Janice steadies herself, crosses and recrosses her ankles. Sister has abandoned the friendly, encouraging approach, the pretense of understanding why Janice might have done such a thing, the willingness to ascribe even the vilest misbehavior to her status as a gifted child, to her "vitality" and need to investigate life. Instead Sister has assumed her best inquisitorial manner——lips pursed, brows gathered above the long waxy nose——but at least this approach is familiar, at least Janice remembers how this part goes.

"Janice, do you remember my 'health' lecture a couple of weeks ago?"

"Yes, Sister."

"And you remember the part about Eve's curse after she tempted Adam, and why women must bleed every month?"

"Yes, Sister."

Janice glances at that picture behind Sister Mary Joseph, that gruesome naked pulsating Sacred Heart——blood, so much blood! At this school, you couldn't escape blood.

She glances back.

"Well," Sister says, her voice softening, "is that what happened to you last Friday, Janice? Had you begun to menstruate?"

"No, Sister," Janice says mechanically, but now she feels something——a burning sensation, a twitching heat between her legs. (Only her imagination, surely, for as her father recently said, Janice is a highly "suggestible" child. Because her mother's fear of leaving the house has increased, sometimes Janice also refuses to go outside, disdaining the neighborhood kids and normal after-school pursuits. Because her mother often develops "sick headaches" and goes into her room and shuts the door for hours against Mr. Rungren, sometimes Janice does the same, claiming she doesn't feel well when her father comes tapping at the door. And when her mother screeches and throws things during one of her demonic binges, using filthy language, blaming Janice's father for her ruined life, why at those times Mr. Rungren has noticed that his daughter also misbehaves, and says disrespectful things, and screams like a banshee if she doesn't get her way—and then he has *two* crazy females on his hands. Yes, he'd said on that rainy weekend not long ago, sighing noisily, draining the last of his fourth beer, or his eighth beer, Janice is so "suggestible" that he really fears her mother's influence—fears what Janice herself might someday become.)

And sure enough the twitching hot pain subsides; Janice recrosses her ankles and yanks her navy wool skirt down over her bumpy knees.

Sister taps the envelope, once. She says, "But there was blood on these panties, Janice, and we know they're your panties. Your mother did confirm it."

Sister's eyelids close, for a long moment. When they open again her irises have darkened to gunmetal gray, thundercloud gray; the room itself seems to darken.

"So," Sister says, spreading her fingertips out on the desk, "it's your obligation to tell me what happened that day. Let's be frank, Janice. You attended my 'health' lecture, this shouldn't be so puzzling to you. *Did* he do something?"

"Do something?" Janice says blankly.

"Did he take advantage of you? Did he try to—to penetrate you?"

Often in future years Janice will look back to this moment, to her eleven-year-old self, and wish she'd been a natural actress, wish she had burst into tears and clasped her hands and cried, "Yes!— yes, Clifford Bannon opened my legs and made me bleed!"

But Janice only looks down, feeling her lashes brush together. She says, "No, Sister. He didn't."

Quickly Sister presses her advantage, knowing Janice is embarrassed and about to cry: "Then why were your panties off, Janice? Why were they bloodstained?"

Janice breathes deeply. In a quiet, respectful voice, she repeats the story she'd told her parents the night before.

Sister looks uncomfortable, skeptical; again her brows come together as though to say, "Cut himself on some hedge clippers! Indeed!" Janice studies the woman's veil, the starched white wimple, the voluminous black sleeves—she's grotesque, really. She's ridiculous. Why had Janice ever been afraid of her?—why should Janice be afraid of anyone?

"Janice?" Sister Mary Joseph says. "Would you like to reconsider your story?"

Janice's own eyes have turned hard—harder than Sister's own. She lifts her gaze to Sister Mary Joseph and feels, all at once, both calm and hateful; her heart scarcely resembles that gory thing on the wall; instead it has shriveled to a bit of stone or gravel, a grain of sand. To nothing—nothing at all! She feels what must be hate, that thing it is a mortal sin to feel, calm pure hate moving out from that absence where her heart should have been, filling her arms and legs, relaxing every muscle and even her skin, the very pores of her skin!

"Well," Janice says, "the truth is—the truth is that Clifford and I went out to the shed because—because he wanted to show me something. And when he showed me, I used my panties to wipe at the blood."

Sister's eyebrows lift in surprise. "Show you something, Janice? What do you—"

"The stigmata," Janice says, looking Sister in the eye. "It's supposed to be a secret, I guess, but Clifford has it—he has the stigmata."

Sister rises abruptly from the desk. She walks to the door behind Janice and opens it, then closes it; she moves toward the telephone stand by the window; she turns back to Janice with a ghastly look, less enraged than simply horror-struck, flabbergasted, disbelieving. She opens her mouth to speak. She closes her mouth. She sinks into her chair, removes her little rimless spectacles, and draws one hand slowly across her eyes.

Janice sits glaring at Sister Mary Joseph, her scuffed school shoes wrapped around the chair legs. She waits.

For a long moment they stare at one another, but Sister doesn't speak and Janice knows now that she won't; that she can't, really.

There is nothing to be said. And Janice knows that they are thinking the same thought, Janice with bitter pleasure, Sister Mary Joseph with guilty relief: the consoling thought that Janice is a sixth-grader now, after all; that this is Janice Rungren's last year at St. John Bosco Elementary School.

3

Janice

One day in November she pauses outside the chapel door at Pius XII Junior and Senior High School, a pretty blond fourteen-year-old in a white lacy blouse and navy skirt, a popular girl, a good student, a hallway monitor and second-prize winner at last year's science fair and a favorite of the nuns, especially Sister Mary Veronica, the school's dainty but intelligent principal; she pauses by the cracked-open door and glances down the hall in both directions—nothing, no one—and obeying a whimsical sudden impulse she eases herself through the door and pulls it shut. Once inside the chapel she turns her head in all directions, in that quick birdlike way of ninth-grade girls, her hair shimmering in the faint light, falling straight from a severe center part and framing either side of her heart-shaped face with its wide-set blue eyes, its dusting of freckles across cheeks and nose, its upper lip rising in two delicate points. Between them the pink tip of her tongue shows briefly, her eyes darting about the dimmed chapel as she wonders where he is, what excuse will she make if she's caught, should she slip back through the door and into the hall as if nothing had happened? Why *is* she taking this risk,

exactly? But she tiptoes away from the door and along the back edge
of the pews, squints up toward the darkened altar—nothing, no
one—and has almost decided that he's not here after all, he must
be serving his "detention" period somewhere else, when she glimpses
a crack of whitish light under one of the doors at the rear of the
chapel, the door to a small changing room, in the far corner, used
by Father Culhane when he says mass each morning at eleven. It's
this room that is lighted from within, a sliver of bright light showing
along the tiled floor, and now Janice Rungren tiptoes in that direction, her voice low, a mere whisper.

"Clifford? Is that you, are you there . . . ?"

No answer.

What if someone else is inside the room, one of the janitors
or nuns or even Father Culhane himself, what excuse would she
make, what does she want, why should she risk getting into trouble
for *him,* anyway? Yet there's a deep hot excitement in her belly, an
illicit thrill of longing and guilty pleasure she hasn't felt in quite
some time, and so she takes hold of the big round knob and gently
turns it, her eyes half-shutting against the sudden glare of fluorescent
light as the door opens, opens.

"Clifford?" she says, confused. "Clifford, is that you . . . ?"

Since entering Pius XII as a seventh-grader Janice has blended easily
into the school. She is better known for her pretty blond hair and
bright giggling laugh and excellent clothes than for her occasional
demerits in the cafeteria or in study hall, where her "liveliness"—
as Sister Mary Veronica likes to call it—sometimes gets out of control; but Janice's occasional roughhousing in the sluggish food line,
or among the rows of battered formica tables, and her bright rippling
laughter that sometimes rises powerfully in her chest for no reason,
or almost no reason, in study hall or Spanish or algebra and which
even her two hands clamped firmly across her mouth cannot stifle—
these minor infractions place Janice among the majority of girls her
age. Here at Pius XII she is pretty and popular, other kids envy her
good grades and expensive clothes, she often gets "plum" assignments
from Sister Mary Veronica or from the ninth-grade homeroom
teacher, Sister Mary Cecilia, the school's sweet-faced instructor in

music. As Sister Mary Veronica told her one day, when Janice had stayed after school to do a book report for extra credit, energy like Janice's was much to be admired, so long as it was channeled in the proper directions—and someone like Janice was to be much more respected than the type of "pasty-faced" girl, as Sister phrased it, who never misbehaved but who never opened her mouth, either, or distinguished herself in any way. Janice had avoided *that* fate, at least, Sister had said with a wink, and Janice hadn't thought it disrespectful, or irreverent, to wink back, though she'd immediately lowered her eyes and thus hadn't caught Sister's reaction.

So nowadays she is surrounded by friends and admirers; she is well-behaved and even pious during mass and theology class; it is well known that last year, during Lent, she gave her homely younger cousin, Ruthie Dawes, her very favorite new sweater, a white angora with pearlized buttons, as an act of humility and self-mortification. Yet she has come to enjoy performing saintly acts and feels a thrill of secret pleasure when Father Culhane gives her a stiff penance after her Saturday afternoon confession. In one memorable instance, she got *five* rosaries when all she'd done was tell her mother a tiny fib, but Janice had gone immediately to the back pew of the church and said the rosaries slowly, reverently, which took more than two hours and made her late for dinner that evening. She has dropped hints here and there that she might even enter the convent, for she *does* believe that she has a vocation and intends to pray constantly about this to the Blessed Virgin during the next school retreat. (Her parents are unable to disguise their horror whenever Janice mentions the convent—and this has, she must confess, only encouraged her to send off for brochures from the most cloistered and mysterious orders, located in far-flung regions of the United States and Canada.) So she is very happy, and these days when Janice thinks back to her days at St. John Bosco Elementary—the black crosses, the knuckle-rappings, the knitted eyebrows of Sister Mary Joseph as she considered the hopeless case of Janice Rungren—her memories seem those of some other child.

And there are boys, suddenly there are many boys, there are more boys in the school and even in her own class than she had realized, for she hadn't noticed most of them before—there are

dozens, hundreds of boys. An infinity of boys. Boys from the high
school cafeteria at the opposite end of the building often wander
over to "the pigsty"—as the junior high cafeteria is fondly nick-
named—for awkward foot-shuffling conversations in the hall with
Janice Rungren and Kathy McCord and two or three other ninth-
grade girls, all of them pretty, all of them good, and sometimes one
of the boys will take Janice's hand for a moment, or brush his
fingertip along her cheek, and she will think to herself, giddily, *Yes,
a miracle,* as she steps back or lowers her eyes, telling the boy no,
she can't date yet, no, but thanks for asking, she won't be sixteen
for almost two years, one year and eight months and three weeks
to be exact, but she does appreciate the invitation, there's nothing
she'd like better than a drive-in movie, she really *loves* drive-in movies—but no, definitely no.

   No is a word she says often and hears often, especially when
the topic is boys. During the "health" lectures given by Miss Finney,
the coltish young gym instructor who puzzles all the Pius XII girls
with her short unbecoming haircut and ugly denim jackets and prominent calf muscles, they learn that *No* is the most important word
they will ever learn, especially when they do begin dating. (Miss
Finney lifts her upper lip sharply whenever she says the word "dating"; clearly, she doesn't think much of boys.) Her father says *No*
whenever Janice asks to meet her girlfriends down at the Dairy
Queen on Friday evening, or on Saturday afternoon, he knows that
it's just an excuse to meet boys, he knows what boys are like at
that age, he's not even comfortable when she goes to CYO dances—
which are chaperoned so oppressively, Janice complains, that there
are two nuns for every girl; she and the other popular kids have
threatened to boycott all the CYO functions because they refuse to
be treated like little babies. Sometimes on weekday evenings the
phone will ring for Janice and Mr. Rungren will treat the poor brave
boy like a criminal, give him the third degree, ask him the most
embarrassing questions before handing the phone to his daughter.

   Five minutes, he'll tell her, and angrily Janice will turn her
back and say a few times into the phone, *I'm sorry, no,* or *I'd like to,
but I'm afraid I can't,* or once in a while, when Mr. Rungren's hovering
behind her back really gets on her nerves, she'll say, *No, I live in a*

*prison, didn't you know? I can't do anything, I have an armed escort around
the clock, my daddy pays him a thousand dollars an hour to protect my
precious virginity!*

Hanging up the phone, she'll turn to glare at her father——but
he will look strangely pleased, strangely satisfied.

"Believe me, I know what they're like," he'll often say.

Not long ago the phone had rung and her father hadn't even
passed the receiver to Janice.

"Who did you say? *Who* is calling?" her father shouted, and
then he said, "No, Janice certainly can't come to the phone, and no,
calling later would not be a good idea"——Mr. Rungren had paused
a beat or two, considering——"and in fact, don't ever call here again,
understand? Got it?"

"Daddy, who *was* that?" Janice had cried, though she knew
perfectly well. "Daddy, the whole school is going to think we're
weird," Janice had wailed, turning her back on her father as she
worked up the tears, though she knew perfectly well that the Rungrens, far from being considered "weird," were well known in the
school as one of the parish's wealthiest families. Mr. Rungren was a
phenomenally successful insurance man, Mrs. Rungren was pretty
and doll-like in her costly dresses and careful makeup, they lived in
that gorgeous split-level out in Lazy Acres——what could be weird
about the Rungrens?

"You stay away from that boy, that Clifford Bannon," her father
had said, addressing his daughter's quivering back without the slight-
est misgiving. "I can't believe he'd have the nerve to call here, after
that stunt he pulled——I can't believe you'd *want* to talk to a boy like
that!"

Curious, wanting to know if her father knew something she
didn't know, Janice delayed her weeping exit up the stairs.

"Like what?" she said sourly, not turning around. "A boy like
what?"

Now her mother's voice approached from the dining room;
obviously she'd been eavesdropping from the kitchen as she often
did whenever Mr. Rungren and Janice argued, and as usual she took
her husband's side.

"Well, he doesn't have much of a home life," Mrs. Rungren said. "And I've heard rumors that Mrs. Bannon—well, that she—"

"That she's crazy as a loon," Mr. Rungren finished.

"Oh, I wouldn't say *that*," Mrs. Rungren said, uncertainly.

"Hell, the way she mopes around church every Sunday, wearing that absurd long mantilla like some kind of goddamned Mexican—and how many years since her husband died, and she's still doing her grieving widow routine? And don't forget"—Mr. Rungren looks down at his wife, severely—"don't forget that business with Janice, over at St. John Bosco. For Christ's sake, he tries to rape my eleven-year-old daughter, drags her off the school property and out into the woods, and then his crazy mother calls up and starts blaming Janice, blaming us, blaming everyone but her own degenerate kid. Holy Christ!"

"Don't swear, dear," Mrs. Rungren murmured.

Without turning around Janice could see them, her father tall and hawk-nosed and scowling, running a hand through his thinning dark hair, her mother petite and pretty in her caramel-colored wool dress and white gingham apron, the outfit she wore to cook and serve dinner this evening; yes, they were a model American couple, Janice thought as she watched her mother slip her narrow shoulders into the crook of her husband's arm. Now that they'd entered their forties they'd "mellowed" a bit, as Janice overheard her mother saying one day to Aunt Lila, and it was true that they seldom argued anymore except when Mr. Rungren brought up the idea of leaving this "godforsaken, spic-ridden town," surely he was capable of "better things" in some city like Houston or Dallas. Though born and raised here, Mr. Rungren often complained about Vyler: what a strange city it was, the oil-rich "society" people on one side of town, the niggers and spics on the other, and everyone in the middle was in limbo, in a twilight zone, as if they didn't exist no matter how doggedly they worked and tried: so how on earth was a normal family man to survive? Doing well in business wasn't enough—the old money still turned up their noses. Moving into Lazy Acres (the most expensive subdivision in Vyler, after all!) wasn't enough: the Rungrens *still* hadn't been invited to join the country club, not only were the oil people snotty about their money and how they got it, they hated Catholics to boot, they were all fundamentalist yahoos, yes it was sadly, disgustingly true that a decent family man hadn't a chance in *this* benighted place. Yet he'd resigned himself, evidently. He'd given up, evidently. Not long ago, in a final spurt of anger, Mr. Rungren applied for a promotion and transfer without telling his wife and then announced at dinner that they'd be moving to a Houston suburb in two months' time, but Mrs. Rungren had locked herself inside her room and cried for several days and finally Mr. Rungren had turned down the promotion and they hadn't had a serious quarrel since.

She didn't want to leave this town, Mrs. Rungren often said. She'd seen a lot of places in her youth, she'd been a military brat and then had traveled to New York and even Europe during her college years, but after all this time she'd found no place better than right here, maybe it *was* just a smallish ugly city in east Texas to some people but it was home to her—no, she didn't like leaving town even briefly, even for vacations!—yes, this was *home* to her and about this issue she wasn't ashamed to be stubborn and ornery. After one of these little speeches Mrs. Rungren would laugh to herself, airily; her husband and daughter wouldn't reply since they'd heard it all before and they knew that Mrs. Rungren not only wouldn't leave town but generally refused to leave the house except for 10:00 mass on Sunday, when Mr. Rungren would close the garage door and Mrs. Rungren in her oversized dark glasses would scurry out into the garage and slip inside the car and lower the sun visor on her side, in preparation for the perilous two-mile drive to church. Mr. Rungren and Janice would flank her on either side in the church parking lot, distracting her with small talk until they got inside the cool dim safety of the vestibule, and then they reversed the whole procedure when mass was over and they had to get Mrs. Rungren home again. . . . So that evening in early November, only a few days before she would renew her patchy but never-quite-ended relationship with Clifford Bannon, it occurred to Janice to stop her parents' speculations about Clifford's "crazy" mother by tossing something smart over her shoulder as she ran up the stairs, something like

People who live in glass houses, or *Well, that's the pot calling the kettle black!*—sayings that were popular among the nuns at school. But Janice bit her tongue. For some time she has known that sarcasm gets her nowhere, that what her father really liked was for Janice to behave sweetly and prettily, to simper and beg and pretend to give in so that *he* could give in; or, conversely, to throw furious tantrums that reminded Mr. Rungren that he was the man of the house and must indulge the irrational, uncontrolled behavior of his women. Sometimes it occurred to Janice that she'd begun copying her mother's behavior, and that made her lip curl. But if it worked, it worked.

So she'd turned around, slowly. Pawing at her eyes.

"I'm sorry, Daddy," she said.

The two sharp creases in Mr. Rungren's forehead suddenly vanished. His cheek lifted on one side.

"Well—that's better," he said.

"We only want what's best for you," said Mrs. Rungren, who could always be counted on to repeat "motherly" lines from the situation comedies they watched in the evenings. Looking off-balance after the withdrawal of her husband's arm, Mrs. Rungren put her hands in her apron pockets and smiled sweetly, her eyes—which were a mild, pretty blue—nearly lost in the wide swath of violet eyeshadow and thick black eyeliner and spiky mascara she applied each morning and refreshed several times during the day. Mrs. Rungren often said that she never felt happier than when applying her makeup, especially her eye makeup, and though Janice still thought that the band of purplish and black paint made her mother look like a raccoon, or maybe a bandit, she wouldn't want her to stop wearing it. Early one morning she'd sneaked into her mother's bedroom to borrow some perfume at the moment her mother had just seated herself at the vanity table, her face looking pale and indistinct, like a mass of whitish clay with eye-holes, a mouth-hole. Her mother had stared at Janice in the mirror, lips parted in shock. Janice had backed away, stammering. Her mother needed the makeup, she thought, the way her father needed his white dress shirt (the cuffs buttoned during business hours, rolled halfway up the forearm after business hours) and Father Culhane his clerical collar and the nuns their billowing black habits. Otherwise the world swerved, went crazy, and you'd cling to anything rather than experience that.

"You're a friendly girl," Mrs. Rungren continued, "and that's nice, sweetheart, but you can't associate with just anyone. If you choose the wrong friends, you can get into all sorts of trouble."

Janice recognized this as a version of the "bad companions" lecture she had heard often from the nuns—long ago, her mother had attended parochial schools not much different from St. John Bosco and Pius XII.

"But I don't think," Janice began—looking from one parent to the other, sweetly—"I don't think Clifford is really *bad*. I think his mother just has some problems, you know?—and so Clifford has some problems. And anyway, it's important to forgive the faults of others," Janice said piously, staring at her father's massive black wingtips. "Even when they harm *us,*" she added, remembering foggily some long-ago theology lecture in which Father Culhane had described ancient Christians being persecuted—at times, even tortured and killed—by packs of vicious Jews.

But Mr. Rungren frowned again; he looked skeptical indeed. He said, "But Janice, it's hard to forgive a boy who would try—I mean, you were only eleven years old—"

"But he was just a baby, too—only twelve," Janice said, looking from one clunky wingtip to the other, imagining how one of them could easily crush Clifford Bannon's shapely skull, "and I don't think"—she paused for a moment, considering—"I don't think he knew what he was doing. I think he'd just come across a bad book or magazine, and he was trying to copy—I mean, he didn't act *mean* or anything, and I don't think he knew—I don't think it was his fault, completely."

"But honey, you can't blame a book or a magazine—" Mr. Rungren began.

"He was trying to act like a grown-up, maybe," Janice said softly. "Trying to act like a *man.*"

Mr. Rungren looked stymied. He glanced down at his wife, whose eyes had misted over, as though she were moved by her daughter's uncanny wisdom and understanding; he glanced at Janice, whose face had paled and whose eyes were downcast, staring at the floor, staring at her father's size-eleven shoes, which had begun to twitch a little, which had begun to grind slowly into the plush buff-colored carpet. After a moment of looking puzzled and uneasy, he took a deep breath and reached into his back pocket. Again the forehead creases vanished. One side of his handsome whisker-stubbled face smiled, then the other. He lifted his eyebrows as he glanced into the wallet, as if speculatively, his fingers moving playfully among the bills.

"Well," he said, "since I've got such a sweet little girl, I wonder how much I'd have to pay for a kiss this evening—?"

Mrs. Rungren laughed in delight; this was a familiar father-and-daughter game, and Mrs. Rungren was always delighted by what was familiar. She even said, roguishly, "A whole *lot,* I would think."

Janice ran forward, as expected. She put her arms around Daddy's waist, as expected.

"Well," she said, drawing back, her cheeks dimpling, "how about—one dollar?"

Her father lifted a dollar out of his wallet, held it up, and laughed gently when his daughter plucked the bill out of his fingers. He crouched until his cheek was in range of his daughter's pursed lips. Janice stuffed the bill inside her navy school skirt, then pecked her father on the cheek.

He straightened, looking genial and pleased. "Worth every penny!" he cried.

He looked down, winking. "How about another?"

He pulled out another bill, Janice snatched it away, her father bent down for another kiss. The process was repeated several times, and ended as usual with Mrs. Rungren saying playfully, plaintively, "Hey, how about *me?* Don't I get to buy a kiss? Don't I get to sell one?"

She laughed, thinly.

Mr. Rungren said something about getting a beer, said something about TV. Janice turned and raced up the stairs, shouting *Thank you, Daddy!*—though she wasn't thinking about her daddy. She was thinking about Clifford Bannon, whom she'd gladly kiss for free.

*   *   *

"Clifford?" she says, stepping inside, shutting the door carefully, quietly, "Clifford, is that you . . . ?"

He's sitting in one corner of Father Culhane's small changing room, perched on a high stool, his books and papers scattered across the simulated wood-grained table where the tiny cruets of wine and water, the server's paten, and other paraphernalia for the chapel masses are kept; Clifford has shoved all these things to one side and has his arms in a semicircle around his work, as though protecting the loose-leaf sheets—ten or twelve of them, Janice estimates— which are covered with Clifford's bold, elaborate handwriting. Clifford uses a black felt-tip pen when he writes, and he always writes rapidly, frantically, bent over his work in study hall, or during an English test, as though his writing were a desperate, private act. Whenever she cranes her neck to see over his shoulder, as she often does these days, Janice expects to see a hasty illegible scrawl, a mess of black marks and blots and smudges, but in fact Clifford's penmanship is fastidiously neat despite the intensity with which his crimped hand assaults the page. His letters are long and looping and carefully formed, all slanted gently to the left like rows of cockeyed soldiers. Now she doesn't try to speak, however; she pauses several feet away, put off by the look of surprise and displeasure on Clifford's face, which says clearly that he wishes she hadn't interrupted, that he'd like to get on with his work.

"I didn't know—I wasn't sure it was you," she says awkwardly.

"Yeah, it's me," he says, neither friendly nor unfriendly, not offering anything else.

"Oh," Janice says.

Strange, stubborn Clifford Bannon!—so smart, so "artistic," the nuns all said; yet not really popular with his teachers or classmates, much too private, too willful, apt to send you cross looks or ignore you outright if you tried to have a simple conversation, if you asked some harmless question about homework or football or the Monkees, or if you praised one of the strange portraits he drew in Sister Mary Matilda's art class, heads or profiles or sorrowful drooping women to which Clifford gave titles like *Magadalene,* or *Beauty,* or *Bereft.* Few people, or perhaps no people, got to know Clifford Bannon very well, as he didn't play sports and his mother no longer pushed him into parish activities and even during recess he stayed to himself, drawing or reading in an empty classroom, doodling on the covers of his textbooks, daydreaming with his clear expressionless brown eyes slanted up toward the top half of the windows, his finely boned face a bit sallow as if drained by excessive contemplation. In fact, most of his classmates ignored him as they'd always done; he might still have been that new kid from back in third grade, looking aimless and disconsolate; and in truth he still didn't fit in, he didn't look the part of a Pius XII ninth-grader. He wore tight black jeans instead of Levi's, and favored white cotton shirts (which were seldom ironed and which billowed around his thin waist and chest) instead of the permapress shirts in plaids and solids worn by the other boys; oddest of all, he wore his dark hair cropped close to the skull in these post-Beatles days, when even parochial students were allowed sideburns and wisps of hair straying over their ears.

Try as she might, and she tried quite often, Janice didn't understand Clifford Bannon. Ever since the puzzling incident at St. John Bosco—only three years ago, though it seemed a lifetime to Janice—the two hadn't really been friends except to say "hi" in the cafeteria or to exchange small neutral smiles when passing in the hall, but neither were they enemies or even particularly unfriendly. Janice had pushed the whole incident to the back of her mind, deliberately letting her memory blur, rejecting that image of her child's self sprawled naked in the gardener's shed on that fateful day—she even laughed to herself about it, thinking that kids did such things, didn't they, experimented with each other, played "doctor," were giggly and naughty but they were still innocent, weren't they? Innocent just the same? She wasn't even sure that the version she'd told her father the other night wasn't the truth, since by now her memory had warped what had happened in a dozen different directions; maybe Clifford *had* planned the whole thing, in some subtle way, had manipulated her out of her clothes and onto her back just so he could look at her with such cool indifference from ten feet away, not wanting to come any closer?

Yes, everything in the way Clifford greeted her—eyes clouded, arms kept protectively over his papers, shoulders hunched as though prepared to butt against her if she dared come any farther—sug-

gested that Janice was wasting her time, that she was taking an
uncharacteristic and stupid risk in leaving her position of responsibility for a few private words with Clifford Bannon. This morning
Father Culhane had come for his monthly conference with Sister
Mary Veronica, and because Sister's "secretary" Mrs. McGreevy (one
of the volunteer moms who helped out around the school) had a
dentist appointment, Sister had asked Janice to sit in her office and
answer the phone, saying Janice could do her reading there just as
well as in ninth-grade study hall. Every day for weeks Janice has
been reading during this period for her term theology paper on St.
Thérèse of Lisieux; she is now halfway through the *Autobiography* and
has already found a title for her paper—"The Little Flower: Portrait
of a Blossoming Soul"—of which she is extremely proud. So that
now, remembering the superhuman patience and sweetness of manner that distinguished St. Thérèse, Janice inclines her arm gracefully
toward Clifford's papers.

"What are you working on?" she says. "Is it—"

"The term paper," Clifford says shortly. "What else?"

The paper is due this coming Friday, and last week Father
Culhane had shocked the ninth-graders by insisting that the paper
should be five thousand words, and that it should be typed. Their
themes in other classes, even English class, were usually five hundred
words, handwritten, and the assignment had thrown the class, as
well as a few parents, into outright panic. But the ninth-graders
were lazy, Father Culhane had decided. The youth of this generation
had begun a frightening descent, he'd told them, running a hand
through his fiery red hair, his ruddy thick-skinned face flushing in
anger, in what seemed a kind of desperation—never mind the hippies
with their disgusting long hair and dirty feet, he went on, their drugs
and their protests and their licentiousness in general—never mind
them, for there was a more insidious kind of moral decadence which
he could perceive very clearly. Nowadays kids were spoiled rotten,
he told them. He saw signs of rot right here in this classroom, in
the fancy clothes and fat cheeks of kids who had no idea what
suffering was like (Mary Frances Dennehy, both well-dressed and
plump, had begun squirming at this point) and didn't know what
Christianity meant, for that matter, since their lives were so easy

and would always be easy. So if they couldn't learn by experience, maybe they could learn through their little intellects—Father Culhane's lips had lifted on the phrase "little intellects," in what must have been a sneer—and by reading and writing on the subject. Each child had been required to come up with a topic in two days, and to begin researching and writing immediately. Their entire term grade would depend on this paper, and the guidelines were strict: he wanted five thousand words, not forty-nine hundred; he didn't want typographical errors; he didn't want errors of any kind. When the students complained to their homeroom teachers, each of the nuns said the same thing: Father Culhane had been under a great deal of strain in recent weeks, not long ago he'd had a meeting with the bishop and maybe he would be transferred—or maybe he would *not* be transferred—but in any case, he'd gotten some bad news and the children would have to weather the storm just like everyone else, they would have to do the colossal theology assignment as best they could.

"But I can't *type,*" Annie Shelton complained to the ninth-grade homeroom teacher, Sister Mary Cecilia. "How can I make an A if I can't type?"

"Annie," Sister said, her delicate little mouth pursed in sympathy, "this time, I don't think even *you* will make an A."

But something had stirred in Janice in the days and weeks following Father Culhane's notorious assignment; she had always admired St. Thérèse and so, fearing competition, she had quickly obtained all the school's library books on the subject and had begun reading her eyes out, taking notes, making outlines; she'd even gotten her father to use the photocopy machine down at his office to reproduce portraits of the sweet-faced saint, which she planned to intersperse throughout her paper as "illustrations." Occasionally, as had happened last year during the science fair, Janice did get very interested in her schoolwork, although her work in general, according to the nuns, was "spotty," as was her attention during class and her deportment during chapel and the weekly hour of contemplation. Spotty, but occasionally "brilliant." Just as Clifford's artwork was called strange by Sister Mary Matilda, but also "brilliant." Often Janice had told herself that she and Clifford were soulmates, that eventually they would become close friends and possibly something more. Eventually you would get everything you prayed for, the nuns had always told them, but you might have to wait, and the waiting was the hard part; the waiting required the patience of a saint.

"What's your topic?" she asks Clifford, smiling. "I'm doing mine on St. Thérèse."

Clifford waits a moment, glancing at the door as though considering whether to bolt out of the room.

"Hey," he says, his voice pleasant but matter-of-fact, "are you supposed to be in here?"

"Are *you* supposed to be in here?" Janice asks, using the nuns' technique of answering a question with a question.

"I'm in detention," Clifford says. "Every day this week."

"I was there when you *got* detention, remember? I came here just to see you, Clifford Bannon. I risked my scrawny little neck."

Janice puts both hands around her neck and squeezes, letting her eyes roll back inside her head. To her extreme gratification, Clifford laughs.

"You're crazy," he says.

"But you're in detention," she says smartly, "not me."

Clifford narrows his eyes, as he'd done the previous Friday when Father Culhane had asked him to stand and recite the Apostles' Creed. Father had been lecturing the ninth-graders on the Immaculate Conception, which was *not* to be confused with the Virgin Birth, he said severely, crinkly reddish eyebrows gathered above his piercing blue eyes; it amazed him how often so-called "good Catholics" confused Mary's virginal status at the time of Christ's birth with her having been conceived without original sin. This explanation had led to a ringing lecture on original sin itself, which he reminded the students that none of *them* had been born without, and which meant that even the tiniest babies had an instrinsic mark of evil upon their soul, and if they died without being baptized . . . At which point Father Culhane, pacing up and down the rows of straight-backed students, had stopped beside the desk of Clifford Bannon, who was clearly not listening; who had let his head slump forward as he doodled aimlessly on the cover of his theology text. Normally Father Culhane's wayward Irish temper and bristling virility kept even the rowdiest kids in a state of wide-eyed paralysis, so he wasn't accustomed to lapses of attention, much less to being blatantly ignored. When he boomed out Clifford's name, Clifford had reacted only with a twitch of his shoulders; he'd shown no alarm, no terror; he'd slowly raised his head, blinking. "Yes, Father?" he said, and his sarcastic tone sent a shimmer through the classroom. Janice's heart had twitched with excitement, admiration, and she supposed that only she saw the sullen hesitation before Clifford obeyed each of Father Culhane's orders—to stand up, to hold his arms straight at his sides, to repeat the Apostles' Creed verbatim, not getting a word out of place, not leaving out so much as an *and* or *the*. After Clifford stumbled over the second sentence, Father Culhane had told him brusquely to sit down; he added that for the next two weeks Clifford would remain in chapel detention during recess, lunch, and study hall. When Father Culhane had finished and turned his back, Clifford's eyes narrowed, his lip curled downward on one side. By the time the priest reached the front of the room and resumed his lecture, Clifford had gone back to his doodling as though nothing had happened.

This, Janice now decides, is Clifford's typical expression—slightly bitter, slightly skeptical, but with an awareness that it's pointless to get excited or make a fuss, it isn't worth the effort. As Clifford sits giving her this look, she feels both excited and resentful. She comes closer, leaning back against the table and crossing her long legs, one of her knees brushing against Clifford's as he sits perched and silent on his high wooden stool. She follows his gaze—the narrowed eyes still a bit leery, a bit sour—down past her skirt to the inch or two of exposed knee to the long navy blue socks worn by most of the Pius girls. (For the idea of school uniforms for students of St. John Bosco and Pius XII continued to be rejected whenever the nuns brought it up. Such protests were usually spearheaded by girls from well-to-do families, like Janice and Mary Frances Dennehy, and by their mothers: especially by their mothers. Yet it turned out that many of the girls tended to copy one another, so that some days they arrived at school in virtually identical outfits.) Inside her brown-and-white saddle shoes her toes are twitching as he passes his gaze down and then up again, assessing, his attitude smug and superior even though her clothes are expensive and relatively new, while there's a small hole in one knee of his faded black jeans and his plain black loafers are scuffed and worn. *That boy is nothing but trouble, believe me,* her father had said. Feeling self-conscious but happy, Janice lifts herself into a sitting position on the table, letting her legs swing free.

"So what are you doing in here?" she says, lightly. "You're not supposed to study during detention. You're supposed to sit in the very back pew and remember your sins."

Clifford blinks, slowly. Lazily. "I hate wasting time," he says. "Besides, I want to do a good job on the term paper, don't I? For good old Father Culhane?"

"Clifford Bannon, you're the most sarcastic boy I've ever met," Janice says, aware that she is speaking in the flirtatious tone she uses on the other boys, and that this tone isn't quite suited to Clifford. She feels her cheeks reddening; her legs swing a bit faster, as if free of her control, and occasionally one of them brushes Clifford's knee.

"Am I?" Clifford says.

"Sometimes I think you don't even try," Janice says, starting to talk fast and without thinking, as she always does when she gets nervous. "I mean, you're the smartest boy in the class when you want to be, and before this year you never got into much trouble, but lately you're in detention every other week—and I think that's really *strange,* Clifford, it's almost like you want to get in trouble and get punished and—"

"And?" Clifford says. When Janice looks over, her cheeks burning—she had been watching the tips of her shoes as they swung back and forth, only half listening to herself—she sees that Clifford has put down his pen and folded his arms in an attitude of intent listening. A mock attitude, of course. A sarcastic attitude. When Janice's blush begins to die away she flips her hair back behind her ear, as she does every few minutes during the school day, with an air of casual disdain.

"*And,*" she says, trying to mimic him, "I'm just a little curious, that's all. Curious as to why—"

Abruptly Clifford unfolds his arms and slides off the stool. "Are you hungry?" he says.

"What?" Janice says, puzzled. "Am I—"

Clifford has turned away, bending down to one of the wood-grain cabinets, where he begins rifling through stacks of boxes and supplies.

"Oh Clifford, you shouldn't—" Nervously Janice checks her watch, amazed to discover that only a few minutes have passed. Father Culhane and Sister Mary Veronica's meeting will last another half hour at least, so there's really no chance of her being discovered; no one ever comes inside the chapel this late in the school day. But nonetheless her stomach is jumpy, she has that feeling of butterflies she gets whenever she has to recite poetry in English class; she discovers, oddly, that although she had a big lunch she *is* hungry, she's ravenously hungry; but her entire body goes cold when she sees what Clifford holds in his hands as he turns back to her, his lip curled downward again as though enjoying her discomfort, her utter shock. Out of a white oblong box he has removed a cellophane bag which contains dozens and perhaps hundreds of hosts—communion hosts, the tiny thin wafers that have been melting on Janice's tongue every school day and Sunday since the morning of her First Holy Communion.

"Clifford, what are you—"

"Here, have one," Clifford says, removing one from the bag as casually as if it were a potato chip. He holds it out. "C'mon," he says. "They're really pretty good. They're better if you chew them."

"But—but you're not supposed to chew them," Janice gasps. "You're not even supposed to *touch*—"

"Hey, relax," Clifford says, smiling. One after another, Clifford removes hosts from the bag and pops them in his mouth. He chews happily. He watches Janice as she recrosses her legs, half sitting and half leaning against the table, her eyes fixed in fascination and dread upon Clifford.

"Clifford, only a priest is supposed to touch those, it's sacrilegious, it's a mortal *sin*—"

"Don't be a dope," he says, clicking his tongue. "These aren't consecrated yet, there's nothing sacrilegious about it. They're just bread, that's all. Little pieces of bread."

Slowly, Janice unclenches her hands from the table behind her;

she tries to smile. Come to think of it, she does remember some long-ago theology class back at St. John Bosco, Sister Mary Joseph saying that before the hosts were consecrated anybody could touch them, that ordinary nuns baked them in convent kitchens, baked them by the thousands like cookies.... No, what Clifford is doing isn't so bad, he's just trying to shake her up, just trying to get a reaction. She takes a deep breath.

"I—I'm not hungry," she says.

He comes forward, reaching into the bag for another host.

"You're such a good girl, aren't you," he says. "These days."

"What? What are you—"

"C'mon," Clifford says, speaking gently, "open your mouth. You can open your mouth and I'll put it on your tongue, just like Culhane does."

"Clifford," she whispers, deeply frightened, deeply excited, "you shouldn't do this, they'll know who opened that box, you'll get into all sorts of terrible—"

"C'mon," Clifford says, smiling. "Open wide."

He has come very close now, so close that she can see the faint stubble of whiskers at his chin. This year the boys often talk about shaving, bragging about how often they have to shave, how thick their beards are, and she sees that Clifford has started, too. She hadn't noticed before. In his cheeks are tiny dents that deepen when he smiles. She hadn't noticed the dimples before, either; she supposes she has never been this close to Clifford, and she doesn't know if the sensation is pleasant or unpleasant as he bends toward her, the tiny host held between his two fingers in the air between them, that queer seductive half-mocking smile on his lips.

"Clifford?" she says. "Clifford, why are you"—but before she can finish this question he has brought the host to her lips and without thinking she puts out her tongue. Out of habit she holds the host in her mouth until it melts, then swallows guiltily.

"Clifford, I've got to go," she tells him.

"Do you? But why?" Clifford says. "You just got here."

Janice smiles, awkwardly. Again she grasps the table behind her, arms rigid, body cringing backward as Clifford steps closer, tossing the bag of hosts onto the table and resting his hands lightly, experimentally, on Janice's shoulders.

"Now that you're here," he says, "why don't you stay?"—his voice husky, gentle, appealing in a way Janice can't quite define. She is pinned against the edge of the table, she can feel Clifford's breath on her face and throat as he speaks, but there is nothing of mockery in his voice, and suddenly he doesn't seem the same person anymore—that strange and devious Clifford Bannon, with his narrowed eyes and skeptical half-smile—but someone much gentler, milder. She still has the pleasant yeasty taste of the host in her mouth and as Clifford brings his lips to hers she thinks of the stained-glass windows down at Sacred Heart Church that show Jesus in his white robes, rising from the dead, Jesus healing the sick and forgiving a fallen woman and summoning the little children onto his lap, Jesus with his face writhing in the passion and ecstasy of the crucifixion, lips parted, eyes rolling back inside his head.... Now as Clifford presses himself against her and prods her mouth with his hot rigid tongue, Janice unclenches her hands from the table and pulls his wiry strong body closer to hers; she keeps her eyes closed as their legs become entwined, as shoulders and elbows and knees bump together, as kisses turn into giggles—so much fumbling, so much awkwardness!—but then turn into moist heated kisses once again. Several times they almost lose their balance and fall to the floor like a single ungainly organism but they don't, Clifford reaches out and steadies them against the door, not missing a beat as his mouth sucks at Janice's in little hungry gasps.

Time passes. An eternity passes. Despite herself Janice can't help thinking of the hushed dim chapel beyond the closed door of this stuffy fluorescent-lit room, and beyond the chapel the rows of classrooms in which the students of Pius XII Junior and Senior High School are in study hall and biology and American history, living through an ordinary seventh period, drowsy and innocent and doomed, and suddenly it seems that she and Clifford have entered some dangerous new dimension, that they have departed time altogether, and abruptly she pulls back, averts her eyes from Clifford's face (so smeared and sleepy-looking, eyes half-closed, tongue exposed), and says in a jocular uneasy voice, "Hey, I didn't come back here for *this*"—and she tries to laugh.

"Didn't you?" Clifford says, taking her hands and lifting them to his mouth, kissing her fingers one by one.

"Didn't you?" he says again, and Janice is startled by the dark pained wondering look in his eyes, and startled by her own response, which isn't to adjust her skirt and leave quickly and quietly, tiptoeing back through the chapel and peeking out the door in both directions before stepping into the hall. No, instead she accepts Clifford when he comes forward again, she stops imagining what would happen if one of the nuns or another hall monitor or her own cousin Ruthie— sweet, pious little Ruthie, who sneaks into the chapel at odd times during the day—should discover them. She stops imagining alto- gether, stops thinking altogether, giving herself to the glowing sensa- tion that arises each time Clifford's mouth touches her body—her hand, lips, throat—and not even bothering to keep quiet, allowing herself to moan and whimper and squirm. When he lifts her skirt and curls his fingers around the elastic edge of her panties and jerks them down, inch by inch, one side and then the other side, she moves as necessary to make the process easier, and listens without alarm as Clifford opens his zipper—looking down at himself for a moment, panting—and pushes against her with a new urgency, jam- ming her hips against the table, so that the sudden white-hot pain is only another sensation she must feel, her head flung back, eyes and mouth contorted. By the time Clifford finally pulls away, fum- bling again with the front of his jeans, Janice has forgotten exactly who and where she is.

She says out loud, in a little stifled gasp, "Jesus!"—but as her hands mechanically adjust her panties and skirt and blouse, she watches Clifford as though waiting for a sign, Clifford who has taken a step or two backward but seems to have receded a great distance, like someone glimpsed through the wrong end of a telescope, and she sees that he is smiling, or half smiling, and shaking his head. He looks amused but also saddened, or perhaps he's just tired?—she'll never know, of course, what he's really thinking or feeling.

"No," he says, shoulders hunched, hands stuffed in his pock- ets—"I'm afraid it's only me."

Clifford

On Friday morning at half past eleven Clifford makes a phone call and then slips quietly out of the house. When he gets to the highway intersection six blocks away, the cab is already waiting. He gives the driver an address not far from Pius XII, then sits back and begins methodically cracking his knuckles. He's very nervous. Although he'd rather not acknowledge his anxiety and excitement, his turbulent wayward emotion, he's neither foolish nor dishonest and so he says to himself, Yes you're nervous but it's only natural, only normal, yes this is an important day but it doesn't have to screw up your life, you know. Because you don't have to let it.

He'd left a note on his pillow that read *I got a little bored, Mom. I'm going for a walk.* Last night his mother had cooked dinner for Mr. Parkins, a public school chemistry teacher who lived down the street, and after he left she had stayed up late, obviously upset. She cleaned the kitchen ferociously, banging pots together and slamming cabinet doors. Clifford hoped she had taken one of her pills and would sleep until one or two o'clock, as she often did; on his way out the door, he had quietly slipped the kitchen phone off the hook. Today was the last day of his weeklong suspension from school, and if the principal's office should call and discover that he'd broken the rules of his suspension by leaving the house, all hell might break loose. They might suspend him for the rest of the term, and though there were only two weeks left until Christmas vacation he'd have to repeat all his courses. That was a thought he couldn't abide, not the way things had been going lately. The other morning while Clifford sat in the den watching a game show, his mother had entered the room in her blue quilted housecoat, weeping, saying that she knew what Clifford was thinking about—he was thinking about *him*, wasn't he? Wishing his own mother would die, wasn't he, so that he could go and live with *him*?

Clifford hadn't responded. Staring blankly as a woman jumped up and down on "The Price Is Right," he felt an inward heaviness at the moment his mother referred to *him* as a living, breathing person——*him* was still a generally forbidden word, one his mother used only during periods of grave instability or during those times of hectic gay insouciance that disturbed him even more. For Clifford himself was disinclined to think of *him*. He'd almost come to believe that his father was dead, to think of himself as an "orphan," as his mother used to call him when they first moved here, her voice tender and aggrieved. But now it appears that he is no longer an orphan, and that neither he nor his mother can rest comfortably in the fiction they have developed over the years. This past Sunday night, around nine o'clock, the phone had rung and it had been Clifford's father. Predictably, his mother had grown shrill and hysterical, pacing the kitchen, stretching the phone cord as far as it would go, blaming her chronic unemployment and Clifford's "troublemaking" at school and assorted other tribulations on her husband, whom she would not allow to speak with Clifford. "After all this time," his mother had whispered into the phone, her eyes shut tight in pain or disbelief, "you have the nerve to ask for your son, as if he'd even *want* to speak to you, as if——" Clifford, who'd been leaning in the kitchen doorway, rubbing one bare foot with the other, had turned and gone back to the den and flipped on the TV, loud. What was going to happen, he thought, would happen. His mother had ruined her life by fighting the inevitable, and that was an error Clifford Bannon would never make.

This Friday the inevitable means waiting for Janice Rungren in an idling taxi, fidgeting in the backseat, rubbing his sweaty palms together.

"Hey kid," the driver says after a few minutes, catching his eye in the rearview. "The meter's still running, understand?"

Clifford leans toward the window. "I've got money," he mutters. In fact, he'd been watching the meter nervously. It reads $3.10 already, and he only has four dollars. He takes his old Timex out of his jeans pocket and sees that Janice is ten minutes late. He replaces the watch, thinking dourly that whatever would happen, would happen, when something catches his eye: down the sidewalk, in and out of the sunlight dappled by massive oaks and elms, he sees the quick tossing motion of Janice's light blond hair. She is running. Galloping. He rolls down the window and calls, "Hurry up!"—even though her gangly, flailing gait is surprisingly rapid, her long legs in their navy blue knee socks a whir of motion, her shoulder bag flapping at her side.

"Here she comes," Clifford says.

"Shouldda known," the driver says, putting the car in gear. "A female."

Janice gets in, apologizes, and then chatters profusely all the way to the Ramada Inn, behaving as if this taxi ride, this outing, is the most ordinary thing in the world. Last night he phoned her house, using their special signal of letting the phone ring once and hanging up, so that Janice would then call *him*, and Mr. Rungren, who distrusted teenage boys in general and Clifford in particular, would be none the wiser. Clifford had said only that he wanted "to meet someone," and could she skip away during lunch, if he promised to have her back before two o'clock? Though leaving school grounds without permission was a grievous offense, Clifford hadn't been surprised when she said *yes* at once, for that was Janice. She loved adventure, danger. She loved the idea of "putting one over," as she phrased it, on the nuns, while retaining her status as the model Catholic school girl, docile and smiling, modestly dressed, devoted to St. Thérèse, maybe even convent material despite her good looks and her popularity with the junior and senior boys.

When they first made love in the chapel anteroom three weeks before, he'd felt a hunger, an urgency in the way she clung to him, thrust herself against him; yet afterward she'd joked about it, referring to the incident—since they'd made love standing up—as their "standing joke," and chiding Clifford for absconding with her virginity. She spoke the words laughingly, as though they held no meaning. It had been Janice who initiated their lovemaking the following week, leading Clifford down the basement stairs, tiptoeing, giggling, saying that it was Jimmy the caretaker's day off and so why was Clifford lagging behind, why should they hesitate when there was no risk, no danger?

"So," Janice says now, her smile dimming when she sees Clifford's strained expression, "where the heck are we going?"

Clifford looks out the window. "Somewhere," he says.

"Hey," she says, slapping at his knee. "Don't clam up on me, you said we were going to meet someone, you've got to *tell* me——"

Her voice is light, teasing. When he doesn't respond she leans forward and taps the driver's shoulder. "Say, where's this car going?" she says playfully. "Am I being kidnapped or something? Is this some kind of plot?"

The driver is fiftyish, unshaven, wearing a soiled and shapeless cap. He's not in a playful mood.

"Ramada Inn," he tells her.

Janice falls back, clasping her hands in pretended shock.

"Clifford!" she cries.

"All right, all right," Clifford says, embarrassed. "Calm down, would you?"

She squeezes his thigh. "Come on, then, you've got to *tell* me, you can't just——"

"My father," Clifford says, looking away. "We're going to meet my father."

From the corner of his eye, Clifford can see her blond head cocking from side to side, her hair whitish and sparkling in a sudden flood of sunlight. They have just turned onto the Loop, a new four-lane highway stripped of trees on either side to make way for commercial development; a garish shopping center with bowling alley attached is already completed a mile down the road, and an enormous mall, Vyler's first, is in the planning stages, to be placed somewhere along the Loop's affluent southern curve. And now everything around Clifford——Janice in her blond exuberance and good clothes, the Checker cab with its mud-streaked hood and doors, the open and barren world spread forth on each side of the highway—takes on a vicious clarity, a reality, that fills him with dread. Here in December this small city, he thinks, is particularly ugly. (*Vyler is at its vilest today,* his mother had said half-jokingly a few days before, making the familiar pun he'd heard so often since moving here. She'd been gazing out the window at the dispirited gray-toned neighborhood and the ice-laden pines, the ancient gnarled pecan trees and mimosas——speaking mostly to herself, Clifford supposed.) Even in this area of commercial development the familiar inescapable stands of evergreen pine remain, now trimmed far back from the Loop on both sides, but the trees appear stunted, deadened, covered with a sooty haze; in the distance the city's large oil refinery is sending its eternal black smoke plumes into the air. Despite everything Clifford's mother often speaks of how beautiful Vyler can be—the azalea trails in April, the Rose Festival in October with its spectacular parade of marching bands and gaily decorated floats, the ostentatious displays of Christmas lights that have recently brightened Lazy Acres and other affluent subdivisions and the old redbrick mansions near the city square—but to Clifford these attractions always seem gaudy, superficial, mere tawdry attempts to dress up the essential barrenness of the place. In Vyler there is no art museum, no theater, no symphony; the single public library downtown—an ancient masonry structure with a desiccated red tile roof—is dank and musty inside, most of its books dating from the thirties and forties, virtually all its tables and chairs unoccupied even on weekends. (Above the broken pediment of the library door waves an untattered and ever-bright American flag: the building's only accoutrement that is replaced with faithful regularity.) Clifford doesn't know which he dislikes more, the crumbling downtown area with its outdated "art moderne" commercial buildings (hideous structures with their flat roofs and curved corners) or the flashy new residential developments like Lazy Acres, sprawling brick ranch-style and French provincial homes, the inevitable sharp-finned Cadillac parked on the inevitable curving front drive, to which middle-aged black maids are bussed out each morning from "colored town," and each evening bussed back again. Suddenly Clifford is assaulted by the distant memory of himself at four or five, treated by his parents to a Christmas production of *The Nutcracker Suite* in downtown Dallas: it had been a rare snowy day and his memory swirls with the bright-hued movement of the dancers' costumes, the hectic lovely snow-filled air as they emerged from the auditorium, he and his parents, chattering happily and innocently about the performance as if they might be attending this ballet every Christmas for the rest of their lives. . . . And now, gulping, he resists his fierce urge to tap the driver's shoulder and tell him to turn around. He sees that the meter says $3.90 and up ahead, to the right, looms the Ramada Inn, a colonial redbrick building with sparkling white columns and a marquee that reads PARDON OUR MESS!

"Meet *who?*" Janice is saying, in that fakey horrified voice used by all the ninth-grade girls. "But Clifford, I thought—"

Clifford says, shortly, "He and my mom got a divorce, but she doesn't want people to know. He still lives in Dallas. He wants to see me."

"A divorce?" she whispers.

The driver pulls up alongside the imposing glass entrance, and Clifford sighs in relief when he reads the meter. Four dollars. Exactly. He pulls the wad of bills from the pocket of his windbreaker and thrusts them at the driver.

"Thanks," he says.

"That'll be four dollars," the driver says, palming the bills smooth in his hands. "The fare is four dollars," he says.

Clifford knows the man expects a tip but there's no more money, *no more money*. Panicked, he turns to Janice and whispers, "Do you have anything in your purse—you know, for a tip?"

Janice veers her longish blue eyes off Clifford's discomfited face and toward the driver, who has turned sideways and raised his eyebrows, annoyed.

"A tip?" Janice says airily. "Does he want a tip?"

Clifford hears the mischievous lilt in her voice and quickly opens his door. At the same instant Janice leans forward and pecks the driver's stubbly cheek, calling out, "There you go! Don't spend it all in one place!"—giggling as she exits the cab. Clifford catches only a glimpse of the driver's slack-mouthed dazed expression and now he finds that he's laughing, too, he and Janice running toward the entrance of the Ramada Inn, shoulders hunched, breathless with daring. They stop at the entrance and turn to see the Checker cab tear out of the lot, so viciously fast that one wheel catches the curb. When it slams down again the hubcap—the cheap bottlecap variety—comes flying off, rolling across the asphalt and finally stopping only a few feet from Clifford and Janice, at the base of a little pine tree, a baby tree still held in place by stakes.

Now they are bent over double, laughing hysterically, Clifford's laughter just as violent and uncontrolled as Janice's. This isn't like him, he thinks, he's got to take hold of himself, he's got to remember where he is—

Janice is holding her sides, trying to stop laughing. "Did you see that guy," she says, "did you see his *face*—"

"Janice, stop," he says, "we've got to—"

"I should have said, *Here's* a tip for you, don't ride with strangers!"—and she erupts again over her own joke. "Get it, Clifford, telling a cabdriver not to ride with strangers? Oh Clifford, I'm so glad we got away from Pius, I feel so"—and before he understands what is happening she has slipped her arms around his waist, she is giving him an open-mouthed giggly kiss right out in public, in broad daylight!—and Clifford is deeply embarrassed.

"Stop that," he says, stepping away.

"Stop that," she mimics him. She turns on her heel, cocking her head one way, then the other.

"So," she says. "Where is this father of yours, anyway?"

Grimly, Clifford leads her through the glass doors, following signs to the coffee shop. His laughter has emptied him out and left him hollow, unprotected. He can't remember what was so funny.

What, has he brought Janice Rungren along? To meet his father?

The coffee shop is off the main lobby and entirely enclosed by glass. Standing near the entrance he feels vulnerable and exposed; he wanted to catch sight of his father before his father saw *him*. That was important, somehow. But the coffee shop is filled with middle-aged men in suits, any of whom could be his father—who might already have glimpsed Clifford, dropped money on the table, walked away. Ever since their phone conversation Clifford had imagined himself doing something like that, after just a momentary glimpse of the man sitting alone, checking his watch, waiting; he would stare hard at the man for a moment, his eyes narrowed, then simply walk away. He'd imagined feeling a dark sort of satisfaction, a sense of triumph. After all this time, he'd have the last laugh.

Though the fantasy was pleasant, he knew this wouldn't happen. Even before his father had telephoned, Clifford had noticed the shiny red Buick driving by the house, slowing, almost stopping; he'd recognized the squarish blond head peering out, squinting so hard that Clifford drew back behind the curtains. These days he often sat at the front window, doing charcoal sketches of the quiet, dim-looking houses across the street, the surrounding pines and mimosas, the phone poles and scattered bikes and oil-stained driveways. The neighborhood was ordinary, neither pretty nor ugly, but he'd grown perversely attached to it, and would sit drawing for hours while his mother watched soap operas in the den, smoking, sunk in melan-choly—Clifford would feel almost that he didn't exist as neighbor-hood kids raced along the street on their bikes, some of them familiar to him and some not; they seldom noticed him.

The more time he spent drawing the more attached he became to objects rather than people, as though the landscapes he drew werc dependable and changeless, while the kids and cars flashed by with the quick impermanence of minnows. He seldom went out into the neighborhood anymore. Even his old intimacy with Ted Vernon had all but ceased now that Ted was engrossed in his public high school life of football and proms and girlfriends; the weekend nights Ted once spent with Clifford in the backyard tent had given way to movie dates with girls or to "dragging Broadway"—the city's main street—with his friend Hank (who'd gotten a cherry red Mustang for his seventeenth birthday) and a rowdy gang of others from the public school. Once or twice Ted had hinted that he'd like to invite Clifford along some night, but the conversation had never gotten very far, both boys knowing it was impossible—Clifford was only fifteen, he went to Catholic school, he was part of a boyhood that Ted Vernon (over six feet tall by now, and already written up in the local paper as college football material) had quickly outgrown.

Clifford didn't really mind, for he'd outgrown Ted Vernon, too. He preferred staying home, reading or drawing. He didn't need people, he often thought. When he was old enough he'd go off to college (in her remorseful moods, his mother had promised him that he needn't worry about college—the money had already been set aside, in trust) where he planned to study art, preferably in some enormous university where he could pursue his life quietly, anony-mously. He could not really conceive of any details of the life he wanted except that he would keep drawing and painting, getting better all the time, and that he'd be living far away from here (he still felt that their move to this city had been an error, an unfortunate accident of fate: neither of them belonged here and neither had been happy, whatever "happiness" was). Yet when he sat at the window, drawing, he didn't feel unhappy or lonely, he didn't regret being a "misfit" (as Janice had once called him, fondly) both at school and in the neighborhood; instead he felt impersonal, detached, flooded with calm. Despite what Father Culhane had said the other day, when suspending Clifford from school, he felt no resentment toward anyone, no need to become a "rebel." He had finally gotten free, he thought, of both corrosive hatred and cringing love. He'd become himself at last, untouched and pure.

So when he spotted his father's car outside the living room window he'd been alarmed by the sudden, violent emotions he felt, lunging this way and that. First panic, then relief. A spurt of rage, then a throe of longing. A desire to protect his mother, to draw the curtains and lock the doors, and then a furious need to drag her out of the den and to the window, pointing and crying *See? See?* As Clifford watched helplessly his father passed the house three times, the third time coming to a full stop at the edge of the driveway so that Clifford's heart pounded in fury, in a kind of vicious joy. When the car pulled away, he knew he had witnessed a beginning rather than an ending, and that night, when the phone rang, Clifford hadn't been surprised by the shrill rise in his mother's voice. Nor had he been surprised when his father called again the next day, while his mother was at work, though he'd managed only a series of dull, robotlike answers: "Oh, hi. Okay, I guess. Huh? On Friday? Yeah, I guess I can. Okay, I will. Okay. Bye."

Putting down the receiver, Clifford had let his eyes fall shut. He'd felt that he might faint.

Now at the coffee shop entrance he feels a similar dizziness— so much noise and commotion, so many glaring surfaces of chrome and glass!—but Janice, as usual, is pulling at his arm, chattering in his ear.

"Well?" she says. "Which one is he? Can you see him?"

They're still outside the coffee shop, gawking through the glass partition.

"Quit pulling at me," Clifford mutters, but reluctantly he leads her toward the entrance.

"I can't *wait* to meet your father!" Janice cries.

When they reach the hostess station the restaurant interior abruptly shifts, comes into focus: the crowd of lunching businessmen fades, becomes blurry, as from a corner table Clifford's father stands partway up, his hand raised. Dressed in a handsome dark suit, a paisley tie. Smiling broadly. But it's Janice who cries out, "There he is!" and begins weaving through the tables, pulling Clifford by the hand.

"Mr. Bannon?" Janice asks, eagerly.

"Clifford, it's wonderful to see you," his father says genially.

Across the table, father and son shake hands. Clifford is embarrassed that his own hand feels sweaty, grimy, while his father's is cool and dry.

"This is Janice," Clifford says hoarsely. "Janice Rungren."

Immediately Janice starts telling Mr. Bannon how much she has wanted to meet him, how much she has heard about him, and so forth—all lies, of course, but now Clifford has a chance to get his breath. He shakes the napkin onto his lap, he takes a sip of water. There are only two place settings at the table and Clifford wonders if his father minds his having brought Janice, then thinks sullenly that he doesn't care if his father minds or not. (But why *has* he brought Janice, exactly?—he can't think, his heart is beating fast and he can't quite catch his breath.) As Janice chatters into Mr. Bannon's ear, leaning toward him confidingly (she took the seat closest to him, of course, so that Clifford has the chair directly opposite his father), Clifford notices that his father is nodding politely while Janice speaks, trying to smile, but his eyes keep darting back to Clifford, to his son. Now Janice is winding down and Clifford feels stymied, helpless: he has nothing to say to this man.

Janice tells Mr. Bannon, in a light flirtatious voice, that he's wearing a "groovy" tie—she just loves the new hippie look, she really does—and then Mr. Bannon laughs and so Clifford laughs, too.

"And you *look* like Clifford, especially around the eyes, I could see it right away—even though Clifford has dark hair," she adds, "and is such a skinny kid!" She laughs shrilly, giving Clifford a little smirk. She says, "But you do favor each other, I really think——"

"Do we?" Mr. Bannon interrupts. He turns his shoulders away from Janice, decisively, and raises his eyebrows at Clifford.

"I take after my mother," Clifford says conversationally to Janice. Once the words are out they sound a bit rude, but he hardly knows what he's saying. He has gotten more and more nervous—wiping his palms against his jeans, shifting from side to side in his chair.

"Well, that's true," Mr. Bannon concedes. "When you were born, you know, you already had this thatch of dark brown hair, exactly the shade of your mother's. Now your baby brother, on the other hand——"

His father breaks off, kneading his large ringless fingers together, his elbows set bluntly on the table as if to steady himself, and Clifford wonders if he's nervous, too. During their last years together—their last years as a "family"—Clifford's father had seemed a blond, broad-shouldered colossus, big and slow-moving, deliberately unbothered by his wife's erratic behavior. For more than a year after her baby's death Clifford's mother had stayed depressed and angry, assaulting her husband with unreasonable demands and recriminations, weeping, literally plucking at his elbow from the moment he arrived home from work. She would insist in a thick slurred voice that she needed another baby, that they *must* make another baby without delay, and as she followed him around, her hair mussed, no makeup, she reminded Clifford of a beggar assailing some well-to-do tourist; and at times, in fact, his well-dressed father behaved with a tourist's slightly annoyed indifference, no longer trying to comfort or mollify her, silently withdrawing his arm. His father had always been the kind of big, good-natured man who could not argue; he could show anger only by leaving the room.

In recent years Clifford has mostly shunned memories of his father, good and bad, but occasionally he allows himself the image (when lying in bed at night, hands clenched at his sides, hearing the tinkling of ice cubes as his mother drinks her brandy and water) of his father slamming out of the house that final time, his fleshy handsome face darkened with blood, while his mother stood screeching at the door long after the car pulled away. (Mr. Bannon hadn't taken so much as a suitcase, and he had not returned: his mother had received from their lawyer the notification of "legal separation," and the next day she let the Salvation Army cart away her husband's clothes and books; what they wouldn't take, she threw out.) During their last breakfast together, at the Adolphus Hotel that Sunday morning of Clifford's First Communion, the three of them had said nothing of substance: his mother had seethed with anger, her voice brittle when she could bear to speak at all, while his father had stayed deliberately, cheerfully obtuse as he chatted and joked his way through the meal. Clifford remembered that his mother had finally dropped her pose, and her incoherent last words to her husband had focused on Dennis, on *my baby,* on *my little one, my lost one,* and Clifford had sat quietly inside the shadow of his mother's grief and felt that he did not exist for her. A quiet, pragmatic nine-year-old, he'd decided not to become upset by his mother's words; nor had he allowed his father's leavetaking to upset him. . . . And now, facing this chunky blond man with his eyes so deep-set, so guarded, with his guilty half-smile that seems ready to express either mirth or sorrow, hope or despair, whatever emotion his abandoned son might deem appropriate, Clifford feels a tug of something like pity, knowing his father has wasted so much of his life, or lost it, while Clifford's still stretches before him in all hope and freshness. It's the same emotion he feels when glimpsing his mother as she sits watching TV in the den, slump-shouldered, or when he sees her fiddling with the garden hose out in the yard. He feels almost that he is the parent, and they are the children; that he is prepared to absolve them of all responsibility if only he could move quickly into the next stage of his life, free of them.

"It's okay," he tells his father. "You can talk about Dennis—you can talk about anything."

"Oh, my God!" Janice says shrilly. "I forgot that you'd had a little brother—you told everyone back in third grade, didn't you? My God, I can't believe I just *forgot.*"

Clifford glances aside, irritated. He had almost forgotten Janice.

"That's when it all began, you know," Mr. Bannon says to

Clifford, leaning forward anxiously. His father is over six feet tall, big-boned, solid; Clifford feels, or imagines that he feels, his father's body heat enveloping him, even in the midst of this crowded restaurant.

"Maybe," his father says, "if it hadn't been for Dennis, what happened to Dennis—she was sick, you know, that he hadn't been baptized. The christening had been scheduled for the following week—"

"Look," Clifford says, taking a deep breath, "she loved Dennis from the moment he was born, it has nothing to do with his being baptized or not. She blotted out everything else because he looked exactly like you, he was like another version of you—" But Clifford stops, confused, not understanding his own words.

"What?" his father cries. "A version of me?"

He reaches out his hands as though to seize Clifford's, like a man taking hold of a recalcitrant woman; then he withdraws them.

"As it turns out," Clifford says, "she could have used a spare"—and though the words sound cruel, and he hadn't meant to sound cruel, he lets them stand. Again he breathes deeply.

"Look," he says, "are we here to talk about this? What did you—"

"What did I want?" his father says, ironic, hurt, and now he does look over at Janice, who has sat pale and wide-eyed during this puzzling conversation between Clifford and his father.

"Don't worry about Janice," Clifford says quickly. "We're best friends, it doesn't matter if she's here."

As Clifford speaks the waitress arrives to take their order, and while waiting for the food they make small talk—about Janice and Clifford, their life at school, their plans for college. Janice says she has no interest in college, she'll probably just get married, but Clifford refuses to commit himself: he doesn't want to talk to his father about his artwork, his hopes for the future. For a few minutes his father becomes light-hearted, expansive, talking about his new job in Atlanta—he has a sales position with a new computer company, a firm that's on "the cutting edge," he says—but after the waitress brings their lunch he becomes serious again, taking small bites and chewing thoughtfully, and finally he says, "Why did I ask you here? What did I want?" And Clifford nods, hoping his boredom doesn't show too plainly in his face.

Slowly, haltingly, his father says he'd been trying to make sense of what had happened. He hopes Clifford understands that *his* life was torn apart, also, that he lost a spouse and both his children within a very short time, and that he'd had a bout of depression himself (though nothing so serious as Irene's, he adds quickly). He went through a period, he admits, of blaming other people. He knew that Mrs. Traynor had never liked him, had considered him a fortune hunter or worse, and had never been satisfied with his "conversion"—did Clifford know that from her deathbed, when they'd already been married two years and Irene was six months pregnant, his grandmother had still been asking Irene to consider an annulment, to acknowledge that a mere physical attraction had drawn her to this boy, who had no religion, no money, no family to speak of . . . ? Irene had laughed, Clifford's father says, and pointed to her stomach—that is, to Clifford—and said, But Mama, what about this? How would I explain to Monsignor Reilly about *this*?

"But no," his father says, "I don't blame your grandmother— and anyway she's dead now, there's no point in blaming the dead. But at the time I thought, She can keep her money and her suspicion and her stuffy narrow-minded religion. . . . I remember feeling so relieved that Irene hadn't inherited that religious stuff, that she was like your Uncle Pete and didn't really believe it—I just assumed they both went through the motions to please their mother, I never dreamed Irene would go *back* to all that. . . ."

He stops, squaring his shoulders; small dents appear in his broad fleshy cheeks as he tries to smile, to apologize.

"Sorry," he says, "I know it's still *your* religion, but I—"

"It's all right," Clifford says. "Go ahead, you were saying how you don't blame other people."

Hearing the sarcasm in his voice, Clifford realizes he's no longer nervous. He sits calm and attentive, like a model classroom child.

"Janet, this must be boring for you," Mr. Bannon says, "all this family talk—"

"No, it's okay, *please,*" Janice says, and Clifford watches in alarm as she reaches out to touch his father's hand. It's the merest touch, light and quick, and then she folds her slender arms and resumes her expression of intent listening.

"Thanks," Mr. Bannon whispers.

"But it's Janice, not Janet," Clifford says. "Her name is Janice."

"Anyhow," his father says, not hearing, his deep-set eyes like dark wedges as he stares down at his big hands curled around his coffee cup, "I finally decided that the fault lay in the marriage itself, Clifford, that it was based on the wrong things—on the wrong, um, emotions. When I met your mother at S.M.U.—we met in the biology lab, did we ever tell you that?—I thought she was the loveliest thing I'd ever seen. So petite and sweet-faced, with those little dimples and her fluffy dark hair. I didn't know her mother was well-to-do, I didn't know she'd almost entered a convent instead of coming to college, I didn't know any of that. . . . I was just a football player, a scholarship boy who was lonely and ready to fall in love, and who thought he *had* fallen in love—but it was an infatuation, really. That was harmless enough, I suppose, but the real mistake came later, Clifford, when I realized how unhappy she'd been, when I started feeling a bit uncomfortable by how intensely happy she seemed *now,* how intensely relieved. We hadn't dated two weeks before she started talking about marriage, and feeling me out about converting to Catholicism, and there was such an appeal in what she was asking me—which was, simply, for me to rescue her. To save her. She was unhappy, she was lonely and depressed and at times, she hinted, rather desperate. She wanted to live a good life, she said, full of love and laughter and children, lots of children. . . . Well, I think it was vanity," he says, his thick blond eyebrows lifting somberly, "I think she appealed to my vanity, because I'd had my own problems with self-esteem, with my identity—you know that my father drank quite a bit and my mother died, Clifford, when I was about your age, and I felt—I felt—"

He breaks off, again squaring his shoulders and trying to smile. "Sorry," he says, "I don't mean this to be 'true confessions,' I'm just trying to—to explain, to justify—"

"We understand," Janice says quickly, and now Clifford feels her foot under the table, nudging him. "Don't we, Clifford? *Don't we?*"

"Sure," Clifford says, coolly. His heart has calmed, his eyes have narrowed, but he doesn't know if he believes his father—that is, he believes the facts but isn't sure about his father's abashed, contrite demeanor, his seeming inability, at the moment, to meet Clifford's eyes. He looks like a football player still, Clifford thinks, his big muscular frame seeming barely contained by the navy pin-striped suit, the thick hair even lighter than Clifford remembered, carefully styled and sprayed like a teenager's hair. Yes, he has an unexpected liking for his father, and doesn't think he's lying, exactly; though he may be lying to himself. For there's an undercurrent of defensiveness and self-pity in his father's manner, which has brought to Clifford's heart tiny spasms of recognition, and the memory of his mother's angry scorn: Yes, you're just like him, aren't you—you're dying to be with *him*.

Now his father says, simply, "I couldn't save her. She thought I could stand between her and her illness, and then she thought Dennis could—but it just didn't work, Clifford. One person just can't save another."

"But what about me?" Clifford asks suddenly.

"What?" his father says, puzzled. "You . . . ?"

"Why you and Dennis? Why not me?"

Again his father lowers his eyes. He says slowly, "Don't get me wrong, Clifford, your mother always loved you, *always*—in fact, I think she considered you an extension of herself, somehow. Like you say, you always took after her, you looked like her and you had something of her personality, you were a rather quiet, tense little boy, you held everything inside. . . ."

"But *she* doesn't do that, you know," Clifford says bitterly. "Not anymore."

His father pauses, as though collecting his thoughts. He says carefully, "Look, I know it's been tough on you, I've been keeping in touch through Rita McCord on a weekly basis, really I have, it's not like I just turned my back on you. I've sent money, too, though she hardly needs it. I've sent child support. . . . Anyhow, I wanted you to know all this, Rita says you're very mature for your age and so we thought this talk would be a good thing, and I especially want you to understand that no one is to 'blame' here, not me or your mother and certainly not you. . . . Sometimes a divorce is just inevitable, Son, and there's nothing to be done about it. I wish that's something the Catholic Church would understand, I think they do their members a disservice when they don't acknowledge—"

"I know that, Dad," Clifford says tightly. "I know all that."

His father gazes across at him, sadly. He says, his voice lowered almost to a whisper, "And Clifford, I wanted you to know that I've met someone, a wonderful woman who works where I do. She was in Dallas for a convention, and we met, and pretty soon I was visiting Atlanta on a regular basis, and I managed to get a position right in her own department. Her name is Miriam and she's—"

"You're getting married?" Clifford says, hating his own stupidity for feeling surprised and displeased. Why hadn't he foreseen this?

"Yes," his father says, looking worried again, "and your Uncle Pete has met her, and really likes her a lot—I hope you can get to know your Uncle Pete someday, Clifford, he's a terrific guy, he's so different from—but anyway, I know your mother won't take it well, I know how she'll interpret it, but she's got to know eventually, I think, at least in order for us—for you and me—"

"Yes," Clifford says quickly, hoping to silence him, but his father keeps talking. His father's second cup of coffee arrives, and the dessert arrives, and the check arrives, but still his father keeps talking in his soft, unhappy voice, still he keeps apologizing and kneading his big hands together, saying he hopes that Clifford will understand. He knows that everything will work out, and before long maybe Irene will let Clifford come out to Atlanta for a visit, he really wants to hear about Clifford's school life, and what he's thinking and feeling—today, unfortunately, he has spent their entire visit talking about himself! And he quickly checks his watch, then reaches into his wallet and pulls out a wad of bills.

"Here you go, Son—I want you to have this," he says. "Buy yourself something for Christmas, and something for your girlfriend here"—he flashes an uneasy smile at Janice—"and remember that I haven't forgotten you, I'll always send money and think of you and try to keep in touch, to the extent that your mother allows. . . ."

His fingers numb, Clifford takes the money: a handful of fifties and twenties.

Walking out to the car Mr. Bannon keeps talking in a rueful voice about the necessity of change, the inevitability of unpleasant things like divorce, and separation from one's own children. . . . "It's human nature, probably," he says, "constancy just isn't the strong point of our species, or maybe just of our gender"—he laughs to himself, walking hurriedly—"or maybe it's just the times we live in," he says. "I mean just look what's happening over in Vietnam, and the racial mess, and kids dropping out of society and taking drugs, ruining their lives. . . . No, you can't pin all your hopes on one other person, one relationship," he says, preceding Clifford and Janice out the glass doors into the brisk December air and then, as Clifford comes out, reaching behind his son's neck and squeezing, as he'd done when Clifford was a very young boy. "And certainly not in any religious institution," his father adds, "they have such a vested interest in resisting change, after all, keeping themselves *blind* to the need for change. . . ." Then, out in the parking lot, next to the candy-apple-red Buick, which already has his father's bags stowed in the backseat, there is a long and awkward pause.

"I'm really glad," his father says, "that we had this little talk."

"Yeah, sure, but what about . . ." but Clifford doesn't know how to finish this sentence and he notices that the wind has picked up during lunch so that his few meager words are torn away. Beside him Janice whispers something, at least he thinks he heard her, but when he glances aside she is only standing there looking very cold, her knees bent and held slightly together, her arms folded against the wind, her face squinting in what might be a hectic smile or a look of extreme anguish. She hasn't said a word since before Mr. Bannon's long monologue about his divorce from Clifford's mother.

Now his father bends down, awkwardly. He hugs Clifford, patting his back and squeezing his neck again. Submitting to this embrace, Clifford feels very little. The urge to speak, to protest, has left him. This leavetaking is a kind of formality, he thinks, that must simply be gotten through.

His father says a few polite words to Janice, who stands shivering violently, her arms wrapped tight around her body, and then he glances at his watch and mumbles something about a plane to catch, and then looks back at Clifford a final time and winks. By now, though his cracked leather jacket is really quite snug and warm, Clifford is also shivering, and he takes Janice's hand and they back away from the curb.

Now his father crosses his own arms and flaps them, penguin-style, grinning. "We're in for some cold weather, it looks like!" he shouts, and he walks around to the driver's side and gets into the car and drives off.

Holding Janice's hand, Clifford stares after the red Buick—which is only a rental car, he sees, not even his father's real car—until it blends into the other traffic out on the highway. Then he looks down at his left fist, which is still clenched around the wad of money. He and Janice watch mesmerized as his fingers slowly unfold—like a blossom, he thinks, like a strange thing of beauty—and the money swirls out onto the chilly December wind.

Staring at his empty hand Clifford thinks *What now?* and then, on impulse, lunges after one of the bills that has landed on the pavement near their feet. Still beside him, still trembling in the cold, Janice giggles and presses closer against his side.

Thank God, the bill is a fifty.

"Come on," he says, and pulling Janice after him he runs back toward the glass doors and into the lobby. He points Janice toward one of the wide upholstered banquettes, hidden from view of the registration desk by a huge ficus tree, and then he approaches the desk, the fifty outstretched in his hand, and tells the man he's Clifford Bannon, he's Jim Bannon's son and his father has changed his mind—he'll be needing that room for one additional night.

The man looks up, briefly, and then consults his papers. He's portly and double-chinned, with bushy sideburns; now his pale blue eyes rise above his half-glasses and focus on Clifford.

"Double occupancy?" he says. "Or single?"

Clifford swallows, nervously. "What did you——"

"It *was* a single," the man says—tapping a bill that bears, Clifford sees, his father's signature.

"Oh, right," Clifford stammers—"well, now it's a double."

"Twenty-two dollars," the man says, "plus tax," and after a minute of staring at the orange-and-red floral design in the lobby carpet Clifford gets his change and a key to room 312.

"Enjoy your stay," the man says.

Though the room is overheated and decorated in the same orange-and-red tones—over the bed there's a bullfighting scene, a gash of red in the bull's left side—Janice is still shivering, saying *Brr* and laughing to herself, walking in little awkward steps as though she's drunk. While Clifford double-locks the door and draws the curtains, she plops into a chair beside the bed.

"Whew!" she says under her breath, as if speaking to herself. "What a day . . ."

Clifford looks around the room, somehow pleased that the maid hasn't come—he sees a partly filled water glass, he sees a wad of used Kleenex on the floor beside the dresser. The bed is unmade but still neat, the covers turned down chastely on one side, a pillow folded and crushed against the headboard. The bed looks snug and inviting, maybe still warmed by the heat of his father's body.

Now Clifford walks over to Janice and pulls her up in a quick graceful movement, as if they're going to dance. "C'mon," he says, and as they walk sideways toward the bed he nuzzles her neck, his eyes closed, and when his leg touches the mattress he grabs her waist and pulls them both sideways onto the bed, where Janice giggles and squeals, and pretends to struggle, while Clifford alternately pulls at his own clothes and hers, getting his jacket off, then his shirt, undoing the buttons of Janice's blouse and tugging at the sides of her skirt.

"Clifford, stop that!" she cries, but he's very efficient and has even maneuvered them under the covers, where the bed is still warm and snug, where the feel of the smooth sheets against his bare skin is delicious, irresistible; he nestles into the warmer smoothness of Janice's legs pulled tight along his sides, his thighs, and though his eyes are shut tight he can tell that she's no longer giggling.

"Clifford?" she says, faintly, "should we be doing this? Should we——"

By now they are naked and under the covers, but Clifford's pleasure isn't complete until he pulls the covers over both their heads and stretches his body tight and heated over Janice's, his extended arms and legs along hers, his mouth clamped tight upon hers. Ever since that day in the chapel anteroom their lovemaking has been furtive and partial; either they kept themselves fully clothed as on that first day, both with an ear cocked toward the hallway in case one of the nuns should happen along; or else, during the few times they've sneaked down to the basement on Wednesdays, Jimmy the caretaker's day off, they've undressed but made love awkwardly and uncomfortably atop their little pile of clothes on the damp chilly cement floor, their bare arms and buttocks turning to gooseflesh within minutes, even their teeth chattering as they moved together frantically in a brief overheated coupling, panting into each other's shoulders, even then half fearful that Father Culhane might come clambering down the stairs (he had a "mechanical bent," as he often said, and liked to "check" the furnace or the plumbing when Jimmy wasn't around) or that they might somehow be missed in all the hectic activity just above.

But today, Clifford thinks, there's no hurry, there's nothing to worry about, and keeping his eyes clenched tight he arches his back slowly and prods at Janice, hearing her little cries and moans as if from a great distance, and entering her Clifford has never felt more powerful, more in control, in all their previous times together they have never generated such heat!——and he presses the side of his face against hers, feeling his cheekbone jam hard against hers, and he hears his own panting from a great distance, too, all his attention upon that terrible friction, that heat, until finally he empties himself into it, shuddering with pleasure, with relief, his mind blank and dark and cool as though he has emptied out everything he has ever felt or known.

He opens his eyes and sees Janice watching him, her blue eyes big and puzzled. Now they're lying on their sides, the covers halfway off, though he doesn't remember pulling away from her; he doesn't remember anything.

"Clifford?" Janice says, faintly. "Are you—"

"I'm okay," he says quickly, trying to look nonchalant with his coolly narrowed eyes, one arm crooked behind his head.

"Clifford," she says, stammering, "I'm not sure we should—I mean, it's getting late, we're going to get in trouble—"

"I'm already in trouble," he snaps, irritated that she's thinking about school—about ordinary life.

"But if they find out you left home, and then they discover I'm missing—"

"Look, we'll make up something," he says idly, staring at the ceiling. This moment will never be repeated, he thinks. Even this place is anonymous, not quite real; he's pleased by the thought that he'll never again find himself inside room 312 of the Ramada Inn. Why doesn't Janice understand?

"It doesn't matter, anyway," he says. "This is a terrific day."

"But what about—"

"Anyway, who cares about school?" he says. "In fact, we ought to *tell* them what we've been doing—we ought to rub their faces in it!"

Janice stays silent; obviously she's shocked, but the sudden bright anger coursing through Clifford is too pleasurable to relinquish, it's somehow fuller and more passionate than his sexual pleasure a few minutes before. Everything he's feeling is suddenly sharper, bolder; all this school year he has been on the verge of this, he thinks, but somehow hadn't been able to pass over the boundary, hadn't been able to break through. He has felt as though a caldron were boiling within him, pulling his attention inward, so that his mother and the nuns at school and even Janice had become two-dimensional, no longer quite real to him. That day in the chapel anteroom he'd been seized by the random gaiety and energy that came so often now, and turning from the theology assignment he had impulsively thrown aside his own and Janice's virginity without caring if someone came upon them or not; for suddenly, wildly, such discovery no longer mattered, the very idea of "authority" no longer mattered. He remembers something his father had said today—*I want my freedom, that's all;* and that's all Clifford wanted.

He's feeling wonderful, but now Janice asks shyly, fearfully: "Why are you so upset, Clifford? Why are you so *mad?*"

"I'm not mad," he says, though now he does feel a spurt of anger at Janice—for her timidity, for the fear in her baby-blue eyes.

Lifting the covers, he looks down her body, from the gleaming blond hair and lashes to the pale freckled shoulders, to the small narrow breasts and slender waist; below her waist, under the covers, she dissolves into darkness, just as he does. He feels how his penis has shrunk almost to nothing.

"What's wrong with you, anyway?" he says. "What are you doing here, if you're so afraid?"

"I'm not afraid," she says, touching his shoulder, "it's just that you're—I don't know, you act like you're mad and like nothing matters, like you've given up on everything—like you don't care about school, or—"

"You want to go back to school, is that what you want? Be Sister Veronica's good little girl?"

"Clifford, we *have* to go back sometime, we can't just—"

"Not me," Clifford says bluntly. "I'm never going back."

Janice laughs, disbelieving.

"Why should I?" he says. "I'm a misfit in that school, I always have been. Look, I really take after my father," he says, groping for the words, "more than my mother—I'm not really a Catholic, even, I don't believe in that shit—"

"Clifford!" Janice cries. "But what about school, what about your *mother*—"

"I can go to public school," he says. "And as for Mom"—his voice lowers, remembering how she'd put her head down on her arms, like a child, at the dining room table the night before, returned home safely from yet another "date" with the dull and hopeless Mr. Parkins—"well," Clifford says, "Mom has her own problems, her own life. I don't think she'll care, at this point."

"But why . . . ?" Janice can't finish this question. Though it's very warm in the bed, she has started trembling.

"Because *I* don't care," Clifford says, and the moment the words are out he feels a thrill of certainty: of course, he must get away from Pius. For months he has spent most of his time drawing, paying little attention to his classes, feeling entirely withdrawn from the ordinary routines and activities of the school. This year, his single major effort outside of art class has been a deliberate mockery, a taunt thrown in the face of the scowling and self-important Father Culhane: for several weeks he had worked feverishly on the priest's notorious theology assignment, producing a painstakingly written and carefully researched paper that had succeeded in getting him suspended from school. Entitled "The Power and the Glory: A History of Corruption in the Vatican," his paper had dealt with the licentiousness, avarice, and violent inclinations of certain popes, mostly in the Middle Ages and the Renaissance, and had focused upon the terrors of the Inquisition. He had enjoyed the project immensely, and had been the only student to meet the five-thousand-word requirement. On the day the papers were handed back, Father Culhane had called his name after class, and had informed him quietly (the priest's face had been rigid with fury, his eyes like small pale blue stones) that he'd made an A+ on the paper; and also that he was suspended from school, so that he would have time to meditate on his impiety and malice. Yet Clifford had seen with satisfaction that the priest didn't really know what to do with him; throughout his years at St. John Bosco and Pius XII, Clifford had never really misbehaved, technically speaking, and he always made good grades; but somehow (as even Father Culhane must have perceived by now) they had gradually lost him. Somehow his case was more serious than Phil Witherspoon's or Jack Snyder's—those kids were little gangsters, constantly in trouble, but they were little *Catholic* gangsters who took communion, went to confession, and would eventually grow up and get married and bring up their little gangster offspring in the Church. Clifford's case was different, for Father Culhane and the nuns knew that despite his intelligence he simply didn't believe, he simply didn't care. It wasn't his behavior but his mind—what they would call his soul, probably—that had veered beyond their control.

Now, he thinks grimly, *he's* in control, but Janice is shaking her head, pulling herself toward him, pressing the side of her face against his thin pale chest; he understands that she's starting to cry, and soon enough she's sobbing, choking out her words so that he barely understands: "If you're a misfit," she says, "then so am I"— and she wraps one arm around his back, another around his buttocks as though she'll never let go.

"C'mon, don't cry," he whispers, and not for the first time he wonders where her energy comes from, and why she cares so much. He knows her better than anyone, he thinks, but she's the only person he doesn't understand, the only one who keeps trying to lunge through the bubble of loneliness and unreality in which he lives, and has lived for so long. Even now, she clings to him so fiercely!—and he cannot understand his own response, for he wants to comfort her, to express his gratitude, but at the same time he longs to push her away, angry and disgusted, thinking how she will resume her place back at school, with her long navy socks and sweetheart locket and shining blond hair, the model Pius XII girl, free of him. As she clings to him now, he feels his own rigid body thrusting back at her, anguished and angry, so that when she looks up shyly and speaks to him, his reply sounds flippant and cruel.

"But you care about *me,* don't you?" she says, in a little girl's voice that sets his teeth on edge. "Clifford . . . ?"

Only now does he notice that he's erect once again, that the flame of his anger and love and frustration has concentrated down between his legs, aimed directly at Janice, and so he takes her white cool fingers and very carefully, deliberately, folds them around his pulsing flesh.

"Does *this* answer your question?" he says, with his sly down-turned smile.

4

Clifford

When Clifford Bannon returns to his tenth-grade class on the second of January, after being absent for the entire fall term, there's a firestorm of gossip and rumor and speculation among his class-mates—the talk is far more intense than the mock-sorrowful, mock-pitying discussions they'd enjoyed last fall, both the boring ones directed by the nuns in class (who said they must *pray* for Clifford, must try to imagine the hellish *ordeal* he had suffered) and the less formal, possibly less hypocritical buzz of conversation in the cafeteria, the hallways, the parking lot, where Clifford Bannon's name had been on everyone's lips throughout September and most of October. (Although, by the first of November, the talk had died down and the subject was discarded, like a piece of Juicy Fruit that had finally lost its flavor.) On Clifford's first day there are cheery hello's sent in his direction, there are plenty of offers to help Clifford "catch up" with his schoolwork, there are a few brave attempts to get him involved in the CYO, or the basketball team, or the planning commit-tee for the Spring Formal to be held in early May—but Clifford, to no one's surprise, greets all offers with a curt shake of his head, a barely audible *Thanks, but I'll pass;* and he gives that enigmatic half-smile of his, mouth turned down on one side, which none of his classmates quite knows how to interpret.

"He's the same old Clifford, if you ask me," Trudy Cravens whispers in the cafeteria one day in late January, her lips puckered in disdain. "He's still got his nose in the air, still won't date any of the Pius girls—"

"Trust me, Clifford is *weird,*" says Mary Frances Dennehy, around a mouthful of ham and cheese. "I mean, anybody who likes Janice Rungren has *got* to be weird."

"C'mon, you guys," one of the junior boys says from the far end of the table, "give poor Clifford a break! That stuff is ancient history, Kathy McCord says he wouldn't touch Rungren with a ten-foot pole. Anyhow, Rungren's been dating some guy from pubic school."

"God, that's so *gross!*" another girl screams in delight. "I mean, *pubic* school, that's the most grotesque thing I've ever—"

"Yeah, well, it fits. In Janice Rungren's case."

"But listen, you guys," Jennifer Jenks says in a heightened voice, "you know he's got to be hurting—I mean, can you even imagine your mother killing herself, and then you just walked into the kitchen one day and found her? Like *that?*"

"You've got a point, Jenny, but you heard what Kathy and Fritzie McCord said, last fall—said he just sits around their house and draws his pictures, which he won't let anybody see, and acts like nothing ever happened. He never cries, never talks about it, just acts like he's been living with the McCords all along. And did you hear about last summer?—Mrs. McCord had to *make* him go to the funeral!"

"See, didn't I tell you he was weird?" Mary Frances says.

"Where is Kathy, anyway? I have trouble believing *that.*"

"I know Kathy better than you guys," Jennifer says hotly, "and she never told *me*—"

"Oh, and get this—guess who Clifford has made friends with, now that he and Janice aren't speaking? Jimmy Tate!"

"The caretaker? *That* moron?"

"You've got to be kidding!"

"He's worse than a moron," says one of the tenth-grade boys, his voice fallen to an ugly whisper, "I heard he's a fucking *queer*. One day when Gallagher and me——"

"Hey, yeah, that's *right*——Witherspoon told me Clifford goes down to the basement and visits Jimmy all the time, during lunch, during study hall——"

"There, I told you he was weird. I rest my case."

"C'mon, Mary Frances," says Jennifer Jenks. "I think he's sort of sweet, and he's got to be upset. I mean, wouldn't it blow *your* mind, if you came home one day——"

"Well, I guess you should know," Trudy says slyly, "since I heard that you and Clifford went out together——it was around November, wasn't it? And you thought nobody knew?"

"What?" Jennifer cries. "How did you——"

"Shush, you guys! Here he comes."

The whispering starts and stops, and starts again, and whenever Clifford turns down a corridor or enters a classroom his classmates in their tightly clustered groups break apart, grinning awkwardly, chagrined, and occasionally he troubles to wonder if they think they're fooling anyone; or if they think he really cares. All through January and part of February——until February 14, to be exact, when Clifford Bannon's career as a parochial school student meets its abrupt and ironic end——Clifford slips back into the persona that has served him so well during his years at this school. *Well-behaved, though a bit reserved,* Sister Mary Veronica had written on his final evaluation last spring, at the end of ninth grade; *Keeps his own counsel, and might do well to interact more with his fellow students.* . . . He remembers standing quietly in the kitchen on that May morning (two weeks before Senator Kennedy's assassination and the start of that final abrupt downward spiral in his mother's condition) while she read and reread the report, frowning. It was certainly far different from the one he'd gotten the previous fall, after Clifford's chapel detention and the infamous term paper and the two-week suspension just before Christmas; in fact, Clifford had thought, Sister might have been describing someone else entirely.

"If you misbehave, they complain," his mother had muttered under her breath, "and then when you *behave,* they still complain."

Signing the note, she'd lifted her dark deep-set eyes to Clifford and, as if on cue, they'd begun laughing at the same moment. They both laughed so recklessly that their eyes filled with tears, and finally his mother had bent over double, trying to catch her breath. A few minutes later, Clifford had gone out to the school bus with a lightened heart; but, as it turned out, this was the last time he could remember that his mother had laughed.

By now, in January of 1969, at sixteen years of age, a tenth-grader at Pius XII Junior and Senior High School, he has lived for over five months in the hectic noisy household of Rita McCord and her genial husband, Larry. Oddly, there hadn't been the "period of adjustment" everyone had warned him about, even though he had to share a room with Fritz McCord, a freckle-faced athletic boy a year older than Clifford, whom he'd never known very well. To please Rita, he joined fully in the household activities, sharing chores with the other children, observing curfew rules (set according to each child's age: Fritz and Clifford were expected home by 10:00 on weeknights, 11:30 on weekends) and television rules (one hour per evening) and rules concerning promptness at mealtimes and personal hygiene and the many details of Catholic religious observance. Because Father Culhane and Sister Mary Veronica and Clifford's father had all agreed that sitting out the fall semester might be the best thing for Clifford, he'd had plenty of time to get to know all the McCords, who had done everything possible to make him feel at home. Clifford felt both flattered and embarrassed by the attention they paid him. Fritz had tried to interest Clifford in coming to the basketball games, and the CYO socials, and at such times Clifford would look up from his book or his sketch pad and smile, saying *Okay, sure*—though at the last minute he usually found some excuse to avoid going, knowing he would be bored, knowing there would be a certain amount of whispering and staring. His name was still Clifford Bannon, after all, not Clifford McCord; it was important to keep reminding himself of that.

One evening, when Larry handed Clifford a button worn by all the McCord kids to school that read STAY TOUGH IN VIETNAM!, he had hesitated, confused; he remembered how hungrily his mother had watched RFK's speeches the year before his death, her eyes welling with tears as Kennedy parted company with Johnson on the bombing of North Vietnam and the escalation of the war in general. As she listened to Kennedy summoning up the uncomprehending terror of the Vietnamese peasants, the tragic spectacle of innocent mothers and their children, all hope gone, trapped in that scorched and ravaged landscape, his mother had stroked Clifford's forearm idly, weeping: "See, honey, there's someone who understands, isn't there? He *does* understand, doesn't he?" He'd felt a brilliant hectic energy in his mother's touch, like an electric charge. Yet Clifford had sensed that she was responding to something other than the man's words, and had quietly drawn his arm away.

Though he'd hesitated, he finally did accept the pin from Larry McCord, and sometimes wore it around the house to please him. Larry was a friendly, energetic, rather boyish man who looked more like Fritz's older brother, Clifford thought, than his father; to provide for his large family, Larry worked long hours as a manager in a toy manufacturing firm. It was clear that he loved his family, that he *lived for* his family—into which he'd welcomed Clifford, it appeared, without a moment's hesitation. Yet Clifford also saw an angry and even bitter side to Larry that only increased Clifford's admiration, especially when Larry indulged in dinnertime tirades against the "decadent liberals" who'd gotten so lax about the communist threat, who wanted to surrender the war effort, who pretended a reverence for JFK's memory but were actually betraying the martyred president's vision of American leadership and integrity. It was clear that Larry, an ardent Kennedy supporter back in '60, had developed serious reservations about Robert Kennedy in the months preceding *his* assassination, though in Clifford's presence he avoided this topic, perhaps unaware that Clifford listened so intently not because he cared about Larry's conservative politics or Vietnam or the drug culture or birth control—Clifford had no opinion about any of these things—but because Larry's innocent adult *certainty* so impressed and pleased him; the certainty that there were right and wrong ways to live, that there existed certain moral absolutes that need only be recognized and followed.

It pleased Clifford also that neither Larry nor Rita had attempted to coddle him in the matter of his mother's suicide—Rita,

as always, moved forward through life with her no-nonsense relentless good cheer, and though Larry, soon after Clifford moved in, had
offered a "sympathetic ear" anytime Clifford needed one, he'd never
again alluded to Mrs. Bannon's death. Nor did they allude to Mr.
Bannon, though for weeks after the funeral last August Clifford had
gotten calls from his father, whose whining faraway voice spoke of
Clifford's coming to Atlanta to live, "anytime he wanted"—of course
he wouldn't fight Clifford's decision to stay with the McCords, he
knew how close Irene and Rita had been, but still if Clifford ever
had the desire.... Clifford had stood in the hallway next to the
McCords' noisy dining room, where kids were always eating or playing cards or talking in high cheerful voices, and he'd turned to the
wall and answered his father in a quick low murmur, *Uh-huh, yeah,
I guess so—no, I guess not—yeah, I'm sure, but thanks anyway. No, Dad—
but thanks.* He'd been patient, not wanting to hurt his father; and to
his relief the calls had tapered off gradually, painlessly.

He hadn't been so lucky with Janice Rungren, who called almost every night in the weeks after the funeral, who wanted to
know how Clifford was *feeling,* if there was anything she could *do*—
and though Clifford tried the same monosyllables on her, the same
practiced indifference, she eventually became angry and shrill, de-
manding to know *when* she would see him, *why* couldn't they get
together, there were two weeks of summer left and why should they
waste this precious time, wasn't this an opportunity to get closer,
and shouldn't they—

No, he'd said sharply, and he allowed himself a shiver of revulsion over the way she'd clung to him all these years, always coming
back, always wanting something he couldn't give. She was so imma-
ture, really. At school she'd started getting in trouble again—the
blond and pretty and privileged but still rather demonic Janice Rungren, the scourge of the nuns at Bosco and now at Pius too, a bundle
of passionate misdirected energy who had, since they met in third
grade, focused so much of that energy on Clifford Bannon—and he
couldn't count the times she'd gotten *him* in trouble. So he'd said
No quite loudly, rudely, hoping to settle this once and for all. Expecting to hear her shrill voice coming back through the line, making
accusations, telling Clifford what his "problem" was, he'd been sur-

prised when, after a long silence, she said softly, even meekly, "Clifford? Clifford, are you still there?"

"What?" he'd cried. "Where else would I be?"

"Clifford?"—again with that peculiar meekness, which grated on his nerves because it was so unlike her—"Clifford, what's happened to you, anyway? What's happened to *us*?"

"Us?" he said, exasperated. "*Us? What the hell do you mean, Janice, what are you—*"

"Everybody's been saying it for years, haven't they?" Janice said. "Haven't they said that we liked each other, didn't everybody just assume—"

"We're friends, Janice, we've always been just *friends*. Don't try to—"

"But what did you expect, Clifford Bannon"—she was raw-voiced, furious—"when you spent all your time at school with me, year after year, and never had another girlfriend, and never contradicted anybody who said we *were* boyfriend and girlfriend—what did you expect me to think? Or the other kids?"

She paused, swallowing hard; she took a deep breath.

"What were *you* thinking, Clifford, during all that time . . . ?"

"Who cares what anyone thinks!" Clifford shouted, but his own words were hollow, in a flash he saw how things had appeared to *her*. She'd been indulging her "romantic" daydreams right before his eyes and he hadn't cared, hadn't really paid attention, he'd simply hung around with Janice because he liked her and because she was always *there*—energetic, laughing, pulling him along. It was true that they'd done many things together, but only because her will to do them was so much stronger than his will *not* to do them. Hadn't she known that they were only playing around, "experimenting"? Did Janice really think he felt romantically drawn to her?—or to any girl, for that matter? So there had been no solution, he thought, and during that last phone conversation he'd listened woodenly, summoning all his patience, as Janice rattled on shamelessly about the "romance" they could have had, and how she'd never thought of anyone else as her boyfriend—and how much the other boys at Pius disgusted her with their stupid remarks, their dirty words and gestures—and how she didn't know what to *do* at this point, since she felt sure that Clifford wasn't leveling with her, that he was still upset over what had happened to his mother, and if only he would *talk* about it, if only they could get together and talk things out the way other couples did—

"No," Clifford said again, not sharply but wearily, absolutely needing this to end. His palms were sweating: he didn't think he could bear Janice's rambling self-pitying voice for another moment.

"Clifford," Janice cried, "will you please listen? Don't you know that I *love*—"

And so Clifford had no choice: very gently, he replaced the receiver.

Though he felt guilty for a few days, he understood how pointless the guilt was, and soon enough began living through his days at the McCords with a new lightness, a sense of freedom. Past was past, he thought. In a polite and reasonable tone he'd said to Rita McCord that if Janice called for him again he'd rather not take the call, and Rita had said of course, of course; but Janice had not called back.

So for Clifford the fall passed in a blur as he comported himself easily with the McCord household and its routines, not thinking of the future and seldom about the recent past. Sometimes, late at night, he would let the familiar procession of images rise to his mind's eye—the discovery of his mother that humid morning of August eleventh when he came into the kitchen for breakfast, staring at her body curled pitifully on the floor next to the wrought-iron telephone stand, a thin greenish vomit oozing out the side of her mouth; the arrival of the ambulance, the police, and finally Rita, who pawed the tears roughly off her cheek and literally pushed Clifford out the front door and into the back of her station wagon; the funeral a few days later, toward which she'd also pushed him, and after which he had to endure an awkward and pointless conversation with his father and Father Culhane, both of whom looked guilty and aggrieved, both of whom tried to explain what had happened, the two men stepping on each other's lines and apologizing to each other and casting the same timorous assessing glances into Clifford's expressionless eyes.

Father Culhane had assured Clifford that his mother must have deeply regretted her act after it was too late to forestall its results, probably she *had* been struggling toward the phone when she died and this did suggest remorse, and the likelihood of God's forgiveness. Mr. Bannon's milder, more tentative voice had woven in and out of the priest's in Clifford's hearing, saying how Rita had told him about Irene's reaction to the assassination in June, that she'd even called periodically and suggested hospitalization because Irene had begun claiming that everything was over now, the world had no chance, there wasn't any hope—that kind of talk—and his father admitted that he hadn't wanted to hear all this and had put Rita off.

"I'm sorry," he told Clifford, "I'm very, very sorry—of course you can come live with Miriam and me anytime you want, or if you'd prefer—"

He'd broken off, bewildered, just as Father Culhane had done when he'd recited his words about God's forgiveness, and then had seemed, abruptly, to run out of things to say.

Then his father tried again, his voice cracking: "Your mother had this sorrow inside her, Cliff, this deep *sadness* that would well up suddenly, without warning—and I guess it overwhelmed her, this time, I guess she couldn't—"

Tears blocked his voice and Father Culhane had touched Mr. Bannon's hand, had given him a reproving glance, and then signaled Rita, who stood waiting at a discreet distance, by the olive-and-white-striped funeral canopy, to come and take Clifford away; which she did, herding him back to the station wagon with her other children, who stayed respectfully quiet all the way home; and Clifford had felt both embarrassed and nearly faint with relief.

It's over, he thought.

Over, he thought repeatedly in the following days and weeks and months, thinking back and remembering only to wonder at his father's and the priest's bewilderment; for if Clifford understood perfectly why his mother had died, why couldn't they? There was no mystery, Clifford thought, and the issue of having hospitalized her, of having "saved" her, was probably irrelevant; just as the issue of God's forgiveness, Clifford thought scornfully, was irrelevant.

Though school didn't seem to matter, either, he did his home-work with faithful thoroughness like all the McCord children, and no longer indulged in blatant daydreams during classes or felt the need to ridicule the religious instruction still given out patiently, year after year. It was even likely, he would later think, that he'd have finished his remaining three years at Pius with all A's (at the time of his expulsion, he had near-perfect averages in all his classes) and perhaps even as senior class valedictorian, if he hadn't happened one day in mid-January to enter the first-floor boys' bathroom at about 8:25 A.M., only minutes before homeroom period began.

He'd assumed the bathroom would be deserted, but he saw something—a shift of the light, a shadowy movement—as he hurried toward the urinals. Then unzipping himself he saw Jimmy Tate, the school caretaker, emerging slowly from the tiny supply closet over by the sinks.

"Oh, hey," Clifford said, as the man stood there for a moment, staring. "How's it going, Jimmy?"

He'd never really spoken with Jimmy before, but the man had worked here for several years, and evidently the kids considered him "slow"; he'd seen Phil Witherspoon mimicking Jimmy's slack-mouthed expression, his rounded shoulders and shuffling gait. Clifford hadn't paid him much attention, had never heard him say anything, but he'd noticed the way Jimmy would stare as kids passed by him in the hall, his lips parted vaguely, his pale blue eyes looking glassy and stunned.

"How's it going, what's new?" Clifford repeated. He felt embarrassed to be using the bathroom while talking to someone, but now Jimmy was giving him that look, too, that baleful blue-eyed stare; when Clifford laughed, uneasily, the man licked his upper lip and smiled back, though his eyes still held their look of unabashed longing.

Keeping his gaze fixed on Clifford, he leaned his mop against the wall.

Clifford turned his head, ignoring him, looking down as if zipping himself, preparing to leave; but he waited a moment as Jimmy stepped up to the urinal next to him, undid his own zipper, then cleared his throat and said in a shy, deep voice, "Not much, I reckon. How about you?"

There were no partitions between the urinals and Clifford could feel the man's body heat, and imagined he could feel him glancing over, from the sides of his eyes. Blond and big-boned, Jimmy was over six feet tall, several inches taller than Clifford, and of course he could see that Clifford hadn't yet zipped his jeans. For a moment Clifford's heart pounded, but he took a breath and looked over as Jimmy stepped back and turned toward him, showing himself to Clifford, and in almost the same movement Clifford turned toward Jimmy, and as the man reached out to touch him the 8:30 bell rang, startling them both.

Clifford laughed, his hand trembling as he quickly zipped his pants, then flushed the urinal; Jimmy Tate didn't laugh.

Unwillingly, Clifford thought about Jimmy all the rest of that day, and the day after that; he kept glancing over his shoulder in the cafeteria, or in study hall, expecting to see the man with his mouth ajar, his eyes vacant but eerily still, in some fixity of longing. All around Clifford his classmates were talking eagerly about Valentine's Day, asking one another if they were sending hand-made or printed cards, and did they plan to send cards to everyone, or just to that "special person"?—and though no one dared to ask Clifford any such questions he felt as much angry resentment as if they had, he shouted into the shadowy threatening corners of his mind *No Janice and I are not an "item," no goddamn it I'm not dating her nor will I ever date her, nor will I* . . . And out of those same mental shadows that were already threatening the clarity he'd achieved these past few months—which Clifford likened to a harsh fluorescent light that showed everything for what it was, reducing the world to a single unlovely substance that didn't bear much scrutiny—out of these shadowy dim corners stepped Jimmy Tate, who simply stared as if waiting patiently for Clifford to acknowledge him; as if he knew something Clifford didn't know but would wait as long as necessary—with more than patience, even, perhaps with something like affection—for Clifford to recognize it, too.

Several days later, when Clifford went to his locker during lunch period, he saw Jimmy at the far end of the hall, dressed in his khakis as usual, holding a broom. He stared at Clifford, his lips slightly parted. When he nodded toward the basement stairs and disappeared, Clifford hesitated only for a moment; in subsequent days

he never hesitated. Sometimes he and Jimmy talked for a while—
friendly comments and questions on Clifford's part (in that new
polite voice he'd developed since living with the McCords), awkward
half-mumbled replies from Jimmy Tate. Over a period of several
weeks Clifford learned a few facts about Jimmy: that he was from
Abilene, that he'd fought with his father a lot and had drifted east,
working odd jobs, getting fired a lot ("I wasn't no good at school,"
Jimmy told him), sometimes getting help from the Salvation Army
or the local rectory. His mother had been Catholic, as a boy he'd
gone to mass and First Holy Communion, and he hadn't been surprised when Father Culhane had offered him a job and found him
a rooming house right around the corner, even though he'd only
asked for an evening meal. That was the luckiest day of his life,
Jimmy told him. He liked working around Catholic kids, and around
the priests and nuns; he liked his job, he was lucky to have this
job. . . . When he touched Clifford his big calloused hands were
almost reverent; he seemed nervous and abashed when he fumbled
with the zipper on Clifford's jeans and looked more solemn than hungry
as he slowly lowered the jeans and then Clifford's Jockey shorts and
approached him with lips parted and tongue extended, like a communicant. He would suck Clifford slowly and thoroughly, a blurry deep
sound coming from the back of his throat like murmuring underwater,
but whenever Clifford's fingers brushed the smooth front of Jimmy's
khakis the man would back away, dropping his eyes.

"No?" Clifford said. "How come?"

Jimmy wouldn't respond, and so Clifford quit trying; whatever
happened, happened, he thought, and he was pleased enough with
things as they were. He'd begun to find Jimmy's company strangely
soothing, as the man seemed to have no capacity for judging him,
or perhaps simply no wish to judge him, and he asked for nothing
beyond what Clifford wished to give. . . . And so, on that February
afternoon, just after Janice Rungren thrusts an envelope into his hand
during library study hall (and just as Sister Mary Jerome turns her
back, bending over an encyclopedia with Annie Shelton), his sudden
impulse feels inevitable: he gathers his books quickly, quietly, and
sneaks out of the library. He goes immediately to the basement door,
raps twice, hurries downstairs, and takes his usual place against the

wall, next to a closet doorway where they could hide if anyone came along. On this particular day, he and Jimmy don't exchange a word, Jimmy coming forward at once and getting to his knees, Clifford not even glancing down as he takes the envelope and rips it open quickly, impatiently. Above the valentine message, *Will you be mine?*, Janice has written his name, "Mr. Clifford Bannon, Esq.," dotting the *i* with an oversized heart, and in a tiny, ornately "feminine" hand she has written "I love you," and beneath that she has scrawled in big block letters, "WHY THE HELL NOT? (Ha ha)."

She didn't sign the card.

Clifford stuffs the valentine inside its envelope and drops it in a huge waste barrel next to him, and at the same moment he hears a noise from the top of the stairs. He looks down at Jimmy Tate's blond head, bobbing rhythmically; he knows that Jimmy's grateful guttural murmur keeps him from hearing, but after his first impulse of alarm Clifford decides to do nothing and at once he's flooded with calm. There are a few moments of exquisite pleasure when he is able to focus only on what Jimmy is doing, the fact that it won't last only increases his pleasure, and when Sister Mary Jerome reaches the bottom of the stairs and peers into the dim light of the basement, not yet with her pale fish-faced look of horror because she hasn't quite focused, her vision hasn't yet quite adjusted to what she's about to see—even at this moment Clifford is able to think, Whatever happens, happens, and why the hell doesn't Janice Rungren understand?

J a n i c e

No one understands what has happened to Janice Rungren. What has "gotten into her," as the nuns like to say. Not that the facts aren't plain, since people talk about her constantly, her classmates in gym class or the cafeteria, the lay teachers chatting in the hallway, whispering through their fingers, the nuns themselves in hushed desperate conferences behind closed doors. Janice Rungren, what to do about.

Janice Rungren, what has happened to, how could she possibly, was it conceivable that her parents condoned, etc., etc. The facts include a long-haired and sandaled boyfriend from the public school across town; a shoulder bag filled with makeup and cigarettes and other items best left unmentioned, no matter that the nuns confiscate the bag on a regular basis and take all its contents, while Janice looks on sullenly, her orange-painted lips pursed in disgust; four suspensions from school this spring term alone, twice for "immodest behavior" with her boyfriend in his parked car, right in the school lot, once for calling her elderly algebra teacher, Sister Mary Jerome, a "dried-up old bitch" because Sister had asked about Janice's late assignments, once for stomping out of Sister Mary Sylvester's theology class because—as Janice claimed, tossing the words over her shoulder—she "just didn't believe this shit anymore." The facts include numerous conferences between various nuns and Janice; between the school principal, Sister Mary Veronica, and Janice; between an exasperated Father Culhane and Janice; and finally a lengthy conference attended by Father Culhane and all the nuns and Mr. Rungren (Mrs. Rungren being "indisposed") and Janice—though Janice, as during the other conferences, sat with one open-toed shoe swinging, studying her nails, her silver-shadowed eyes glaring briefly into the distance (utter boredom, utter disgust) whenever her name and her various misdeeds were mentioned.

Janice, why do this to yourself? they asked.

Janice, why destroy your reputation? they asked helplessly.

She had to laugh over that one, though generally the laughing stage—the laughing-in-their-faces stage—was over. Now, like Randy said, she had best ignore them. If you laughed or got mad you were playing into their hands, putting them on an equal footing. She loved Randy for his intelligence and daring, except for Clifford Bannon she hadn't met anyone worth knowing at this shit-ass nun's school— here all the boys were pansies or dim-witted athletes or religious nuts, now that Clifford was gone the place was totally hopeless.

She knew a good man when she saw one and she'd hung on to Randy. He was older, anyway—eighteen, nineteen. Still a senior at the public school but he'd been held back a year or two, maybe for behavior not much different from Janice's.

"So you think I should ignore them, huh?" she says coyly, brushing her palm along his slender pale chest. He wears shirts but doesn't button them; several strands of love beads, some made by Janice and others acquired she doesn't know where, dangle from his long skinny throat. She loves the way his Adam's apple bobs when he talks or laughs.

"Jesus," she says, touching her fingertip to the point of the Adam's apple as she often does, curious, exploring, "Jesus," she says in the harried tone she has copied from Randy, "did they give me hell today."

They sit in Randy's old '56 Thunderbird in the school lot, empty except for the faded yellow schoolbus and the little dun-colored Volkswagen van that the nuns drive to and from the convent. Despite the brisk wind they have the windows down, as always. Not caring who sees them, as always. Randy once said he liked the way Janice's long straight blond hair—cornsilk blond, he called it—would blow across her cheeks and nose in the wind, it reminded him of Mary Travers, it looked so peaceful and natural and he really liked it a lot, and Janice likes what Randy likes.

"Well, that's the business they're in," he says in that low intelligent voice that drives Janice wild.

"Bitches," Janice whispers as she nibbles his ear. "Damn dried-up old bitches," she says irately, drawing back.

"Hey, little one. Hush now," Randy says. Then he smiles over her shoulder, adding, "And speak of the devil."

So she looks around, not that she needs to, and here they come, the six of them struggling against the wind with veils flying, holding their wimples in place with one hand, moving briskly, cheerfully. Like a flock of dumpy penguins, Janice often said, and she knows they won't glance over here, they won't give her the satisfaction anymore. "We'll take a wait-and-see attitude," Sister Mary Veronica said today, tapping her fingers on the desk in a surprising show of tolerance. "Yes, fine," Father Culhane and Mr. Rungren said, in unison. Janice laughed, briefly, feeling a little thrill of victory, but of course they won't acknowledge her now, of course they won't look over to see her huddled up with Randy, perched half on his knees and half on the steering wheel, right here in broad daylight.

"Who cares what they think, anyway," she mutters, rubbing her cheek against his shoulder. "I mean, do they really think I care?"

Don't you *care* about your appearance, don't you *care* what people think, her mother had whined all during the school year, beginning early last fall when Janice had started spending so much time down at the new mall just a stone's throw from the entrance to Lazy Acres, had gotten to know some kids from the public school like Randy and Julie and Mitch and Evie, kids she could *relate* to (unlike those stuck-up Pius jerks); and had started changing the way she dressed, her hair and makeup; and even the way she walked and talked and acted. She'd started wearing halter tops and jeans, she'd gotten fond of ordinary cotton dresses in flowered prints and bright solid colors, "psychedelic" colors, and depending on her mood she either went with the natural look and wore no makeup at all or else she played around, she used white lipstick or blue mascara or iridescent silver eye shadow just for fun, it wasn't so weird, everybody did it, so why should her mother get so upset? And her hair: it wasn't light enough, something wasn't *right* about it, so when her cousin Ruthie came over to spend the weekend they'd bleached Janice's hair, and it had turned practically white except for an orange-tinted sheen that looked sort of odd, Janice admitted; but she hadn't expected the tears that rose to her mother's eyes the next morning as they were all getting ready for church, she hadn't expected her to wail about what *beautiful hair* Janice had once had, and now had destroyed. "Okay, fine, then I won't go!" Janice had said, furious, hating the hair herself but refusing to admit it, and she'd trounced out of the house and stalked along the highway toward the mall where she'd called Randy to come and pick her up, and poor Ruthie had gone to mass with the Rungrens as though replacing Janice as their daughter, and this was the first time Janice had ever deliberately skipped church on Sunday; which had upset her mother more than anything, she knew, but now that it had happened, it had happened, and Janice seldom went to church after that.

Though she complained to Randy and her other public school friends that she didn't have anything in common with her mother, that her mother didn't have a clue as to who Janice was and what she was all about, Janice admitted even to herself that she resented her and was jealous of her, both at once, that somehow over the years her mother had "found herself"—a phrase Mrs. Rungren picked up from the self-help books she was always reading—and had gotten everyone to like her, even some of Janice's new friends, even Randy, who was always the perfect gentleman when he arrived for one of his dates with Janice. Yes, everyone said how "sweet" her mother was, how "pretty" she looked on Sundays or during family get-togethers or even on her weekday shopping trips with Aunt Lila—lovely Phyllis Rungren, who'd softened her makeup over the years to a shimmer of frosted coral lipstick and "a touch" of rouge and mascara, who smiled sweetly when anyone addressed her but didn't say much in return and didn't *have* much, as Janice thought, to say in return, oh yes her mother had softened, mellowed, could become "charming" and even socially adept when all the conditions were right. No more running from the doorbell, no more fear of everyday outings to the mall or Aunt Lila's house three blocks away, no more weekends spent in her bedroom with the door closed and no more explosive tearful arguments with Mr. Rungren (who now called her "bunny," evidently a nickname he'd used before their marriage), oh hell yes Janice sees what her mother has done, she has turned into Jane Wyatt and June Lockhart and Barbara Billingsley all rolled into one, she's a department store mannequin and a freak and a very sweet lady, and how can Janice Rungren fight against that?

So naturally Janice's clothes, charged without permission at various expensive shops down at the mall, have gotten wilder month by month; and naturally she has continued bleaching her hair, until it is finally the right "California" shade; and naturally when questioned about her latest suspension by her exasperated mother (Mr. Rungren, who now cheerfully admitted he didn't understand "the kids these days" and who had mellowed a good bit himself, left the matter of disciplining Janice to his wife) or about the cigarettes that had been found in her purse, or about the arrest of one of Janice's public school friends for possession of marijuana, of course Janice gave her the same disgusted glare she gave the nuns at school or just said, contemptuously, "You wouldn't understand—believe me, you would *not*."

And her mother always replied, "I *might,* if you'd give me a chance," and Janice would laugh her little flippant laugh and glare briefly into space and that would be that.

These days she often feels vivid and rebellious and free, but just as often she's hurt and confused and unhappy, and it bothers her that other people—her mother, for instance—stay themselves day after day, never changing, while she rides this roller coaster of crazy moods and feelings, barely hanging on, not knowing where she's headed. Thank God there's Ruthie to talk to, at least, when she's trying to figure it all out, when she needs to think out loud about Clifford and Randy and all the rest of it—she knows enough to be grateful for Ruthie now that her so-called best friends at Pius have deserted her. . . . And she often admits to Ruthie that Clifford, as usual, is the focus of everything she thinks and feels, no matter what ugly rumors have spread throughout school since February, no matter that she's supposedly going steady with Randy these days and free of this place, free of the past (*free* being Randy's favorite word, half-sung in her ear when they're making love, or passing one of his funny-looking joints back and forth between their lips), no matter that Janice Rungren, for all Clifford knows or apparently cares, might have dropped off the face of the earth. Yes it's Clifford, she won't deny it, despite everything she just won't give it up.

"If I could just *see* him . . . ," she says to Ruthie one Friday evening, standing before the full-length mirror hung outside her closet door, brushing her hair down on each side, hard, so that the brush sends out tiny electric sparks. Behind her is an ironing board and behind that Ruthie sits on the bed, looking forlorn after the 45-minute ordeal of ironing Janice's hair—Ruthie's own dark curls have drooped against her clammy cheeks and forehead, the tips damp with perspiration. "I mean," Janice says, "if we could just *talk,* you know? I'd feel so much better then."

As always Ruthie says very little, and when she does speak it's usually to ask a question, shyly. She begins, stammering, "But is he—is he still there, with the McCords? Because I heard—I mean, some of the girls were saying—"

"Don't listen to *them*," Janice says brusquely, glancing at her cousin's slump-shouldered image in the mirror. Tonight, for some reason, Ruthie looks more pathetic than usual—her plump face is pale, her eyes look shadowed and indistinct behind her thick rimless glasses. She sits in her plain sky-blue dress with its girlish white collar, her hands fiddling in her lap, like an anxious handmaiden; Janice is amazed, as always, by the extent to which Ruthie makes Janice's sorrows her own.

"But," Janice adds, "what did you hear?"

"What?" Ruthie says, startled. "Oh, it wasn't much—just that he might be leaving the McCords soon, that Mr. McCord had gotten upset and asked him to leave again—you know, like that other time, after what happened——"

"What supposedly happened," Janice corrects her, and as the image of Jimmy Tate's woebegone face darts into her mind, she pushes it out just as quickly. She hasn't told anyone, not even Ruthie, that she went down to the basement the day after Clifford's expulsion, the day gossip was rocking the school so violently that Janice thought she might become ill, and she'd looked all over for Jimmy only to be told by a smirking seventh-grader half a foot shorter than Janice, who'd seen her reentering the hallway, that Jimmy Tate had been fired and given bus fare to Houston. "Want to know how come?" the boy had said snidely, cupping his hand to whisper in her ear, but Janice had recoiled, lifting her pert upper lip in disgust, and hurried off in the opposite direction.

But then, she reasoned, Jimmy was supposed to be a retard, wasn't he? He wouldn't have been able to tell her anything.

"Um," Ruthie says, blushing now, "I heard that he'd been staying out late, sometimes until morning, and Mr. McCord checked the mileage on Clifford's car and figured out he'd driven up to Dallas, he found a gas receipt or something, I don't know——"

Janice turns around, slowly. "Clifford has a car? Who told you that?"

"What? Oh, it was Kathy McCord, I guess," Ruthie says, swallowing, "her and some of the others, they said that he'd gotten a lot of money in his mother's will, and that his father sent him money, too, and that the McCords couldn't control him, that he and

Mr. McCord don't get along anymore—but I'm not sure, Janice," Ruthie says, in a whining, defensive voice, "why don't you ask Kathy?"

"Because Kathy's a little bitch," Janice spits out. "She's just like all the others. Too good to talk to *me*."

Janice throws the brush down onto the floor; she stalks over to the bed and plops down next to Ruthie, her eyes averted from the closet door and its mirrored image of herself in bra and panties, hair hanging into her face and shoulders slumped lower than Ruthie's.

"They're all too good, much too good," she whispers.

And she looks at Ruthie, who seems both shocked and saddened, Ruthie who has expressed her "envy" of Janice so many times, in such wistful tones, Ruthie who has never had a date and never will and who seems willingly headed for the convent to her parents' delight and Janice's parents' delight—Janice's mother, in particular, secretly prefers Ruthie to Janice, as is painfully obvious to Janice whenever Ruthie comes to spend the weekend.

Behind her thick glasses Ruthie's eyes look misty and perplexed.

"I wish there was something I could do," she says sadly.

Tentatively she pats Janice's smooth bare shoulder while Janice toes aimless designs into the carpet, staring down.

"At least *he* likes to draw, he has something else to think about," she mutters, her mind's eye recalling Clifford bent over his paper in art class, or study hall, not troubling to glance around no matter what went on in the classroom, "whereas I can't draw a straight line," she adds, laughing.

And she's thinking, though she doesn't share the thought with Ruthie, that Clifford has not only talent to console him but evidently money, too, and freedom, and the whole future opened wide before him. Why should he think about *her,* after all?—especially when girls like Kathy McCord and Jennifer Jenks, who are both pretty and good, seem so eager to forgive him anything, attracted by that sexy half-smile or the secret coiled intensity and power they sense in Clifford but cannot know. At least, not the way Janice knows, beginning that afternoon in the Ramada Inn when Clifford had stretched his hard tense limbs across hers, pinning her to the bed, prodding so deeply inside her, so repeatedly, his breath hot against her throat.

They can't know the life she'd had in the months following that day,
how she'd lived for her brief urgent meetings with Clifford, the
occasional fifteen or twenty minutes down in the basement with its
damp floors and overheated air and clanking hellish machinery. Suddenly Janice's days and nights and weekends had blurred together,
had become a haze of memory and longing, punctuated by her occasional long looks into the mirror, staring at her feverish pale-cheeked
self and thinking *I'm in love* and yet knowing that perversely the
world had not changed; she was expected still to do homework and
attend mass with her parents and accept phone calls from other boys
and watch slide shows on convent life in the school auditorium, her
mind scarcely able to concentrate, her blood frantic and confused in
her veins. No wonder that she'd finally gone "awry," as Sister Mary
Veronica put it, exasperated, no wonder the other girls wouldn't
give Janice the time of day, called her slut and bitch and whore,
narrowed their eyes and turned away each morning when Randy
drove her into the school lot. Yes she should be angry, no it isn't
fair, she must keep that flame of rage and resentment alive even if
it gets her into trouble, even if no one takes her seriously. Like
Randy says, If you don't look out for yourself, then nobody else will.

"Janice?" Ruthie asks timidly, peering into her face. "Are you
okay?"

Janice's smile is quick and chagrined, she rises abruptly and
crosses to the stereo.

"Sure, why wouldn't I be fine?" she says, pawing through her
records, tossing "Yesterday" aside because she'd cried herself to sleep
to that last night, Paul McCartney always makes her cry, tossing
"Monday, Monday" aside because it's too melancholy and she hates
to think of a pretty girl like Michele Phillips singing that song (and
hadn't Ruthie said that Janice looked like Michele, sort of?), and
finally reaching for the Stones, "Satisfaction," she wants something
loud and crazy and wild. She twists the volume knob to HIGH.

So Janice is energetic, she's "revved up" as Randy often says,
she and Ruthie go through the closet putting together an outfit for
tonight, scarcely able to hear each other over the music, making
faces as they go through the clothes, giggling. Soon enough Mrs.
Rungren comes in, her lips pinched in distaste as she rushes toward

the stereo and turns it down, saying that if it weren't for that racket Janice might have heard the doorbell and know that her date had arrived.

"You can say 'Randy,' Mom," Janice says, throwing her eyes to the ceiling. "I don't date anybody else."

Mrs. Rungren is passing her mild but slightly critical gaze up and down Janice, her lips twitching in distaste. "Janice, is that what you're wearing?" she says. "On your *date*?"

Janice glances into the mirror one more time, pleased by the calf-high black leather boots and the silver-studded jeans and the tie-dyed "peasant blouse" and the several strings of multicolored beads and the big floppy hat of black felt, which for some reason Randy loves. Tonight she has decided to skip the makeup but her jewelry is so plentiful (there are several rings, too, a turquoise-and-silver, and a "mood" ring, and a "peace" ring, and a delicate gold rose ring with a tiny diamond in its center, a birthday gift from her parents last year; and a pair of gold studs in her ears) and her blond hair hangs so straight and heavy in front of her shoulders, that she'd decided she was colorful enough.

"Yes, Mom, this is what I'm wearing," she says in her mechanical bored voice, but this is only a ritual they go through every few nights, it doesn't mean anything, already Mrs. Rungren is backing away. As usual, she throws a commiserating glance toward Ruthie.

"I wish she'd dress more like *you,* dear," Mrs. Rungren says. Ruthie smiles neutrally and Mrs. Rungren disappears.

"Well, kiddo," Janice says, giving Ruthie's shoulder a squeeze, "guess we'd better go down and meet my 'date.' "

And when they get downstairs Randy, as usual, is perched like a model schoolboy on the edge of the sofa while he talks with Mrs. Rungren, never mind his ripped and faded Levi's and the Levi jacket with its psychedelic mushroom and tulip decals on the back, never mind the scraggly dark-blond hair parted in the middle like John Lennon's; it's clear that Mrs. Rungren is accustomed to the way he dresses—or, more precisely, no longer quite sees the way he dresses—and so they sit conversing politely, Randy his usual charming, grinning, deferential self (the persona he adopts around "straight" adults) and Mrs. Rungren erect and gracious in her yellow linen dress, doing her motherly duty in entertaining her daughter's date until the daughter herself arrives downstairs. (Also as usual, Mr. Rungren has retreated quickly to the den, after laughing over the handful of unfunny remarks he always delivers to Randy when he first arrives, like "Take care of my daughter, you hear?—somebody's got to," or "If the police stop you, just say you're going to a costume party," laughing uproariously but uneasily, not quite meeting Randy's eyes.)

Not that Randy is anything special: he's a skinny scrappy public school kid from across town, indistinguishable from hundreds of others except for his grin that could melt a girl's pants, and often has, and Janice wonders at her parents for not grasping the irony of Randy's "polite" behavior when he's around them, his flirting with Mrs. Rungren and laughing out loud at Mr. Rungren's jokes, as if they don't see the cool mischief in his eyes or worry at all about the trouble he's had in school. (When they started dating, Janice made sure her parents knew all about Randy, his being non-Catholic and his getting kicked out of school over drugs and his bad reputation generally—but to her surprise and chagrin, they hadn't uttered a word against him.) But despite everything Randy is ordinary, she sees now, reaching the bottom of the stairs and able to observe him for a few moments before he sees her; no, there's nothing special about Randy, but nonetheless she rushes forward as if on cue and throws her arms around him.

"Hey baby," Randy says, extricating himself from Janice's embrace and struggling to rise from the sofa. "Well, see ya, Mrs. Rungren. See ya, Ruthie."

And they're moving toward the front door, Mrs. Rungren issuing her usual warnings about being careful, and not driving too fast, while Janice as usual says nothing, giving the little private twist of her mouth toward Ruthie, who smiles back mistily, and a brief wave—a careless wiggle of her beringed fingers—as she and Randy move out the front door.

"Have a good time!" Mrs. Rungren calls from the doorway, as her daughter and Randy half-stumble through the balmy spring air and climb into Randy's T-bird, both of them a bit giddy, laughing for no reason, slamming their doors shut at the same moment.

"Jesus," Janice murmurs, under her breath, "will she *ever* let me alone?"

"Aah, she's okay," Randy says, reaching into the glove compartment for his stash. He adds, "She sort of flirts with me, you know? I sort of like it."

"Oh yeah?" Janice says. "Well, do you sort of like this?"

She slips her hand underneath Randy's T-shirt and gently strokes his flat hard stomach with her nails—one night he'd said that drove him wild—but now Randy twists away, frowning.

"Cut it out, Janice. Not *now*."

He's peering into the cellophane baggie, his lower lip stuck out. "Shit, I could have sworn I rolled two numbers this afternoon. I swear, I'm going to beat Chris's ass when I get home."

Chris is Randy's younger brother, only fourteen but a carbon copy of Randy in both looks and behavior.

"What the hell?" Janice says. "You've got plenty, don't you? Just roll some more."

So they change places, Janice getting behind the wheel and Randy settling his paraphernalia on his lap, his brow severe and businesslike as it gets, Janice has noticed, only when he's bent over his dope.

"Drive, go ahead," he says irritably. "I'm doing fine."

So she pulls away from the house and then out of Lazy Acres and past the mall, then through a few residential areas where friends of theirs live, checking cars in the driveway but everybody's out, supposedly they're all meeting around midnight at Charlie's place out by the old Dallas highway, but now it's only 8:30 and too early to drop by Charlie's—he's one of Randy's older friends and he throws great parties, but he's a little "paranoid," Randy says, and doesn't like unexpected company—so she just drives around, aimlessly. Letting the car go wherever it will. She's always a little jumpy when Randy rolls his joints, mainly because he's such a perfectionist, and takes so damn long, and snaps at her if she says anything, breaking his concentration. She's not even that crazy about marijuana, it makes her feel too giggly and uncontrolled, and it tastes horrible, and puts an itchy dry feeling at the back of her throat that lasts for hours. But Randy likes to smoke, and she tries to like what Randy

likes. He smokes a joint before and after school, at the beginning of
their evening and once or twice during the evening, and always just
before they make love; and though Janice can't possibly keep up,
she does take little frowning puffs at the joint whenever he hands
it over, she pretends to enjoy the stuff, he doesn't notice or doesn't
care that usually she's not inhaling but letting the smoke come
tumbling back out her mouth. Nonetheless she gets high. Spending
an entire evening with Randy you can't help but get high.

Now he's running his tongue along the edge of a completed
joint and so she says, casually, "You hungry or anything? You want
to stop somewhere?"

"Naah, not yet. Maybe after we smoke."

Janice laughs, turning the corner where St. John Bosco Elementary School stands dark and hulking back among a thick stand of
pine, turning with elaborate slowness though she does not glance at
the school. She says, "When we get the munchies, right?"

Randy looks over, briefly. "Yeah, right," he says.

He begins rolling another joint.

She keeps driving, feeling bored. She can't deny any longer that
she feels bored most of the time she's with Randy. They never do
anything, these days; never see movies or attend football games or
eat at nice restaurants. Only fast food places, once they've gotten
the munchies. They drive around, mostly, stopping to visit Randy's
friends around town, mostly male friends, and the talk centers on
new dope in town, hash or acid or psilocybin, who's got what, who
can get what; and eventually a party at somebody's smoke-filled
house or apartment, garish posters on the wall, black lights that
transform everything into ghosts with pale bodies and dark mouth-
holes, eye-holes, Led Zeppelin or Joe Cocker pulsing against the
walls and inside Janice's skull so that she can't think, can't really
hear when someone speaks to her. She just nods, smiles vaguely and
nods in the usual manner of pretty girls at such parties. Only male
voices can be heard above the music and through the mucous-thick
smoke, and here too the talk is about dope, or sometimes of music
or travel. "Getting out of this town" is a phrase she often hears. At
first it was all glamorous, maybe, a bit thrilling, she would draw
slowly on whatever joint came her way and try to flow inside the

music, but nowadays, after months and months of this, she's bored. And that's allowed for the confusion, she supposes, and the sense of panic. And her renewed obsessive thinking about Clifford Bannon who, it appears, has shut her out of his life forever.

Now they're driving through a subdivision called Pleasant Valley Woods, not quite as expensive as Lazy Acres but still very nice; several of the kids from Janice's school live on these streets named after trees, like Pine Tree Trail and Weeping Willow Way and Cherrywood Circle and Redbud Drive. Just as she's turning off Pine Tree onto Redbud (they'd just passed Jennifer Jenks's house and Janice had allowed herself to glare briefly at Jennifer's bedroom window and put out her tongue as far as it would go), Randy knocks his arm sideways against her shoulder as he's so fond of doing lately, it's so rude, it hurts her feelings but she won't let on, and she looks over and sees the lighted joint cupped protectively in his hand.

"Not *now*," she says, irritably. "Not while we're driving."

Randy shrugs and exhales mightily and returns the cigarette to his lips for another draw, quick and delicate, hissing, his lips pursed daintily like someone trying to play the flute.

But now as they're driving along Redbud something happens, Janice's expression changes and she draws in her own breath quick and light, and feels her heart begin to pound; for there, up ahead and to the right, is the McCord house, the chunky redbricked place on the corner with its ungainly addition of two extra bedrooms on one side; and of course Janice knows that Clifford's room is upstairs, that he shares a small bedroom with Fritz McCord, it's the right upstairs corner, she'd gotten that much out of Kathy McCord at least. Now, approaching the end of Redbud, Janice slows the car and directly in front of the McCord house, unable to help herself, she pulls over. She turns off the ignition, breathing deeply.

"Hey, why're we stopping?" Randy says.

Janice wiggles her fingers. "Here, don't hog it," she says. "Give me some."

Randy grins, handing the joint over. "Good *girl,*" he says.

The corner streetlight sends a faint band of illumination slant-wise into the car, rippling down from the dashboard onto their laps, but their faces stay masked in near-darkness and Randy can't tell

that her eyes have drifted past him. Anyhow he doesn't know about
the McCords, or Clifford Bannon, or the real reason they've stopped
at this particular corner. As she draws on the joint Janice allows
herself to squint hard past Randy's shoulder at the house, all of
whose downstairs windows are darkened. Upstairs there's a small
window illuminated—a bathroom, probably—but that light goes out
the moment Janice fixes her gaze upon it. A quick rude chill passes
through her; she shivers uncontrollably and hopes Randy doesn't
notice, but of course he doesn't. She has handed the joint back and
he is sucking greedily, oblivious of her. Already, or is this only her
imagination, she can feel the drug lightening her head, smoothing
out the clenched muscles in her shoulders and stomach. She smiles
faintly to herself, moving her eyes slowly toward Clifford's window.

The window is illuminated, of course. Clifford is alone up there,
probably; Janice has already noted the new Mustang (black or dark
blue, dusty-looking) that Ruthie mentioned, parked in the driveway
behind Mr. McCord's Oldsmobile '88 and Mrs. McCord's station
wagon, and she can imagine him bent over his desk at this moment
with a pencil gripped in his hand, drawing or writing, oblivious of
her, unaware if it's 10 P.M. or 2 A.M., yes he is free in a way she'll
never be free. Now a lazy and languorous rhythm has been estab-
lished between her and Randy, they are passing the joint back and
forth quietly, not speaking, not looking at each other, Janice for her
part drawing deeply on the joint each time and keeping her eyes on
Clifford's lighted window. Only a few yards away, she thinks; and
yet light years away. How odd that she'd been driving aimlessly
through the night with Randy and yet had ended up here, uncon-
sciously, as if guided by that light.

Now she's aware that Randy has said something—what? something about wearing a brooch?—but she'd tuned out, she hadn't
heard, and now it's too late; he has bent closer and squinted into
her eyes, and now he turns around and follows her gaze across to
the McCords' house.

She knows Randy: even when he's stoned his eyes are sharp,
he doesn't miss a thing. Though her heart jumps, she isn't really
surprised when he turns back around and says flatly, matter-of-factly, .
"Bannon. Clifford Bannon."

"What?" Janice says faintly.

"That's his car," Randy says, adjusting a tiny remnant of his joint inside the little metal clip he keeps in the cellophane baggie. "Look," Randy says, "do you want to share this roach or not?"

Janice shakes her head, turning her body so that she's looking straight through the windshield at nothing. Massive clumped trees in the darkness, at the end of Redbud; nothing distinguishable except the ghostly shine of pavement, gradually fading beyond reach of the street light.

"Yeah," Randy says, hissing at the roach, "I know because I was riding by here not long ago, with Edie and Charlie and stuff, and Edie points to that Mustang and starts talking about this kid who got expelled from Pius and now he goes to our school, I don't know him or anything but Edie said he got expelled because—"

Now Randy breaks off, looks over. "But hell, I guess *you* know. Your school is so small, you couldn't not know."

"I knew him, but I barely knew him," Janice says evenly. Now, sitting so still, she can feel how powerfully the drug has overtaken her; she feels that she has shrunken inside herself, neither happy nor unhappy, and everything else is very distant. Randy might be speaking from a hundred yards away, or a mile away. She can scarcely listen.

Randy laughs, grinding the few particles left of his roach into the ashtray. "Shit, can you imagine?" he says. "Getting sucked off in the basement of Pius, and by a guy? I mean, whatever anybody wants to do is okay by me, but shit, I mean, like it's really—"

Randy is babbling like he always babbles after smoking dope, she can listen or not listen, for her the important part of the evening is over anyway. In a few minutes she'll turn the key and drive them away from here, and she'll look back at Clifford's window or she won't look, it really doesn't matter; she can't feel pain and she can't feel sorry and so why does it matter? In the morning, she'll barely even remember this. In the morning, the quality of Randy's dope being what it is, she'll still be a little high.

She says, making a great effort to form the words clearly, "Well, are you ready to go? Ready for something to eat?"

But Randy has come closer without her quite knowing it. He

stretches one arm along her shoulder, playing with the ends of her hair, and he bends closer and whispers something in her ear.

"What?" she says, thinking she misunderstood, and she lets her eyes fall to Randy's lap. Her head feels heavy, like a piece of crockery. Her eyeballs feel heavy and warm. But she hasn't misunderstood, for with his other hand Randy has undone the buttons of his Levi's and begun gently stroking himself; the ripple of light across their laps gives the illusion that they're both underwater. As he gets harder and bigger his stroking hand slows and relaxes and diminishes and finally falls away.

"Come on, baby," Randy whispers. "Why not? I mean, if two guys can do it—"

So she moves quickly, not wanting him to say any more. Lets her legs go limp, melting down toward the floorboard, surrendering to gravity. Although Randy has begun pushing her head downward, his hand cupped over her skull, she has time to glance one last time toward the light in Clifford's bedroom window, which is still shining and will probably shine all night, long after she has satisfied Randy and they've driven away. But she feels nothing as she thinks about this, and she lets her eyes fall from the window to Randy's lap without regret, her mouth opening as she reasons that she wants to make him happy; and if he's happy, she thinks vaguely, then she is happy, too.

5

Janice

Rumors about Janice, always Janice, the plain and overweight and
stodgy girls in the senior class perpetuate the rumors even as they
complain. (The pretty, popular girls never mention Janice's name,
they'll have nothing to do with *her;* but they keep track of the
rumors, too. They have their sources.) Lately the boys have gossiped
right along with the girls, one big rowdy gang in the cafeteria or
during study hall, braying with laughter, shrieking in disbelief, testing
new theories, discarding old theories, the speculation focused on
Janice's absence from school since mid-February, an absence that had
stretched from two weeks, to four, to six—and here it's the final
term, graduation takes place in early May. Or maybe she won't
graduate, after all? Maybe they'll keep her back another year?

"Never," one girls says. "Every teacher in school will pass
Janice, just to get her out of here."

"Maybe she's already gone—her cousin keeps worrying about
that, she's afraid Janice will run off with that boyfriend of hers—
Ronnie or Randy, whatever his name is—"

"Naah, he ditched Janice—and besides, Ruthie's out of it. *She*
doesn't know."

"Does anybody know, then? Has anybody—"

"Maybe they put her away somewhere, it'd serve her right!"

"In a convent, maybe. Or the funny farm."

"Sure, I can see Rungren in a convent. Sure thing."

"The funny farm, though. That sounds about right."

"Lucia said *she* thinks Janice is pregnant, she said Janice was asking her about her periods, what was the longest Lucia had ever gone without one, those kinds of questions—"

"Pregnant with a *baby*? Rungren? God, I pity the poor kid."

"Maybe she's getting rid of it—you know, an abortion."

"Shit, the Rungrens wouldn't go for *that*."

"Maybe she's hooked on something—marijuana or something."

"Maybe she's a junkie!"

"I mean, it got to where she'd smoke a joint after every class, right out in the parking lot."

"In the bathroom, too. She offered me some, but I just walked away."

"Jimmy Gallagher's father saw her downtown one Saturday, late at night. You know, all made up like a hooker, just hanging around—"

"Janice Rungren may be bad, you guys, but she'd never be a prostitute. I promise you that."

"Look, why would Mr. Gallagher make up a big story? I mean, he must've seen *some*thing."

"It wouldn't surprise me. I wouldn't put anything past Janice."

"I didn't mean she wouldn't *do* it, I just meant she wouldn't *sell* it. She enjoys giving it away too much."

"You should know, McElroy!"

"*I* think she's crazy. *I* don't know why they let her get away with—"

"Listen, you know she's got to be miserable. I mean, inside."

"Oh hell, she's probably sitting at home right now, listening to the Stones and laughing her head off."

"Well, I wouldn't be surprised if she's dead, would you? I mean, if I were Janice Rungren, I'd kill myself."

"So would I. You got it."

"I mean, just think about it for a minute, having to get up and see Janice Rungren's face in the mirror every morning. What would be the point?"

She sits on Clifford's porch steps one mild April afternoon, ready for her new life to begin. It's 4:45 and her lover won't be home until 5:30, but she couldn't wait, she was anxious, she doesn't know if her life will really change—so completely and irrevocably, by this time tomorrow!—or if this is all some kind of ugly joke. She knows better than to get excited, but still she is excited. Last night in his bed she'd told him, finally; they'd been lying quietly together after making love, both feather pillows propped under their shoulders, idly caressing, not talking, and she'd tensed as his hand paused along her abdomen, gently feeling, assessing, and in sudden panic she'd blurted out the truth. Yes, pregnant, she'd told him. Four months and counting, she said, trying to make a joke of it, and when Clifford hadn't laughed she'd started to cry.

Though he rubbed her shoulders and murmured soft comforting phrases, half an hour passed or maybe an hour before he said anything about what they would do, before he would commit himself at all; she'd lain beside him, sniffling, waiting, and had endured a small lifetime before he'd calmly explained that he'd been thinking of moving to Atlanta, his father had been after him to come take a job with his company and now that school was almost over he really had nothing to keep him here, he couldn't think of a reason *not* to go. That is, nothing to keep him here but Janice, he'd added hastily, and if she wanted to come along, if she thought she loved him enough to give up everything else for him and the baby, assuming she wanted to keep the baby—well, then she was certainly welcome.

Since late last night when she arrived home until this moment she has not slept or eaten or done much of anything but think of Clifford's words, replaying them in her head, twisting them this way and that . . . hearing subtle hesitation one moment, suppressed emotion the next . . . feeling ecstatic and then doubtful; hopeful and then doomed. Naturally today was one of those days her mother kept after her—when was she going to start on that history project, how far had she gotten in that novel for English class?—but all morning and afternoon Janice had simply drifted from one room to the next, escaping her mother's presence not rudely but dreamily, wondering was this real, was this happening, was she drifting out of this life and into some other life? She'd felt gooseflesh along her arms and legs, and several times had become so dizzy that she'd had to sit down, rubbing her fingers gently along her temples, feeling herself hurtling forward into an unknown future, irresistibly, just as her baby five months from now would succumb irresistibly to the pull of the daylight world.

If you'd like to come along, her lover had said, shyly, then you're certainly welcome.

She'd known by February that she was pregnant and she'd told her parents at once. It had been a cold drizzly morning, a Friday, and when she came out of the doctor's office, for the second time that week, she'd asked Ruthie to drive her straight home. They'd gone to a gynecologist in a neighboring city, thirty miles away; on Tuesday Janice had picked his name at random out of the phone directory and asked could she come now, it was an emergency, she couldn't wait for an appointment. To her surprise, the doctor had *not* been surprised; evidently he'd had such patients and such emergencies before. When she came out of the office she told Ruthie to take her home, she was going to tell them, she would tell them everything—and Ruthie had simply nodded, white-faced. For the first time in her life Ruthie had skipped school, telling Sister Veronica she felt ill, and letting her parents believe she *was* at school (a lie by omission), and had done all this lying and deceiving twice—and all for the sake of her pretty cousin, Janice, who had now gotten herself into so much trouble.

"But what—what will happen then?" Ruthie had asked, timidly.

"I don't know," Janice said, still dazed by the news. "And I'm not sure I really care."

Her father had fumed, her mother had fretted, and after an obligatory hour spent cursing Clifford that "degenerate kid" (Mr. Rungren) and Clifford that "awful boy" (Mrs. Rungren), they'd both looked at Janice as if realizing for the first time that she, too, had contributed to the problem, and had asked once again the question they'd asked all this past fall and winter—*what* did she see in him, exactly, *how* could she possibly have dated a boy who'd been kicked out of school under such frightful circumstances and who no longer went to church and whom even the benevolent McCord family had disowned? Didn't she care about her own reputation, or at least about the embarrassment she was causing her mother and father? That Randy character, her father added, had been bad enough, but despite his scrapes with the law and his not being Catholic, Randy had at least seemed—well, *normal*—whereas they'd always known Clifford Bannon was a rotten kid, hadn't they? And surely Janice had known?

As her father ranted Janice had felt all her ancient steely resentments take hold of her, settling especially in her arms, which she folded defiantly over her breasts, and in her jawbone, which she jutted aggressively toward him.

"I'm going to keep seeing him," she said. "We're *not* breaking up."

So the furor in the Rungren household had only begun, and had lasted through eight tumultuous days of raised voices and ragged weeping and curses flung in all directions, and finally even Father Culhane and Sister Mary Veronica had gotten involved, brought to the house by Janice's desperate parents after they'd reached, seemingly, a hopeless impasse; and to the surprise of all concerned, the priest and school principal had discussed the matter with remarkable calm and had helped arrange a compromise that was accepted, after a good bit of haggling, by both the elder Rungrens and their daughter. The one point of negotiation upon which Janice would not budge was her resolve to keep seeing Clifford Bannon, and the tide had turned when Janice, exasperated, had pointed out that she couldn't get any *more* pregnant, could she? Despite the horror-struck faces of her parents, Sister Mary Veronica had said that Janice had a point, and that while intimate relations were "out of the question, of course," it might be possible, if the Rungrens would agree, for her to continue seeing Clifford Bannon on a limited basis, for a limited period of time. Janice had heard the subtle emphasis on the word *limited* and knew something else was coming, but it didn't matter, she reasoned: they'd have no way of knowing whether she slept with Clifford or not, and if they didn't try to keep them apart then she'd agree to anything else.

What she agreed to, finally, was that in May or June—that is, when she'd begun to "show"—she would quietly leave town for a Catholic institution in Fort Worth designed especially for girls with Janice's particular problem; there she could have her baby privately and safely, and it would be given up for adoption, and she would be back home shortly afterward. In the meantime, it might be best if Janice stayed out of school and did her last-semester assignments at home, occasionally meeting privately with her teachers in the evenings or on weekends. For his part, Father Culhane agreed with everything Sister Veronica said, and so Janice's parents had no choice but to agree, though they blanched visibly at such phrases as "drop out of school" and "home for unwed mothers," spoken in Sister Veronica's clipped and reasonable voice.

But Janice wasn't perturbed; Janice smiled, in fact, whenever she encountered the word *dropout* on television programs or in magazines she flipped through idly, waiting for the long days to pass and for the moment when her life would resume. Nowadays the word had broader connotations than simply dropping out of school, but quickly enough this spring she'd felt how lucky she was, being away from that school and its foolishness about proms and graduation and the senior trip; how happy she was to have escaped all that! Sometimes her mother would come upon her in a remote corner of the house and see the dreamy distant smile on Janice's lips, and ask impatiently why wasn't she doing anything, what was she smiling about, and after a moment's pause she might add, resentfully, that *he* hadn't cared enough, had he, to keep from getting her into this mess, so there was no point in thinking about *him*.

But Janice would only smile at her mother as if drugged or entranced, drawing her knees up under her chin and turning to look out the window, and at first her mother would turn away angrily, murmuring under her breath, but finally she had burst into tears, releasing a few blurred phrases about "my baby" before hurrying from the room.

Glancing at her watch, the only jewelry she wears these days, Janice now feels that smile of dazed astonishment widening her face again; for somehow time has passed quickly and it's 5:25, and Clifford will be home soon; and then her waiting will be over. Despite the warmth of this late afternoon, the cement steps are cold, sending a chill through the worn fabric of her jeans, so for the third or fourth time she adjusts herself, moving one step higher, wrapping her arms around her knees in the pose she strikes often these days, feeling very alone but strangely happy. She has a powerful sense of well-being, of being alive and healthy and conscious at this moment, this particular moment and no other; and feeling anonymous, even name-less; and yet purely herself. She looks like hundreds of other girls her age, she knows—not the girls at Pius, of course, but girls from Randy's crowd of friends or girls she sees downtown or girls from California and New York whose pictures appear occasionally in the magazines her parents receive, blaring news about the new "youth culture" with pictures of hippies and rock stars and their girlfriends, usually blond, looking dazed and pretty and interchangeable. These girls are happy being themselves, Janice feels, just as she is happy. She no longer needs to pretend, to transform herself pathetically into someone else. Today her hair and skin are clean, shining, her brown sandals and faded jeans and loose-fitting white cotton tunic are ordi-nary, unstriking. Late at night, during their last hour in Clifford's bed before her midnight curfew, she often feels that he is not making love to her, necessarily, but to any pretty blond anonymous girl, or to all such girls at once; and the thought is strangely pleasing, sooth-ing; and often he whispers not her name but simply *Baby, baby,* and always she answers *yes* pulling him closer, unable to get him close enough, thinking that she has never been so happy.

When she hears the familiar chortling of his '69 Mustang she rises quickly, embarrassed as always when he finds her sitting here, so obviously waiting. For there's always the moment when he pauses on the sidewalk and looks at her, blinking, as if uncertain of who she is.

"Clifford . . . ?" she says, shifting her weight back and forth.

Only now does she notice that he's carrying something, a white bulky sack he pulls from under his arm and holds forward, smiling openly, not grudgingly, holding the sack out from his body as though to place it in her arms.

"Hungry?" he says, and she rushes forward and puts her arms around him, not caring who sees, half-crushing the sack of warm food between them as she hides her face in his shoulder, feeling foolish, inane, why should she choose this moment to begin crying, a sudden harsh ache in her throat and her eyes scalded with tears, like a child's?

"Yes," she whispers in Clifford's ear. "Yes, I'm really starved."

This is possibly the most important evening of their lives, but actually it's not much different from other evenings they've spent together these past few months, which Janice feels is a good sign. Though they're planning and discussing their entire future, their baby, their move to a city they've never visited before, the general tone of their conversation is frank and intimate, oddly casual. They sit side by side on the couch and eat the cheese enchiladas and rice Clifford picked up on his way home from his job at a branch library (an easy job, he insists, where he likes his co-workers and spends much of his time reading), and as usual Janice, shoving the food in her mouth with her white plastic fork, endures his jokes about her ravenous appetite and her inability to cook and his hope that Atlanta has plenty of fast-food places, or else they will surely starve. Janice mouths the syllables "ha ha" without pointing out, as she often does, that she is eating for two; for she *is* ravenously hungry tonight, and the Mexican food is delicious, and the burgundy wine Clifford has opened only adds to her sensation of mellow pleased contentment, a glowing warmth she feels in her belly and breasts and in her slightly flushed cheeks, her dampened eyes. Every few minutes she glances at Clifford, making faces at his jokes, or shrugging her shoulders, and in the heavy pleased sensuality of their eating and drinking and their togetherness in this overheated snug apartment where they've made love so often, she thinks suddenly of her mother and feels that she has found herself, too, poor crazy Janice Rungren has found herself at last, and impossible as it seems her dreams have all come true.

She is scraping the last bit of rice out of her styrofoam plate when Clifford says, idly, "When did you get here, anyway?"

"Here?" Janice says.

Clifford is bent over the small pipe he sometimes uses to smoke hash, giving Janice a sudden unwelcome memory of Randy, who had abruptly "taken off" (as his brother Chris had informed her, laconically) one day last October. Which was more than a month before she'd planted herself on Clifford Bannon's doorstep for the first time, and at least three months (as she had calculated anxiously, breathlessly) before that gynecologist told her she was two months' pregnant. (Two months? she had asked, her voice quaking. It couldn't actually be three months, she forced herself to ask, it isn't possible ...? The doctor had given her a curious look, almost a scowl. *Two* months, he'd said, and her eyes had slid shut in relief.)

"Here at the apartment," Clifford says, tamping the hash delicately into the pipe. "Today."

She watches him, puzzled. "I don't know, about four-thirty I guess, or quarter to five ... what difference does it make?"

Clifford holds a match to the pipe, puffing. "I don't know," he says, "it sort of makes you look like—well, a groupie."

"A groupie?" Janice says, amazed.

Their eyes meet through the sudden haze of smoke and they begin laughing, hysterically and uncontrollably laughing, at exactly the same moment. Clifford puts down the pipe and grabs her, and they laugh and tussle for a while, and they make love on the couch for a while, Janice remembering a joke she'd cracked a few weeks ago, to the effect that they didn't *need* to smoke dope because they giggled and carried on quite sufficiently without it; and Clifford had agreed; and since then, they hadn't used any of the handful of Colombian joints they keep in a little sandwich baggie in Clifford's underwear drawer. Janice has no idea where Clifford gets the hash, or even why he uses it.

Nor does she care, she thinks. After their languorous hour on the couch, Clifford pours some more wine and they sit huddled together in one corner of the sofa, still naked but wrapped in a quilt Clifford has dragged out from the bedroom. Again Clifford has begun fiddling with his pipe as Janice snuggles against him.

After a few moments of dreamy silence, the wine bottle drained and Clifford puffing idly, Janice says with a smile, "You know what we remind me of?"

"What we remind me of?" Clifford says in a light mocking voice. "No, what do we remind you of?"

Janice laughs abruptly, a quick unbidden laugh, like a hiccough, and laying her head against Clifford's shoulder she says, "An old married couple, that's what . . . I mean, we just had a big dinner and we're sitting here on the couch and you're smoking a pipe— we're like an *ancient* married couple," she says, "we're like Grandma and Grandpa."

"Hmm, very interesting," Clifford says, narrowing his eyes in a parody of extreme pensiveness, sucking on the pipe. "But I think there's a flaw in your theory, my child," and he nods sagely. "Several flaws, in fact."

"Oh?" Janice says, giggling, playing along, "and what might they be, Father Bannon? Please do tell me, Monsignor Bannon, please do enlighten me, Pope Cliffie the First . . ." but her voice dissolves into laughter, her blond head tilted back against Clifford's shoulder as she laughs.

"In the first place, we aren't married," Clifford says.

"Not yet," Janice says.

"Nor do we own the couch," he says, ticking the items on his fingers one by one, "nor did you cook the meal, nor *could you* have cooked the meal, if our lives depended on it."

"Oh, pooh," Janice says airily. "You're such a nitpicker."

"Furthermore," Clifford says, in a tone of priestly gravity, "I don't believe that too many grandfathers smoke hash, at least not in our civilized country, and I'm quite sure that very few grandmothers ever find themselves in your—ahem—condition."

On the word *condition,* Clifford wrinkles his nose in fussy distaste, sucking on the pipe rather fiercely, and that sends Janice into a paroxysm of laughter, so that she has to sit up and bend over and try to catch her breath as she laughs, she can't remember laughing so hard in all her life. . . . And when she does recover, there are tears in her eyes, and her stomach aches a little, and she turns back to Clifford with a look of wild intensity, as though the roller coaster of her life were taking a sudden plunge, a delicious plunge, and she touches his face with the tips of her fingers like a blind girl trying to read him, to understand him, and she cries, "Clifford, we *are* going to be happy, aren't we?"

This close she can see that her lover's eyes are pink, he's totally stoned, he's wrecked, and she's hardly surprised when he gives her that tilted half-smile of his, making him look a bit sly, a bit drunken, and she thinks to herself, wondering, Does she know him at all? Will she ever know him, really?

"Well, what do *you* think?" Clifford says.

Clifford

On the morning of the happiest day of Janice Rungren's life, her best friend and lover and fiancé and soulmate, Clifford Bannon, wakes very early and blinks his eyes several times. Often he wakes in this manner, abruptly and fully conscious, his senses heightened, his vision in particular strengthened by a harsh and vicious clarity: it's almost painful, this access of vision; the muscles of his eyes seem to strain outward, in a visceral confrontation with all he sees. There have been times when he has wondered if it's the dope, if somehow during sleep the drug works a chemical change in his brain that gives such rest and freshness to his eyesight that he might be seeing everything for the first time, like a baby.

He looks over and sees Janice's doughy-pale face looking puffy in sleep, her eyes clenched tight and lips parted slightly, her head pressed down hard into the feather pillow as if in the intensity of her dreaming. He sees from the bedside clock that it's 6:30, and the whitish clear light slowly filling the room reveals Janice's sleeping form without grace or apology, focusing the small mole at the side of her neck, the tiniest hairs along her forearms, bringing each strand of her coarse straw-blond hair and each tangled eyelash to her lover's detached but unswerving attention. Without thinking Clifford gently lifts the sheet and puts it aside so that her full nakedness is revealed, the breasts flat and small, the belly slightly distended, the pallid flesh of her hips and thighs unhidden; her legs are spread frankly in sleep, her cleft parted but dry-looking, its surrounding bush a dark uncomely blond, even the tops of her thighs looking nerveless and unhealthily pale. Clifford glances away, despite his erection feeling almost nothing and remembering one night recently, when she'd fallen asleep on the living room couch with nothing on, one arm flung backward over the armrest: I want to draw you, he'd thought, more than I want to fuck you. At that moment she'd awakened and smiled, reaching out her arms.

Now he replaces the sheet and gently nudges her side.

"Hey," he says. "It's time."

Always she smiles vaguely before opening her eyes.

"Hmm?" she says, and since he knows what part of him she'll reach for first, he backs to the edge of the bed and swings his legs over.

"C'mon, it's nearly seven. We're going to be on the road by eight, remember?"

While he dresses she rouses herself, yawning, talking her sleepy early-morning talk which is like a gentle background noise as he packs his toiletries into a plastic garbage bag. He has so few possessions; last night Janice had insisted that they finish packing his things (her stuff had been ready for days, she reminded him, stowed neatly into the trunk of the Mustang) and so he'd relented, finally; but the packing had taken less than an hour. A few canvases and sketch pads, some bed linen and cooking utensils, a few dog-eared paperbacks and a shoebox full of old photographs and, to Janice's squealing delight, a copy of their 1969 yearbook from Pius XII, The Recorder, which showed Bannon, Clifford, short-haired and unsmiling near the alphabetical beginning of the sophomore class, and a few pages later Rungren, Janice, with her blond hair straight as a curtain on either side of her face, grinning manically for the handsome yearbook photographer. Now Clifford has a mustache, and longish hair nearly covering his ears and his back collar, so Janice had spent some time laughing and pointing from the yearbook picture to him, asking where had that innocent funny-looking little boy gone, that clean-cut altar boy and future priest and bishop and cardinal and pope: what had happened to him, exactly? Clifford had wanted to say, in an ugly snide voice, "The janitor sucked him off, remember?—and that's the last we saw of him." Instead he'd squinted sarcastically and said that Janice hadn't looked so hot herself.

When he finishes gathering his things out of the ancient peeling medicine cabinet, tossing containers and tubes helter-skelter into the white plastic bag as though eradicating every sign that he'd lived here or had lived at all, he closes the cabinet door and stares into its yellow-tinged mirror. He's nineteen years old, but this is April already and in September he'll be twenty: since finishing his senior work at the public high school last fall there had been a sudden change in time, it had begun careening forward as if shoving him rudely ahead, saying to hurry up, saying to grow up or else. He'd been attending his final classes in the mornings and doing a work-study program in the afternoon at the public library, and he'd been so busy that days melted into weeks and into months without his noticing or even caring very much. He'd gone to summer school and taken a heavy load during the fall so he could graduate in December; he concentrated purely on getting out of here. During those rare evenings when he wasn't loaded down with homework or didn't feel exhausted or demoralized, he'd stolen the few precious hours for his drawing, seizing whatever was at hand: a vase of crumbling dried flowers left behind by a previous tenant, a plate of apples and cheese which he would eat the moment he finished drawing them, an old photograph of his parents in the early days of their marriage. Sometimes he did self-portraits, quick ruthless sketches of a gaunt raffish unsmiling man who looked older than nineteen or twenty, much older: he might be a street bum, Clifford had thought one night, tossing one of the sketches aside, he might be some kind of felon or mental patient or religious fanatic. Nonetheless, the self-portraits and the stern renderings of his young parents and the grimly desiccated flower drawings did not make him unhappy; he never felt more absorbed and purely contented than when he was drawing, and experienced dismay only when he finished a sketch and came out of his trance to discover that so much time had passed, or so little, and nothing had really changed.

Then one afternoon in November he'd gotten home from work to find Janice Rungren perched on his doorstep looking woebegone, waifish—like an orphan, he'd thought; like one of those pagan babies they'd been asked to adopt back in grade school. . . . He hadn't really been surprised to see her, and he couldn't deny that since that day she had brought to his life a certain shapeliness and energy which he'd begun to associate only with his drawing, not with his life; and a rather harsh sensuality which had always been part of him but which he'd somehow lost along the way, as if absentmindedly; and, for good or ill, a link with his distant past that comforted him slightly more than it frightened him.

When she comes up behind him, circling his waist with her arms, his stomach and heart contract for a moment; he wants to pull away. She has developed the disconcerting habit of catching him off guard—sneaking into the bedroom when he's sketching, for instance, and clasping her hands over his eyes; pulling back the curtain while he's showering and giving a loud wolf's whistle and then, naked herself, stepping into the tub without invitation. Now he pushes her arms away, good-naturedly. Only when he turns around and says cheerfully, "Come on, we've got to get going," does he notice that she's still naked.

She presses herself against him. "Cliff," she says, her voice trembling, "this is the happiest day of my life—it really is."

"I—I'm glad," he says awkwardly.

Briefly she kisses his chin, then his lips. "Honey," she says, "this is the first place where we—well, lived together. We've got time to make love, don't we? One more time?"

He wants to pull away but doesn't dare.

"Cliff," she says, standing on tiptoe to whisper in his ear, "couldn't we—"

"No," he says, more sharply than he intended. "No kidding, Janice, we don't have time—I mean, who knows when your parents will read your note, they could be over here in an hour for all we know—"

He stops himself, chagrined; his own dishonesty alarms him and makes his stomach contract further; even his skin seems to tighten, as though desperately holding him together.

"Look," he says—and now he does pull away—"I guess I'm uptight, I feel a little queasy this morning. Let's get going, okay?"

In her nakedness Janice looks so frail, so undefended; now that she's standing he notices how clearly she is "showing," her belly looking swollen and hard and triumphant as though draining the life from her pale slender limbs. She's smiling vaguely, her eyes fastened unmoving to his.

"I guess you caught it from me," she says.

"From you . . . ?"

"Nausea, the morning sickness," she says, but her voice has lowered; he feels how intently she's watching him.

"Cliff?" she says. "Is something wrong?"

Behind him, Clifford's hands have grasped the sink. He feels light-headed, woozy. When had she started calling him Cliff, he wonders vaguely, few people have ever called him that; he'd always disliked nicknames and he asked people to call him *Clifford*, always that, nothing but that.

All at once he feels very ill.

"No," he says, "just a little—like I said, it's just a nervous stomach. I'll eat something, maybe. Or light up a toke."

"There's nothing like grass for nausea," she says lightly. "It got me through *my* morning sickness"—and now she goes to the tub and twists the faucet to HOT; within seconds the room begins filling with steam.

Over the splashing water Clifford shouts, "I'll finish loading up the car"—and he pulls the door shut behind him; he escapes.

From inside the bathroom he can hear the faint sound of Janice singing in the shower—one of her favorites like "If I Fell in Love," probably, or "Sing for Your Supper"—so evidently she's all right. Evidently he hasn't hurt her feelings. Despite her relentless high spirits and her perversely insouciant approach to the sudden changes in their lives she will sometimes pause like that, sensing in his voice or eyes something that doesn't quite please her, doesn't quite fit; at such times a chill runs through him and he understands how much he needs Janice. Sometimes he wonders if it isn't Janice who has adopted him, rather than vice versa.

One day this winter his heart-stopping sense of vulnerability had impelled him out to the cemetery, his first visit since the funeral on that muggy-hot dour day when he'd behaved so childishly, as if his mother's suicide were only an inconvenience, an empty ritual that held little interest for Irene Bannon's son and only companion

during the last seven years of her life. Returning to the cemetery
this past January, early on a frigid, bright-blue Sunday morning, he'd
thought back upon that former self without remorse, and had stared
down at his mother's headstone without rancor. Shivering, he nonetheless felt a stony peaceful assurance as he stared and, very shyly,
remembered; he saw her last grimace with its greenish string of
vomit and her last wink over their morning coffee and her last
crunching desperate lovely hug before he left for school and her last
laugh. He smiled to himself, recalling the laugh. For a moment he
felt a catch in his throat and he didn't try to stop, but then the
tears didn't come, after all; or else the frigid wind that morning met
them as they appeared, as he looked down with his wide-open gaze,
and instantly dried them to nothing.

    After that day he knew he wouldn't return to the cemetery
again, it wouldn't be necessary, but he did seek out other places, as
if sending forth tender young new shoots of himself, experimentally,
to see if they might survive into some other dimension. He'd followed
the strongest such impulse even while still at the McCords, leaving
at seven P.M. for a "date" and then driving the two hundred miles
up to Dallas in under two hours, his senses sharpened by panicky
dread and excitement. Once during a murmuring aimless conversation with Jimmy Tate, he'd heard of Jimmy's abashed visit to a "gay
bar" in Dallas—how easily the phrase had come off even Jimmy's
awkward tongue, when Clifford hadn't known such places existed!—
and how frightened Jimmy had been the first time he went, but how
very excited. The first time Clifford drove to Dallas by himself he'd
gone into a phone booth and begun calling numbers under "Cocktail
Lounges," beginning with The A-OK Saloon and proceeding alpha-
betically, methodically, asking the same steely-voiced question each
time: "Is this a gay bar?" He got snide laughter in response, once a
"Hell no!" followed by a hang-up, once a "Chile, whatchoo talkin
about?" followed by an impatient silence upon which Clifford hung
up; only when he reached a "B" listing, the Bayou Landing, did he
get a forthright, "Sure is. You from out of town?"

    He'd gotten directions and by the time he arrived it was nearly
midnight and the place was packed with men, most of them only a
few years older than Clifford, and for a while Clifford had stood on

the edge of the dance floor, staring. He'd been literally open-mouthed, he supposed, and had probably attracted a few stares of his own, a few titters from the sidelines, but he'd been astonished by the spectacle of several hundred men packed into a massive dance floor beneath roving lights and a sequined ball representing, he supposed, the moon, and all of them *dancing:* all of them men, and dancing together. He might have been set down into some other world, and for a while no reaction was possible, neither alarm nor delight, neither distaste nor pleasure. Very slowly, tentatively, some buried and half-acknowledged part of himself, featureless and remote, lacking even a name, began to make sense, began asserting itself in his blood as if in rhythm with the beating, ear-shattering music. When a tall boy with an earring tapped him on the shoulder and yelled, "Wanna dance?" Clifford had come back to himself, startled, had focused on the boy—his own age, roughly, red-haired and bony, with pale hopeful eyes—and had quickly shaken his head, and croaked out, "No?" The boy gave no reaction. He turned quickly and melted back into the crowd. Clifford then tried to smile, feeling an ache at both sides of his mouth, and he said a bit louder, "Yes?"—though by then the boy had been gone for quite some time and Clifford was only talking to himself.

From that night on, he returned to the Bayou Landing every weekend, sometimes on Friday and Saturday nights both, until the McCords began to tease him that he'd found a girlfriend, hadn't he, and who was she? When would they get to meet the lucky girl? Embarrassed but still relentlessly polite, Clifford mumbled noncom-mittal replies until Larry, disturbed that Clifford had begun getting home later and later, began checking the mileage on Clifford's car and waiting up for him: and finally they'd had it out, one Sunday morning at five o'clock, just after Clifford had stumbled inside the front door. Exhausted, Clifford had told him everything. Asked if he would promise to stop, and if he would agree to set up counseling sessions with Father Culhane, Clifford had declined, and Larry said he had no choice but to ask Clifford to leave ... and so it had ended, that phase of his life, without much fanfare and with only mild regret. Since moving to this duplex apartment, Clifford thought back upon the McCords in much the same way he thought back upon his mother and, before that, upon his life with both his parents as a very small child: these memories seemed less his past than a dream of his past, just as late on Sunday afternoon he would wake and think back in amazement to the crowded, pulsing dance floor he'd visited the night before, the sea of male faces bobbing among the slashing lights and sudden gaps of darkness, the music and smoke and blended smells of liquor and cologne, and especially the emotion—the random, hectic, unceasing emotion; all that hope and dread and craving so thinly overlaid with an air of primordial festivity.

For a while this dreamlike setting entered Clifford's blood like a response to his own hidden passions and he became, he supposed, an addict, living through the bland weekdays for the moment on Friday night when he paid his money and stepped into that other world. Despite the seemingly large number of men, he began quickly to realize that he saw the same faces again and again, and that he himself had become a recognizable part of the landscape. After the first few weeks, people seldom asked him to dance; he'd developed a half-scowling persona—hands stuffed in his pockets, chin lifted slightly as he surveyed the crowd—that kept any hopeful others at a distance. A couple of times he did fall into conversation, once with a handsome choirboy type who went to the University of Dallas, once with a hawk-nosed blond man in his early thirties, very thin, raffish-looking; and both times he was invited to bed. He declined the student but accepted the fringe character, as he thought of him, with his predatory sharp blue eyes, prominent nose and Adam's apple, his air of having stopped into the bar only briefly, homing in for the kill. Riding home with the man, Clifford had thought clearly that he could be either an accountant or a mass murderer, there was no way to know, but he turned out to be Nick, a thirty-two-year-old elementary school teacher with an apartment full of exquisite English antiques and a large collection of X-rated color movies. They'd spent about ten minutes watching the movies and then more than an hour having sex, Nick moving quickly all over Clifford's body, his tongue probing Clifford's mouth, his navel, his buttocks, before he sat unceremoniously on Clifford's chest and masturbated while keeping his trembling eyelids closed. Clifford had turned away, closing his own eyes, when Nick came, and a minute later Nick was up and dressed, rattling his car keys. He had, he said, to get up very early in the morning.

Delivered back to the bar, Clifford had the idea that he must have done something wrong, but a few weeks later, accosted again by the choirboy, he agreed to have coffee with him and confessed what had happened on the night they first met.

"Oh, *her,*" said the student, whose name was Brandon and who rolled his eyes at almost anything Clifford said.

"You know him?" asked Clifford, who'd kept hoping against his better judgment that he'd run into Nick again very soon.

"Everybody knows him—once," Brandon said, keeping his round-eyed gaze on Clifford.

"Once?" Clifford said bleakly.

"Well, he's not husband material, if that's what you're thinking," Brandon said with the mildest of scorn.

He blew on his coffee and sipped, wincing.

They sat in a crowded Denny's only a few blocks from the bar, and Clifford had noticed several other gay couples, and over by the windows a rowdy squealing group, several of whom he recognized from the dance floor. But most of the clientele filling the garish orange-and-pink vinyl booths were straight—older couples with thin hunched shoulders and eyeglasses; a few redneck types and their girlfriends, in jeans and baseball caps; hard-looking men of indeterminate age (truck drivers? insomniacs?) who sat alone, chain-smoking, unfazed by the clanking dishes and chattering people all around them. What did the straight ones think, Clifford wondered, when they glanced at Clifford and Brandon, or at any of the other male couples? Perhaps they didn't know, or didn't care?

Now Brandon was giving him a soft, sympathetic look, as if reading Clifford's mind were the easiest thing in the world.

"Honey, you've got to relax," Brandon said. "Ain't nobody gonna gobble you up."

Though very intelligent, and a doctor's son from Jackson, Brandon went for the deliberate, droll effects of a Mississippi rural accent. After half an hour Clifford was bored with him, and he was discom-

fited by the boy's knowing, jaded air, its implication that Clifford
had so much to learn. He wasn't sure, really, that he wanted to
learn.

"Listen," Brandon said, "I'm having a few folks over for dinner
next Saturday, and I promise you that we'll be the only Catholics
there. How's that sound?"

Clifford had mentioned, idly, that *his* mother—of whom he
spoke in the present tense—wanted him to attend UD, and they'd
talked for a while about their Catholic upbringings. To his surprise,
Brandon still went to mass, and he'd abandoned his big-eyed drollery
when speaking of the Church. When Clifford asked, bluntly, "You
still believe in that stuff?" Brandon had shrugged and said, "No sense
in throwin the baby out with the bath water, darlin."

"Thanks," Clifford said now, "but I'd better—"

"Come on," Brandon said, reaching across the table to touch
Clifford's hand. Clifford resisted the impulse to draw back. "Really,"
Brandon said, "these are *nice* people. Not like that number who ran
off with your virginity."

While Brandon cackled at his own joke, and poured more sugar
in his coffee, Clifford looked around in alarm. For all his innocent
looks, Brandon had an overloud, raucous voice, and Clifford didn't
want anyone to overhear. Did the boy have no shame?

"It's nothing to be ashamed of, you know," Brandon added, as
though reading Clifford's mind again. "Most of us give that precious
commodity to someone entirely unworthy. I met my degradation
early, in a most unromantic setting—a boys' locker room in Tupelo,
if you please, with a two-hundred-pound *black* football player for the
opposing team. Now darlin, don't look so shocked, I didn't actually
play football, I was only the—what did they call it—oh yes, the
manager, the job they always give the sissies. Anyhow, we were
visiting this team in charming Tupelo, home of the immortal Elvis,
and during the game I'd wandered back into the locker room, bored
to death, and somehow I found myself near the showers, one of
which was running, and there was this gigantic black creature standing blissfully under the water, playing with himself like he'd discovered the delightful thing that very day. I shouldn't say 'thing,'
though—I should say *hose*. And I'll be damned if instead of being

embarrassed he didn't just *wink* at me. Turns out that he was a
bench-warmer for *their* team, and knew every song that Billie Holiday
ever recorded, by heart—but I'm getting ahead of myself. See, when
he first invited me into the shower, I didn't—"

But Clifford tuned out, he was embarrassed, uncomfortable,
and when he caught the eye of the waitress he signaled for more
coffee.

"Honey, you're going to be up all *night,*" Brandon said, delighted. He dropped the narrative of his lost virginity without further
ado. "Now look," he said, "I do want you to come to this little
dinner, you've *got* to meet my friends—in fact, why don't you plan
on staying over that night, and then Sunday we can go to brunch
and—"

"The bathroom," Clifford said. "I've got to use the bathroom."

And while Brandon, shrugging, picked up his cup of fresh coffee
and blew at it, wrinkling his nose as he sipped, Clifford headed back
toward the restrooms but at the last moment turned in the opposite
direction, toward the exit. Out in the cool night air, he inhaled
deeply, nearly overcome with relief. He half-walked, half-jogged back
to the bar's parking lot, vowing that he was finished with bars.
When he got home it was almost light, and this was the morning
he had his confrontation with Larry McCord and refused to promise
that he wouldn't keep going into Dallas, going to gay bars. He
refused to promise anything at all.

It had been with some relief, in the following weeks, that he'd
finally accepted his father's invitation to Atlanta, where he could
work full-time or part-time, where he could live at home or in his
own apartment, where his father's wife, Miriam—"your new
mother," Mr. Bannon had said, hurrying past the phrase—knew
some midtown gallery owners who would be happy to look at Clifford's work. Why was his father being so agreeable, going out of his
way to bring Clifford near?—it was hard not to wonder, not to be
suspicious, since Mr. Bannon had never seemed particularly interested
in custody when Clifford was younger; but on the other hand, Clifford thought, it was surely better not to bear a grudge and not to
ask questions but simply to move ahead, do exactly what you wanted
so long as no one else got hurt. So he'd felt relief in finally accepting

his father, let bygones be bygones, and he'd felt more relief than dismay when he returned from the library that afternoon to find Janice Rungren sitting on his porch steps, her hair coarse but shiny, falling nearly to her breasts, her face fresh and almost plain without makeup—really a pleasant face, he couldn't help but think, so pleasantly familiar. That night he'd said they'd better use a rubber, did she have a rubber, but she'd laughed in mock-outrage. "Do *I* have a rubber?—do *I* carry a rubber around with me, ready to lie down and spread my legs for the first available man? I guess you've still been hanging around with those Pius jerks, haven't you," she said. "Listening to their vicious gossip."

He'd had to laugh at her horror-struck tone, her comically widened eyes, and he'd said, "Sorry, I mean it, *sorry*." And he'd thought: What if we *did* have a baby? Weren't young kids these days having babies left and right, weren't the communes filled with happy naked babies toddling around, in the sunlight, under the smiles of their liberated long-haired parents? It wouldn't really be so awful, would it? If *we* had a baby?

When she told him about the pregnancy, he did feel a mild jolt of panic, but almost at once his thoughts about the baby she carried—*his* baby—blended in his mind with distant childhood memories of that lost baby brother, Dennis Ray Bannon, over whom his mother had grieved so profusely. When he imagined himself, only months from now, holding a tiny infant in his arms, he thought of the six-year-old Clifford holding baby Dennis with exaggerated care, seated between his parents on the living room sofa, both of them beaming down at him. . . . Somehow it felt right to Clifford, this sudden bold idea of becoming a young father; there was an emotional logic behind it that pushed aside any practical considerations. And, he thought, he did love Janice, however guardedly, however fearfully at times, and surely this baby would bring them closer, maybe they *would* be a blithe carefree "counterculture" family—Clifford working at his art, Janice happy at home in her long hair and sandals, the baby plump, naked, babbling. Straining to imagine this, he felt his vision and his eyesight itself beginning to mist over: only when he woke in the morning did the ruthless clarity of his seeing return to him, and the world seemed bleak and ungiving, he and Janice pitiful and deluded in their homely physical bodies. Blinking, he would feel paralyzed before the day looming ahead of him and the long stretch of days and months and years, his life itself, looming beyond that. At such times, he felt that "love" was the most pitiful delusion of human beings, and in response to this thought his body would twitch, or he would cough loudly, wanting deliberately to wake Janice, and a few terrifying seconds would pass—heartbeats, pulsebeats—before she would reach out and grab hold of him, grab him *there,* and he would turn toward her with an abrupt sense of youth and strength and power, forgetting everything else.

Janice took forever to get ready, she was slow and disorganized and forgetful, always asking for "just one more minute"—she needed to do "just one more little thing"—before disappearing into the bathroom again. By the time Clifford finishes loading the car, checking the doors and windows, putting the key under a large white rock in the backyard to be retrieved by the landlord, Janice is still "not quite" ready, she isn't even dressed yet, her hairbrush and face cream and body oil are still spread along the top of the sink, and so Clifford returns to the bathroom door and says smartly, "Hey, what happened to the natural look? Come on, Janice, we're just going to be driving all day—no one's going to see you."

She looks over, smirking, wrinkling her nose in a way that reminds him of that college kid, that poor sweet-faced doomed Brandon, and so Clifford hurries forward with an empty garbage bag and begins unceremoniously dumping Janice's things inside. He takes the bag and stuffs it inside the trunk with all their other things, and then takes the wrinkled map of "The Southern United States" out of his back pocket and unfolds it for the umpteenth time—for he's nervous, unaccountably nervous, his hands shaking as he holds the map so that he can't quite focus. He finds southeastern Texas but can't make out where *they* are, exactly, much less where they're going, and as he sits sideways in the front seat with his sneakers digging aimless patterns in the graveled driveway, Janice finally comes out, hesitating on the front porch, squinting out at Clifford.

On this mild balmy gray April morning Janice is a vision, abrupt and powerful, a sudden unexpected apparition in a white jumper and skirt, the skirt very short, and a pair of white sandals, and a matching necklace and bracelet—oversized white-and-crimson beads, Janice calls them her "bangles"—and a white leather handbag with a long strap, flapping at her side. On either side of her face she has brushed her hair long and straight, the part very neat in the center of her head, and as she grins and starts toward him Clifford thinks, She looks like a kid, still—like that girl back in junior high, like a little girl at her First Holy Communion. He's wearing an old pair of jeans and a black T-shirt, he hasn't shaved in a few days, and when Janice gets to the car he stands awkwardly and asks, "Why're you so dressed up?"

She puts one palm on each of his cheeks and brings her face toward him, crushing the map as their bodies press together and Clifford's arms respond, reflexively, gathering her close, and after a long wet kiss she steps back and says, "Why the hell not? This is a pretty big day, isn't it? Like, the biggest day of my life?"

She's jocular and grinning but also serious, he sees that; he sees the look of hope, of childlike desperation, in her wide longish blue eyes.

"Of course," he says, his tongue still moving along his lower lip, still feeling Janice's kiss—"of course," he says quickly, "of our *lives*."

"Well let's get this show on the road!" she cries, laughing at him, hurrying around to her side of the car. He hears the door open and slam.

"You didn't forget anything?" he asks, getting inside, blinking his eyes as though to clear his head of this strange dreaminess, a sudden loss of orientation that makes him feel woozy and more than a little stupid.

"Nope," Janice says, pulling the map from his numbed fingers and efficiently refolding it. "I'm ready, babe—come on, it's almost nine. Don't forget—I left that note in my mailbox at home. We don't want to get caught by my dastardly parents, do we?"

Janice rolls down her window, laughing brightly.

A few minutes later they've shared a joint between them, passing it back and forth, staring out the windshield as though there were something to see. He's seeing all this, he realizes, for the last time: jolting through the redbricked streets of the older part of town, driving along the Loop with its new shopping centers and fast-food places, then rushing through the unchanged countryside with its ridges of pine, black gum, elm, its sagging barbed-wire fences, its weathered farmhouses and sheds, and the occasional oil well looking solitary but smug out in a field, pumping implacably, eternally: yes, it's likely that he's leaving Texas for the last time, and for a moment he feels a startling tug of nostalgia, something very like sorrow. But only for a moment. Feeling the drug lightening first his abdomen and chest, then in a swoon of utter blissful relief his mind itself, he strains to remember if he has ever been to Atlanta—but no, he has not—and then to recall any visual images that attach to the city, for surely he has seen photographs, perhaps his father has sent a snapshot or two . . . ? But no. There are no images in his mind of the future, it all spreads before him blank and featureless. That had been the source of his panic, he supposes—he's a visual person who can't, at the moment, see where he is going.

Only a few turns and they're on the old highway that will take them to the interstate. The sky has darkened slightly and a light mist is falling, the kind of intermittent rain that forces Clifford to turn on the wipers and then, when they begin squeaking loudly, to shut them off again. Beside him, Janice has begun chattering. Always after her initial period of relaxation the dope makes her more talkative, her words disjointed and hectic, addressed toward him but not precisely at him. He can listen or not listen. Today, not surprisingly, she's talking about her baby, *their* baby, discussing articles she has read in *Family Circle* and *Redbook*—for she has begun buying such magazines—that tell how to raise your babies, things to do, things not to do. She rattles off a list of things she will do, things she will not do, saying she's going to be a damned good mother, she's going to be the best damned mother in the world if it's the last thing Janice Rungren ever does.

"Janice who?" Clifford asks, lazily.

Janice gives a quick abrupt laugh: "Oh yeah, Janice *Bannon*," she says, as if listening to this name, its unique sound, for the first time. She says, "I forgot about that."

They haven't discussed the details of the marriage, the when and the how of it; they haven't even discussed getting married, really. Gradually phrases like "once we're married" and "after the wedding" had crept into Janice's conversation, and Clifford hadn't said anything, hadn't reacted at all—but he didn't mind, really. Clifford supposed that if they were going to live together, with a baby, then they might, as well be married.

Now he says, as if to settle the issue, "We ought to get married right away, I suppose. Before you really start to show."

"Yes," Janice says at once, not glancing aside. "I think that's best for the baby, too. I want to do everything right, Clifford, everything by the rules. That'll be best for the baby, don't you think?"

"Yes," Clifford says.

"I think all this is happening at the best possible time," Janice says, confidently. "I mean, they know so much more these days about bringing up kids, don't they? So much more than our parents knew."

"What do you mean?" Clifford says.

"I mean that nowadays everything is *natural,*" Janice says, her white fingers gesturing as she speaks. "I mean, I'm not bringing up my baby the way we were brought up"—Clifford has the fuzzy perception that she sounds angry, but why should she be angry?—"you know," she says, groping for the words, "with all that Catholic bullshit, and if it's a girl she should act prim and proper, and if it's a boy he should go out and cut all the other boys' throats to get ahead, to make money and to fucking *win.* God, I hate the fucking establishment!" she cries. "It's so fucking *gross.*"

Now he sees that Janice is bending forward, fiddling with the air conditioning controls. "It's getting hot in here, Cliff, turn on the AC, would you? I'll get wet if I even crack the window."

Clifford reaches down, idly, but he doesn't really move the controls, he can't quite remember how the air conditioner works. And suddenly his stomach and chest are heaving, and he understands that he has started to laugh. Janice looks over, annoyed, and asks what the hell is he laughing about? And will he turn on the fucking AC, for Christ's sake?

Now the windshield has gotten wet again, and he reaches down for the wiper knob but turns on the radio by mistake, then quickly snaps it off. They'd heard a blaring split-second of "Hey Jude" and after that the silence seems more intense, more ominous. Why is he laughing, exactly?—he's laughing so hard his eyes have begun to water.

Wanting to mollify Janice, he manages to say, "I'm sorry, I don't know why I'm laughing—I guess it was just so funny, what you said—"

"What *I* said?" Janice cries, turning her body to face him. He knows that she's angry, she's absolutely furious, but he can't stop laughing and so he tries to make her understand, make her hear what she'd said the way he'd heard it.

"I mean—I mean," he says, trying to catch his breath, trying to stop laughing this deep half-painful dry-throated laugh, "I mean what you said about the establishment, about hating 'the fucking establishment,' and its being *gross,* I mean that struck me as so damned funny that I couldn't—"

"Listen, Clifford Bannon," Janice says hotly, "this may all be a big joke to you, but it's my baby I'm talking about here—*our* baby, in case you've forgotten—and if you think I'm not serious about—"

But he can't listen, he *must* tune out or else he'll become hysterical, his stomach is already knotted in pain from so much laughter. Now he does manage to find the wiper knob and when the windshield clears he sees that there, up ahead, is the entrance ramp to the interstate, they're here already, they're on their way!—maybe smoking the dope was a bad idea, it does tend to make you giddy, but God he feels so much better than he did half an hour before. Now, as he turns the signal indicator for entering the high-way, he feels something grasping his forearm—of course it's Janice, her small white fingers flexing tightly, almost painfully, as if trying to throw them off course.

"Cut it out, Janice, I'm trying to make this turn—"

He hears the wild curses—*Goddamn you! How dare you!*—in Janice's shrieking voice, he understands that she's furious, she's out of control, and in her rage she has a fierce strength, greatly overpow-ering his. He enters the expressway, looking behind him at the stream of other cars, but she has grabbed his arm and the wheel swerves abruptly, sending them sideways across the interstate—he hears the blaring of horns, and screeching tires—and that's when he loses track of what is happening. They're going only twenty or twenty-five, his foot lunges at the gas pedal, but there's only Janice shrieking in his ear and the windshield again covered in mist so that he can't see, can't understand, and before he can straighten the car he hears another loud blaring of horns and an instant later comes the impact, unbelievably sudden and brutal, that sends him and Janice flailing toward the windshield, Janice's tight-grasping hand still affixed to his forearm. And for the next few minutes he knows nothing, understands nothing at all.

Though the information has no meaning, nothing he can relate particularly to himself, he sits outside the emergency room and stares at a clock that reads 11:40; a gray pearly light enters through a small window, at the far end of the hall. For nearly two hours he has sat here, interviewed first by the police, who were amazingly polite, who said they knew how rocky he felt and what a bad time this was: they had only to get some information and then they'd leave him alone.

Had he and Janice been drinking? asked the older cop, a blunt-featured man with a gray crew cut so short his scalp showed through.

Despite Clifford's bloodshot eyes, the man didn't look skeptical or ask about drugs when Clifford said hoarsely, almost inaudibly, *No.*

The cop wrote Clifford's answer in his notebook.

Was there any explanation, then? asked the cop, who'd informed Clifford that the other driver, now down at headquarters, reported that Clifford's Mustang "careened" across the expressway onto the grassy median, and directly into a line of oncoming traffic. Clifford, elbows on his knees, had looked down at the floor as the cop asked gently, "Did you lose control of the car, then? Was it unavoidable?"

As if feeding Clifford his lines, Clifford thought, and he mumbled gratefully, "Yes, yes that's right—I lost control of the car."

The cop wrote this down and straightened; he'd been crouching next to Clifford, in the posture an adult assumes toward a confused child. He said, "We'll ask your girlfriend, once the doctors are through. I'm sure she'll tell the same story."

"She will," Clifford had said, hoping the cop and his quiet younger partner would now walk away, which they did, leaving him alone until he heard the fast approach of footsteps and looked up in despair, knowing it was Janice's parents but unable not to look up, even though he half expected to see Arthur Rungren with his fist raised, barreling madly toward Clifford. Instead Mr. Rungren looked pale, his face blurry and distraught, while the petite honey-blond Mrs. Rungren wore sunglasses and Clifford couldn't see much of her face. Perhaps they didn't recognize him? Perhaps they'd spoken with the doctor on the phone and already knew something he didn't know? They went through the swinging double doors on Clifford's right, doors only immediate family members could enter, and once the doors finally became still—which took, Clifford thought, a very long time—the silence and the eerie half-light from that distant tiny window seemed almost impossible to bear.

So he waited, and still he waits, looking from the clock (now it's 11:48, the nurse promised to come out and tell Clifford the moment she knew anything) down to his bloodstained hands and to his shoes, also spotted with blood, and down to the gleaming black-and-white-tiled floor. So silent and motionless, he is nonetheless assailed—his head ringing, echoing—by the events of the past two hours, Janice's contorted screaming face and her mangled posture as she slumped against the car door, bleeding from a gash in her forehead, her hands and lap covered in a thicker, darker blood, so impossibly profuse that it covered her exposed thighs and knees in gleaming moist red, and the sight of his own clenched hands on the wheel as he steered them somehow, God knows how, off the expressway and onto the service road and back toward town, toward this hospital that thank God was only a couple of miles away. Though his head had hit the dashboard, too, he didn't think he was bleeding, he felt dazed but basically all right; his left ring finger had been smashed back against the steering wheel during the impact and the finger throbbed with pain, and his head ached dully, but otherwise he felt fine and he was quite sure that none of the blood in the car was his. Blinking his eyes, trying not to panic, he drove right up to the emergency entrance and after bending toward Janice, adjusting her legs so that she looked more comfortable (for she was unconscious by now, her face deathly pale, her lower body a mess of thick dark blood), Clifford had wiped his hands on his jeans and torn inside the building and within seconds the nurses had taken over, had brought Janice inside on a stretcher and tried to comfort Clifford as best they could. So it had begun, or so it had ended, but in any case here he sits, numbed, unattended, waiting as the minutes tick past. He ignores the throbbing pain in his head, his finger; strangely, he's almost grateful for the pain.

When the double doors swing open again and he sees Janice's father, Clifford looks mechanically at the clock—12:01, it reads—and then stares blankly into Mr. Rungren's face, which looks creased and pale, and suddenly rather old; Clifford feels less afraid of him than sorry for him.

"How is she?" Clifford whispers.

Mr. Rungren stands with his hands in his pockets, not quite looking at Clifford. He says, "She's in shock, but they say they've seen worse cases. She lost some blood, but not too much."

"Some, but not too much?" Clifford says.

"Whatever that means," says Mr. Rungren.

"But I mean—will she—"

"She'll be okay," Mr. Rungren says in a flat resentful voice. "A day or two in the hospital, but she'll be okay."

Clifford looks back at the floor. "That's a relief," he says.

He thinks that maybe it's over and Mr. Rungren is about to go back inside when the man says, in a tone that sounds oddly sarcastic, "She miscarried, of course. But I guess you knew about *that*."

Clifford gapes at him.

"Here," Mr. Rungren says roughly, pulling money out of his wallet, "call a taxi, I'll gladly pay if you'll just—"

"No, it's okay," Clifford says. "My car still runs, Mr. Rungren. I drove us here from the—the accident."

"What *were* you doing out in the interstate, anyway, at this time of—" but before Mr. Rungren finishes this question he seems to lose interest, he goes back through the doors with one hand to his forehead, like a man in an aspirin commercial.

Clifford thinks, dully: They haven't read Janice's note.

Shakily, he rises. She's all right, he thinks, and he decides that he should get cleaned up; he can go back to his place and retrieve the key and take a long hot shower. Then he'll go buy some flowers and return here and endure whatever he must.

He moves slowly out to the car, rubbing gingerly at his forehead with his uninjured hand, but even though it's raining he pauses for a moment by the trunk. He takes out his keys, rummages through one of the white garbage bags, and brings out a towel. Gazing up into the rain, he soaks his face and hands and rubs them briskly. He feels better at once, so he takes a fresh towel and continues wiping himself until his face and hands are free of blood. But it's not enough. He bends back inside the trunk and finds a fresh white T-shirt and pair of jeans and right there in the parking lot, not caring who sees, he takes off his bloodstained clothes and dons the fresh ones. Then he finds a pair of clean white sneakers and replaces his bloody shoes with those. He empties one of the garbage bags and throws the soiled clothes and towels inside it, and sets the bag down on the asphalt. Armed with several more towels, he approaches the passenger side of the car.

Cleaning out the car takes a bit longer, and he wishes he had waited before changing clothes, but he's very careful and doesn't get any of the blood on his shirt or hands. He wipes slowly, patiently at the car seat, at the dashboard and floorboard, and finally at the windshield where some of the blood had spattered on Janice's side. Every few seconds he holds the towel outside the car, wetting it with rain. While cleaning the car seat, where the blood is thickest, he holds his breath and lets his brain go blank, for the blood is mingled with a whitish mucous substance, which he takes special care not to touch with his naked hands. Twice he has to return to the trunk for more towels, but at last he's done and he puts everything into the garbage bag and twists the top of the bag deftly. He runs back into the hospital and deposits the bag in a trash receptacle by the door.

Inside the car, he turns on the radio but doesn't really hear the music, just as he isn't really conscious of himself driving the car quite crisply and expertly, following pure instinct as he heads back toward the service road and the expressway. Hours later he is past the Texas border and well into Louisiana before his mind begins relaxing, his senses begin returning, and before he's aware that his head and finger throb mightily and that his throat is constricted in grief. It's no longer raining but the windshield is blurred nonetheless and he understands that now there's no turning back, it's over with, it's done. He has that consolation, at least.

Part
———————————

T W O

6

Clifford

Around five o'clock he comes out of his apartment building, jacket collar raised against the wind, and hurries the two blocks down Ponce de Leon Avenue to Fourth Street, where he'd been lucky to find a parking place late last night—in fact, around three in the morning. Sometimes he has to park five or six blocks away when he gets home that late, but even though midtown is semi-dangerous after dark he prefers this to using the overpriced parking garage across the street with its monitored security system where businessmen and rich old ladies park their cars. He doesn't mind the danger, he likes taking chances, he tends to walk fast with his head lowered, collar raised—in this posture he feels anonymous and protected even though he knows better. Today, in fact, someone accosts him just as he's unlocking the car door, a loud husky black voice from the alley behind him—"Hey you, hey man I'm talkin to *you*, goddamn it!"—but nothing happens, probably the guy is just peddling dope, it's nothing, Clifford Bannon ignores him and gets in the car and drives away down the street, scot free.

Late winter. Late afternoon. He isn't due at his Uncle Pete's until seven o'clock, but he'd been restless today. He'd slept until noon and felt that the day had escaped him, plummeting toward nightfall by the time he showered and changed and read the Sunday papers. On weekend nights Clifford stays out late, very late, and often sleeps until one or two o'clock, but he likes to get out of the apartment by late afternoon, especially on these winter days when it gets dark so early. Now it's already dusk and he has more than an hour to kill before he drives the two miles to Pete's, so he starts driving along Piedmont Avenue rather slowly, idly. Clifford has lived in Atlanta for five years now, he has a degree in art history from the state university downtown, he's on good terms with his uncle and his father and his father's new family, and he has already made a name for himself, somewhat, among the city's gallery owners and other artists—but despite all this, he doesn't yet feel at home here. Driving around town in his battered '63 Chevy, he looks about him with the appreciative eye of a visitor, someone who won't be permitted to stay here for long, and in fact all during these past five years his life has felt provisional, as if something might easily call him away, as though he weren't properly anchored in his life the way other people were in theirs. Yet nothing has called him away, and in fact he pursued his degree and produced his own work at a steady clip and developed a routine, he knew, that differed little from that of other students. He has lived in several midtown apartments and though he has accumulated very little—a few dozen books and old canvases, all packed into cardboard boxes—he has begun to feel weighed down, overburdened with possessions. He likes his present apartment, with its blend of seediness and piquant faded glamor, but he doesn't know how long he'll be living there, especially now that he has finished his degree. He has no plans to unpack those cardboard boxes.

When he's a few blocks away from Pete's house, he glances at his watch, then checks his jacket pocket for the envelope: half hoping he might have forgotten it.

Yesterday he'd gotten a letter from Janice Rungren, one of several he'd received lately. He has no idea what he thinks about these letters. The first one had shocked him—he'd recognized her handwriting at once, his face blanching—but its tone had been lively, friendly, cheerful, lacking even an oblique reference to their awful parting five years before. The letters contained droll descriptions of her recent life, of her comical attempts to pass business courses at the local junior college, of her "plagued" romantic life and the "delicate equilibrium" of her relationship with her parents, with whom she still lived. When she did refer to her and Clifford's past it was only to the distant past, their school days at St. John Bosco and Pius XII and all their "shenanigans," their "less than saintly" behavior. Though Clifford did not answer the letters, and would not dream of answering them, Janice never asked for any response and seemed perfectly willing just "to ramble," as she put it, enjoying their common memories, getting off a witty phrase here and there, and giving Clifford the eerie feeling that Janice, at long last, had grown up; that she had come to terms with her past in a way Clifford himself had never done. And this pleased him. He'd finally been lulled into a sense of complacency, of safety, and had begun to entertain the idea of dropping her a card, or perhaps even giving her a call one evening, to thank her for the letters. But then came yesterday's letter, which had an Atlanta postmark and, beneath her usual signature, "Love and hugs, Janice," a local phone number.

No other reference to her move. No request to call. The letter had been almost wholly focused on her relationship with her cousin Ruthie, who was now a Dominican nun, and how "sad, but proud" Janice felt about Ruthie's attaining her goal at last, even though it meant "losing her best friend, in any *real* sense." Clifford narrowed his eyes when he read the phrase "best friend," wondering if this were a little dig, remembering how often back at school she would call Clifford her "only friend" or her "one true friend" or, most often, her "best friend in the whole wide world" while Clifford grinned awkwardly and glanced away.

Because this particular letter is quite long and therefore bulky he now removes the envelope from his jacket pocket and places it on the seat beside him, but it keeps catching at the corner of his eye as he drives so he puts it in the glove compartment and even then he senses it there, as if the letter were throbbing, glowing, and he laughs at himself, uneasily. He's not sure why he's bringing the letter to Pete's, but suspects he must want advice, or reassurance;

or perhaps just to hear someone say, out loud, that Clifford is not responsible for anything Janice Rungren says or does. He takes a deep breath. He smiles weakly and exhales, watching his breath turn to frost on the air. Outside it's below thirty degrees and he keeps meaning to have this car's heater fixed—he keeps meaning to get a better car, in fact, Christ he has six hundred thousand in the bank so why shouldn't he have a new car?—but when he thinks of going to a garage, or a car dealership, it never seems important enough, somehow; it never seems quite worth the trouble.

A few blocks ahead is the turn for Pete's house, but impulsively he turns off Piedmont and into the park, glancing at his watch as he slows the car to three or four miles an hour. Past six o'clock and freezing outside and the sky darkening quickly, but still he sees them, a flash of red flannel here, a sudden pale face there, a whitish flare among the dark thick trees, and now Clifford is driving very slowly, the car has crawled nearly to a stop. Soon enough, of course, there's another car behind him, cruising, slowing; then with sudden impatience it pulls alongside him. The driver is a burly red-faced man in his forties, looking annoyed but slowing to Clifford's pace, glancing over, assessing. Clifford stares at him briefly, impassively, then with a decisive turn of his head he looks away. The man revs his engine and drives off.

It's a scene that replays several times as Clifford's car follows the winding lanes more deeply into the park, the trees with their gnarled massive bare limbs adding a bleaker shadow to the dusk in here, and every few minutes he glances at the driver of another car that has slowed beside his, or watches as a young man's figure emerges briefly from the woods—most of them young, wearing mustaches, looking very cold inside their green army jackets or nylon windbreakers but pausing nonetheless to give Clifford the same dull-eyed glare he gives to them—and at some point he couldn't have predicted and doesn't really choose (the man he sees now differs little from the rest, perhaps he's a bit older, a bit meaner-looking) he does bring the car to a stop and rolls down the window. Though he keeps the engine running.

The man approaches the passenger side, ducks his head to look through the glass, and when Clifford makes no move to reach across or open the door he comes around to Clifford's window. Now Clifford rolls the window halfway down, but he keeps a tight grip on the handle.

"Hey, what's up?" the man says. His tone is friendly enough, though he isn't smiling. Neither is Clifford smiling.

"Not much," Clifford says. "What about you."

Asking this question, his voice flat, uninflected, Clifford looks away. Stares ahead through the windshield.

He'd seen enough: the man is in his thirties, tall and lean, no mustache; his face handsome but gaunt, weathered-looking. Exactly Clifford's type.

"So, my name's Earl," the man says, reaching inside the car and drawing two fingers along the back of Clifford's neck. "So," he says, "what're you looking for, exactly?"

Clifford cuts off the ignition as Earl steps back from the car. When Clifford gets out and pockets the keys, Earl does smile at him. But slowly. Warily. Clifford moves one side of his mouth upward in what he hopes will resemble a smile and tilts his head toward the woods.

"I don't have a lot of time," he says to Earl.

All through dinner Clifford fights the urge to talk about what had happened in the park. Pete always urges him to talk, just as tonight he insists that Clifford eat, eat, he's getting too thin, his color isn't all that good, and so Clifford takes a second helping of the shrimp thermidor and the asparagus in hollandaise and chews, nods, smiles: but their conversation stays relatively light and Clifford fears that his uncle might be shocked to hear his young nephew discuss sex so openly, bluntly. Though he knows his uncle is gay, and vice versa, they've never talked about it; their understanding of one another is based upon the various omissions, assumptions, and indirect or even wordless references—a quick glance, a small fixed smile—by which two men who are blood relatives and of Catholic background and of different generations and of a rather quiet, self-contained disposition must communicate about anything very personal, much less sexual. They don't even discuss family matters very often, so that when Pete abruptly changes the subject over dessert—they'd been discussing a new contemporary sculpture exhibit over at the High Museum—Clifford is startled, even a bit fearful.

"I saw Jim the other day," his uncle says, offhandedly. "He stopped by the office, in fact. He's looking very well, I think."

Clifford drops his eyes and forks off a bite of Pete's delicious blackberry cobbler; but he's full, he's not accustomed to big meals and suddenly he knows he can't take another bite. Though he and Pete have become quite close over the past few years, gradually but genuinely close, Clifford can count on his fingers the number of times they've spoken of his father—and, of course, they seldom refer to Clifford's mother. Clifford knows that Pete and his sister had been very close at one time and that Pete still grieves over her death in a way that Clifford had never done. Not that Clifford has wanted to bring up the subject, either.

"Really?" Clifford says, his voice even. "How's he doing?"

"Fine, fine," Pete says, sipping at his coffee. "He asked about you."

"I haven't seen him in a while," Clifford says quickly. "I need to get over there."

It had been two months since Clifford's brief visit on Christmas day. His relationship with his father and his wife, Miriam, and their two young daughters, Kerry and Eve, had become a matter of the obligatory holidays—Father's Day, Thanksgiving, Christmas—with an occasional birthday or other "special occasion" thrown in. Three years ago, after Eve was born, he'd agreed to serve as godfather at her christening (thereby entering a church for the first time in many years), and when Clifford turned twenty-one his father had thrown him a small party, attended by Pete and a couple of Clifford's friends from the university. On the whole such occasions were awkward and somehow embarrassing, even though he and his father got along well and though Clifford enjoyed being around his little half-sisters. On this past Christmas they'd gathered around the tree after dinner and Clifford had opened his presents, his deft fingers hurrying, and they'd had a toast of champagne and then Clifford had said he had to be going. Miriam, a tall and handsome but perplexed-looking woman (her thick glasses made her cool gray eyes seem overlarge, she appeared to watch with questioning curiosity everything he did), had said at once, disappointed, "Already . . . ? But Cliff, what about some fruitcake, or maybe another glass of champagne?" Yet his father had stood at once. He came over and embraced him. "Thanks for coming, Son," he told Clifford. Although his father had put on some weight, especially in his face (his deep-set eyes now seemed embedded in sockets of flesh), and wore his blond hair longer at his ears and collar, Mr. Bannon was still the same formidable well-dressed man with whom Clifford and Janice had shared that decisive lunch, all those years ago in the Ramada Inn. They didn't resemble one another physically, and had little to talk about: though Miriam always expressed disappointment when Clifford left, and the girls clambered over his knees begging him to stay a bit longer, Clifford knew his father felt a certain hollow chagrin if not outright embarrassment that was similar to his own. Their good-byes were tinged with a sense of mutual relief.

Now he says to Pete, idly, "What was he doing there, anyhow? I didn't know that you two—"

"Oh, we don't keep up, not really," Pete says, in the tone of airy disappointment he uses often, "but our paths have started crossing at the office these past few years—haven't I mentioned that? We're getting downright automated," Pete laughs, "though unfortunately we haven't bought anything from Jim yet. I hope he doesn't take that against *me,* I've got nothing to do with buying computers, God knows!"

For many years Pete has worked for a large management consulting firm, where he produces an in-house trade magazine, designs pamphlets and brochures. It's a pleasant, undemanding job, Pete says, and occasionally he does get to use his "artsy" side. As a young man Pete had wanted to be a cartoonist and magazine illustrator, but has told Clifford that the competition was just too severe, that he'd been only "talented, not brilliant," but that he's quite satisfied with the little niche he'd found for himself. (And of course, as Clifford knows, Pete doesn't need the money: he and Irene had each inherited half of their mother's estate, and Clifford suspects that Pete, who has a good business head, has probably doubled or tripled his own share by now. He keeps after Clifford to let his broker invest Clifford's money, too, he says it's a waste for it just to sit there, in CD's; but Clifford always changes the subject. He has more than enough money, he has told his uncle bluntly. He doesn't want any more.)

Yet Pete has gotten his nephew, whom he does consider "brilliant," several freelance illustrating assignments for the magazine he edits, and has introduced him to a number of gallery owners and well-known artists around town. There was even, last year, a small show in one of the galleries on Highland Avenue, called "Young Atlanta Artists," in which Clifford's work was featured alongside that of four other local painters and sculptors. Several visitors to the gallery took note of Clifford's work, comparing his elongated heads to those of Modigliani, admiring his spare, even "minimalist" use of color, commenting in hushed tones on the stark isolation of his still lifes, the small gatherings of fruit or flowers that were deliberately flattened out, ungiving, seeming to hover provisionally on the surface of the canvas. . . . He'd gotten a good deal of attention, a glowing newspaper review, even a couple of letters from a New York gallery—and he owed all that to Pete, he knew; and though Pete, he suspected, didn't really like Clifford's work, he genuinely seemed to respect it. Several times Clifford has asked to see some of Pete's youthful work, which Pete once let slip that he keeps hidden away in the basement, carefully boxed and preserved, but Pete always laughs and says, "You probably won't see that stuff, kid, until you inherit it. You can shed a few tears at the funeral, then come over here and have a good laugh!" Clifford will shrug and smile, but whenever he visits he thinks idly about that buried artwork in Pete's basement, wondering what it says about his uncle, his youthful dreams and longings. He suspects that Pete's work, whatever its level of accomplishment, is much more optimistic and fully textured than his own.

What he enjoys most about his evenings at Pete's is their predictability: always a glass of wine while Pete puts the final touches on the dinner, Clifford sitting on a bar stool on the other side of the kitchen pass-through; the meal itself at Pete's glass-topped octagonal table; then leaving the table for a long talk over coffee and brandy, Clifford feeling pleasantly intimidated by Pete's rather fussily overdecorated living room. There are matching china cabinets filled with porcelain vases, bisque figurines, exquisite objects of crystal and brass; there are two overstuffed armchairs, both upholstered in Chinese red silk, and a small matching sofa; there are cherrywood tables laden with photographs in elaborate frames, silver candle holders, crystal lamps. Normally Pete and his nephew sit in the two chairs, with their coffee and brandy on the table between them, but tonight Pete plops himself down on the sofa and pats the cushion beside him. "Okay, c'mon," he says. "Let's talk about that letter."

Clifford looks at him, startled. He'd mentioned the letter during dinner, he must have said something about wanting Pete's advice, but now he can scarcely remember; he fights a sudden urge to flee.

"No, it's all right—I—"

"Don't be silly," Pete says, his head craned upward. "Sit down," he says, frowning. "Show me."

"It's in my jacket, Pete, and anyway I don't think—"

"Well, then *get* it," Pete says smiling, rolling his eyes. "For heaven's sake, it's just a letter."

"It's nothing," Clifford says. "Really."

"It's *not* nothing," says Pete. "That much I know already."

Woodenly, Clifford crosses to the coat closet and takes the letter from his jacket pocket—out in the car, once he'd arrived at Pete's, he'd sat skimming the letter for the fourth or fifth time, and now he suddenly can't imagine anyone else reading it. . . . *Did I tell you I got a promotion?—granted, not much of one, from secretary to "administrative assistant," if you please, I guess it's still what they call a "shit job," but for a girl who neglected to finish college it's the best I can do, at least for now. . . . There's a guy at the office who reminds me of you, kiddo, every time I pass his cubicle he's hunched over drawing something, or writing something, and once when I paused too long he glanced over his shoulder and you'd have thought I was Miss Medusa, 1976, he looked so shocked and appalled. Sister Mary Joseph would have denounced his "guilty conscience" on the spot! But I smiled and moved along, moved along. . . . When it gets lonely I do get a kick out of remembering the old days, Clifford, and how our fiendship made the whole ordeal bearable, or at least a bit more REAL— didn't you think so? Growing up in a Catholic school was just so fucking Gothic, wasn't it?—ordinary adult life seems so thin and empty somehow, it doesn't bear comparison. . . . Well, I'd better get back to work, kiddo. Love*

and hugs, Janice. . . . And then that phone number, whose prefix he
recognized as from the Emory area, since he'd lived there during his
first year in town, in a ratty student complex. He'd thought that
the Atlanta postmark might have been a post office fluke, but the
phone number stunned him. He couldn't deny that the letter had
made him feel both elated and helpless, and more than a little fearful.
When he hands the envelope to Pete, his fingers are trembling.

   He sits close to his uncle as the older man reads the letter;
several times Pete nods to himself, or says *Humpf,* or laughs in a
tone that might be sardonic or appreciative. Or both. It was probable,
Clifford has often thought, that Pete would like Janice, since he
shares her sense of the outrageous, an ability to view life as a colossal
joke of which they were the helpless but willing victims.

   Clifford has begun reading over his uncle's shoulder when Pete
points to the last page and says, "Whoa! What's *this?*"

   Clifford squints, rereading the passage: . . . *the old days, Clifford,
and how our fiendship made the whole ordeal bearable* . . .

   "What?" Clifford says. "What about it, Pete?"

   "Look how she spelled it," Pete says, glancing slyly at Clifford.
"Look how she spelled 'friendship.' "

   Clifford looks closely and now he sees it, too—Janice had left
out the "r." He hadn't noticed before.

   Fiendship. Clifford can't help smiling.

   . . . *how our fiendship made the whole ordeal* . . .

   "I believe," Pete says primly, smiling at his nephew, "I believe
that's what's known as a Freudian slip."

   "Knowing Janice," Clifford says, "it was probably deliberate."

   "Oh, is she that clever?" Pete says, turning back to the letter.
He begins studying the pale lavender sheets, turning them in his
hands like artifacts.

   "I don't know," Clifford says uneasily.

   "Because she doesn't strike me as clever," Pete says. "She seems
too *intense* to be clever."

   "That's about right," Clifford says. "I guess."

   Again he regrets having mentioned the letter to Pete. Feeling
self-conscious, he leans toward the coffee table and drinks from his
snifter of brandy. The liquor burns pleasantly in his mouth and

throat; his insides glow with warmth and now he feels a bit less hollow. All during the evening he has been recalling, off and on, how angry Earl had gotten today, in the park, when Clifford wouldn't let him come inside Clifford's mouth. "Hey," Earl had said, jeering, still unable to give it up while they tramped out of the woods and back to the car, "what are you, a virgin or something? Too good for it, eh?" But Clifford hadn't wanted the warm salty liquid inside him, didn't want to feel it or taste it; though he had plenty of partners these days, usually two or three a week, he seldom let anyone come inside him, and so it was true that even his rather impulsive sexual activity was somehow chaste. Clifford hadn't responded to Earl's anger and hadn't even glanced at the man again. He unlocked his car quickly and drove off.

"So you think it's nothing?" Clifford asks, feeling unaccountably nervous. "I mean, I really *don't* want to get involved with her again, it wouldn't be good for either of us. . . ."

He'd briefly outlined for Pete his prior relationship with Janice, including their attempt to run away, but he hadn't mentioned that Janice had been pregnant. He hadn't mentioned how he'd had to scrub the blood and tissue from his floorboards before he could leave town by himself, unfettered.

"I said she doesn't sound clever," Pete tells him. "I didn't say she wasn't dangerous."

"Dangerous?" Clifford says bleakly.

"Well, the Atlanta postmark, the phone number—and yet her not mentioning, in the course of a long letter, that she'd moved here. There's something odd about it, Clifford. Something creepy."

Pete shudders. He hands the letter back.

"Well, you may have the wrong idea," Clifford says, in a strange impulse to defend Janice. "I mean, she's not crazy or anything."

Pete looks at him. "What do *you* think about it?" he says.

"Do you mean—"

"I mean, what do you want from Janice? Do you know?"

"Not anything," he says. "I don't want anything . . ."

Hurriedly, he folds the letter into a bulky square, stuffs it inside the pocket of his jeans. As he's doing this, tears start to his eyes. He'd just taken a long swallow of the brandy and it must have gone down the wrong pipe, he feels that he's about to choke, his throat is closing, and suddenly his vision blurs as the tears rise up, stinging, running jaggedly along his cheeks. Clifford wipes at his face roughly with two fists; he sits breathing deeply and slowly, trying to calm himself.

"Hey now," his uncle is saying, one hand clamped on Clifford's shoulder. "Just relax, okay? Just relax and we'll talk about it."

He doesn't understand what is happening; he heard the raw, wrenching sobs but couldn't recognize them as his own. For some reason he has never been one for crying. Even making that frantic first drive to Atlanta, five years ago, he'd stared dry-eyed through the windshield all the way, like a man with tunnel vision; his eyeballs had felt seared and hot, but he hadn't cried. Now he says to Pete, brokenly, "It's not what I want, it's what do they want from me, what do they *want*—"

"They?" Pete says gently. "Who is—"

"But it's nothing, never mind," Clifford mutters. He keeps glancing at his uncle, feeling apologetic and guilty, knowing he should stop. His uncle deserves better than this. Pete is a fleshy but still-handsome man, balding a little, a few strands of his dark hair arranged strategically over his head; the pinkish scalp shows through. Pete has the sorrowful deep brown eyes Clifford had inherited from his mother, but the extreme vulnerability Irene had expressed in her wildly erratic behavior shows in Pete as mere kindliness, very ordinary, very sweet; he seems bewildered yet stalwart, determined to understand what is happening to his nephew.

Now Clifford breathes deeply. He gives an awkward laugh.

"I'm all right, really," he tells Pete. "It's just—"

"You're *not* all right. Now tell me what's wrong, Cliff. *Now.*"

He widens his eyes at Clifford, in a look of mock stubbornness, and all at once Clifford lets his guard fall and thinks he may as well confess, he doesn't have anything to lose, does he? Yet it isn't easy, and he tells Pete very slowly, gropingly, what had happened in the park—and of the various men he'd met in recent months, many of whom called repeatedly on the phone despite Clifford's discouragement, wanting to see him again, never seeming quite satisfied—and of the mingled bitter elation and quaking dread he feels when one of them gets upset, accusing him of various emotional misdeeds and limitations, usually ending by slamming down the phone. Yes, he says, elation and dread, the same contradictory response he has when he opens one of Janice's letters, not really knowing what might be inside: he's happy to have gotten the letter but doesn't really want to read it. He tells Pete that his past relationship with Janice has been chaotic and painful (he spares his uncle the worst details, but makes clear that there's more he isn't telling) and now the sound of her familiar voice, even in a letter, renders him limp and fearful, he doesn't understand what she *wants* from him, exactly. If he could understand that, he says, he could understand just about anything.

"Do you react this way because," Pete asks, hesitantly, "is it because you're, well, attracted to Janice?"

"What?" Clifford says, startled. "No, Pete, you know that I'm—"

"I know *that,*" Pete says smiling. He squeezes Clifford's shoulder and adds, "I guess it runs in the family."

"I guess so," Clifford says hoarsely, but he keeps thinking about that man in the park and how he'd sneered at Clifford, *too good for it, eh?*—he hadn't quite explained all this to Pete. So he says, in a near-whisper, swallowing hard against the tears rising along his throat, "You see, Pete, that guy I met today, he got mad because I wouldn't let him—I made him withdraw before—"

But he can't finish, he loses control again, and the next few minutes pass in a painful hot blur: Pete hurrying out of the room, saying he'll get some Kleenex, he understands that he and Clifford need to have a long, *long* talk, Clifford rising the moment his uncle leaves the room and thinking that he must flee. But standing, wavering, he knows that he has drunk too much, far too much—several glasses of wine at dinner and then the brandy he swallowed too quickly, gulping it down—and almost simultaneously he thinks all this is the liquor's fault and that he drank so much precisely so this could happen. Rubbing the tears off his cheeks, he lurches over to a small side chair and without even thinking, or without daring to think, takes the letter out of his pocket and sits down beside the telephone table. His fingers trembling, he dials quickly.

She answers on the first ring: "Hello? Hello?"

Out in the kitchen Pete is scurrying around. He has the tissues, *a whole box,* he calls cheerfully—and now he's putting on some coffee, how does that sound? And is there anything else Clifford needs? Anything at all . . . ?

"Hello?" Janice says, her voice lowered to a whisper. "Is that you, is it—"

Panicked, Clifford hangs up. He stares at the sweaty mark he left on the receiver.

"Yeah, sure," he calls to his uncle, moving woodenly toward the kitchen doorway. "Some coffee is fine, but don't rush," he tells Pete, "really don't, because I'm okay now, I don't know what got into me."

"What's that?" Pete calls out, clanking cups and saucers together.

"Thanks, but I'm all right," Clifford calls back in a louder, more jovial voice. "Really, I'm perfectly fine."

And it's true: for Clifford feels much better now.

J a n i c e

She'd stuffed the letter in her purse, she'd only skimmed the letter because she was late, very late. *We're so proud of Ruthie, the party was so lovely and everyone asked about you, we all wished you could have been here. . . . Ruthie always says to tell you hello, different as you two are she's always liked you, Janice, I guess because neither of you had a sister of your own . . . she says that she's written several times to your new address, but no answer yet, I guess you're staying pretty busy, still getting settled and all. . . . Anyway, guess we'll have to get used to "Sister Barbara" now, though it's hard to imagine calling her that, she'll always be little Ruthie to us. . . . And how are you doing, dear? Hope the job is going well and that you'll have a chance to come home soon. . . .* Yes, she'd only skimmed it, her mother's letters were always the same, they were interchangeable, you could always tell she'd rather be writing to Ruthie. To "Sister Barbara." Expelling her breath with a little *pfaw* sound, her way of dismissing irrelevant thoughts, pointless daydreams, Janice stuffed the letter inside her black-patent shoulder bag—later she could read it more carefully, if she wanted to; when she hadn't anything better to do.

Slinging the purse across her shoulder Janice takes a long look in the mirror, squinting. Dirk had said eight o'clock and here it's a quarter till, she'll be late if she doesn't hurry; the anxiety that blossoms in Janice at the thought of *being late*—or more precisely, of *failing to be prompt*—is maybe a poison still in her blood, she sometimes thinks, from that godawful parochial school. This idea pains her, since she likes to think she's gotten all that crap out of her system, that it hadn't poisoned her because she was too strong for it, too independent, unlike poor Ruthie. Dimpled little Ruthie, meek-eyed, doleful, Janice remembers how her cousin would stand back in the shadows of the bedroom while Janice stood just like this before the vanity mirror and its circle of glaring bulbs, brushing her hair frantically in her race against the clock, applying mascara with brisk rapid strokes, putting dabs of cologne at her wrists and behind her ears and, winking in the mirror at Ruthie, down between her breasts. "Holy water," she'd say, and Ruthie's moon face would swell as she tried not to giggle, one hand clasping her mouth, and she'd watch with shining eyes as Janice rushed out the door for a date with Randy, or Pete, or Ted Golden, poor Ruthie who never had a single date in high school and never would, and at the last minute Janice felt a thrill of pity and would call out, "Wait up, Ruthie, and I'll tell you everything!"—knowing that Ruthie would live on that crumb of anticipation all evening, waiting alone in Janice's messy bedroom and listening to Gene Pitney on the radio, listening to Gary Lewis, waiting for her daring and glamorous cousin to come home.

Although, at three or four that morning, Janice really told her very little; even Janice wouldn't have dared to tell more. Although that little, for someone like Ruthie, passed easily for "everything."

How long ago that was!—squinting into the mirror she applies mascara with the same rapid strokes, she brushes her hair long and straight in the style of her high school years, though it has grown thicker, coarser, and has darkened to her natural dirty-blond shade— a "slutty" shade, a boyfriend had recently whispered, apprecia- tively—and her cheeks are fuller now and require a bit more rouge.

On "The Mary Tyler Moore Show," which she watches religiously, Mary's hemlines have steadily descended, and Janice knows that this minidress—a tight-fitting pink linen sheath, shot with silver threads— is really out of date, but still it looks good on her, her legs are still great, she'd decided to hell with fashion and she still wears the dress. Attention comes her way whenever she wears it—out on the street, or squeezing among the little tables down at her favorite disco, Crazy Days, and of course from Dirk and all his fraternity pals. So she smiles, smoothing the nylons one last time before rushing out of the apartment, her shoulder bag flapping.

Dirk meets her at the front door, all smiles, a glass of Chablis in one hand and the little blue tablet in the other, between thumb and forefinger. Beyond his shoulder Janice can see that one of his friends has arrived—or are there two?—but the lights are so dim, there is only a vague flickering from the fireplace and a distant fluorescent glow from the kitchen. This is one of the nicer "garden apartments" in the university area, one of many complexes catering mainly to students, to college kids with well-to-do parents like Dirk. Since arriving here six months ago Janice has fallen in easily with the college guys, she meets them at the clubs or even at the Kroger's down the street from the university. Although Janice is twenty-three now, she looks and dresses and behaves much younger. Since that nasty break-up with Ted Golden that had so gladdened her mother's heart (God forbid she'd be the mother-in-law of a Jew, much less a forty-year-old Jew with hairy arms and an eighteen-karat medallion nestled in his matted black chest hair), ever since their knockdown-dragout fight on the Rungrens' front porch one Saturday morning four months ago, their voices carrying to the neighbors and inside to Janice's parents on the crisp October air, Janice has felt like a new person entirely, has cast that old life away: a used-up skin, a husk.

Dispatching Ted Golden, she'd suddenly wondered what she was doing still at home, the hell-raiser Janice Rungren who'd gotten pregnant twice more after that first miscarriage, both times by boys she met in her classes at the local junior college, who almost died after the second of her (top-secret) abortions, who for the last three years had slept with her middle-aged Jewish boyfriend no matter how her mother pouted, and withdrew, and sank into black depressions lasting weeks or months—finally it occurred to Janice, what the hell was she doing with her life, anyway? Most of the girls from her high school class were married, or college graduates who had started careers, or both. Even her dippy cousin Ruthie had made progress, she'd done well in her convent studies and had just taken the veil and begun teaching a whole new generation of Catholic brats. And here Janice had frittered away her time. First one boyfriend, then another. Refusing to marry Ted Golden and then, once he'd gotten to like the arrangement, hysterically insisting that he marry her, screaming every obscenity she knew at the top of her voice that October morning, to the mortification of her parents—who listened helplessly in the kitchen, held together in a cringing embrace. Taking a course or two in "business" one semester, a course in "fashion merchandising" the next. Quitting school to work part-time in one of Ted's three "lounges" in the Dallas-Fort Worth area, spending her tips on miniskirts and makeup and albums by the Grateful Dead (as though she were still a high school kid!), not giving a thought to the future despite periodic grim-faced lectures from her father, who would end by sighing that he still *loved* her, no matter what she decided, and she must always remember that.

So a few days after Ted had shuffled down the sidewalk toward his wine-dark Mercedes, she packed two bags and told her parents she'd gotten a job offer in Atlanta; yes, she knew how far that was but one of Ted's friends had called and said the job was waiting, an executive secretary's position that could lead to something really big—how extravagantly, how fluently she had lied!—and so she'd moved to this city, she told her new friends, just because she'd overheard a conversation about it once, at a party: how pretty it was, how "progressive," how mild the winters and how spectacularly the dogwoods bloomed in spring. She arrived knowing no one but had fixed that soon enough, managed to find an office job near the university that was dull but didn't demand much other than promptness, since the phones began ringing exactly at nine, and she thought maybe she *wasn't* so different from Mary Tyler Moore, maybe she *would* make it after all, and at least she'd put all her anger behind her, she was moving forward, and wasn't that what counted?

Now she moves forward into Dirk's arms, accepts his kiss and opens her mouth for the Valium, which he places ceremoniously on the tip of her tongue, which then darts inside and makes them both laugh. They take long swallows of the Chablis, and Dirk leads her gently back toward the "wet bar" where two of his friends—but no, there are three—wait on bar stools, smiling. Each has a glass in one hand, scotch or wine, and one says conversationally that he's heard a lot about Janice, and she lowers her silver-painted eyelids and says *Only good things, I trust* in that girlish self-mocking voice that always gets a laugh, and then she hears the doorbell but doesn't bother to glance around. One of Dirk's friends has risen from his stool to give Janice a peck on the cheek: "I'm a business major," he says, his eyes crinkling, "and I guess you'd say, well, I like to get down to business," and he runs the tip of his finger down her cheek. Janice thinks this is a bit much, so she looks at one of the other boys—the handsomest one, the lanky blond-haired swimmer's type she really prefers—and jerks her thumb toward the business major and makes a little face. This gets another, bigger laugh; as if on cue, they all take a long swallow, and Janice feels the beginning effects of her "cocktail," the wine and Valium combination really *is* unbeatable, and now she hears more laughter behind her and feels a pair of large hands circling her waist. Dirk? Or no, one of Dirk's friends, doesn't she recognize the voice, whispering and half-sighing into her ear, from the last time . . . ?

"C'mon, sweetie, I'm first," he breathes against her neck, and as they move slowly down the hall she can hear the gaggle of male voices from the living room, somebody claiming that the toss wasn't fair, somebody else claiming that Brian always takes forever (was this Brian, then?) and somebody else saying there isn't enough to drink, they'll have to go out for more, does the treasury have enough money for the really *good* scotch, or should they settle for . . . But Janice no longer hears them, not really, Brian has gotten them inside the bedroom and closed the door and the rest of the evening will continue as planned, Janice doesn't even have to think about it.

What, had her mother written her a letter?—*and you know how Ruthie admires you, so if you'd just drop her a line . . . I think about you often, honey, and I say a little prayer . . . how we wish you hadn't left the*

way you did, not saying good-bye to anyone, we didn't know what to tell
people. . . . Hello Janice?—this is Ruthie, I hope you don't mind my calling
but . . . Hello Janice?—this is Larry, we don't know each other but I'm a
friend of Dirk Pittman, and he . . . Hello Janice? This is—Hello Janice, are
you there, hello, hello? Janice Rungren, is that really you, is everyone correct
that you're really such a little bitch, that you really don't care, what's gotten
into her, anyway, where could she be, who has she become, how could a girl
from such a good home, with such excellent training. . . .

In time, just in time, the drugs turn her body to air: she opens
her mouth for Brian, she spreads her weightless limbs and thinks of
nothing at all.

"Do you mind?" the man says. "I mean, are you really mad?"

Janice laughs at him. "Of course not, you silly goof!" she cries.
She doesn't glance over; she wants to keep her eyes closed, but she
gropes for his hand and gives it a little squeeze.

"Like I told you," the man says anxiously, "this has never happened before, I guess I had too much to drink or something—those
Long Island Teas you ordered, I'm not used to that shit, you know?"

"Listen, I said it's *okay,*" Janice says, hearing the edge of impatience in her voice.

Late Friday night, the week after Dirk's party. She'd spent a
couple of hours getting ready: the tight white leather skirt and jacket
she'd charged last month at Rich's, silver studs in her ears, lips and
eyelids a pale pink, an almost natural pink, her hair a streaked blond
mane, deliberately messy, deliberately "wild." Just before leaving for
the club around 10:30 she'd paused before the mirror, thinking she
hadn't looked this good in years. She'd had a bad week, yes the
night at Dirk's bothered her despite herself, she was tired of that
crap, so she'd decided to head for Crazy Days and say yes to the
first man who asked her: she needed some control back in her life
and wanted someone who was attracted to her, specifically; who
took the trouble to approach *her.* And it hadn't taken long. This
man, she thought his name was Leo, had materialized out of the
shadows near the quieter end of the dance floor and since she liked
his looks—tall and broad-shouldered, dark hair, an abrupt and hawk-
ish profile she found pleasing—she smiled and suggested they have

a drink, which they did; in fact, three or four drinks. By the time they got to Janice's place Leo was slurring quite badly, he'd hit the doorframe coming out of the bathroom, and she guessed she wasn't surprised that he'd turned out to be impotent, though this was the first time this had happened to her, too; but no she wasn't surprised and not really displeased. She was still a little sore, after all, from that night at Dirk's; maybe Leo was exactly what she needed.

"Are you sure?" Leo says.

Janice laughs, harshly. "Yes, I'm fucking sure!" she cries. Now she does glance over and tries to keep her smile from looking mean. Since he'd finally climbed off her, half an hour ago, they'd lain there without speaking, heads propped against folded-over pillows, Leo contemplating his failure, evidently, while Janice thought about the letter she'd sent earlier in the week to Clifford Bannon, a mistake she regrets keenly. Truly her life since arriving in this city has been chaotic, impulsive, wayward, she supposes that anyone from her hometown or old school would think that Janice Rungren had at last achieved the utter degradation she'd been seeking even in high school. The faces of Mary Frances Dennehy and Sister Mary Veronica and even her own mother, all of them wearing bitter knowing smiles, had taunted her dreams these past few months as if saying See, Janice, now do you *see*? Now don't you see that you're getting what you deserve? In her dreams she tries to talk back to them, her jaws grinding, her eyes tensed as if straining to see what they saw, as if willing to acknowledge that possibly—just possibly—they might be right. But she says nothing. She sees nothing. She wakes feeling uneasy, bruised, ill-treated, a vague soreness in her belly that had nothing to do with her night at Dirk's apartment, and despite every-thing she can only protest that she's coping the best she can; evi-dently this behavior is an escape for her, she believes firmly that she'll get all this out of her system—though what "this" is, exactly, she can't really say—before she gets very much older. She *is* only twenty-three, after all. Almost anyone observing her life *would* judge her according to a double standard, after all, since men her age were expected to sow their wild oats, they were praised rather than criticized for it, so she's damned if she's going to listen to those voices in her head. She's herself, nothing more. She won't apologize.

Her life will get better if she gives it time, she thinks, but she has to follow her own way; and that's a way, she knows, that does not include reliving the past. The past meaning Clifford Bannon and those years of useless passion. She would give almost anything if she hadn't sent that letter, but now it's done, it's too late, and at least she knows she'd made a mistake; and isn't it a small victory that she knows this, at least? And Clifford, of course, won't answer the letter, he certainly won't use the phone number she'd hastily written beneath her name; so the mistake will end there.

Hoping to rectify another mistake Janice now releases Leo's hand and moves her own hand along his belly and downward, but he's still soft, in fact the flesh of his penis feels chilled, somehow *dead,* and so she quickly withdraws the hand.

"Listen," she begins, "maybe we should——"

"No," he says, easing closer, "now *you* listen, I'm going to make it up to you," and he grazes her throat with his opened mouth, then moves down to her breasts, her belly, finally positioning himself between her legs where he begins using his tongue on her—his tongue which is quite sufficiently hard, she thinks drowsily, letting her eyes close again. As she lies there she imagines herself sitting again at her dining room table but instead of writing the letter to Clifford she is *un*writing it; she replays the scene in reverse so that her hand moves up instead of down the page, the words disappearing one by one, and the mental satisfaction of this image surpasses even the quite intense physical pleasure Leo is, at last, managing to bring her. After fifteen or twenty minutes he finally stops and rests his cheek against her belly, murmuring, "So how was *that,* have I redeemed myself?" She's so drowsy that although she opens her mouth to reply, "Yes, oh yes," she's never quite sure if she does. Leo continues to lie pressed against her belly and Janice stays motionless with her eyes closed, her mouth just slightly ajar, and finally they fall asleep that way.

One Saturday afternoon she's in a small drugstore near the university, refilling her prescription for Quaaludes. (These are the "sleeping pills" an internist recommended by Janice's boss had reluctantly prescribed for her, saying that really the best way to cure insomnia was to take hard exercise and abstain from both alcohol and caffeine; but Janice, of course, doesn't waste the pills by using them for sleep. She chose this drugstore because she'd heard they weren't picky about refilling prescriptions on weekends, when doctors could not be reached—Janice's doctor had indicated "no refills" for this prescription—and so every time Janice comes to the drugstore, always on Saturday, the pharmacist-owner says vaguely, "Well, if you're *sure* Dr. Holcomb wants you to have these," to which Janice always responds emphatically, "Oh yes, he certainly *does*.") While she's waiting for the prescription she picks up a copy of *Mademoiselle* and some baby shampoo and some dental floss, and just as she's about to turn back to the pharmacy counter, something catches her eye at the plate glass window. A man, peering inside, his hands splayed on either side of his face. Holding her breath, Janice feels certain that the man is Clifford Bannon, and her first thought is to wonder whether Clifford is looking at *her,* or whether he's peering inside for some other reason. The store's interior is rather dim and she doesn't suppose he can see her, not really, but still she can't be sure. She stands frozen as though trapped in a dream. It seems that several minutes pass but of course it's not more than ten seconds, perhaps even five seconds, before the man—and yes he's a tall slender man, with short-cropped dark hair—drops his hands from the glass and turns away.

"Miss?" the pharmacist says, from behind her. "Did you want anything else?"

Janice turns, quickly; her heart is pounding, but for some reason she feels angry rather than afraid. She strides over to the counter, confused for a moment, glancing around, and then she blurts out, "Condoms? You sell condoms, don't you?"

The man points wordlessly to a rack directly in front of Janice. Hardly seeing what she's doing, she grabs several boxes of the condoms and puts them on the counter with her magazine and floss and shampoo.

"Cash or charge?" the pharmacist asks blandly.

Janice twists her mouth at him. "What do *you* think?" she says.

These days when the phone rings Janice will stare at the receiver, hesitating. (Not that it rings so very often; Janice has lived in this city for a few months, she still knows relatively few people and even fewer to whom she has been willing to give out her number.) Back at home, in that other life, she would snatch up the phone on the first ring, say *Yeah?* in that casual half-bored voice she had cultivated during her high school years, but now she lets it ring four times, five times, then says hello in a soft even tone as though trying to disguise her voice. One night in February, not long after sending that letter to Clifford Bannon, that dreadfully foolish letter, his image rises into her mind's eye the minute the phone rings and she thinks, panicked, *No, please no,* and when she speaks into the phone her voice is a bare whisper.

"Honey? Janice dear? Is that you?"

Janice closes her eyes, exhaling in relief—or is it disappointment—and says, "Hello, Mother, yes it's definitely me—is that you?"

But then she bites her tongue; she has to curb, always, her impulse to speak sarcastically to her mother, to indulge in word games, or mind games, of the kind her mother could never grasp. Which is to her mother's credit, she supposes. They talk idly for several minutes, the usual back-and-forth of mother and daughter, how are things at work, Janice, how are things at home, Mother, when are you coming home to visit, Janice, I was just there at Christmas, Mother, I've got a *job,* you know, how is your health, dear, how is *your* health, Mom, and so on, and so forth, it's the kind of conversation Janice can carry on in her sleep—so why does she clutch the receiver so tightly, her palms moist, why the cool dribbling of sweat down her sides?

"Guess who called us last night, honey," her mother begins. "We were so—"

"Was it Ruthie?" Janice says quickly, determined not to get angry, not to play the "child" role with her mother. It's virtually inevitable that her mother calls after hearing from Ruthie—as if Mrs. Rungren's fantasy child reminded her of her real child—and that within five minutes she begins talking about Ruthie in a rushing elated voice, not at all meanly, not at all intending Janice to feel how poorly she compares with Ruthie. Her mother is entirely uncon-scious of any such subtext, of course, a fact which disarms Janice and makes her frustrated anger far more acutely painful than if her mother were to attack Janice outright. . . . "Ruthie is so happy in her work," her mother is saying, "just the other day she sent a few of the holy cards her students made in class, along with some cookies she bakes during the one 'off' afternoon the nuns are allowed each week, Ruthie is so wonderfully thoughtful, so wonderfully *sweet*. . . . And what about you, dear—have you heard from Ruthie?"

"No, not in a while," Janice says evenly, not pointing out that she'd failed to answer Ruthie's last couple of letters. She hadn't deliberately ignored them, she thinks to herself, defensively—she'd just been so busy lately, so stressed-out.

"Ruthie was so disappointed that you missed each other at Christmas, dear."

"I missed her, too," Janice says contritely. "Next year, I'll make it a point . . ."

"What, do you mean you're not coming home before *next* Christmas? What about Easter, honey, what about this summer?"

"I don't know, Mom, I just meant that I probably wouldn't see *Ruthie* before then. She comes home just once a year herself, doesn't she?"

"Well, the convent has rules," her mother says. "She'd come home more often if she could, I'm sure. But at Christmas you only stayed two days, and I was afraid Ruthie's feelings would be hurt, Janice—you did leave the very day before she got here, if you remember, and it just looked as if—I mean, I know you didn't deliberately—"

"I had to get back to work, Mother. I'd just started this job and I couldn't—"

"I understand, dear."

"I'm glad you understand, Mother."

So the conversation proceeds, Janice standing in her tiny fluorescent-lit kitchen, then sitting on one of the vinyl bar stools tucked beneath the pass-through to the dining area, staring at the tiny green malachite clock on the countertop, it's 9:08, it's 9:13, how she wishes she'd taken the call in her bedroom where she could stretch out—she's so drowsy lately, the stress of her life has become almost more than she can bear. She imagines her mother in the sitting area of her bedroom, talking into her white marbleized "French Provincial" telephone, perfectly dressed and made up here on a Tuesday evening; she sees her father down in the den, polishing off his sixth or eighth beer, thumbing through one of his sports magazines or flipping the TV remote control, life as usual at the Rungrens, nothing special about it, nothing particularly depressing; and so why is Janice beginning to feel depressed? Something in her— yes, the child in her—wants to cry out: *Mama!* Nothing more than that, just that loud helpless primal wail, though of course she doesn't, she takes a deep breath instead, she nods, she is an adult person now and she plans to act the part. Yet she's tired, very tired, and when her mother veers into discussing church activities—for her mother has made great strides these past few years in conquering her agoraphobia, she has joined two church organizations and is even an officer of one of them, and Janice is very proud of her mother's persistence in therapy and her declared intention no longer to be a "burden" to her family—nonetheless when Mrs. Rungren launches into a detailed analysis of the floral arrangements down at church this past Sunday, her daughter cuts in, as gently as she can, saying, "Mom, excuse me? Listen, I'm really beat—I've really got to go."

"Oh, of course," her mother says quickly. "I know you work hard, Janice dear. Try not to overdo it."

"I will, Mom. Good night!" Janice says cheerfully, wanting to end on an upbeat note.

"Oh, one more thing," her mother says, and Janice hears that timid catch in her voice: which means that Janice isn't going to like what's coming next.

"Yes?" Janice says.

"I just wondered, you know, if you'd met anyone . . . anyone nice? I thought, you know, if you attended a young singles group down at church, maybe you'd meet someone, a nice young man—"

"A nice Catholic young man?" Janice says.

"Well, I mean, there's no reason why you shouldn't—"

"Mother," Janice says in a melancholy voice, "I wouldn't foist myself on a nice Catholic young man."

"Why Janice, what a thing to say!" And though her mother tries to take it as a joke, to sound amused, almost at once she's

whining at Janice: "But why don't you *try,* Janice honey, even if the
mass itself isn't meaningful to you, there's no reason you can't go
there to meet nice people, there's nothing wrong with that, dear,
there's no reason to think a young man wouldn't—I mean, that
you're a—"

"A lost cause?" Janice says. Again she hears the little wail from
somewhere inside (*Mama!*) and her eyes fill abruptly with tears.

"Mother," she says, keeping her voice firm, "I've really got to go."

"All right, then. Good night—and thank you, dear."

Janice pauses: Thank you? Her mother had thanked her?

"Yes, Mother," she says quickly, "good night. And *thank you.*"

In bed, in darkness. In her lover's arms. They're awake, they're half
awake, they're sated with slow dreamy lovemaking and now they lie
quietly, each drifting in and out of the other's consciousness, dipping
into sleep and back out again. Smiling. Half-smiling. Their small
bedside candle has fluttered out and the darkness is total, enveloping,
they can't see one another's faces but they sense the smiles, the half-
smiles, they are alert to what is happening no matter that they drift
in and out of sleep and no matter that their arms are limp along
one another's shoulders, no longer tense in the fierce grip of passion,
that's over for a brief sweet while. Every few minutes in such luxury,
such perfect languor, they adjust arms and legs, hers easing between
his, his between hers, arms and hands grazing shoulder blades, backs,
buttocks, lips brushing as if accidentally the other's lazy smiling
mouth or hooded eyes.

This pleasure so fathomless and deep, even deeper than when
he'd thrust inside her, more profound now that their bellies are
pressed close together divided only by a film of cooling sweat as she
feels his slow hand move down her spine as if counting the vertebrae,
one at a time oh very slowly downward and reaching at last the
cleft of her buttocks where his fingers nestle companionably as he
releases a long sigh against her throat. Then he inhales in a way she
recognizes so well, she knows him so intimately after all, this slender
dark-haired lover with his wry smile and fierce passions, she knows
he is about to say something, to whisper some small endearment or

bit of mischief, and now he does open his mouth to speak and presses his lips against her damp hair and he says—

Janice wakes, startled. Somehow she'd fallen asleep again with the lamp on, the book splay-backed on the pillow next to her, damn how she hates it when this happens, how sorely she yearns to get back inside the dream, to escape this sudden raw twist of her insides, as if she'd been cut open and manhandled, cruelly disarranged. With an angry *oof!* she raises herself up in bed, shivering, goes out to the kitchen not bothering with a robe, not caring that the kitchen window is uncurtained, if there's some poor guy so desperate that he crouches in the backyard of this crummy duplex at three in the morning just hoping for a glimpse of Janice Rungren in her panties then let's give him a thrill, why the hell not, and she reaches into the back of her junk drawer for the aspirin bottle that hasn't contained aspirin in quite some while. She taps the pills onto her palm and debates for a moment, one or two, then looks at the oven clock and sees that it's almost 5:00 A.M. so she thinks just one, but then she reasons that tomorrow is Sunday after all and what if no one calls, what if she gets into one of those blue funks that are so common on long formless Sunday afternoons, so she thinks two, definitely *two,* and she swallows them down without water and flips out the light and returns to the bedroom and wills herself not to reenter that dream with all its seductive imagery, its abiding torment.

Thirty minutes, she figures, until the Quaaludes do their work, so she picks up the book and reads for a while in the biography of St. Thérèse of Lisieux she'd ordered from her book club; it's a very thin book about a very short life, "one of the most beloved saints of the Catholic Church," the dust jacket says, and since childhood one of Janice's favorites. She'd once done a school paper on Thérèse and even now she still thinks of her, daydreaming at odd moments about the feisty young girl who devoted her heart to Jesus while only fourteen, whose sanctity so impressed the local Mother Superior that she was allowed to take her vows early, and who wrote a meekly pious autobiography before succumbing to tuberculosis at the age of twenty-four. . . . Reading this new biography, which is a perfunctory account of an uneventful life, a recounting of the "facts"

in a skeptical modern voice, Janice keeps being distracted from the
text by photographs of the saint which are also included. She stares
at St. Thérèse as a happy, chubby child; as a girl smiling forthrightly
and almost mischievously into the camera at age fifteen, just before
entering the convent; as an ailing and withdrawn-looking nun in her
early twenties, clearly aware of her impending death, eyes dark and
luminous, seeming to exist in some hushed inner world far removed
from the ordinary daylight noises of her childhood. Lately, unable to
sleep, Janice will lie in bed staring at these photographs, reading of
Thérèse's happy childhood among her loving parents and sisters, then
of her cloistered life inside the convent walls, and finally of her
prolonged, painful death; she reads mesmerized as if imagining this
life as one way her own life could have gone, somehow. If she'd
been born eighty years earlier, in a small French village? If she'd
gone through a certain type of schooling, if she'd had older sisters
who had entered the convent, if she'd lived in a setting so pervaded
by Catholicism that the rather Gothic fate of St. Thérèse would
have seemed rapturous instead of bizarrely tragic, if not grotesquely
shameful? *Then* might she, Janice Rungren, have traded places with
Therese of Lisieux?

As usual Janice smiles at her fantasies, her self-indulgence, but
since moving here and experiencing a sudden piercing loneliness
she'd never felt before, a sense of isolation she finds challenging but
also, at times, almost unbearable, she allows herself these idle bouts
of nostalgia for her childhood, especially for her parochial schooling
and her upbringing in the Church and all its elaborate rituals and
paraphernalia. If it wouldn't get her mother's hopes up, in fact, she
might have asked that her mother send her old school missals and
holy cards and First Communion flower, and the yearbooks from St.
John Bosco and Pius XII; all that junk must be packed away somewhere, and it would be amusing, she supposes, even consoling to
thumb through such items during her idle hours, remembering, reas-
sessing. One relic of her childhood she did bring with her, though
quite by accident (it had been pushed into the back of her makeup
drawer at home, hidden under a pile of old handkerchiefs for who
knew how many years), was the crystal rosary Grandma Rungren
had sent for her First Communion, and as she packed her bags on

that rainy October day four months ago, she had smiled grimly and tossed the rosary into her makeup case along with everything else. Now she keeps it in her bedside drawer, along with whatever book she might be reading, along with the strawberry-scented candle and a packet of condoms, and sometimes she will take out the rosary, fondling it for a few moments, feeling a sharp influx of both revulsion and longing.

Hail Mary, full of grace. . . . How was it that she could reject all the brainwashing she had endured and now, as an adult, despise almost everything the Church stood for, its treatment of women and its absurd views on sexuality and its arrogant claim to hold the monopoly on "truth," whatever that was—and yet feel such a powerful attraction to its symbolism, its artifacts, even its shameful history of greed and bloodshed and splendor? For she handled the rosary with great care, as if it were sacred indeed. She read and reread the life of Thérèse of Lisieux with a deep, unaccountable pleasure, as if the idea of some kinship between them were really not so laughable, as if they might have switched identities—switched fates—as easily as not.

She understands what's been happening, of course; she understands that she's going through a "transition," an important "passage" of her life, she knows the jargon from the self-help paperbacks she sometimes buys at the drugstore, along with the Quaaludes and the condoms. Also she understands, at least she supposes she does, her ongoing absorption in Clifford Bannon, for wasn't he the single remaining link with her childhood self, hadn't he known her more fully than any other person, and didn't she love him as authentically as she'd ever loved anyone? (Assuming that she knew what "love" was; the self-help books combined with her own wistful brooding had served only to confuse Janice on that point.) And five years had passed, after all, so why should she and Clifford be enemies? Why couldn't they be friends—or at the very least, friendly—in some carefully negotiated and civilized way?

Ever since moving here she'd gotten through her insomniac nights, the weeknights when she hadn't had a few drinks down at Crazy Days and had no temporary companion, by reaching into her night table drawer and writing a letter to Clifford; though at first

she had no intention of mailing these letters, she wrote and rewrote
them as though they were the genuine text of her life and she'd
better get it right. She *had* sent him a few letters back in Texas that
were harmless enough, she felt, bright and cheery, undemanding, but
after arriving in Atlanta she knew she'd better stop, she knew the
Atlanta postmark might shatter whatever fragile return of goodwill
her letters of the previous few months had inspired. In the five years
since their terrible parting she'd not heard a word from him, and
had no idea where he'd gone until last fall, when she'd impulsively
called his father after waking in a muggy hangover next to Ted
Golden and feeling, all at once, awash in despair; and seeing, all at
once, what she considered for good or ill the true shape of her life,
a story that did not include an overweight Jewish boyfriend or the
childish rebellion she'd been waging—defiance being the point of
Ted Golden, after all—under her poor parents' noses. She saw at
once that she had to get out of this place, start some new life of
her own, some authentic life, and simultaneously she thought of
Clifford and felt an overpowering urge to find him.

   Though her heartbeat thudded in her chest and throat, though
her hand felt so weak she could scarcely hold the phone, the call
had been surprisingly easy: for Clifford's father still lived in Atlanta
and had answered on the first ring, remembered her at once, and
cheerfully volunteered the information that Clifford was also living
in Atlanta, in midtown, that he was studying art and had begun to
make a name for himself. . . . Janice thought at once, *He doesn't know*
but of course that was to her advantage so she listened, she urged
him on, greedy for facts, and as she scribbled Clifford's address and
phone number on a matchbook Ted had left by the phone she could
scarcely believe her good fortune.

   Mr. Bannon had faltered a little when Janice, having learned
all she could, asked him please not to tell Clifford about this call, it
was all too complicated but he should trust her, could she have
his word that he wouldn't tell?—and, knowing Mr. Bannon's past
noninvolvement in Clifford's life, his button-down distaste for emotional mess, she'd felt she could trust his promise. When they hung
up Janice had felt the stunned immobility that comes with a riot of
contending emotions, of intense joy roughly balanced with intense

fear, and she'd removed herself numbly from the bed—Ted hadn't woken, having drunk far more than she—and slipped out of his apartment for the last time and groped blindly through the rest of that day, squinting through the fog of her hangover as if trying to glimpse her future life. When her headache abated she sent Clifford the first of her bright chirpy notes and, a few mornings later, had her final raucous argument with Ted Golden on her parents' front porch. She talked to her parents about Atlanta as though she'd always planned to move there, really, but through some oversight had simply neglected to tell them, and she was surprised by how little resistance they offered, how willing they were to let her go; she supposed that anything was acceptable, from their point of view, that separated her from Ted Golden, even the prospect of losing her altogether.

October, that had been; and here it's four months later, a Sunday, an overcast glowering February day that seems designed to press down upon Janice's spirit. The Quaaludes taken at five o'clock had knocked her out until almost noon but now that she's up the afternoon passes slowly. Sunday always troubles her; the day forces her recognition that she's really made no friends here yet; despite her frantic partying and many male acquaintances she still lacks a confidante, a true *friend*, and she needs to remedy that. During the week her job keeps her fairly busy, on Saturday there's shopping and cleaning the apartment, but Sundays do get to her: they're so long and so patternless.

Today she decides impulsively to take a walk, despite the cold weather; she strides quickly along Briarcliff, then down North Decatur Road toward the university, her eyes downcast as if she has a destination, a scarf over her hair and held tight under her chin with one hand. Janice Rungren, what to do about. Janice Rungren, whatever happened to ... Having escaped the apartment, she ends up having one of those times when she's eerily happy; the pills have worn off and she didn't drink last night so her head is clear, she feels good, she feels healthy, the harsh cold air filling her chest brings a sense of vitality and well-being that Janice hasn't felt in quite some while. Humming a stray tune, her eyes moist from the cold wind, she stops into Kroger's and buys herself a chicken breast and fresh asparagus, thinking that she'll make a hollandaise when she gets home and pour a glass of wine and sit down to watch "60 Minutes," yes all at once she doesn't feel lonely at all but hopeful, quite unreasonably happy, and when she leaves Kroger's the bag boy calls out, "Have a nice evening!" and Janice turns around, smiling, and she calls back, "You too!"

She has her dinner cooked and halfway eaten when the telephone rings. She had really gotten into watching Mike Wallace nail a corrupt meat-packing executive to the wall and so Janice lets out a little groan, pushing the TV tray aside. Her mother has heard from Ruthie, she supposes; today is Sunday after all, and so she decided to give Janice a ring, see how she's doing *this* week, maybe she did decide to attend mass, after all, maybe she did meet some nice young man . . . ?

Janice gingerly picks the kitchen phone off the wall, her fingers still greasy from the chicken. She tucks the receiver beneath her ear as she grabs for a paper towel: "Hello? Yes, hello?"

Silence. She hears a slow intake of breath, but then nothing. In the background someone is talking, a male voice from a distant room, maybe a TV or radio. But up close, breathing into the phone: nothing.

"Hello?" Janice whispers. "Is that you, is it—"

She hears a click, then a dial tone. Nothing.

Methodically Janice turns off the TV, rinses her dishes and places them in the dishwasher. Carefully, she wipes the kitchen counters, ignoring that roiling sensation in her stomach, the sense of vertigo that has all but overcome her. She feels that she may lose her balance, she may fall, so she grips the kitchen counter, reaching for her glass and draining the last of her wine. Moving cautiously, warily, she opens the refrigerator and takes out the bottle and pours herself another glass, and then she goes to her address book, which she opens to the "B" section. She dials; the phone rings six times, eight times; she hangs up. Once she has finished the glass of wine she vows not to have any more, and then she lies down for a while.

An hour passes. Two hours. It's ten o'clock. She would normally start getting ready for bed about now, but instead she lies there fully dressed and after a while reaches for the bedside phone and again dials the number.

A male voice, low and suspicious: "Hello?"

She says nothing.

"Hello, Janice? Listen, Janice, why don't you——"

She hangs up. In a few seconds the phone rings and she answers.

"Janice? Listen, don't hang up, all right?"

"I'm not hanging up," Janice says.

He pauses, as though shocked by the sound of her voice.

"Well," he says, trying to sound amused. "Hello."

"Hello yourself," she says.

So they talk for a while, their voices brittle, wary; they ask the usual questions about jobs and apartments and family. After a while Janice begins to breathe evenly, thinking that she'll be all right, after all, they'll exchange news until there's nothing more to say and then they'll say good-bye, politely. It was good to hear your voice, hope everything goes well for you, I wish you the best . . . I bear you no ill will, I don't hate you love you hate you . . . please call again sometime if you're not doing anything if you ever get nostalgic about the past if you're ever this goddamned desperate.

No, she can't quite imagine an ending, she can't see any kind of neat and graceful closure, but nonetheless she's shocked when Clifford asks, out of nowhere:

"So, what are you doing tonight? Anything special?"

"What? Well, I've got work in the morning, and so——"

"You want to get together? Have a drink or something?"

"Tonight?" Janice says, startled. "You mean *now*?"

"Of course now, why not *now*?" Clifford says, mocking her. Before she has quite assented, he's giving her directions to a bar-restaurant on Peachtree Road—does she know where 26th intersects with Peachtree, could she meet him there in half an hour? Shelly's, the place is called.

"Come on, Janice, just one drink," Clifford says. "For old time's sake."

There's only one ground rule, Clifford tells her, once they're seated at a table: Nothing about the past.

Janice stares at him. "Nothing . . . ?"

"There's no point in it," he says hastily, hands folded on the table, looking earnestly into Janice's eyes. "I mean, don't you agree? That there's no point in rehashing the past?"

She gives him a wry smile. She lifts one eyebrow.

"I don't understand why *you're* laying the ground rules," she says. "It was you who called me, after all. It was you who wanted to come here."

"Okay, okay," he says, smiling. "But you have to admit it's a sensible rule, don't you? You'd have thought of it yourself, wouldn't you?"

"Maybe," she says curtly, glancing around. They're seated in a small restaurant area but it's past eleven, the other tables are empty; from here Janice can just make out the long bar in the next room, and a small strobe-lit dance floor. The room is filled with smoke, lights, blurry dark shapes; she can feel the disco music pulsing in her chest. Across from her, looking diminished inside his high-backed leather chair, Clifford seems oblivious to the noise from the other room, his attention focused almost uncomfortably on Janice. Does she look so different after five years? she wonders. Does she look older, harder, is she the same Janice or someone else entirely? She must admit that Clifford has changed very little. Though his hair is shorter now, cropped close to his skull, he has the same dark mustache, the restless dark eyes. If anything, he has lost weight; his face is bony, gaunt, there are shadowy creases in his cheeks and beneath his eyes, but yes he's still beautiful and he still favors black clothing—tonight a leather jacket with a fur collar, a black-and-white-checked shirt, his usual black jeans—and black looks good on him, lends him an air of mystery. As always his hands are exquisitely clean, fingers long and tapered, nails trimmed to the quick. An artist's hands, Janice thinks. She looks at her own hands and sees that they're overlarge and graceless, the nails unpolished. She hadn't bothered with primping or makeup and hadn't changed clothes, deciding she didn't need to impress Clifford, after all; she would just present herself at the appointed place and time.

"This is a nice place," Janice says idly, as the waiter delivers their drinks. A tall red-haired boy with a diamond earring, the waiter seems to know Clifford. He tends to Janice's brandy and soda with exaggerated care, and asks Clifford in a syrupy overdone voice, as if mocking him, "Will there be anything else, sir?"

Clifford ignores him and the boy turns away.

"I go to one or two places," Janice adds, "but I've never been here."

"I thought you might like it," Clifford says.

Silence. They sip at their drinks. Several times their eyes meet and they both glance away. Janice thinks how ridiculous this is, they're old friends, they know each other thoroughly, but she supposes this initial awkwardness is to be expected, an obstacle they'll have to fight through. They're enduring this silence, she thinks, because they won't resort to small talk, they respect each other too much for that; but on the other hand they're afraid to discuss what's really happening in their lives. She supposes she should take the initiative, break the ice. After all, she's got nothing to lose.

She says, "Maybe I shouldn't have written, Clifford. I'm sure you thought that I shouldn't have."

"Oh, I wouldn't say——"

"But the fact is that I've been lonely, and that I think about you a lot. That might sound self-pitying, but it's the truth."

"It doesn't sound self-pitying," Clifford says. "Self-pity is not admitting that you're lonely."

Janice laughs. "And love is never having to say you're sorry?"

At once she regrets her words: Clifford's face has reddened and he keeps his eyes downcast, kneading his hands together on the table. She says, "I'm sorry, Cliff, I——"

"Never mind, you're right," he says. "I'm not good at this kind of discussion."

"Neither am I," she says. "That's how we grew up. It's not anybody's fault, you know."

He looks up at her, wistfully. "So you thought about me, huh?"

"Yeah, but not in——not in *that* way," she says, wondering if she's lying or not. Clifford doesn't look particularly reassured.

"That's good," he says.

"Look," she says, suddenly feeling impatient, and a bit angry, "look, this is the issue. We live in the same city now. We're grown-ups now. What we have to decide is what we want to do about that. If anything."

"Right," Clifford says. "What we want to do, if anything."

"Well?" Janice says shrilly. She's tired of competing with the noise from the next room. "Clifford, do you have an opinion on that?"

"Janice, the main reason I asked you here—I mean, what I wanted to be sure you knew—"

He breaks off, perplexed. He takes a long swallow from his drink and sits back in his chair.

"Look, do you want to dance?" he says.

"No, Clifford," she says, glancing again toward the dance floor, "I really think we should—"

And that's when she stops. That's when she notices. The strobe lights are pulsing brightly, it's a record by the Bee Gees and the dance floor has filled and she can see much more clearly; she can see that the flailing bodies and smiling faces belong to men. Her eyes dart quickly from the dance floor, to the bar, to the group of patrons just entering the door of the club; all of them are men, well-dressed, in their twenties and thirties. Not a woman in sight.

She looks at Clifford. "We wouldn't quite fit in, would we?" she says. "On the dance floor."

"I wanted to be sure you knew," Clifford says.

"What you mean is, you wanted to rub my nose in it." She takes a deep breath, her hands clenching in her lap. The fury in her chest comes in bright hot surges, as though keeping time to the music. She wills herself to stay calm. She has no reason, she tells herself, to get this angry.

"That's not true, Janice."

She says, in a quieter voice, "You could have just told me, Clifford. You didn't have to treat me with disrespect."

"I don't see how this is disrespectful, Janice. I come here all the time, so I wanted to bring you here."

"You—you wanted to embarrass me," she says, losing control despite herself, "you wanted to humiliate and embarrass—"

"Do you see?" Clifford says, and she's aware that he's angry, too; she remembers that clenching of his jaw, the way his eyes seem to lose color and focus. "*Do* you see? This is why I was afraid to call or write, Janice—I was afraid that nothing would have changed, that you would refuse to listen and understand who the fuck I *am*."

Never before has he shouted at her, and now she has a glimpse of what he'd wanted from this meeting. He'd wanted a new Janice, a changed Janice; he'd wanted a friend. Someone to accompany him, she thinks scornfully, to places like this? Someone with whom to discuss his little boyfriends?

She says, "You're one to talk about listening, you never—"

"Look, Janice, this is pointless." He grabs the check and takes out his wallet. "I'm really sorry," he says, "I really did hope that we wouldn't argue."

"But what *did* you hope for?" Janice says.

He gives her a blank look. The question seems to have stumped him.

"I don't know. I guess—I guess I was hoping that we'd have both grown up by now."

"You didn't want much, did you?" Janice laughs. All at once she feels better; all at once the situation no longer seems so bad or unworkable.

"Janice, I don't think—"

"Okay," Janice says quickly, smiling. "The answer is yes."

"Yes?" he says, puzzled. "The answer is yes . . . ?"

"Yes, I'll dance with you," Janice says. "Or have you changed your mind?"

Janice

Every Friday evening Janice makes dinner for her boyfriend, her future husband, the love of her life: it's one of their many rituals. Tonight he arrives promptly at seven—like Janice herself, Jack is unfailingly prompt—and they have time for a drink out on the porch before Belinda and Graham arrive. The dinner, most of it prepared last night and early this morning before Janice left for work, is under control; the table is set, the house is impeccably clean; Janice has changed into navy wool pants and a crimson silk blouse that she knows is Jack's favorite. For several years now she has lived in this small redbrick house in the Morningside area, an older neighborhood known for its quiet streets, yards filled with trees, big porches. Fortunately it's warm for November and so they sit on the yellow-lit porch for a long while, nibbling cashews, sipping wine coolers, talking idly of what happened at work that week, people they know in common, items in the news. Janice purposely invited Belinda and Graham for eight o'clock, since this quiet time with Jack is another of their rituals, and perhaps her favorite: with great effort and discipline she has at last managed, she often thinks, to achieve a semblance of control in her life, to understand what matters and what does not, and more than anything Janice wants to preserve that.

Tonight Jack seems a bit dreamy and abstracted, so she mentions a girl they both know from Janice's office, Millie Proctor.

"She still talks about that magazine story, you know," Janice says in a sly voice. "I guess I really ought to be jealous."

Jack looks over from his white wicker chair, smiling wearily. "Yeah, sure thing," he says. "Maybe I ought to just give her what she wants, and have done with it."

Janice sits on the porch swing, rocking herself back and forth with one foot. She says, "Very funny, mister," and tosses a cashew piece in his direction; but it misses him, evidently, for Jack doesn't flinch. Ever since they sat down he has been staring straight ahead of him, gazing out into the darkened street.

"Today she comes into my office," Janice says, "and she goes, 'How *did* you catch that guy, anyway? It said in the magazine that he's never been married, that he's, let's see, *what* was the word' "— Janice mimics Millie's high chittering voice perfectly—" 'oh yeah, one of the more *elusive* bachelors in town. So tell me, Janice, how'd ya do it, huh?' " Janice laughs, reaching for her cigarettes. She says, "I really ought to fire her ass."

Jack doesn't react; normally, it's easy to get a laugh from him. In August, the month *Atlanta* magazine had done its piece on the city's "singles scene," featuring a close-up look at its ten "most eligible gents and ladies," Janice had taken Jack to a party at her boss's house, where Jack had met Millie and everyone else from Janice's office, and much had been made of his inclusion in the article; she supposes he's sick of discussing it by now. Still in his thirties, Jack is a successful builder of office and condominium projects in the Atlanta suburbs, and yet he's essentially quite modest and shy. He hates being the center of attention, he doesn't really like parties—Janice had seen his tight grimace when she'd told him that the Jensens would be coming for dinner tonight, he much prefers to spend his evenings alone with Janice—and she'd been surprised that Jack had allowed himself to be profiled in the first place. Now he glances at his watch, downs the rest of his wine and puts the glass on the table.

"What time are the Jensens coming?" he says.

"Eight," she says, "and remember, honey, don't say 'The Jensens' in front of Belinda. She still uses 'Dr. Comstock,' and she's pretty sensitive about it."

Jack gives her a little smirk, as he often does when they discuss women's issues. Occasionally he and Janice like to argue—intellectual arguments they conduct just for fun, just for the exercise—and one of their recurrent topics is feminism. Just a couple of weeks ago Janice had said, smartly, "Well what about *me*, kiddo? Do you expect me to call myself 'Janice Lassiter' all of a sudden? At my advanced age?" He'd given her that same little smirk then, she remembers; he hadn't really given an answer.

"I'll try not to abrade her rarefied sensibility," Jack says. He grabs up a handful of nuts and begins chomping on them.

"Jack?" she says. "Is something wrong? The sarcasm isn't like you, babe."

His face softens, but he doesn't look at her. "Sorry," he says. "It's been a tough week."

"You want to talk about it?" she asks, but at that moment headlights flash into the driveway. Jack stands and walks to the end of the porch, waving. The gesture isn't like him, either, Janice thinks, watching from the swing. In response, Belinda Comstock toots her horn three times.

It occurs to Janice that the dinner is going quite well, considering. Jack has perked up noticeably, and is more forthcoming than usual with both Belinda and Graham, as though compensating for his detachment out on the porch; Belinda is bright and enthusiastic, as always, and though Graham has been downing martinis ever since their arrival, he seems to be holding his own. Often during the dinner Belinda makes deliberate eye contact with Janice, as though to confirm Janice's perception that everything is going well. For several years now, since the late seventies, Belinda has been Janice's closest friend, and though Belinda refused to become Janice's therapist, Janice routinely credits her with saving her life, if not literally then at the very least spiritually. (They'd met one day while jogging in Piedmont Park, at a low point in both their lives: Janice had been

estranged from Clifford and hadn't yet met Jack; Bel had been enduring a particularly difficult period in her stormy relationship with
Graham. The friendship had become so close, and so quickly, that
Bel referred Janice to a therapist-friend of hers, pleading that she
couldn't be both Janice's personal friend *and* her therapist; and she
wanted Janice's friendship very much. Janice had been touched, and
in fact the psychiatrist Bel recommended had greatly reassured and
helped her: the woman had told Janice confidently that she was not
a "suicide risk"; the life force was too strong in Janice, she said, for
good or for ill; what mattered was to channel Janice's extraordinary
energy into positive, as opposed to self-destructive, channels. Janice
would often ponder this insight: it was true that, in spite of everything that had happened, the thought of suicide had never entered
her mind.) Yet it was Belinda's friendship, not the therapy (which
lasted only a few months), that sustained her: not only had Belinda
guided her, week by week, through the perils of her life, including
the fervent promiscuity of her "disco years," or her "crazy days" as
Janice often calls them, and her on-again off-again friendship with
Clifford Bannon, and her conflicted relationship with her parents;
she had also introduced Janice to Jack Lassiter, the brother of one
of Belinda's grad school friends, so that the three of them—or four
of them, if you included Graham—had become what Janice liked to
consider a family of sorts, a group she thought would remain close
to one another all their lives.

In the early years of their friendship, Janice often supposed
guiltily that she was taking advantage of Belinda—that actually Belinda *was* her "unpaid therapist," in a sense—but whenever Janice
made this joke Belinda would give her throaty laugh and say that
Janice had helped her, too, in ways too subtle even to be expressed.
And that's what friendship meant, wasn't it? . . . In any case, Belinda
insisted, people often entered a kind of emotional "plateau" when
they reached their thirties, and Janice should give some of the credit
to herself: she'd survived some difficult years, after all. In retrospect,
Janice sees that her life *has* gradually become calmer, even serene at
times, allowing her to be promoted steadily at the advertising firm
where she has worked since moving to Atlanta. As office manager,
she now makes more than double her original salary and has discov-

ered that she is quite good at running an office efficiently, hiring
and firing people, practicing business economies; and she is known
as a fair-minded manager. One evening she had boasted to Clifford,
over the phone, "Listen, kiddo, let's show a little respect—I'm a
model employee, after all. I'm a fucking *manager*." Obligingly, Clifford
had laughed. Not long before that, in fact, he'd said abruptly, apropos
of nothing, that he was proud of Janice; despite her pestering he'd
refused to explain what he meant, but no compliment from anyone,
she felt at the time and feels still, has ever touched her quite so
deeply.

And yet, as Belinda recently said: "Remember, don't get complacent. When you start congratulating yourself on your progress,
life has a way of sending a bulldozer straight toward you."

Janice had laughed, though knowing well that Belinda wasn't
joking.

In the past year or so, it would appear, Belinda and Janice have
traded places, since it is now Belinda who has serious problems in
her life: her husband of seven years, Graham Jensen, has declined
steadily into alcoholism. Once a successful dentist who has now all
but stopped practicing, who lives off his wife and talks vaguely about
going back to college to study literature, or Eastern philosophy, or
the history of the American West, Graham is someone whom Jack,
at least, considers a lost cause, and a testament either to Belinda
Comstock's superhuman loyalty or to her outright foolishness. Janice
hadn't mentioned to Jack that long ago, responding to some despairing remark of Janice's, Belinda had laughed and said, winking, "Believe me, honey, I'm addicted to lost causes." The remark had hurt,
though Janice knew that Belinda hadn't intended her any pain; Janice
had quickly changed the subject and she certainly hadn't repeated
the remark to Jack.

Tonight, on the surface, both Belinda and Graham seem far
from lost: Belinda is a shapely, dark-haired woman, only eight years
older than Janice, whom Clifford Bannon had called (after meeting
her once, at a small cocktail party Janice had given) "smoky-looking,"
an odd phrase that captured, Janice felt, Belinda's dark-complected
sensuality very well. Though Belinda is both talkative and candid, a
woman who tends to nod and smile during conversation, who listens

intelligently, she has nonetheless an air of mystery that surely height-
ens her appeal to men. She wears her heavy dark hair long and
straight, more in the style of the late sixties than the mid-eighties,
and she uses little makeup, and she favors Mexican or Indian jewelry.
Clifford had asked Janice whether Belinda might have some Indian
blood, but in fact Belinda is a farm girl from Wisconsin, and has
deliberately cultivated, over a period of many years, the "self" she
now possesses (or rather, as Belinda would undoubtedly prefer, the
self she now *is*). Tonight in her loose-fitting cotton dress of bright
aqua, and her heavy turquoise-and-silver jewelry, looking eager and
interested as she listens to some convoluted anecdote Jack is telling
them, Belinda looks to Janice like someone supremely at ease,
healthy, comfortable in her life; a passing observer would scarcely
imagine her deeply troubled connection to the pale and rather prim-
looking Graham Jensen, who sits quietly beside her, a handsome yet
gaunt, almost cadaverous man who is paying more attention to his
wineglass than to Jack's story.

Yet Belinda has seldom seemed more radiant; and Janice sees
that Jack, directing his anecdote mostly toward Belinda, has shrugged
off completely his rather dour mood of an hour before. She glances
at his wineglass, then at Belinda's, and sees that they're both empty;
and of course Graham's is empty.

"For heaven's sake!" she cries, leaping up. "I'm not much of a
hostess, am I?"

Though Belinda glances her way, smiling, neither Jack nor Graham looks over; while Janice pours more wine, and urges Graham
to have a bit more of the chicken cacciatore—he has scarcely
touched his first serving, and Janice has the idea that the more he
eats, the less drunk he will get—she listens as Jack finishes his
anecdote about a couple of women lawyers who had been to see
him recently, about buying one of his office duplexes. It seems that
after a gingerly and, to Jack, rather puzzling discussion in which Jack
had tried to determine how the women wanted to handle the pur-
chase, and exactly what their business relationship was, one of the
women had blurted out: "Listen, Mr. Lassiter, we're lovers, all right?
Lesbian lovers. Now, do you have any problem with that?" And as
Jack describes his awkwardness, his many apologies, his stammering

and blushing before the women—one of whom was a "diesel dyke,"
Jack says, "she ought to be recruited for the Falcons"—as he talks
on and on about the incident, garrulous, his cheeks ruddy with the
wine and his own good humor, Janice thinks again that he isn't
himself tonight; he's normally far more restrained. Jack is a robust,
healthy man who spends a couple of hours each day at the gym; he
has short-cropped blond hair, a virile square-cut face, and amazingly
gentle, even bland blue eyes. He's the type of man whose physical
impressiveness contrasts in an appealing way with an almost boyish
reticence. Yet now he's far from reticent, and for the first time in
their relationship Janice wonders if he'd had something to drink
before coming here tonight. She remembers that his eyes had seemed
a bit glassy out on the porch, after only one drink of wine. Whatever
the reason, Jack is far more sociable than usual: Belinda's smiling
attention is still fixed on him, and even Graham is looking his way,
with a quivering thin-lipped smile.

"Really, Bel, I'm amazed that you're putting up with this,"
Janice says facetiously, feeling a bit left out. "Some of your activist
friends are lesbians, aren't they?"

"Of course they are," Belinda says, also in a kidding way. "But
after all, the man said that he apologized, didn't he? What more
should we expect?"

"Well, I feel sorry for the poor women," Janice says. "I mean,
think what they must have to deal with, on a daily basis. All the
little remarks and innuendoes, the 'innocent' assumptions. . . ."

"From neanderthals like me, do you mean?" Jack says airily.

Belinda reaches over to pat Janice's hand, and when she says,
"He's not serious, honey, he's just kidding around," Janice understands that she'd sounded angry rather than facetious. Yet why should
she be angry? She has never, to her knowledge, known a lesbian in
her life, and she has no particular sympathy for them. Although she
has gotten over the aversion to homosexuality that she'd felt in the
year or two after learning that Clifford was gay—and once again it
was Belinda who'd helped her with that—she doesn't, on the other
hand, have any strong feelings about the issue, even after meeting
several of Clifford's boyfriends over the years. In the past Janice has

tended to get angry when she's unsure of herself, and this is what disturbs her now; for she is, these days, very sure of herself indeed.

"Well, somebody needs to take up for the poor girls," Janice says, smirking.

"Believe me," Jack says, "these two didn't need *your* help. I wouldn't want to meet either one of them in a dark alley."

"Oh, Jack," Belinda says in mock-reproof, laughing.

"Did you know," Graham says now, abruptly, "that certain Native American tribes used to actually worship their homosexual population? They thought that homosexuality, among men at least, indicated a high degree of spirituality, since homosexuals refused to demean themselves with women. So, in these tribes, queers were given the finest material goods the tribes could offer, and were not expected to work."

"What?" Jack says, surprised. "Are you serious, Graham?"

Graham looks quite pleased with himself; though bony and pale, and wearing an oversized dark suit, he can look extremely handsome at times, even what Janice would call "glamorous": it's largely his bone structure, she supposes, and the contrast of his coal-black hair and heavy brows against the white unblemished pallor of his skin. He sits fiddling with the napkin on his lap, clearly pleased to have their attention. He adds, his mouth pursed in distaste, "Of course, certain other tribes took a quite different view of the matter. The Iroquois, I believe, would cut off the penis of a man discovered in a homosexual act, and then they would roast the thing and serve it up to the queer man's father: it was considered to be the father's fault, you see."

"My God!" Janice cries. "How horrible—"

"Graham, why don't you admit that you're making all this up?" Belinda says, her lips tightly pursed.

"Darling, I don't have to make things up," Graham says, lifting his nose as though repelled by his wife's stupidity. "Because I *read,* my dear, and I assure you that everything I've just told you is absolute fact."

"You read it?" Belinda says impatiently. "Read it where?"

Graham turns his head in a slow, deliberate way toward Janice;

the movement is stiff, careful, and Janice can see that he's very drunk indeed. "Beginning in January," he says, "I'll be taking a course in Native American history at Georgia State—a graduate level course, I'm entering an American Studies program there—so I picked up a few of the texts ahead of time, and I've been browsing through them."

"Graham, you have *not* bought any textbooks," Belinda says, her voice quavering, "so why don't you—"

"Listen, how about some dessert?" Janice says, alarmed. The change of subject is awkward, but she doesn't know what else to do; from across the table Jack stares at her, aghast. He has never been able to deal with emotional scenes, and now looks as if he might flee the room at any moment.

"Jack?" she says quickly, "do you want to help me with the strawberries? I haven't whipped the cream yet, and I—"

"How would you know what I've been doing," Graham says, his voice eerily gentle. He is not looking at Belinda, but at his near-empty glass: he sits twirling the stem between his fingers, as though reluctant to take that last swallow of wine. "After all," he says, "you spend all your time down at the office, with your nut cases, so who knows what I might be doing during the day? Or with whom."

Janice thinks that Graham's words, spoken in his hoarse near-whisper, sound even nastier than they are.

Belinda has crumpled her napkin, her fingers trembling; her dark eyes are moist with anger. "Come on," she says, "we're leaving. We're not putting Janice and Jack through this."

"Oh, please don't go!" Janice cries. She tries to get up but she feels locked in place, as in a dream she can't quite shake off. Across the table, Jack too seems frozen, and has turned very pale. "No, don't go, please," Janice says feebly, "I think we've all just had a rough week and—"

"*I* haven't had a rough week, Janice," Graham says. He smiles at her, politely. "I've had a lovely time, in fact. You see, in the morning I do my reading, and in the afternoon I go out, see people, do as I please. In the evening, when I get home, Dr. Comstock is generally waiting for me, tapping her foot, and so then I have several dozen drinks in quick succession. Isn't that right, dear?"

he says to Belinda. "Now why don't you tell them about *your* typical day."

Belinda refuses to look at him; glancing between Jack and Janice, she says quickly, "I'm sorry, really sorry, but we've got to go. Obviously this can't continue. He knows I won't engage with the child in him, I absolutely *refuse* to play the role of his punishing mother, and so——"

"This is so pathetically transparent," Graham says ruefully, and now he does finish the wine in one swift and oddly graceful motion. He says, "Both Jack and Janice can see, good Dr. Comstock, that you *are* engaging in a dialogue with me, even though you're addressing your words to them. And really that's more childish, isn't it, than anything I might be doing?"

Belinda has stood, shakily; she keeps her dark anguished eyes fixed on Janice, as though their mutual gaze is sustaining her, helping Belinda keep her balance from moment to moment. She says in a queer strangled voice, "You see, I won't be his mother, and so he retaliates by not allowing me to be his lover or friend, and tries to humiliate me in front of others. This is a fairly new tactic, born of desperation, I suppose, and of——of the fact that Graham is near death, that he's truly killing himself with booze."

Graham leans toward Janice, politely. "Might I trouble you," he says, "for another glass of wine?"

"So we've got to leave," Belinda says raggedly, and all at once Janice sees that the tears are coming, that there's nothing else to be done, and so she looks hard at Jack and says, "Honey, would you drive them home? I don't want either of them to drive."

"What?" Jack says, clearly horrified, but then his habitual male politeness takes over. "Of course," he says, standing. He takes Belinda's arm. "Come on, Bel," he says. "I'll drive you."

"What?" Graham says. "We're leaving so soon?"

Jack shoots him a quick look. "It's for the best," he says. "You can see Bel's upset, can't you?"

"You mean we *have* to leave?" Graham says. "You mean we're being *kicked out?*"

From the kitchen Janice hears the telephone, but it rings only once and then stops. Or is she imagining this?

"Graham, please," she whispers, watching as Jack leads Belinda toward the door. "Please help your wife," she says, "please don't do this."

His mouth twisting in contempt, Graham gets up. "Thanks for the lovely dinner," he says over his shoulder, "*do* invite us again," and before Janice can quite register what has happened they're gone, all three of them gone, and Janice is sitting there alone.

She thinks suddenly that *she* should be the one to drive Belinda and Graham home, not Jack; and she understands that she had felt herself unable to cope with the situation a moment longer. She's not accustomed to seeing Belinda in a vulnerable, victimized state; Janice has admired her friend so deeply, and during her own rocky times had transferred onto Belinda an intensity of longing and belief that was almost religious in nature. Now she sits at her wrecked dinner table alone and disbelieving, stunned. She does not even feel much surprise when Jack, only a couple of minutes after leaving with Belinda and Graham, comes back inside the house and sits down on the living room sofa, his face in his hands.

"Honey?" Janice calls, and when he doesn't answer she leaves the dining room and hurries out to him. She sits on the sofa, too, but keeps a discreet few inches between them. She has never seen Jack like this.

"Honey?" she says again, faintly.

He drops his hands and says, "God, what a wretched scene."

Though his color has returned Janice sees that he still looks rocky, his eyes threaded with blood. He sits there shaking his head.

She doesn't understand why he's this upset; *she's* the one who ought to feel badly. She whispers, "Why didn't you drive them, Jack?"

"Once we got out to the driveway," he says, "Bel insisted that she was okay. She said she was going to phone a treatment center, have Graham committed—she said it was the only way. She really did seem all right, once we got outside. But God, Janice, did you know it was this bad? That Bel was going through this shit?"

"I sort of knew," Janice says guiltily. She wishes Jack had insisted about the driving, but there's nothing to do now but hope for the best. Belinda *is* a competent woman, after all. She's not normally the type to lose control.

Again, in the kitchen, the phone is ringing.

"I'll get it," Janice says hollowly, but she makes no move to rise.

"I will," Jack says. "I want to make a drink, anyway. You want anything?" he says, going out.

"Yes," Janice calls, "a drink. And then I'll make our dessert."

While Jack is on the phone Janice goes to the front door and steps out onto the porch; she stares at the place in the driveway where Belinda's gray BMW had been parked, as if supposing that she might have imagined the entire incident, that perhaps it's Belinda calling on the phone, saying they're very sorry, they're running a bit late, they'll be there as quick as they can. . . . Janice stares disconsolately at the driveway; the asphalt gleams whitely under the mild November moon. She knows that she must call Belinda in a few minutes, that perhaps she'll have to go over there tonight, that maybe there'll be another scene if Belinda really does call a hospital and try to have Graham committed. Janice feels weary, bruised. She doesn't know if she can face all this. It occurs to her that in her own life, when she had been in the midst of turmoil, some sort of superhuman energy—she supposes it was adrenaline, or what that psychiatrist had called her "life force"—had seen her through; but for other people's crises she had no energy, they left her feeling drained and helpless. She remembers shouting at Jack one evening several months ago, during their first and only argument, that she never felt that he *needed* her, she never felt that she was indispensable to his happiness. He'd looked at her, puzzled, and said, "Contentment, not happiness—that's all I'm after. But really, Janice, what's your point? I don't want you to feel that I'm indispensable, either. Why put ourselves in that sort of jeopardy?" At the time the words had sounded heartless and they'd slept apart that night, and Janice had cried herself to sleep as she hadn't done in years; but now she saw what he meant and might even admit that she agreed. *Contentment, not happiness.* After all, she thought, she didn't have as much emotional energy, these days; she didn't know if she had the strength for happiness.

When she goes back into the kitchen, Jack is pouring cream into a bowl.

"Here, I'll do that," Janice says, reaching into a cabinet for the mixer. "Who was that on the phone?"

Jack says nothing. His shoulders look a bit slumped, and very still. "Hand me the mixer," he says.

"Jack?" she says. "Was it Bel? Honey, who was it?"

He turns around, his eyes downcast, and takes the mixer from her hand, then puts it on the counter. He takes the bowl of cream to the sink and carefully pours it out, then rinses the sink with tap water. Janice feels a leaden coldness in her chest; she cannot speak. Slowly Jack turns toward her, leaning back against the counter and folding his arms.

"When it rains," he says, "it pours."

"Jack," she says in a croaking whisper, "please, what's wrong, was it Bel—"

"It wasn't Bel," Jack says. "It was Clifford."

The word has a foreign sound. *Clifford.*

"What about him?" Janice says. "He's all right, isn't he?"

"I guess so," Jack says. "With Clifford, it's hard to tell. He called about that new friend of his, Will something or other, or is it Bill—"

"Will," Janice says. "Will Prather. What about him?"

"Clifford's at the hospital—he called to say that Will is very sick. That he's got AIDS."

"What? His boyfriend has it?" Janice says, panicked. "But what about—"

"He sounded pretty tense," Jack says. "He'd called and left a message on my machine, then remembered about Fridays and figured we'd be here."

"Why didn't you call me to the phone?" Janice cries. "Why didn't you—"

"He sounded tense," Jack says again, "so I let him do the talking. He just asked if I'd check his mail and bring him some fresh clothes. He's been down at the hospital for a couple of days now—evidently his friend doesn't have much time."

"Oh God, this is horrible, poor Clifford—but why did he leave a message at your place, why didn't you call me to the phone, Jack, I don't—"

In her distress Janice has reached out for him, has grabbed onto his folded forearms, and now slowly, mechanically, Jack puts one arm around her shoulder and leads her back to the living room. Janice has begun to cry, murmuring "Poor Clifford," remembering the lunch they'd had together, just a few weeks ago, when Clifford had told her about Will: he was an art history student at Emory, Clifford had said, they'd met at a gallery not long ago and hit it off well, they were already talking about moving in together. . . . Janice recalls in panic how excited and happy Clifford had seemed, she'd never really seen him like that before, so enthusiastic and smiling, using phrases like "the real thing" and "the love of my life," which she'd been amazed to hear coming out of Clifford Bannon's mouth. And now this. Now *this*. She remembers herself saying, "And I've found the love of my life, too, it looks like everything has worked out after all, kiddo," and now it is Janice's turn to put her face in her hands, muttering, "Poor Clifford, his mother killed herself when he was just a kid, you know, and now *this*," and she sits there for a while, sobbing, and Jack keeps his arm around her, telling her that she's got to look out for herself, not to work herself into hysteria over the problems of her friends. She really ought to go upstairs, Jack says, and take a hot bath, then try to get to sleep early. Does she have a Valium or something? Does she want him to make her that drink before she goes upstairs?

"I can't take a bath," Janice says, straightening, "for heaven's sake I've got to call Bel, I've got to call *Clifford*—"

"No, you can't," Jack says. "You wouldn't be of any help, not tonight. Listen, I'll clean up the dishes while you draw that bath. Then I've got to be going, myself."

Janice looks at him, wiping away tears with the back of her hand.

"Going?" she says. "Aren't you—?"

Jack always slept over on Friday nights: another of their rituals.

"I don't think so, Janice. It's been a rough night."

"That's all the more reason—" but she stops herself. She's not going to plead. There had been something different about Jack tonight, she'd noticed it when he first arrived, out on the swing. . . .

"You want to leave?" she says faintly.

Jack stands up, stretching his arms; he looks down at Janice as though from a great distance. "Look, Janice," he says, "there's no point in falling apart, you know, just because everyone else is. Now get down the hall and into that bath. Doctor's orders."

Without waiting for her response Jack goes into the dining room, begins clearing away the dishes.

From the sofa she says, very clearly, "Maybe you should go now."

"What?" Jack says, turning around. "What did you—"

"Just go now," Janice says. "It's what you want to do, isn't it?"

"C'mon, Janice, don't get neurotic about it," Jack says. But he doesn't turn back to the table.

"I mean it," Janice says.

Jack shrugs his shoulders; he comes toward her, one arm outstretched.

"No," she says, cocking her head toward the door. "Go. I've got things to do."

"All right, I'll call you later," Jack says, his tone conciliatory, though she can see that she has angered him; it's in the hard set of his jaw, the sudden cold sheen to those mild blue eyes.

"Thanks, but I've got my own calls to make," Janice says, getting up and heading for the kitchen.

"I hope you'll take my advice!" Jack calls. "It really is for the best!" And a moment later she hears the door slam, then his car speeding away from the curb. Janice is already in the kitchen, her hand on the phone, but now she pauses. What to say to Clifford? How to console him? She remembers those words he'd said to her, long ago: "I don't like losing people. . . ." She thinks of Jack on his way home, his eyes grim, his squarish forehead tilted forward as though to butt aside anything that dared get in his way. What if he hasn't called, by this time tomorrow? Or the next day? Janice takes the phone from the wall, then puts it back. She ought to call Jack and make peace with him; she should try to reach Clifford; she should ask if Belinda wants her to come over this evening, does she need any help, is there anything she can do . . . ? These are the three people in her life to whom Janice is closest, she thinks, they *are* her life, yet now she is suddenly afraid of them. All of them. She stares at the phone a moment longer, then begins snapping off lights and hurries back to her bedroom.

Not long ago, at a flea market, Janice had bought a near-exact replica of the bed she'd had as a little girl: a canopied four-poster, the headboard and posts painted white, carved with whimsical shell designs. Later she'd found a white cotton canopy and comforter, and some fluffy lace-edged pillows; only after showing the bed to Jack did she feel embarrassed and wonder why she'd recreated this little girl's room, which *did* look a bit odd when glimpsed through her lover's eyes. He hadn't helped by making such a joke of it, stretching his arms and saying, "Is *this* where I'm supposed to violate you, on this snowy white bed?—this looks like a nun's room, Janice." At first she hadn't reacted, thinking at once of Ruthie and wondering what *her* room looked like; surely it was much simpler and barer than this one. Then she'd stretched her own arms, mimicking Jack, and had said offhandedly, "What are you talking about, Mr. Lassiter? I thought I was going to violate *you,*" and for a moment he'd been startled, abashed. But only for a moment.

After standing under a hot shower for several minutes and brushing her teeth and then, after a moment's debate, swallowing down the Valium tablet without water, she goes into the bedroom and puts on an old cheap nylon nightgown, her favorite for sleeping, and crawls beneath the covers. She keeps the bedside lamp burning, expecting that the phone will ring at any moment, but somehow knowing that it won't; it never rings when she hopes it will, she thinks nervously, people never behave in a way she can predict. So she lies there for a while thinking that she ought to read something, there's a paperback thriller in her nightstand drawer, there's a copy of Vanity Fair, but instead she stares at the underside of her canopy and thinks about Clifford Bannon. She knows that Belinda, for all her look of angry frustration tonight, is a capable woman and has Graham under control by now; she knows Jack's ability to shrug off

conflicts, arguments, she can see him curled in a fetal position in his
bed, already asleep. Of course he will call her in the morning. Of
course their relationship is stable, they don't often behave childishly,
by tomorrow everything will look different to both of them. . . . But
Clifford. Poor Clifford, as she'd thought a bit earlier—she *is* concerned about him. Though their friendship has been on a back
burner, she supposes, for quite a while, she finds herself still thinking
about him at unexpected times; and yes, thinking of him with a
childlike abandon and longing that sends her thoughts hurtling back
to her adolescent and childhood years. Janice had, of course, discussed Clifford endlessly with Belinda, who had helped Janice to see
that because Clifford was gay, and therefore unavailable, he was the
ideal "withholding father" for her; it wouldn't be surprising, Belinda
said, if Janice hadn't fulfilled a similar role in Clifford's life. So Janice
saw that they'd been the ideal punishment for one another—a never-
ending "penance," she had mused, ironically, as she confessed her
past life to Belinda Comstock. She had wondered aloud, holding her
breath as she awaited Belinda's reply, whether she ought really to
sever her tie to Clifford, sever it permanently, even though the
friendship had become relatively innocuous, a matter of an occasional
lunch together, or a concert?

Janice had stared at Belinda, her wide blue eyes unblinking, as
if startled by her own question. But, as it happened, Belinda said
no; as long as Janice kept the relationship in perspective, there was
really no danger. In fact, Belinda had said thoughtfully, it might be
considered a beneficial discipline to maintain "difficult" or previously
unworkable relationships; they offered a sense of achievement, and
were a way of practicing one's skills and keeping one's emotional
objectives clearly in view.

Janice had nodded, gratefully, had even made a joke of sorts.
She told Belinda, "I've never been too good at 'discipline,' you
know," and Belinda had said, with her kind smile, gently mimicking
one of Janice's phrases, "Well, kiddo, here's your chance."

The friendship with Clifford had begun working, Janice often
thought, because for the time being neither of them cared much
about it—this was a cynical notion she supposed, but their widely
spaced and untroubled visits with one another were so far preferable,

she thought, to the agonized contortions of their past relationship that she really didn't mind if what they shared was "meaningful" or not. And it was clear that Clifford didn't mind. Though his artistic career hadn't quite taken flight in the way those newspaper stories and one-man shows of a few years back might have suggested—for one thing, Clifford insisted that he wasn't "ambitious," he hated New York and refused even to visit there any longer, much less live there, he just wanted to be left in peace to do his work—despite this, or perhaps because of it, Clifford did seem happy, he certainly wanted for nothing, and he seemed to enjoy the "new" Janice, as he often called her. Janice has felt gratified that in the last couple of years Clifford has confided in her about his love life, occasionally introducing her to some handsome young man over drinks at The Country Place, or Peachtree Cafe; he no longer appears concerned that Janice might harbor some jealousy, even now, or might let slip some unsavory detail about their own past relationship. Though she hadn't met the young man named Will Prather, she knew Clifford well enough to understand that the relationship was serious; she'd gathered that from his demeanor at lunch the other day. It amazes her, now, that despite all the publicity about the AIDS epidemic, she'd never seriously considered the possibility that it might touch Clifford's life, much less her own. Perhaps this is why, lying here, she cannot imagine what she will say to him; what words she might contrive that would not sound trite or inane. It is easy, too easy, to resist calling the hospital and having Clifford paged; somehow she can't relate herself to what Clifford is now going through. Of course, what she can't face, she thinks bleakly, is that Clifford truly has moved beyond her. *I don't like losing people,* he had said, and now she thinks to herself, childishly, guiltily, *Well I don't, either.*

But she does reach toward the nightstand and lift the telephone. She remembers an old ritual of hers, from those first couple of years in Atlanta when things between her and Clifford had been touch and go, tentative, neither of them knowing whether to call the other, what to say when they did talk, how to approach one another in this new place and time. Janice would often call his number when she felt certain he would be out, just to hear his voice on the answering machine; she's amazed that she can even remember this, much less that she used to make such calls on a regular basis. Sometimes she would leave a mocking or facetious message, like that taunt she and her friends had used when they were kids: *I know who you are, and I saw what you did,* she would say in a heightened, forbidding voice, breaking into awkward laughter and feeling her cheeks redden as she hung up the phone. The next time she saw Clifford, he would not refer to the message she had left. Now, as though to make up for all their tangled and senseless past, she dials his number and sits waiting, her heart pounding, as she listens to the message: "Thanks for calling," says Clifford's curt voice, "please leave your name and number at the tone."

She doesn't know what to do, but when the tone sounds she says at once, firmly, "Clifford—Clifford, I'm so sorry," and when she hangs up the phone her emotion threatens to choke her.

She lies there in bed for a long while, very much alone, staring at the blank underside of the canopy. She has never felt more helpless in her life.

Clifford

All that November, spending most of his time in the I.C.U. waiting room, his mind benumbed, Clifford Bannon has felt strongly that he does not want to be alone; the perception doesn't frighten him—he is beyond fear, he's fairly certain of that—and so he allows himself the curious lapses into uncharacteristic behavior, wondering if through his lover's death, in some cruelly relentless process of nature, a new self of his own is being born. When another of Will's visitors or one of his nurses or Dr. Federman, the polite but subtly arrogant internist assigned to Will's case, stops by the waiting room to ask Clifford how he's doing or to offer any crumb of news they might have, Clifford will stand and shake hands, invite the visitor inside, indulge in the most sterile kind of small talk. Gradually he's become dazed by the elaborate, repetitive discussions of symptoms and prognoses, treatments and therapies. By Thanksgiving week—Will had been admitted on the second of November—Clifford finds himself avoiding any discussion of Will's case, even with the doctor. He wanders the hallway outside the I.C.U., he buys junk food from the vending machine downstairs, he sits tensely in the waiting room hour after hour, hunched forward, staring at his hands. It seems that these conditions will never change, that he has entered a version of hell, until the night when one of the nurses, a pretty small-framed black woman from the afternoon shift, comes into the room, sits down beside him, and asks Clifford if he isn't becoming "overwrought."

The waiting room is squarish, painted a bruised yellow, furnished with an institutional couch and chairs of orange vinyl. While waiting in this room Clifford has taken up smoking, and the small gold-metal ashtray beside him is heaped with butts. He sits in his usual posture: leaned forward, elbows on his knees, hands working awkwardly as he fiddles with another cigarette and matches. Beside him the nurse sits prim and erect, like a messenger from some impeccable world of health.

"I don't know," he says, shaking his head. "I'm tired of this, but—"

"But?" the nurse says. He hears the hopeful note in her voice; she assumes he is weakening. For some time now, he knows, the medical staff has wished silently that Clifford would just go home.

"Somebody's got to sit here, don't they?" he asks, not for the first time. "Other friends of his stop by, but they only stay a minute or two, they don't seem to—"

"Mr. Bannon," the nurse says, briefly touching his hand. "There's nothing to be gained by waiting out here. Will is comatose, so your visiting the room isn't really helpful, and it seems to be harmful to you. The strain is very great. We can all see that."

She sounds both cold and compassionate. Clifford knows that she's a woman he'd have liked very much, back in his other life.

"It's just that I—"

"We have your phone number," the nurse says, bending closer to Clifford's ear. "The moment there's any change, we would call Will's mother and brother, and you. We wouldn't hesitate."

"His mother and brother? They're here, then?"

The nurse stares, lips parted in surprise. "Why yes, they flew

in several days ago, when it seemed that Will was—that he might
be in danger. They spoke with Dr. Federman for a while, and they
stepped into Will's cubicle—you were asleep on the couch, I think.
In any case, they're staying at the Hyatt, just down the street. Dr.
Federman felt it would be best if they waited there."

"Why didn't Federman tell me?" Clifford asks, hurt. "Why
didn't—" But he stops himself. He understands why. He can imagine
Will's mother and brother—a doctor's widow, a preppie from Dart-
mouth—glancing into the waiting room and seeing an unkempt
youngish man in black leather jacket and jeans. He can imagine the
woman whispering something to Federman, her mouth wrinkled in
distaste, and the doctor whispering back, "Fine, don't worry—please
don't worry." Then mother and son scurried back to the hotel.

Clifford has become vulnerable to paranoia, these past few
weeks. If you know that you're being paranoid, he has thought dully,
then are you? Asking unanswerable questions has become a way of
life in this place.

He says, "But they'll be back today, won't they? I want to
speak with them, I want to—"

A man has appeared in the waiting room doorway, and though
he looks familiar Clifford can't quite bring him into focus. After a
moment the man walks away.

"Please," the nurse says, rising. "Please think about what I
said—you need a break. You're harming yourself, and you aren't
helping him."

As she walks away Clifford reaches out one hand, as though
imploring her to stay; it's a gesture he tends to perform automatically, these days, whenever anyone leaves the waiting room. Clifford
himself leaves the room only for meals and to use the men's room
down the hall, where he gives himself awkward sponge baths and
shaves with a disposable razor he'd bought in the pharmacy downstairs. Uncle Pete had brought him some magazines, but Clifford
can't concentrate well enough to read, nor has he been able to make
even the most rudimentary sketches in the pad of unlined paper he'd
also bought downstairs. For more than three weeks now, the little
pharmacy has provided all his needs: toiletries, cigarettes, an occasional candy bar. Pete brings him fresh clothes every couple of days,

and alone of all the people attendant upon this ordeal Pete has seemed to understand why Clifford is here, why he must not leave: but even he can't be persuaded to stick around and keep his nephew company.

"I'm too easily depressed, too vulnerable," Pete had said, the other evening. "I've lost too many of my own friends this way."

Clifford had nodded, soberly; had said he understood. On that day his uncle had also brought Clifford's mail, which included a card from Janice Rungren—the third or fourth she'd sent since that Friday evening three weeks ago when he'd phoned her house, in his first panic, and had spoken to Jack. (And Jack had seemed so uncomfortable and chagrined by Clifford's request to check his mail, and run a few errands, that Clifford had phoned him again at home, later that night, and told him that someone else would be helping him, after all: in the end his Uncle Pete performed these tasks quite competently, and Clifford knew that he should have called Pete in the first place.)

Janice writes long sympathetic messages to Clifford, apologizing for not coming to visit but saying how often she thinks of him. In fact, she does little else but think of him. Clifford would like to write back and say it's all right, he expects nothing from her or from anyone, but even though he bought some stationery downstairs he has not been able to write a note to Janice. He holds the pen above the paper, but nothing happens. He cannot put the words together.

He is sitting in the room, smoking and thinking of these things, when the familiar man appears again at the doorway.

"Clifford?" the man says, abashed. "Do you mind if I come in . . . ?"

Now Clifford recognizes Jack, but all at once his body clenches and his tongue becomes thick in his mouth. He is afraid that if Jack is here, then Janice must be, too; and Janice is the last person he wants to see. She does not belong in this new world he has entered, he thinks; she would not recognize the new person he has become.

But it seems that Jack is alone, and the two men sit chatting idly for a while. They have met several times before, usually over dinner at Janice's house, and Clifford has found the man affable enough and even, at times, quite kind, though in a quiet, undemonstrative way. There's a gentleness at the heart of him that Clifford suspects few people see, perhaps even Janice herself. For Jack is a fair-haired, rugged man, a bit shorter than Clifford but more powerfully built. Once or twice, while Janice was tending to dinner in the kitchen or answering the phone, Clifford's gaze had lingered on Jack's square-cut face, broad shoulders, well-molded hands—a fascinated gaze, of course; one might say an artist's dispassionate scrutiny if Clifford thought of himself, any longer, as an artist. Jack piqued an interest in Clifford that was, he supposed, aesthetic and sexual at once. When he first met Jack, he was frankly surprised that Janice had done so well, and that the relationship had apparently "taken"; the two of them seemed never to quarrel, and to have a genuine rapport. They had even discussed a possible wedding date quite openly in front of Clifford, just a few weeks ago. Apart from Jack's physical appeal, what interests Clifford most about him are his eyes: something evasive and hidden in their boyish blueness, he has thought, although that might have been wishful thinking on Clifford's part. He remembered a phrase Uncle Pete had used one night, when he'd taken Clifford out for a nightcap; they'd been discussing a handsome kid at a nearby table and his uncle had said, winking at Clifford, "He can be had, I'm willing to bet." Clifford had been surprised at the crudity of the expression, coming from Pete, but had laughed it off. Pete had had several drinks, after all. On the night of the wedding conversation, Clifford found himself watching Jack and hearing the words again in his mind's ear, spoken in Pete's confiding whisper.

As they sit here in this waiting room these things flash through Clifford's mind as images from a distant past, a distant life: images that seem frivolous and vain and that fill him with a nearly unbearable longing.

"Anyway," Jack is saying, "we got worried, so I decided to stop by. You're sure you don't mind?"

The "we" isn't lost on Clifford, who says, "So Janice knows you're here?"

Jack's face reddens. "Well, no," he says, "I was afraid she'd feel—well, obligated to come with me. And she's had enough to deal with, lately, so I didn't think—"

"That's all right," Clifford says quickly, embarrassed himself. "I just wondered."

"I'll tell her, of course. Tomorrow," Jack says vaguely.

He sits in the armchair closest to Clifford's corner of the sofa, and Clifford is now aware that the man's posture is like his own: his body bent forward, elbows resting awkwardly on his legs. He has noticed before that Jack is an active, twitching man, not nervous so much as physically restless, yet now in this waiting room he seems quieter, more subdued, as if the room's atmosphere of grief and endless waiting has slowed him down. Clifford has thought that this room's very air seems thick, viscous, difficult to breathe or move through. He has the urge to prevent Jack's leaving, yet he doesn't really understand why Jack is here. They aren't close friends, and Jack has never met Will. The furtive anxiety Clifford glimpses in the man's eyes seems to confirm that he feels bewildered and out of place.

Clifford says, bluntly, "So what brings you here, anyway?"

"What? Well, I—" Again Jack blushes, his neck and ears an especially fierce red. He says, "To tell you the truth, Clifford, your uncle called the other evening, over at Janice's. He asked us not to tell you, but—but he's worried about you, says you've been keeping this vigil or whatever and that it's wearing you down. He thought maybe we could help. He thought—"

"Thanks," Clifford says quickly, "but I have to do this. We had a—a relationship, Will and I, and he doesn't seem to have anybody else."

"Oh, I understand that. We understand that. I just thought you could use some company. You know, some moral support."

Jack gives him an awkward smile, but Clifford doesn't smile back. He has suddenly understood why Jack had looked familiar yet incongruous—momentarily unrecognizable—when he'd first appeared in the doorway: Jack's blond thick-bodied figure had put Clifford in mind of that young priest back at St. John Bosco Elementary. Father Milliken, who'd been Father Culhane's assistant only for a short while, two or three years, and who'd been assigned the "menial" duties of tending to the schoolchildren, coming once a week to say mass and hear their confessions. Like Jack, Father Milliken had been young, blond, stocky, and though his face had been much smoother, blander, he had the same aura of vulnerability about him, almost as if he were afraid of the children. Clifford recalled seeing the anxiety in Father Milliken's eyes when Clifford entered the small anteroom used for those face-to-face Friday confessions; though he could not recall what "sins" he might have told the priest—that he'd been disrespectful to his mother, probably, or that he'd indulged in "impure thoughts"—he remembered an impulse that he could never have confessed, the almost overpowering attraction he felt for the priest. He'd been only eleven or so, and except for his infatuation with Ted Vernon he'd never experienced such feelings before. Certainly never for a grown man, and least of all for a priest. Clifford had felt suffused in shame and excitement, and he'd gone to confession every Friday whether he had anything to confess or not. Father Milliken had been good-natured but shy; he and Clifford seldom talked otherwise. Remembering all this, Clifford feels again the paralysis that came from recalling the past, whether the past were twenty years or twenty days ago. His mind has begun playing such odd tricks on him!—imagine thinking for a moment that Father Milliken had stood in the doorway, as though ready to hear his confession, to take his hand and lead him back to innocence.

"Sorry," Clifford says, again in that quick helpless voice, "I didn't mean to stare. It's just that you—you reminded me of someone."

"What?" Jack says, startled. "I reminded you . . . ?"

"One of the priests," Clifford says, "from back in grade school. A priest who used to hear our confessions."

Jack looks perplexed, even a bit displeased. He says, frowning, "Janice made the same comment once, she said I looked like—his name was—"

"Milliken," Clifford says.

Jack says vaguely, as though he hasn't heard Clifford, "Janice used to play this game, she'd say, 'Bless me, Father, for I have sinned'—you know Janice, she's always joking around. And she'd invent some elaborate sort of penance for herself, if you know what I mean."

, "Penance?" Clifford says blankly.

"You know—in bed," Jack says, and then it seems he comes back, comes to; he looks at Clifford and again his face reddens.

There's a long, uncomfortable silence. Clifford sees the faint sheen of perspiration on Jack's upper lip, his forehead. Jack is cracking his knuckles methodically, almost brutally, and for a brief perilous moment Clifford fears that he's about to cry. The air in this room is warm, heavy, an almost palpable weight upon their shoulders. Yet Jack's eyes are dry, anguished and hot but nonetheless dry, when he straightens his shoulders abruptly and gives Clifford a strained look, as though gathering all his strength.

Jack says, in a dull monotone, "I'm the one who should be 'confessing,' I guess—I do feel guilty as hell." He pauses, taking a gulp of air.

"Yes?" Clifford says.

"I mean," Jack says, rushing it all out, "I mean that this is one hell of a time to bother you, with your friend here in the hospital, but—but I had to tell somebody, to have a talk with some kind of— It's about Janice, you know, and not just about her—and so I thought—I thought if you had time—"

"Go ahead," Clifford says, unexpectedly moved, reaching forward to touch Jack's hand. "Really," he says, "it's okay. In this place, there's always plenty of time."

On that night when he first visited the hospital, Clifford had intended to stay only for a few minutes. Will had a case of pneumonia which the doctor described as "treatable," it was expected that Will's family would be arriving soon, and in any case Clifford had always hated hospitals. The antiseptic smells, the officious white-clad workers, the eerie mingling of monotonous routine and incipient horror—everything in Clifford's somewhat withheld and fastidious nature recoiled from these images, and especially from the melodrama of fatal illness, the jangled nerves and the runaway emotions and the stark confrontations with pain, with the grisly facts of the body. He'd intended to speak briefly with the doctor, give Will a few cheerful words and a peck on the forehead, then make his way out again, rushing past the rooms with their stink of ammonia and dying flowers, their supine white-sheeted forms and doleful visitors. He had no part in this, he thought. The family would resent him, and Dr. Federman had agreed that visitors often brought more stress than comfort to the patient. So Clifford had rationalized the situation, wanting to get out of here, until he'd actually seen Will. It was clear at once that Federman hadn't told him the full truth about Will's condition. (The next morning, Federman had apologized, but said he had no idea that Will would deteriorate so rapidly; the morning after that, Will was transferred to the I.C.U.) Even that first day, Will was having trouble getting his breath. He would say a word, then a wracking cough would lift him halfway out of bed, his entire body convulsed and trembling. Helplessly Clifford had thought that he had to leave, that he didn't know this boy with his colorless dry hair and thinning cheeks, his moist gaping eyes. Yet Clifford had stood holding his hand for an hour or more, waiting patiently as Will took ten minutes or longer to get out a sentence, a raucous cough punctuating each phrase, followed by several gasps for air that made Clifford wonder if each breath might be his last. Clifford waited, with no further thought of leaving; he knew now that he was here for the duration.

The most wrenching effect of Will's illness was the way it heightened an essential boyishness of his face and manner that had captivated Clifford from the beginning. They'd met at a gallery opening eight months ago, when Will had walked forthrightly up to him and introduced himself, saying he recognized Clifford from a self-portrait hanging in a gallery over on Highland: Will had admired his work ever since he'd moved here two years ago, he said, to study art history at the university. Since this was a program similar to the one Clifford had completed years before, they had a lively discussion of courses and department politics, local artists and galleries, Clifford aware as they talked that the boy—for he thought of him as a boy, even though Will was twenty-two—had inspired in Clifford a degree of openness and spontaneity that he seldom achieved with anyone. So they'd gone for coffee, a bit high on the gallery champagne and their own newfound friendship, and then for a late dinner at The Country Place, and by the end of dinner it was clear, it was an unspoken certainty, that Will would come home with him, that they would fall into bed together as easily as they'd fallen into their first exchange of words that evening. In the ensuing months Clifford spent most of his time with Will; when Will was busy with his classes or his own watercolors, Clifford wondered at the speed and relative ease with which they'd formed a bond that Clifford already considered the most significant of his life. The essential thing, Clifford thought, in these moments of perplexed analysis, was that for some reason Will did not threaten him: it was something in the boy's lack of self-consciousness or manipulative skill, his spontaneous flow of talk (for Will talked a great deal, though never unintelligently) expressing rather than concealing an emotional intensity that Will had, for whatever reason, channeled into Clifford's very being.

In the beginning, Clifford had made the unavoidable comparison with Janice Rungren, for she had the same intensity, the same relentless focus upon Clifford: yet he'd always felt, with her, that she was waiting for something, for some appropriate response or action on his part that might satisfy her voracious need, fill some yawning emptiness that seemed large enough to swallow Clifford and a hundred others like him. For Will's part, he seemed to expect nothing; he seemed pleased by whatever Clifford said or did, never expressing anger or disappointment on those nights when Clifford preferred to sleep alone, or to stay home reading or sketching; a day later, or three days later, they would resume precisely where they had left off, without rancor or emotional tension of any sort.

This freedom Will had accorded to Clifford had permitted Clifford's own passion to bloom with an intensity he'd never known he possessed. He could not sleep for thinking of Will: his full, bright-eyed face with its shock of thick blond hair, a choirboy's face, as Clifford often teased him, with a choirboy's tendency to shift his expression from naive wonderment to shrewd mischief, and back again, with dazzling speed. And despite Will's fair, rather girlish face, his smooth and hairless body, also girlish perhaps in its firm plumpness—he'd never exercised a day in his life, Will laughed, and certainly never would—despite all this Will had an astonishing sex drive, a capacity for outright lust that had alarmed Clifford for a while, since he wondered if he could respond in kind, or if Will would not find him an inevitable disappointment; but only for a while. Every stage of their involvement brought them closer, and quickly; for the first time in his life Clifford felt himself entirely out of control and what shocked him most was that he'd willingly surrendered that control, as though it were some piece of useless baggage that he'd been carrying around for years so that now, letting it go, he felt a welcome sense of lightness and relief.

Their passion had been so intense that neither had wanted to share the other: as a result Clifford had introduced Will to no one, and Clifford knew one or two of Will's friends only in the most passing and superficial way. They seldom spoke of one another's families—Will's family lived in New England, they didn't approve of his "life-style," he'd come south partly to get away from them. Like Clifford, he had a trust fund, and also like Clifford the money meant little to him. Clifford understood vaguely that Will, after first arriving in Atlanta, had gone through the obligatory rites of frenzied promiscuity, at a time when AIDS was a fearsome but not yet well-understood word, not yet a word one applied to oneself or one's own life. When Clifford had first heard Will's diagnosis, his first thought had been to shrug it off, to assume that a treatment would be found very soon; but soon enough he understood this as the "denial" phase of the crisis, and as Will grew thinner, and lost much of his familiar volubility and good cheer, a leaden certainty had begun spreading out from Clifford's heart, almost a paralysis, which reminded him of the days immediately following his mother's death.

I've already done this, he heard himself thinking, though whether the implication of this thought was that the second time should be easier or that he couldn't endure such an ordeal again, he wasn't quite sure.

What surprised him most was the sort of desperation, entirely new to him, that had finally grown out of his paralyzed vulnerability: his urgent need not to be alone, not to pass through this ordeal in the kind of isolation he'd endured throughout his adolescence. At the end of such a road he glimpsed a permanently cold and bitter man, and evidently some life force in him—the force that Will himself had awakened, perhaps—wanted to abort that possibility at any cost. Perhaps what he saw in Jack Lassiter during their tense but exhilarating conversation in the waiting room was a form of that same desperation, that same alarmed awareness that one must not toil in isolation too far down a single path, that one could take a sudden turn and pass out of sight and be lost.

So he tells Jack that he'll be glad to listen; he tells him he has all the time in the world. "After all," Clifford says in a low voice, feeling guilty as he says it, "I do know what Janice is like, you know. I've known her for a very long time."

They've been talking for more than an hour, dancing around the subject, getting nowhere. Clifford has assumed that Jack is feeling smothered by Janice, that he can no longer placate her tremendous neediness, that he wants to withdraw from the relationship but doesn't quite know how to go about it. Yet Jack keeps wearing his puzzled frown, never meeting Clifford's eyes for more than a second or two. Clearly there's something more on his mind.

"I know that," Jack says. Then he adds, cryptically, "And I know why you broke up."

Despite the gravity of Jack's tone, or perhaps because of it, Clifford can't help laughing. He says, "We never 'broke up,' Jack. There was never anything but a friendship."

"A friendship?" Jack says blankly.

"Or a fiendship, as Janice once put it." Clifford laughs again.

"But do you mean, you never . . . ?"

"Oh yes, occasionally," Clifford says. Again he pauses, feeling that same scruple about betraying Janice, offering more than is really necessary. He says without mirth, "But it wasn't any good, really. We made love at her instigation, usually, and looking back on it, I think I did it out of some form of anger. Instead of making love, I was expressing anger. That's what really changed when I met Will. I'd had my share of one-night stands, and I'd had Janice, but I'd never really made love before. He taught me that."

A long silence. Clifford is stunned that he has said something so intimate to Jack, who is at least technically Janice's fiancé; but for the first time, he sees, Jack seems to have relaxed. He is sitting back in his chair, glancing around the room.

"You're really going through hell, aren't you?" he asks Clifford. "Listen, this little room is depressing, would you like to get out for a while? Have a drink, or some coffee?"

Clifford hesitates; waiting outside Will's room has become an addiction, and he fears that the moment he leaves Will's condition might immediately worsen; or else that he'll come out of his coma and ask for Clifford, and be told that his lover could not wait any longer and has gone away. But he pushes these thoughts aside as destructive and irrational. It will do him good, he thinks, to get out of here for a while, so he suggests to Jack that they go across the street to the Pleasant Peasant—actually he wouldn't mind a bit of decent food for a change. Once they're in the restaurant—which is packed and noisy, even though it's past ten o'clock—the grim severity of their earlier conversation dissolves, and they talk of ordinary, inconsequential things, as if entering into an unspoken pact that they need a break from the current stress in their lives. Clifford finds, somewhat to his surprise, that Jack is good company: affable and talkative, especially after a couple of glasses of wine, and surprisingly knowledgeable about contemporary art. As they near the end of the meal, Clifford begins to dread the idea of going back to the hospital, and says as much to Jack, who suggests that they have a nightcap somewhere else.

"A drink?" Clifford says doubtfully, glancing at his watch. "I don't know, I suppose I should get back—"

"But you live around here, don't you?" Jack asks. "Over in the Ponce?"

Clifford recoils slightly from Jack's urgent manner—somehow, in the last hour or so, Jack has become another person. He sits with his thick body jutted forward, his face flushed and perspiring, his forehead scored with deep lines that Clifford doesn't recall noticing before. Clifford sits erect and still, his finger crimping the edge of the tablecloth. Though he seldom drinks, he remembers a bottle of Remy Martin he'd bought for Will's birthday dinner, a couple of months ago; so he supposes he should invite Jack, find out what's troubling him, even though he'd much prefer that they ordered a brandy here so he could get back to the hospital. All through dinner Clifford kept seeing Will's face, a ghostly image flitting across his eyesight but somehow more real than this boisterous restaurant and the many patrons squeezing past their table, crisscrossing endlessly, and Jack's busy gesturing, talking, eating, just across the table; even sitting here Clifford had whispered to himself, as he did aloud each time he visited Will, "Please wake up! *Please!*" Yet the boy's face remained still, unchanging, rendered by the snakelike breathing tubes and drug-induced puffiness into someone beyond his power or sympathy, someone he no longer quite knew.

"All right, let's go," Clifford says, and the moment he speaks Jack grabs the check with one hand, his wallet with the other.

"I'll drive," Jack tells him.

For several years, Clifford has lived in a small one-bedroom on the ninth floor of a venerable old high-rise off Ponce de Leon; it's an address that combines a certain seedy glamor with a knowing, even "camp" sophistication, and has been tenanted for years, in roughly equal numbers, by elderly ladies whose residence dates from the building's opulent heyday and by very young people, mostly gay men and women involved in dance or theater, who shun ordinary singles apartments with their wall-to-wall carpeting and built-in appliances. This building, whose rents are amazingly cheap (perhaps because maintenance is all but nonexistent), boasts an ancient black doorman who seldom goes near the door, preferring to sit in a glass cubicle just off the dim-lit lobby, smiling toothlessly at all who enter as he sips from a brown paper bag; and a creaking elevator which often stops at floors where no one is waiting, a phenomenon an elderly neighbor of Clifford's ascribes to the ghosts of former residents. Most of the apartments, like Clifford's, have water-stained ceilings and clanking radiators and windows blurred by dust and time. Nonetheless the place has its charm—there are elaborately carved moldings, arched doorways, hardwood floors burnished by use to a rich golden-brown—and as Jack strides through the living room to the picture window he rubs his hands together and cries, "Hey, this is a great place!—you can see the whole city from up here."

"The view is pretty impressive," Clifford says, "but the last time they employed window washers, I believe, was before the stock-market crash."

Jack laughs, keeping his back to Clifford, elbows jutting out from his hips.

"Cognac?" Clifford asks.

"Sure, I'd love a drink," Jack says, and as Clifford goes back to the kitchen he can hear Jack following, his tread heavy and thudding, as if he's deliberately making his presence known. But to whom? Clifford wonders. He has been told many times that his own footfall is noiseless, and now he has a sudden memory of Janice Rungren, walking next to him down the main hallway of Pius XII Junior and Senior High and saying, her nose wrinkled in mock-disgust, that Clifford moves along like a cat, so nimble and clever that you had to keep your eye on him; otherwise he might suddenly dart away. Janice had laughed, pleased by her own fanciful notions. Like a mirage, she'd said, giving Clifford a sharp sideways glance. Like someone who had never been there at all.

"So," Jack says, "do you own this?" While Clifford pours their drinks, Jack stands to the side nervously, shifting his weight from foot to foot.

"No, it's an apartment," Clifford says. "But there's a rumor that the building is about to be sold and turned into condominiums. If that happens, all the little old ladies will have to leave. And I'll be leaving, too."

"Really, that's too bad," Jack says, glancing around the kitchen. "This is a great place," he says again, lamely.

Clifford leads them back into the living room, where they sit on the small oatmeal-colored sofa he'd bought from a couple down the hall. Almost all the objects in this apartment Clifford has acquired haphazardly, never quite getting around to actually shopping for furniture. Janice, visiting once or twice, said the place looked like a rummage shop with its antique cherrywood hutch, its gathering of Danish oak tables, its rattan chairs and battered rolltop desk, its lamps and pillows of various styles and sizes. Now he says, just to be saying something, "I guess you could call the decor . . . eclectic."

Jack laughs, swirling the cognac in his snifter. He takes a small sip every few seconds, puts the glass down on the coffee table, picks it up again.

"I like it," Jack says. "It's all your own, you know? It's all you."

"I'll take that as a compliment," Clifford laughs.

"No, really, I mean it," Jack says, turning sideways to face Clifford. "I mean, I got married right out of college—you knew that, didn't you?—so my wife handled the house and everything. It's been three years since the divorce, but the house is exactly the way she left it, and it has never really felt like home, you know? I wish she'd taken the house, instead of the money."

Here Jack pauses, and though Clifford realizes that he'd intended to make a joke, he can't quite bring himself to laugh. Again he hears that nervous edge to Jack's voice, as if his words were more important than they seemed.

Clifford says lightly, experimentally, "So now you and Janice can redecorate, right?"

Jack gives him a wounded look. He says, "I told you, I'm not sure about Janice and me . . ."

"Not sure?" Clifford says. "Sure about what?"

As Jack stares into his glass, which he has just emptied in one swift gulp, Clifford hears that the echo of his question is shrill and peremptory, almost as if he were parodying Janice, or somehow taking her place. Yet he has no desire to meddle in her and Jack's relationship, nor does he really care to become Jack's confidant. His first allegiance is to Janice, after all, and this is a bad time, as Jack had admitted, for Clifford to think about anything but Will; and the sudden discomfort he feels as he sits next to Jack, whose face now wears such a glum, hangdog look, forces Clifford to rise and stretch his arms and say, "Look, Jack, this isn't really my business—"

And yet, despite his unease, despite the images of Will's motionless eyelids and wasted body that keep haunting his vision, so that he can't focus exclusively on Jack, evidently can't provide whatever it is the man wants from him—despite all this Clifford isn't really surprised by what happens next. He has often thought that he's beyond surprise, that nothing any longer can startle or even much displease him, so it's the paralysis of inertia, or indifference, rather than horror or simple distaste that prevents his recoiling from

Jack, who has reached toward him in a fairly swift but dreamlike movement. Still sitting on the couch, he has drawn his arms around Clifford's legs and buttocks, almost knocking him off balance. Jack's body is trembling as he sits there, his face pressed against Clifford's stomach, his arms clenched around him tightly, so that Clifford can't help thinking that no one, not even Janice Rungren, has ever held him this desperately before.

Clifford stares down at Jack's dark-blond head, as though from a great distance. He murmurs, "Jack, you shouldn't—"

Now Jack stands, again in a movement that seems to Clifford dreamlike, inevitable, and he sees that Jack's face is wet but wears a childish blissful look, a look that says he has abandoned all but his terrible longing, and he takes Clifford's arm without speaking and leads him off to the bedroom, already pulling at his shirt buttons with one hand, at Clifford's belt with the other, even though Clifford keeps murmuring, "No, Jack, we can't do this, we've got to—"

"Be quiet," Jack whispers, keeping his cheek next to Clifford's, for which Clifford is grateful, as he can't bear that look on Jack's face, that complete abandonment and dazed unthinking insistence, "please," Jack says, "please be quiet. . . ."

So that when Clifford says (though he knows he's lying), "But it might not be safe, Jack, remember I'm Will's lover, how can you jeopardize . . ." even then Jack puts one palm over his mouth, mumbling what sounds like *I'll be careful* although Clifford knows at once that he won't be, really. Already he has eased Clifford back onto the bed and lowered his jeans and is sucking him, and of course Clifford was aroused before Jack even began and of course by now he can do nothing but lie back, his eyes shut, as someone appears to his mind's eye but not Will, or Janice: rather he sees the face of that young priest, Father Milliken, from so long ago. On those keenly anticipated Friday mornings Clifford would whisper *Bless me, Father,* not caring what happened next, and as he and Jack make love for the next hour, or two hours, Clifford understands that he is still open to whatever might happen next. Once or twice his own face is wet, his own body is trembling, and he feels with Jack—he almost tells him, but holds back at the last moment—that he has never felt so blessed or so afraid.

8

Clifford

It's ironic, Clifford supposes, that in the first months of their affair
they talk of little else but Janice. Playing racquet ball at the Colony
Square Athletic Club, which Jack coaxed Clifford into joining; taking
long walks through Piedmont Park or the Botanical Gardens; sitting
over drinks at Zasu's, Camille's, the Silver Grill—seldom does half
an hour pass without one of them mentioning Janice, glancing into
the other's eyes as if checking for signs of guilt, signs of strain. Both
men claim that their relationship with Janice hasn't really changed;
Jack still goes to her house for dinner on Fridays, they still sleep
together once or twice a week, and he insists that they're really
"better friends" than ever before, most likely because Jack himself
is so much happier now. As for Clifford, he hasn't spent much time
with Janice these past few years, but they still talk on the phone,
have an occasional Saturday lunch when Jack is tied up with one of
his construction projects, and he continues to be amazed by how
well she's doing, how strong and confident she seems, her former
wildness evident only in an occasional outrageous remark or raucous
laugh, or in the way she'll suddenly, perhaps impatiently, claw the

fingers of both hands back through her dark-blond hair, then shake her head as if dispelling bad thoughts or dreams. But really, both men are quick to add, she has never seemed happier in her life. The situation as it stands, they tell each other, is really best for all concerned.

There have been some sticky moments, of course, and Clifford berates himself (flagellates himself, he thinks dourly, wondering if maybe he hasn't retained that old Catholic guilt, after all) for the way he's handled them. At Christmastime, less than a month after Will's death on December second, he'd endured the loneliest and most vulnerable days of his life, acutely aware that he had few close friends: he'd begged off the usual party at his father and Miriam's house, and instead had impulsively called Jack and Janice. It was Christmas Eve, around 9:30, and they were in the midst of opening gifts; of course they insisted he come over, they had something for him, but when Clifford arrived he felt so awkward and out of place that he'd downed one glass of eggnog and opened his gift and departed. He hadn't failed to notice that Janice seemed truly happy to see him while Jack's smile was strained, a bit ragged—how well Clifford knew him, already!—and Clifford went home feeling hurt and ashamed, vowing never to make such a mistake again. But on Valentine's Day the mistake was Jack's: he'd stopped by Clifford's after work, with a bottle of Dom Perignon, and though Clifford supposed that Jack would be going directly to Janice's and would undoubtedly have to stop for another bottle of champagne, neither of them mentioned her name. They drank a glass, Jack impulsively embraced him in the kitchen, and within half an hour they were in Clifford's bed, their lovemaking more passionate than ever before. And that's when the phone rang.

Had Clifford spoken to Jack lately? Janice said shrilly, her voice audible to both men through the wires. It wasn't like him to be more than an hour late and she was worried, she was sick with worry, she knew they'd become friends lately and thought he might have spoken to him, or have some idea where he could be . . . ?

The questions were innocent, Clifford knew; there was no question of Janice suspecting anything. More than once, in fact, she'd said how pleased she was that Jack and Clifford got along—they'd told her about the racquet ball and Clifford's joining the health club, knowing she would approve—and had talked in her usual way of their being a "family" of sorts, of how much she wanted them to grow closer as time passed. Clifford had gripped the receiver, giving Jack a panicked look. The desperation in Janice's voice, the startled look in Jack's eyes, the blunt fact of the two of them here in bed, naked, perspiring, as they listened helplessly to Janice—all at once the situation seemed intolerable. Jack had showered and left quickly, muttering something about forgetting the time—he thought he'd told Janice 8:30, not 7:30—and hadn't even kissed Clifford good-bye. Clifford had stood quietly at the sink, the Dom Perignon bottle upended, watching the champagne swirl down the drain. He'd made several of the angry, guilt-ridden decisions that lovers often make— he wouldn't see Jack again, he'd move away from Atlanta, he'd write a letter to Janice confessing everything. He'd fallen into a miserable, soggy sleep and the next morning when Jack called and asked Clifford to meet him at the health club at six, Clifford said he'd be there. Neither of the men referred to the night before.

When Clifford and Janice have lunch together at Houston's, one bright cold Saturday in early March, he almost blurts the truth. That morning Janice invited him to help her shop for Jack's birthday, and despite Clifford's protests she insisted on buying Jack a gold Rolex, at a prestigious jewelry shop in Buckhead, though Clifford knew she couldn't afford the watch. "Oh hell, it's only money!" Janice cried happily. "So what if it takes five years to pay it off!" While they're eating lunch Clifford keeps trying to convince Janice to take the watch back, insisting that Jack won't be happy that she spent so much, that the gift is much too extravagant—it's inappropriate, in fact. She shouldn't feel that she has to—

"Inappropriate?" Janice says, a forkful of spinach salad paused in midair. Something in her eyes—a certain hardness that isn't like her—makes Clifford regret his words. And why *had* he been so insistent, after all? Was he really thinking of Janice?

"Well," he stammers, "I just meant—"

"For heaven's sake, Clifford, he's my *fiancé*, isn't he? So I don't see anything inappropriate."

"Okay, Janice, that was the wrong word," Clifford says. All at once he's nervous, guilty, ashamed—images of him and Jack in bed flit through his mind, as tends to happen at the most inopportune moments—and he's forced to catch his breath. "I just meant—it's just that Jack won't like it, Janice. You know how modest he is—he won't like a flashy watch like that, he's not into status symbols, and besides he knows you can't afford—"

But Janice has resumed her eating. "That's the problem, he's *too* modest. He deserves nice things like everyone else, and I want him to have them. Besides, I just got a big raise, didn't I tell you? Hell, I'm getting rich!"

She laughs, a bit loudly; people in the next booth look over. Janice had ordered a glass of wine before lunch, and now she's halfway through her second. Clifford says guiltily, knowing he's taking advantage of her exuberant mood, "I haven't heard you use that word in a while, *fiancé*. So things are still on, then?"

Again she stares at him; again her eyes seem to harden, though it's a look he can't really interpret. "Of course things are 'on,' " she says. "Things were never 'off,' you know."

"But I thought you said something, one day—"

"Oh, we have our little tiffs, like everybody else," she says airily. "They don't mean anything. I just had to learn, I guess, that Jack has his moods—sometimes he goes away for a while, emotionally, and I can't reach him. Once I resigned myself to that"—Janice snaps her fingers—"everything was fine."

Clifford puts down his fork; he's almost sickened by her false security and good cheer, and that's when he weakens, forms the words in his head and swerves perilously close to saying them, *Janice, there's something we need to talk about*—

Yet that would destroy everything, of course; not only for Janice, but for him as well. Jack has made clear that he will tell Janice, in his own way, when he feels the time is right. In the meantime, there's no reason for Clifford to worry, or feel guilty, or have the idea that he's betraying Janice. People fall in love, they fall out of love: sometimes with one another's friends. It's a fact of life, a fact of nature. These phrases in Jack's rushing complacent voice fill Clifford's head as he sits there. It's true that they talk of Janice constantly, obsessively, and Clifford has begun to feel that they both have an investment in keeping things as they are. Somehow Clifford can't imagine Jack committing himself fully to a gay relationship; can't imagine him, a well-liked man, a construction boss, a subject of feature stories on Atlanta's "singles scene," allowing himself to become the target of gossip or dislike. Nor can Clifford let himself off the hook. Sometimes in his most abandoned daydreams he imagines living with Jack, no longer having the safety of Janice's claims on his lover to keep that innermost part of Clifford free and inviolate, safe inside the circle of isolation he'd drawn around him throughout his life. But when he tries to imagine it, his mind blanks out, as has happened often lately when he tries to intuit his way into a new painting (for since beginning the affair with Jack, his artwork has suffered; in fact, it has come to a standstill). At such times he supposes that they're playing games, the three of them; that they're simply getting what they deserve. So why not tell Janice, after all? Why not let her see what is happening as clearly, at least, as Clifford himself sees it?

Now Janice is asking him, "Clifford, is something wrong? Is the food okay?"

"Yeah," he says quickly. "Yeah, it's fine."

"Listen, kid, if you're worried about that watch—"

"No, not at all. Really, I shouldn't have said anything. It's your money. It's your fiancé."

All at once Clifford laughs.

"Clifford . . . ?" Janice says, puzzled.

He puts down his fork; there is no question of eating anymore. He tells himself that he shouldn't see Janice for a while; perhaps he won't see Jack for a while, either.

"Sorry," he tells her, and he looks down quickly, feeling the tears starting in his eyes. "Please believe me," he mutters, "I'm really very, very sorry."

He looks in the mirror, denying what he sees. Eyes anguished, red-rimmed. A hollow look to his face, the cheeks pale and creased.

Is this love? he wonders. *Clifford Bannon, in love?*

It seems a mocking self-portrait, a parody of sorts. This isn't a face he dares to recognize.

*   *   *

One balmy evening in mid-April Clifford learns that Jack has had enough. They've been to the club, they've played an especially prolonged and strenuous game of racquet ball, neither man speaking for more than an hour, only straining, grunting, lunging madly for every point. It's the first time Clifford remembers truly wanting to win, though of course he never wins—Jack is far stronger and better coordinated than he—and he doesn't win tonight. After they've showered and dressed, Jack suggests they get a quick dinner at the Pleasant Peasant, his face solemn and downcast. Clifford feels a clenching sensation in his stomach; he knows what is coming. He says okay, fine, but only as they approach the restaurant does he remember that here they'd shared their first meal alone, and that across the street is the hospital where Will had died; the setting is appropriate, he supposes, for what is about to happen. Another milestone, Clifford thinks; another death. After their drinks arrive, Clifford sits with his hands folded, waiting.

After some preliminary stalling, Jack finally says, "It's gone from bad to worse, wouldn't you agree? We can't keep this up."

"No," Clifford says quietly. "I know it."

Jack talks in a droning, mechanical voice, as if he's been practicing his speech and it's already gotten stale; Clifford can't help feeling amazed at his own calm, his resignation. *Whatever happens, happens . . .* He sits docile as a schoolboy, ready for whatever penance he must endure.

"Somehow I thought I could keep them separate," Jack is saying, "I didn't think that the two—that the relationships necessarily conflicted with each other, since they affected me so differently. I told myself that I was bisexual, I guess, that I needed both and could be responsible to both. But it's obvious that I can't. In retrospect it seems ludicrous that I ever thought—I mean, in a way it's almost funny, you know? My dashing from your place to hers, juggling times and dates? A comedy of errors."

Clifford smiles thinly. "Someday, maybe. Someday it will be funny."

"Someday, right," Jack says nervously, glancing around him. The restaurant is crowded and noisy, there's no chance that anyone is listening, but nonetheless Jack looks frightened, even paranoid; more than anything Clifford wants to calm him. *It's all right,* Clifford would like to whisper, bending close; *you don't need to worry about me....*

"So I've decided," Jack says, hoarsely, "I've decided that I won't see Janice anymore. That I just *can't*."

Clifford stares.

"Wait a minute, what are you——"

Now Jack bends close, his blue eyes damp with emotion. "I can't play the hypocrite, not anymore," he says. "It's not fair to you. Or to Janice, either."

Clifford sits paralyzed, in shock; only his heart seems alive, pounding wildly.

"What do you— I don't understand——"

Just then the waiter arrives to take their order. As he recites the menu Clifford tries to compose himself, not once glancing at Jack. The moment the waiter stops, Jack orders his meal quickly, brusquely, and Clifford says he'll have the same. Now they do look at each other. Clifford sees that Jack is uneasy, as though fearful of Clifford's reaction.

Clifford says, trying to smile, "I guess you have the advantage," he says. "The advantage of surprise."

"Surprise?" Jack says, bewildered. "Do you mean . . ."

"I thought—I thought it would go the other way," Clifford says awkwardly. "Christ, I don't know how to talk about these things.... What about the other week, in that bar? You said you couldn't stand it. You said you felt like someone from another planet."

Clifford had taken Jack to Back Street, one of the largest gay dance bars, on a Saturday night; he remembers their standing at the edge of the dance floor and watching the hundreds of gyrating men, most of them in jeans and tank shirts, many of them naked above the waist. Jack had been wearing khakis and a crisply starched shirt, his usual conservative attire; but even more anomalous had been the look of stunned disbelief on his face, his paleness that had been noticeable despite the roving, multicolored strobe lights and the viscous dark surrounding them on all sides. They'd gone back upstairs, to a quieter part of the bar, where they had one beer together but said very little; they'd left within half an hour.

"That's a separate issue," Jack says now. "I don't spend time in bars, straight or gay. That had nothing to do with you."

"But what about your—your self-image?" Clifford says, again groping for words. "I mean, aren't you afraid . . ."

"That people will find out? Maybe, but that's my problem, not yours. I'll have to take these things as they come. I can't just run away."

"But how will Janice react?" Clifford says. "Do you think she'll just accept—"

"Look, what's going on?" Jack says angrily, jutting his body forward across the table. "Are you saying that *you* want out—"

"I'm not saying anything," Clifford says, his own voice raised. "But I'm not sure that you've thought this through."

"Maybe not, but I've *felt* it through. Have you?"

Stung, Clifford stares at him. Into this silence the waiter intrudes, delivering the food, asking in a hesitant voice if they'd like another drink . . . . ?

"Yes, please," Clifford and Jack say, at the same moment. Both men lift their forks and begin to eat.

Janice's reaction, in fact, is what surprises him most; for she doesn't react at all. Jack had broken off their relationship the day after his and Clifford's dinner at the Pleasant Peasant and had reported to Clifford that she took the news very well; there had been a few protests, a few tears, but in the end she'd behaved maturely, as Jack had known she would.

"You might not know it, but Janice is a rather proud person," Jack says. "And she's quite strong, too. She's been through a lot."

"I know that," Clifford says, trying not to show his irritation. "I've been through most of it with her."

Then he wishes he hadn't spoken: he'd never told Jack much about his and Janice's school days, and certainly not about their attempt to run away, the car accident, the lost baby. And he's fairly sure that Janice hasn't told.

Wanting to face the music, to get it over with, he calls Janice a few days later and makes a lunch date, and to his surprise her voice sounds normal; she says the lunch is a good idea, since she has "something to tell him." It's only then that Clifford understands. Jack had broken off with Janice, yes, but hadn't told her why. He'd very considerately left that to Clifford.

"It wasn't my place," Jack says defensively. "You two have been friends since the third grade, so I thought *you'd* want to tell her——"

"So it will look as if I've come between you, rather than you making an independent decision. Very brave of you, Jack."

"All right, damn it, then we'll both tell her. Together. Maybe that's the best way, anyhow. Get everything on the table all at once."

"No," Clifford says, "then she'll feel we're ganging up on her. I'll do it, but don't you think we should have discussed this first?"

"I guess so," Jack says. "There's just been so much confusion that I——"

"It's all right," Clifford says impatiently. "I said I'd do it."

They conduct this mild argument in Clifford's bed, of all places, and as they talk it's in the back of Clifford's mind that an argument might kill their desire, might cause one or both of them to roll over on his pillow, refusing to say any more. But there had been little anger in their words, and in any case their togetherness is new enough, and exciting enough, to supersede all obstacles; so Clifford isn't surprised when Jack reaches both arms around his waist and pulls him close. The hardness of Jack's body, and its intense male heat, are still capable of astonishing Clifford, making him light-headed with desire. Without much preamble Jack wants to enter him, not taking the time for any lubricant, and despite himself Clifford cries out in pain.

Jack pauses, arched over him. "Cliff?" he says. "Do you mind . . . ?"

Clifford is holding onto Jack's waist, and now he urges him downward, grimacing. "No," he whispers, his eyes closed. "You should know by now——I'm not the type who minds."

Yet Clifford never meets with Janice, since the next day Janice cancels the lunch, saying breathlessly to Clifford over the phone that she's at work, she can't talk right now, but she really needs to see Jack that day—she hopes he doesn't mind, but as Clifford might already know they've been having some problems and they really need to talk, she and Jack, they need to try and iron things out, she hopes Clifford understands and won't misinterpret—

Clifford says no, of course not; he understands completely. When he hangs up with Janice his first thought, of course, is to call Jack, but the impulse passes quickly. It's likely, he knows, that Jack is giving him and Janice two very different versions of what he wants, who he is; Clifford understands that the situation hasn't stabilized at all. Lately there have been stray, renegade moments when he wonders if his and Janice's involvement with Jack isn't some roundabout way for them to deal with one another, if it isn't still *Clifford and Janice, Janice and Clifford,* as the taunting singsong had gone in their grade school days. He spends long hours sitting in his rented midtown studio, trying to work, but inevitably he lets his eyes drift to the window, thinking of Jack one moment with passion and longing, with what he supposes must be love; the next moment wondering if he isn't fooling them both, playing some elaborate sick game at Jack's expense. And Janice's, of course. He should be relieved, he supposes, that she canceled the lunch. He'd have undoubtedly been awkward, inarticulate; she'd have undoubtedly flown into a rage. He's never felt less in control of himself, never had less idea of what he should do. This is one of those rare times in his life, he tells himself, when he can do nothing but hope for the best, hold tight, and brace himself for the ride.

It doesn't help matters that Jack's way of coping with all the craziness has been to grow more intense, playing the role of the besotted lover; he now phones Clifford not once but four or five times each day, usually just to "say hello," to ask how Clifford's work is going, to tell him once again what time he'll be "home" that evening. For Jack has begun spending almost every night at Clifford's place. Even though his own house is much larger and better-furnished, Jack whispers into Clifford's ear that he hates that place, it reminds him of his past life, his false life, and he can't go back to that; it won't be long, he supposes, before he puts the house on the market.

Clifford can't quite pinpoint the moment when Jack began making references to their owning a house together one day, perhaps one of the older homes in Virginia-Highlands that they could fix up themselves, or else Jack could build them a new house, complete with a studio for Clifford, perhaps they should go ahead and speak to an architect, start thinking about a location. . . . Clifford's response to all this talk has been evasive and noncommittal. There are evenings when he finds himself wishing guiltily that Jack would not come over, for despite his long and mostly idle days in the rented studio, he feels the need for more time to himself, time to think, to sort all this out; he does not understand himself, cannot interpret the mingling of joy and dread he feels when the telephone rings, when he hears Jack's confident thudding footsteps outside his apartment door. He'd never guessed how intense a lover Jack could become, that his virile competent exterior had concealed such voracious need; nor had he supposed that Jack would give himself to Clifford so fully, unreservedly, nor that such an intelligent man as Jack could keep himself unaware, with the blindness of any lover, that Clifford was still holding back, the essential kernel of himself still inviolate, ungiven. Lately when Jack whispers harshly against Clifford's throat, *I love you, you know that, don't you,* he no longer waits that eerily suspended moment for a response. Evidently he needs to say the words, Clifford supposes, more than he needs to hear them.

And every morning Clifford returns to his studio, doggedly, mechanically, opening the sketch pad on his desk, arranging a blank canvas on the easel, knowing that almost certainly nothing will happen, that his mind has turned as blank and opaque and ungiving as the canvas itself. Recently he'd been tremendously moved by a book of photographs, done by a local artist, of several AIDS patients and their families, and to fill the time he holds the book on his lap and does quick sketches of those gaunt male faces, their bewildered mothers hovering in the background; but even these sketches have nothing of Clifford in them, they're simply bad copies of the photographs, and in disgust Clifford rips each sketch in half the moment he completes it. He would like to do some artwork on the subject, but he tries not to think about AIDS, since that leads to thinking about Will; nor is it a subject he cares to contemplate in relation to himself and Jack. They had a brief, embarrassed conversation early in their affair, Clifford feeling it essential to remind Jack that Will did die of AIDS, after all, and though Will and Clifford's lovemaking had been, so far as Clifford knew, of the "safe" variety, he hadn't been tested and so could not be entirely sure. He'd supposed that Jack would ask him to take the test, and he'd decided in advance that he would comply; but Jack hadn't shown much concern. "If you think we're safe, that's good enough for me," Jack had said. Clifford had responded, "And of course there's Janice, and anyone else ..." "There isn't anyone else," Jack had said, annoyed. "Nor will there be."

And so the subject was dropped. Only in recent weeks, reading accounts of new research, has Clifford become aware that he really should be tested, that the disease is spreading at a previously unsuspected rate, that it might not be as "difficult to acquire," after all, as the early reports had suggested; but still he has put it off. Last fall he'd had enough of doctors and hospitals to last him a lifetime. And lately, in any case, he can't bring himself to care. Lately, he has come slowly to understand, he is becoming depressed, in a "settled" way that becomes more uncomfortable with each passing week.

One afternoon in early May, having gone through the book of photographs yet another time, he sits sketching at his desk for a while, idly, yet feels so completely soulless and detached from his work that he stops and allows the charcoal pencil simply to fall from his fingers. He gets up, stretches, and goes for a long walk down Piedmont Avenue, passing by the park (he has no interest in entering the park, all that is long behind him), and when he finally arrives home he sees that the light on his answering machine is blinking. There's a message from Jack, saying he may be a bit late tonight, but it's Friday so why don't they plan on a movie, and then Clifford hears Janice's voice, that ragged voice of old, telling Clifford that she needs to talk to him, that Jack has canceled their Friday night dinner and she's afraid they've reached a "crisis" in their relationship, did he have any free time this evening, did he want to stop by for dinner, or ... Janice paused too long and the machine must have cut her off, for he hears Jack's voice again, saying he won't be late, after all, and if Clifford is finished at the studio maybe they can go to the gym, then try to catch that movie, and he ends the message with a cheerful *See ya!* so Clifford thinks that's all the messages but no, there's one more, and of course it's Janice again, and of course she's been crying, he hears his own name, "Clifford, Clifford, are you there? If you are, please pick up, I've got to——" and though there's more, clearly there's more, Clifford snaps off the machine.

He glances at his watch: 5:45, and Jack had said he'd be here by six. Clifford goes into the bathroom, brushes his teeth, stares at his eyes in the mirror and understands that he must leave. Impulsively he goes to the telephone and calls Pete, who answers on the first ring. Would Pete mind, Clifford asks, feigning a casual tone, if Clifford came over for a while? Perhaps they could go out for dinner, take in a movie . . . ? And Pete says fine, fine, he'd been thinking about Clifford all day—worrying about him—and had no plans for dinner, no plans for the evening at all.

So Clifford goes. And they have a drink or two, chatting about nothing in particular—an amusing feud between two managers, both women, where Pete works, a story Pete tells rather waggishly, his plump cheeks flushed after two glasses of burgundy wine—and then they decide on a restaurant in Ansley Square. After just a couple of hours in Pete's company Clifford feels better, and asks himself why he doesn't seek out his uncle more often: Pete is his only relative, after all, with whom he can be entirely open, entirely himself. In an odd way, his comfort with Pete resembles that he'd experienced with Will: he'd found the company of both men somehow soothing, nonthreatening. Halfway through their meal, when Pete excuses himself to visit the restroom, Clifford allows his mind to wander back to Will, though in recent weeks he'd so rigorously avoided thoughts of his former lover: the choirboy's face, the mischievous grin, the full-throated laugh all return to him in a rush, bringing a fist-sized lump of sorrow into Clifford's throat that threatens to choke him. Will had loved him spontaneously, freely, completely, almost from the moment they met, and for the first time in his life Clifford had not felt the need to run away; had felt himself deliberately staying, settling in, a responding love already glowing inside him, coming to life slowly and cautiously, perhaps, but coming alive all the same. The full abandonment of his passion had begun only three weeks before Will's diagnosis, after which he felt himself careening wildly, like a driverless car headed out over a precipice; and he supposes that this, now, is the free fall, churning into an unknowable future with no one to guide him. Certainly Jack cannot guide him; they've merely been keeping each other company—he sees it now, bleakly— as they flail together in their separate confusions. How could they pretend to help one another, to "love" one another? All this runs through Clifford's mind as he half-listens to Pete, and soon enough Pete understands that his nephew is troubled, that this is more than a social evening. After the waiter brings their check Pete reaches out and takes hold of Clifford's wrist, gripping him so hard that Clifford winces in pain.

"Pete . . . ?"

"Listen, Clifford," his uncle says, "I know there's something wrong, and I wish you would—"

"It's Will," Clifford says quickly. He grabs the check and stares at it.

"Of course, that's understandable," Pete says, nodding vigor- ously, "even though it's been six months, these things take time, it's not easy to get over—"

"Listen, do you want to go somewhere?" Clifford says. "You know, for a drink?"

"Of course," Pete says, "whatever you—" And already Clifford is rising, having laid a couple of twenties on top of the check. Once they're in Pete's car, Pete says he knows a little place not far away, right in the heart of Ansley—maybe Clifford has been there? But the place is new to Clifford: a small, dimly lit bar with a fireplace, a few wooden tables and booths. The decor is vaguely medieval: a suit of armor at the entrance, a row of ancient-looking tankards along the mantelpiece. Clifford and Pete sit at a table not far from the bar, and as Clifford glances around he's aware that most of the patrons are either men like Pete, in their fifties and sixties, or else very young men who might not be out of their teens. Most of the men, young and old, are alone, though there are several desultory conversations in progress, an occasional laugh or exclamation audible through the tinkling piano music—a recording, Clifford supposes, since there is no piano in sight. Almost every patron holds a cigarette,

and the smoke hangs thickly all through the bar, though it's scarcely
nine o'clock. Clifford finds the place seedy, depressing, and when he
looks back to his uncle, Pete gives him a questioning smile.

"Nice place, Pete," he says grimly.

Pete shrugs his shoulders. "It's fun, once in a while. You know,
when you just want to get away."

"You come here?" Clifford says, surprised. "I mean, by
yourself?"

"Sure, sometimes," Pete says, glancing down. Clifford sees that
he has embarrassed his uncle. "You meet, you know, some nice kids
here. Some of them are down on their luck, but—"

Pete doesn't seem to know how to finish this thought. Clifford
can scarcely believe that Pete doesn't know the young kids are
hustlers, out to make a buck off the older guys, and suddenly he
wonders if Pete . . . but he doesn't pursue the thought. They order
a couple of brandies, and Clifford dreads the moment when Pete
will resume, inevitably, their conversation from the restaurant: for
he doesn't want to talk about Will, doesn't want to dredge up the
anger and sorrow and stunned disbelief of those terrible weeks last
fall. When his uncle finally lowers his voice, as he does when speaking of serious matters, it's Pete who looks sorrowful and confiding,
his eyes cast downward as he swirls his brandy idly inside the snifter.

"Remember, I've lost several friends myself," Pete says somberly. "None of them lovers, of course, but all good friends. One of
them I'd known for more than twenty years."

"Was it recent, Pete? I meant to ask you . . ."

"You were dealing with your own loss," Pete says. "But yes,
last year was pretty severe, the first one came in February, when a
fellow I know from work . . ." Pete continues in his mournful, slightly
monotonous voice, seldom meeting Clifford's eyes, but Clifford feels
his own attention wandering: not because he doesn't want to hear
this, but for some reason he's fascinated by the row of men at the
bar, the scattering of men at the tables and booths. The older ones
are much like Pete: balding, a bit overweight, wearing sport shirts
and polyester slacks. There's something so vulnerable about them—
their wisps of white hair combed over scalps as pink as a baby's,
the rolls of soft fat protruding over their belt lines. Their eagerness

to laugh. Their incessant smoking. Almost all the men, either in groups or singly, are talking to hustlers, and of course these younger men are dressed in muscle shirts and jeans. They talk in low rumbling voices and don't smile much, but they're all smoking, too, and downing beer after beer. Though the older men are fastidiously groomed, the hustlers look vaguely unkempt, as if they haven't bathed for a while. As Clifford watches, one particularly obese man of about sixty rises unsteadily from his bar stool, supported on one side by a hustler wearing a purple tie-dyed undershirt and a baseball cap. From under the cap his greasy blond hair sticks down in spikes, but Clifford sees that his skin is smooth, hairless, and he sees the small hard satisfied grin on the kid's face as he helps the older man down off his stool. This peculiar couple hobbles to the door, and just before exiting the older man lifts one pudgy hand in a wave and calls out, "Ta-ta!" to his friends at the bar, but without looking around. Neither does the hustler look around. Then the pair is gone. No one at the bar said "Ta-ta!" in return, or even seems to take much notice.

Clifford looks back at his uncle, who is talking about the horrible final sufferings of a friend of his. The brandy Clifford had been drinking seems to churn inside his stomach, and all at once he's afraid he'll be sick: he's not accustomed to hard liquor, or to smoky airless bars like this one. He'd like to suggest to Pete that they leave, but a look of contentment has come over Pete's face during his droning monologue, almost a kind of serenity, and so Clifford hasn't the heart: he supposes that Pete has as few friends as Clifford himself and that perhaps he needs to talk. Nonetheless Clifford feels ill. He shifts his feet under the table, he taps his fingers on the side of his glass. Next time the waiter passes, he'll order some club soda, and a slice of lemon. . . . At a nearby table he now sees another man, though the man isn't much older than Clifford himself, lean drunkenly to the boy next to him, a grubby-looking kid in a black T-shirt and cutoffs, and kiss him sloppily on the mouth. Clifford watches in repelled fascination as the older man's tongue probes the kid's mouth, licks along the top lip, then the bottom lip, as all the while the man laughs to himself, idly. (The hustler isn't laughing or smiling; Clifford sees that he is barely tolerating this, his eyes open and vacant-looking.) Clifford wants to stand up and shout, What the hell are you doing, you guys! Do you want to fucking die! Do you—

At that moment Pete reaches across the table, exactly as he'd done in the restaurant, and grips Clifford's hand.

"Clifford?" he says. "Are you . . . ?"

"These people must be crazy," Clifford says, his stomach roiling, "don't they know what they're doing to themselves?"

Pete quickly glances around them, as though he hadn't noticed before. He focuses on the kissing couple at the next table.

"Listen, don't worry," he says to Clifford, "it doesn't go much further. They buy the kids some beer, they exchange a few kisses—believe me, people know better than to go much further than that."

Clifford remembers the pair who'd left a few minutes before, but he says nothing. He supposes there's nothing to say. Now Clifford stands, shakily. He says to Pete, "Um, this might not be such a good idea, I think I ate something that didn't agree with—"

"My God, Clifford," Pete cries, "you look as white as this tablecloth! Shouldn't you sit down? Maybe put your head between—"

"Yeah, we'll leave in a minute," Clifford says. "I'll go to the men's room, okay?—and then we'll leave."

Clifford lurches from the table, hoping his uncle will not follow. Just around the corner, outside the restroom door, there's a small vestibule with a phone and cigarette machine, and off to the side there's another door cracked open. Clifford sees that the door leads to the outside—he can smell the fresh night air—and feels a powerful urge to flee. He remembers some bar he'd gone to, long ago, when he'd fled out the door . . . but he can't hold on to the memory. Of course, he can't abandon Pete like this. So he pushes the men's room door and stumbles inside. Standing above the sink, he contemplates his face in the mirror: ashen, a stubble of whiskers along his jaw, the eyes as vacant as any hustler's. He takes deep breaths, hoping that his stomach will begin heaving, that he'll be able to throw up; but nothing. He stands waiting for several minutes, his hands clenched on the sink. *No one to guide him,* he thinks helplessly. *No one . . .* He remembers how comfortably he'd once scorned Janice Rungren for her frequent inability to control her life, her roller-coaster emotions, her seeming need for self-destruction; now the tables have turned, he thinks. Now it is Clifford Bannon who feels consumed with need, voracious and raw, indiscriminate, now it is Clifford Bannon's life that has careened out of control. . . . Trying to breathe evenly, one breath at a time, one moment at a time, Clifford feels inside the pocket of his jeans. There's some change, there are several quarters, so he backs away from the sink, not glancing again into the mirror, and shoulders his way out of the restroom. In the vestibule, he approaches the phone and puts a quarter in the slot.

"Hello, Jack? Hello . . . ?"

Yet his ears are ringing, he feels faint; he can scarcely hear the other man's voice, his lover's voice, coming back at him through the wires.

"Jack?" he says, interrupting. "Jack, listen, I think I'd better hang up, all right? I think we've got a bad connection."

He can still hear that faraway voice—a bit louder now, more frantic—so he hangs up the phone. He goes to the cracked-open door and stands there, breathing quietly, wanting some of that fresh night air inside his lungs. After a few minutes, he does feel better; he turns and goes back inside the bar to find his uncle.

J a n i c e

"Tell me the story," she whispers, "of the Adam's apple."

"I beg your pardon? Young lady . . . ?"

"Don't you know, there's some story connected with it," she says, her voice rising, quaking, "don't you know the story, aren't you guys supposed to know everything?"

"Young lady, I really don't—"

"Something got stuck there, right in the throat, you know, like a bobbing apple—and it wouldn't come out, it wouldn't budge—and he was—he was choking—"

She has choices, Janice tells herself, it's 5 P.M. on a Saturday, it's the last day of May, she guesses—or the first of June?—but she knows roughly what day it is, roughly where she is, she'd tapped the cabbie's shoulder maybe a bit too hard and said, "Here! Let me off here." That was one choice, and now she must make another. Must get her head clear, she thinks vaguely, must stop asking idiotic questions of this man, must apologize quickly, make her escape, get away. . . . A mistake to come here, surely, quite a laughable mistake!——but at least the choice was her own.

"It's my life," she whispers, as though the priest were arguing with her. "It's my decision, and I'll do whatever I——"

Childish, she sounds so childish. She stands, wobbling in the dark. Bangs her leg against something, turns the wrong way and walks into solid brick instead of the thick velvet curtain——

"Ow! Goddamn it!"

"Young lady"——his voice turned weary, defeated, just like Father Culhane's back in parochial school——"young lady, please . . ."

On the wall hangs a small crucifix, ghostly blue.

I know how you feel, she thinks, as she rubs her throbbing knee.

"I know how you must feel," Jack had said an hour before, tonelessly.

"Do you? *Do* you?"

Jack possessed infinite patience, in arguing as in lovemaking; already they'd "discussed" the matter for more than an hour. Nothing she said would ruffle him, much less send him flying off in a rage. Maybe they'd sit side by side, on these stools in this uptown yuppie bar where they are the only patrons this sunny afternoon, forever and ever.

Their version of hell. But *theirs.*

A bar? You want to meet in a bar? any other man would have protested, but even though she'd wakened him and had shrieked into the phone Jack hadn't argued, her handsome logical Jack hadn't even paused to consider.

"Okay, fine," he'd said. "What time?"

Yes, she'd made the choice to arrive at one o'clock though she'd told him two; she drank Chardonnay steadily during that hour and smoked ten or twelve cigarettes and avoided her reflection in the mirror behind the bar. Puffy eyes, she knew. And she hadn't used lipstick, her cheeks were pale, and her roots were showing like hell. She'd snapped at the bartender once or twice—she didn't want idle conversation—and then each time he refilled her wine, word-lessly, she smiled at him the moment he glanced away. When Jack finally arrived she was ready to kill.

An ice-blue sweatshirt, new-looking jeans, his hair still wet from the shower: he drank Perrier and listened attentively. Spoke, when it was his turn to speak, politely. Expressed his regret, his sympathy, his understanding, keeping his lips pursed in a thoughtful grimace. More than once Janice imagined what he must be thinking: how lucky for him that he'd broken off things last month, before getting this news; how that absolved him from all blame (a word she was careful not to use), and allowed him to go his merry way, scot free. By his reckoning, in any case. Although, to do him justice, he *had* agreed to meet her here, even though they'd agreed on "no contact" for six months. He'd responded to the urgency in her voice, evidently, to the plea that something had happened, something she'd never have predicted—she supposed he must have guessed, by then. She supposed that, driving over, he must have carefully reviewed his options, charted his course of action. By the time he arrived, she wasn't sure why she had felt it so important that they meet, but she liked to think that she wasn't vengeful: that she hadn't wanted merely to see him sweat.

In any case, he wasn't sweating.

"When we first met, if I remember, I asked if you used any-thing—"

His voice timorous. Not placing blame, the tone said, just trying to sort things out.

"And I said yes, didn't I?"

"Well, I seem to *remember* your saying yes—"

Where did her jokiness come from, today of all days? "But I don't use birth control," she said, "I'm a Catholic," and that did get his attention: he threw her a quick sideways glance, a testing glance. She smiled. He smiled. Then her smile vanished and his eyes swerved away.

Jack swallowed, mightily. That's when she noticed his Adam's apple, bobbing above the round sweatshirt collar.

He tilted his Perrier bottle this way, that way. Smallish hands, well-shaped, deft. Absolutely clean.

On and on they droned, Janice trying to keep calm, Jack trying to understand, claiming he *did* understand, both of them using words like *freedom* and *responsibility* and *relationship*. Especially *freedom*. Helplessly Janice drank wine, it seemed to calm the howling void inside, it seemed to make bearable the patient, logical tone of Jack's voice— and the vision she kept having of Jack walking out of here, anonymous and free and sober as a church—and the sight of his Adam's apple that, as he talked, kept bobbing, bobbing.

But not bearable, surely, the shapeless clump of cells, deep in her belly. Bobbing and bobbing, near weightless. But *there*.

Then, at a certain point, the choice to remain calm no longer made sense. Why submit herself to him, anyway? To his way of doing things?

She'd submitted enough, these past two years.

But when she said for the first time, shrilly, "*Do* you," Jack surprised her by signaling the bartender, who approached Jack with a look of sympathy and brotherhood: "Sir?" he said. And Jack requested the check. And turned to Janice, his ruddy face glowing, his eyes sharpened to a sudden bright blue. "All right," he said, "then maybe I don't understand. After all."

As Janice watched he put money on the bar.

As Janice watched he walked out, both hands in his jeans, opening the door with a shoulder turned sideways as though to fend off the world; and his posture was so odd, somehow so humbled and solitary-looking, that she understood she'd hurt him, really hurt him, and that she didn't know him at all. And he was gone.

Now she should be gone, too, but of course the priest comes after her. Follows as she quicksteps through the vestibule, not stumbling a bit, her heels clicking. Follows halfway down the church steps, into the still-brilliant spring afternoon.

"Is there nothing I can do?" he cries after her, and he sounds so pathetic that she stops and turns, no longer feeling drunk or even particularly unhappy. She climbs a few steps and looks into the priest's face, which is round and puzzled and amazingly young.

"It's nothing," she says, squinting against the sun-brightened pale stone of the church, her splayed hand keeping her hair from the brisk wind, "it's just that I—I've been upset about missing Easter with my parents, they had invited me and I—well, I wanted to go but they live in another state, and to be honest the idea of Easter doesn't mean that much to me. . . ."

It occurs to her that she is lying rather badly but that, after all, maybe she isn't lying, for her mother had written her this year, and Janice had considered going home. Yet the thought of shopping with her mother for new Easter dresses and how uncomfortable she would feel, how hypocritical—somehow the idea had seemed impossible, once again; and once again she'd scrawled a note to her mother, declining, making some excuse. (Five years, she thinks, since her last visit home. Maybe six years.) And now, as the priest listens patiently, nodding, evidently believing everything this rather haggard-looking young woman says, she suddenly remembers about the Adam's apple: some story the nuns had told them, long ago, of how Adam had eaten of the forbidden fruit but then, as he swallowed, it had turned to ashes. He'd begun choking, he hadn't been able to get the ashes down, and for the rest of human history men suffered this protuberance in their throats, this obstacle, stuck there like some kind of reminder, Janice supposes. Some kind of taunt.

A silly story, she thinks, disgusted. And so typical.

"Every Saturday from five to seven," the priest is saying. "I'm always here. Always."

"Thank you, Father," Janice says, backing away. "That's really good to know."

It was pointless, she thinks, to visit the confessional; almost as pointless as phoning Jack had been. Since getting the news on Thursday morning, she hasn't known where to turn. The first person she'd telephoned, oddly enough, had been Clifford, but she'd canceled the lunch date soon after making it, for she could imagine how uncomfortable Clifford would be with the idea of *a baby,* considering their own past history. So she'd canceled the lunch and had gone to work on Friday, as usual, impersonating her usual brisk efficient self, her "new" self: for it had begun to seem that all the progress she'd made in the past few years has been canceled, all her success at work, her relative stability, her feeling that she has reached, at last, some hard-earned plateau where she might keep her balance, more or less; that somehow she'd been impersonating a successful adult person, all along, while deep inside she remained that stumbling mischievous little girl, that bad girl Janice Rungren, who had been biding her time, simply waiting—and rather cleverly, as always—to reemerge. She remembers what Belinda Comstock had said, that time: *Remember, don't get complacent. When you start congratulating yourself on your progress, life has a way of sending a bulldozer straight toward you....* And yes, here it was, lumbering toward her; she supposed she was lucky that she *could* still work, still function, despite this turbulent ache of emptiness she'd begun to feel, paradoxically, at the pit of her belly since the moment she learned of the pregnancy.

It was true that she'd become careless about taking the pills at some point, she supposes around the time she began sensing Jack's restlessness, his lack of focus—though this hadn't, of course, been a conscious decision. She'd have despised such a tactic in another woman, and had no intention of trying to entangle Jack by getting herself pregnant; the very idea disgusted her. Thus her dismay, in retrospect, to suppose that she'd been doing exactly that, on some unconscious level, and by Friday afternoon her confused desperation had been such that she'd phoned Clifford again, leaving that incoherent message on his answering machine that she now deeply regrets—for she doesn't want Clifford, any longer, to see this side of her, to think that she's anything but fully mature, and fully in control of her life—and then, at last, she'd called Belinda Comstock. And she'd wondered: why hadn't she phoned Belinda in the first place? Why, when "salvation" seemed required, did she think solely in terms of men?

Yet the conversation with Belinda hadn't gone well, and in fact they'd quarreled for the first time in all their years of friendship. The moment Belinda answered Janice felt the tears welling in her throat, her eyes, Belinda's husky soothing voice was such a godsend, but after Janice blurted out the facts she'd been shocked when Belinda paused, for several long seconds, and then bluntly asked, "Well, Janice, what did you expect?"

"What, Belinda? I don't understand—"

"What did you expect would happen," Belinda said, her exasperation audible through the receiver, "after getting involved with
yet another withholding male? Did you think he'd come rushing
over, with flowers and a marriage license? Really, Janice, I thought
you'd learned a few things."

"Wait a minute," Janice said, angry and baffled, "I never said
that. I'm just trying to understand why—why I allowed myself to
get pregnant. That's all."

Belinda snorted with laughter. "Oh, is that all? But that's quite
a lot, isn't it? To allow yourself to get pregnant, without quite
knowing it?"

"Wait a minute, Bel, hold on," and Janice had detached the
receiver from her ear; had taken a few deep breaths. Then she'd
decided to change the subject, to get off this perilous course, and
after a few guarded moments Belinda did confess that she'd had
Graham committed, at last, that the past few weeks had been the
most hellish of her life, and yes, perhaps she was taking her difficult-
ies out on Janice, "projecting" onto her; and she was sorry about
that. But still there had been no words of comfort, no commiseration
with Janice's plight. Near the end of the conversation, Belinda had
mumbled something about "the abortion" as though it were a settled
fact, had offered Janice the name of a clinic, whenever she was
ready, and Janice had said, "Thanks," rather bleakly. The idea of an
abortion panicked her, and she knew at once that she *wasn't* ready,
and again had wanted to change the subject. "I guess I should talk
to Jack, then," she said, hoping at least for a word from Belinda,
some sign of approval, but Belinda had only said, wearily, "I suppose
so, if you think it'll do any good. But he can't wave a magic wand,
Janice, any more than I can."

"A magic wand?" Janice repeated.

"He can't save you, Janice. Only you can do that."

So they'd hung up, both women feeling sorrowful, both angry;
neither had mentioned "getting together" soon, as they invariably
did when they talked on the phone, and Janice regretted, the moment
she heard the dial tone, that she hadn't said a last word about
Graham, wished him and Belinda well, offered to help in any way
she could. Yet Belinda hadn't offered to help her, after all. *Only you*

can do that came the words in her friend's tired voice, and Janice knew that the phrase—a mere cliché? a profound and terrible truth?—would echo in her mind, tormenting her, like the taunts of her classmates when she was a child, or some withering remark by one of the nuns. It's true that in the confessional, on that interminable Saturday, still dazed from her glasses of wine and her meandering, inconclusive discussion with Jack, she'd wanted the priest to come out of his cubicle and enter hers, put his arms around her as though she were a small child, tell her that everything would work out, that she wasn't a bad girl, that no wrong had been committed that couldn't be rectified. So when she leaves the church and goes to a corner phone and calls another taxi, she feels that she can't go home, that nothing is settled, and for half an hour she tells the driver simply to wander the streets, she needs to think, there's a big tip for him if he'll simply drive, drive, and not ask too many questions. He smells the liquor on her breath, evidently, for he says he'll need twenty dollars, the meter is already approaching that and he's been stiffed twice this week, so she reaches in her purse and gives him fifty dollars: "Here, now will you please just drive?" But at that moment she knows what she must do, and so she leans forward again and gives him Jack's address. "The change is for you," she says, "but just get me there. Get me there fast, all right?"

For she feels, all at once, that she knows what she is doing. Perhaps Belinda's harsh comment had been what she needed, after all; she simply needs to take her destiny in her own hands. Her sense of resolve fills her with elation, fills even that void in her belly, and she knows that she must simply tell Jack that everything is fine, that the news was a shock but she is recovered now, and she knows what she must do. She doesn't blame him, she will say. She doesn't hold him responsible. Perhaps she'll have an abortion, or perhaps— who knows?—she'll decide to have the baby, but in any case that's a separate issue from their relationship, which she understands is severed, at least for the time being. Does he understand? Is there anything he wants to ask her, or that she can do for him . . . ?

Her fantasy is somewhat improbable, of course, for she can't quite picture such forbearance, such near-saintly behavior, but really she does want to prove something, to demonstrate her self-

sufficiency. Less for Jack's sake, perhaps, than for her own. So when
the taxi pulls into Jack's driveway she takes a deep breath, as she
did on that morning before her First Holy Communion, as she did
the first time she and Clifford made love, as she does each time she
must fire someone down at the office; and she gives the driver a
hectic smile and cries out, "Thanks!" And the driver, looking
stunned, still with the money in his hand, merely stares after her.

She decides not to knock; it had become a convention of their
romance that neither of them knocked at the other's door, they'd
been too close for that, too intimate. She breezes into the foyer and
living room with that overly bright smile still plastered on her face
and yells out, "Yoo-hoo! Hello!" Her voice echoes through the large
well-furnished rooms. But no response. She goes out to the kitchen
and checks the door to the garage: his pale-gray Nissan is there. Of
course he's home, she's thinking, or else the front door wouldn't
have been unlocked, so now she hurries to the base of the stairway
and cranes her neck upward: "Hello, Jack? It's me!"

Now she does hear something. A muffled voice. Or voices.
She's halfway up the stairs when she sees Jack come out into the
loft area, shirtless, fiddling with his belt buckle. He looks both startled and chagrined, his face settling quickly into a scowl. It takes a
moment, a short moment, before Janice understands; before her heart
begins hammering coldly in her chest.

"Jack?" she says, feebly. "Did I—did I wake you—?"

"No, you didn't wake me," he snaps. "What are you doing
here?"

She knows him well, she can see in his face that he doesn't
know how to react. Invite her to have a drink? Throw her out? She
waits on the landing, her face twisted upward, her eyes focused
beyond Jack's bare shoulder on the half-open bedroom door.

"I came—I came to talk—"

"You should have called first," he says, and now he succumbs
to his true reaction: simple weariness. His shoulders slump, he speaks
faintly as though knowing his words are pointless. For Janice isn't
listening, really. She has kept her gaze fixed just beyond his shoulder,
and it stays there for several seconds after Clifford Bannon, also
shirtless, walks out the bedroom door and stands beside Jack.

A moment passes. An eternity passes. While Janice stares the two men murmur a few words to one another, and Clifford returns to the bedroom for his shirt, bringing one for Jack when he comes out again, and after donning the shirts they start downstairs, each taking one of her elbows when they reach the landing. All the way down, and out into the kitchen, they're mumbling into Janice's ear, but of course she cannot listen. She sits numbly at the kitchen table as Jack makes them all a drink, and while he works there are more blurred exchanges between Jack and Clifford, who has also sat down at the table. Evidently some of the words are addressed to her, but she cannot hear. Only as she manages to get some of the cold stinging liquid (a martini, she later learns) down her throat, and only after Jack is also seated, the three of them ranged around the glass-topped kitchen table in Jack's lovely breakfast room with its big bay window and hanging ferns—only then does Janice manage to focus on what anyone is saying. And that's because Clifford reaches across the table, very slowly, and takes one of her hands. Begins massaging her knuckles. Looks tenderly into her eyes.

"Hello, Janice?" he says, leaning forward. "Honey, do you think we could have a little talk?"

Hours lying in bed, dry-mouthed, unmoving. Mucous caked along her lips, her eyes bone-dry, seared. Light spills along the ceiling and brightens, then slowly fades. She rises for a glass of water, she gets a slice of bread from the kitchen, tearing the moldy crusts away with numbed fingers and stuffing the rest in her mouth, she visits the bathroom where her body functions implacably, despite her, and where she takes long tepid baths and no longer avoids looking in the mirror. *Janice Rungren, what has happened to. Janice Rungren, how could she possibly* . . . She returns to bed and watches the ceiling, the windows. Brightening. Fading. While days pass. Weeks. Or is it years, decades . . . Then, one day, at the brightest moment of the afternoon that always causes a spasm in both her eyelids, an infernal twitching, a cloud intervenes far beyond her own drawn curtain and the room dims, darkens. Startled, Janice emits something like laughter. A little croak. She feels a pang of disappointment, but she rises and showers briskly and gets dressed and fries herself two eggs. She stares at the eggs that for a moment seem to stare back, protuberant yellow eyes, possibly malevolent, but she croaks again and lifts her fork. Eats.

Certainly the worst, and really the only major depression of her life. For a couple of weeks she'd called in "sick" to the office, thinking that after nine years of perfect attendance she'd surely earned a reserve of goodwill, but she'd stopped calling after the miscarriage, her depression deepening, plunging her ever downward, never mind that the doctor said she should be "grateful," since the abortion she'd planned could have been much more traumatic than anything she'd endured thus far. Eventually her boss, who didn't know about the miscarriage, who hadn't known about the pregnancy to begin with, had called with bewildered but solicitous queries, to which Janice gave monosyllabic replies. Later she'd received written queries, then warnings, then probation, and during the past couple of weeks—which had been the worst time, a period of near-total debilitation during which Janice hadn't been able to answer the phone—she had received no letters from her employer at all.

The pink slip will arrive any day, she supposes, though when she finally plays the answering machine tape she hopes that each beep might bring her boss's brusque, gravelly voice. But no. Instead the machine had recorded four calls from her mother, whose voice sounded cheerful in the first two messages, then snippy, then whining; two from her gynecologist's office, first suggesting and then insisting that Janice's follow-up was past due; one from Belinda Comstock, who apologized for her "bad behavior" and hoped they could get together soon; one from her cousin Ruthie—that is, Sister Barbara—who usually called only at Christmas and Easter and whose bright, rambling, incoherent message had puzzled and exhausted Janice; several hang-ups, which for some reason she ascribed to Clifford Bannon, who had kept his distance ever since that fateful Saturday at Jack's house; and then—of course it was the last message—a few words from Jack himself, *Just called to see how you're doing,* his voice subdued, chastened, and he had paused as though to add something and Janice had waited a heart-stopping moment before the machine clicked, the dial tone hummed.

She rewound the tape; twisted the dial to OFF.

. . . She buys groceries, she cleans her house, she scans the
newspaper and circles the office jobs, double-circles the ones involv-
ing supervisory duties. Thirty-two years old, she thinks, recalling
those old Mary Tyler Moore shows, *You're gonna make it, after all,* and
she laughs her new, throaty laugh, her croaking laugh—for she
smokes more and more these days, but she will stop as soon as she
gets another job, gets her life back in order; she laughs that she'd
ever thought herself anything like Mary. Starting with the blue-veiled
statue down at her hometown church Mary had been a good girl's
name, the name of someone who made it to heaven or at least onto
TV, and Janice was, well, only herself. Yet she told herself that the
depression hadn't lasted long, after all, that surely she *had* made
progress in her life, that this whole situation was only a mere brief
stumble; or would seem so, in retrospect. Once she had regained
perspective. Yes, she felt the grown-up Janice Rungren returning
already, a resurrection announced by that odd croaking laugh she'd
emitted on the day she rose from bed. . . . Immediately after the
miscarriage, after all, she understood what she'd been reaching for
with Jack's baby, how she hadn't wanted to punish him but had
merely hoped it might turn her into someone else, some kind of
grotesque madonna appearing in the university hospital's maternity
ward, with her frosted hair and mint-green eyeshadow, her long thin
pale body (the breasts small, surely dry) that had endured all the
parties, the sleepless nights, exposure of all kinds—but of course
that hadn't happened, she'd gotten only a bloody mess for all her
daydreams, her fantasies, and her doctor had approached her bed
the next day with that pseudo-cheerful expression . . . and so, now,
she'd lost her one ghost of a chance, someone like Janice would not
be giving birth, someone had seen to that.

"Can I try again?" Janice had asked the doctor, that first morning. "Will I be able to . . . ?"

"We'll see," the doctor said quickly, edging away.

As for the depression that followed, that was "to be expected,"
the doctor tells her. And "understandable," Jack says. And "something we all go through, at some point," her mother insists, confusing
her own menopausal blues of some years ago with what has happened
to Janice. They all understand, of course, why she didn't return the

calls. They wish they could have done something, if only they had known. Janice whispers the appropriate thanks, yes things are much better now, yes she got the first job she applied for—my old boss gave me a great recommendation, he was so glad to get rid of me, she laughs—and no she doesn't feel depressed any longer, she's *not* suicidal, there's no danger of that, no danger.

I just need a little peace and quiet, she tells them. A little time to think.

"Okay, but don't *brood,*" Jack says, and she flinches because during these first weeks of her "recovery" she's been brooding quite a bit, thinking back to her first years in Atlanta, that college boy Dirk and his fraternity parties and the vast throbbing headaches she would endure on Sunday mornings, half-remembering the night before. She thought of her "disco years" and the faceless men she couldn't even half recall, the dozens of strange apartments she'd traipsed through, the dozens of men who traipsed through hers, her mother's endless letters and the few embarrassed visits home, eating more food than she wanted and being dragged to Sunday mass and hearing all about relatives she scarcely remembered, except for "Ruthie," as Janice's mother still called her, nostalgically, "dear Ruthie." And her resumption, brave or foolish, of friendship with Clifford Bannon, which coincided with the years with Jack—those hopeful, frantic, despairing, tender years—that had wrung her inside out, finally. Literally. And so here she was, "recovered," she supposed—but yes, brooding.

"Well," she says, still jokey despite all that has happened, "better brooding than breeding, right? For a girl like me?"

Startled, Jack laughs. Then quickly changes the subject.

9

Janice

She almost misses Ruthie's call, for she spends most of that evening at her friend Laurel's place downstairs. Though Janice doesn't drink much anymore, they do have a glass of burgundy, then another; Janice knows that Laurel already had several before she arrived. Less than a year ago, Laurel's husband left her and their infant son, Buster, just two days after telling Laurel that he was having an affair. She moved into these apartments to save money, and also because she hated the idea of living alone in a house and thought she could stand to meet a few new people. She was determined to look toward the future, and now it's a standing joke between her and Janice that they waste all their time together mulling over the past.

This very night, in fact, they spend nearly two hours going through Laurel's photograph albums, which amaze Janice because they're so complete, so carefully ordered. Laurel's whole life is here. She's a south Georgia farm girl, tanned and lean despite the baby, and something of a tomboy (she wears jeans and boots, and doesn't bother much with makeup or her hair), and Janice is continually surprised by her capacity for sentiment, a deep and boundless vulnerability in Laurel's tawny-brown eyes that frightens Janice just a little. In his photographs Laurel's ex-husband looks like a cad—dark mustache, narrowed scowl—and Janice tells her so. Laurel gives her braying laugh, squinching her eyes shut.

" 'Cad' is too polite," Laurel says, "for what *he* was."

Lately it has occurred to Janice that she'd like to spend a bit less time with Laurel—almost every evening, she arrives home to at least one message from Laurel on her machine—but she does like her, and knows that this particular type of loneliness can drive a person nuts; and in the last few years Janice has started to believe, informally, in the idea of karma. If she's good to Laurel now, maybe she'll have someone around the next time *her* life screws up, the kind of friend she didn't have—unfairly, she can't help thinking—when she suffered the breakup with Jack and everything that followed.

But Janice tries not to think any longer in terms of what is fair, what is unfair; she credits this attitude for enabling her to see Clifford Bannon occasionally, and even Jack himself, without any upsurge of her old jealousy and rage. (It helps, of course, that the two men severed their own relationship soon after Janice discovered them, on that terrible afternoon at Jack's house; and that Jack remains uninvolved with anyone else.) So Janice isn't angry, she isn't bitter, and though her current job, managing a small suburban branch of an accounting firm, pays about half of what she'd be making if she hadn't broken down and lost her former position—a cut in salary which forced her to sell her house and move into this apartment in the Emory area—nonetheless she's not unhappy. Most of the other apartment residents, like Laurel, are much younger than Janice, and they make her feel young, too. On the few occasions when she's invited to Jack's house for cocktails, or to a companionable lunch with Clifford, she tends to feel older, less energetic, and to think too much about the past. Despite the jokes she shares with Laurel, she really would like to focus on the future, even though she has sensed herself living day by day, has felt that her life has begun slowing down, stalling; "the future" is a concept she still can't quite imagine.

"How about 'deadbeat,' then?" Janice asks, smiling. She worries about the way Laurel overreacts to everything, laughing hysterically at Janice's jokes and weeping openly when some song comes on the radio that recalls her lost husband. She worries about Buster, too, who had his first birthday last month and spends a lot of time staring dolefully at his mother.

"How about bum, dirty rotten bum?" Laurel says, still laughing, touching Janice's forearm. "Hey, how about another glass of wine?"

But Janice says, "Wait, I'll go up and get *my* album," though she doesn't have an album, of course, only an old shoebox stuffed with pictures dating back two decades or more. And it's while she's back upstairs, at the rear of her bedroom closet pawing through stacks of old boxes, bundled letters, and other junk she hasn't touched in years, that the phone begins ringing. She decides not to answer, for it's probably Laurel wanting nothing at all, saying to hurry up—but then, after the beep, she hears that timid, breathless voice, still familiar after all this time.

Janice stumbles out of the closet and snatches the phone.

"Ruthie? Is that you?"

"Janice, thank goodness, I didn't think you—"

"My God, Ruthie," Janice says, not quite understanding her own excitement, "you sound so close, are you here in town? Are you *here?*"

Within half an hour Janice has phoned down to Laurel and begged off, has gathered up newspapers and soiled clothing and towels and thrust them out of sight, has freshened her makeup and brushed her coarse mane of hair and changed three times, into a dress that seemed too provocative and then one that seemed too demure and finally into an ordinary yellow sundress with spaghetti straps, though Janice hasn't sunbathed since the early part of the summer. Does she look too pale, too washed out? And why is she so jumpy? She'd felt so calm and peaceful down at Laurel's; she doesn't know, really, why a visit from Ruthie should make her nervous.

Their last meeting was two years ago, and she remembers Ruthie's dim blue gaze behind the regulation convent eyeglasses, rimless octagons just like the nuns wore back in grade school, and her shy smile from where she sat on the floor, on the other side of the Rungrens' great flocked Christmas tree, dumpy but sweet in her "modern" navy-blue habit that made her look, Janice thought, like a meter maid, a bit stern, a bit hopeless. She'd been flanked by Uncle Jake and Aunt Lila in identical armchairs on either side, and a few times she'd smiled vaguely across at Janice (who was playing Santa Claus this year, handing out gifts with a roll of her eyes, making droll remarks that kept everyone laughing), but they hadn't spoken much. They really *had* lost touch except for occasional phone calls during which Janice would strain to hear Ruthie's vague rushing words all the way from south Texas, but somehow Ruthie was part of her past, too, the voice was fading, she could scarcely listen at all. . . . So she's nervous, yes, and to calm herself she takes the box of old photographs to the dining room table, thinking she might as well glance through them; but the moment she sits down the doorbell rings.

Exclamations—of course. Hugs and kisses—the usual. But who is this person, is this her cousin Ruthie, that little girl in bobby sox who had a shrine to St. Francis in her bedroom closet and who had collected holy cards the way other girls collected pictures of Paul McCartney or the Stones? Janice is a grown-up now and manages not to appear shocked, *not* to let her mouth hang open as she watches Ruthie cross the room in bright yellow flipflops, white short shorts only a shade lighter than her doughy pale legs, a black halter top spotted with Day-Glo patches in yellow, lime green, bright pink. Janice catches only a glimpse of the face—also pale and doughy, but lurid with makeup, dark lipstick and rouge, and paint smeared on the eyelids—and of the fine auburn hair frizzed up around the forehead and ears: catches only a glimpse because Ruthie herself is clearly nervous, hurrying inside the apartment and exclaiming over Janice's ordinary furniture, over the boxlike and nondescript rooms which are virtually identical to every other apartment in the university area, and continuing to look everywhere but at Janice.

"Oh look, look at these!" Ruthie cries, in the dining alcove now. She takes up a handful of the snapshots and quickly sorts through them, laughing and mumbling vaguely.

From the door, her hand still on the knob, Janice says in an amazed clear voice: "Ruthie?"

And Ruthie turns, letting the pictures drop. And Janice creeps forward, stopping about five feet away.

They stare at each other.

"Ruthie," Janice says, "what on earth . . . ?"

Blushing, Ruthie says in a brittle voice, "I've left the order, Janice. But I didn't think *you'd* be surprised."

"What? What did you——"

"You look wonderful, Janice," and Ruthie lowers her eyes in the old way. In shyness. In admiration.

Except now the eyelids are brilliant with turquoise paint.

For a couple of hours they sit at the dining room table, Ruthie doing most of the talking, answering Janice's questions as best she can. Yes, she's thought it over carefully, she's been thinking of little else for the past several months. Yes, she'll miss teaching the kids, but that's probably the only thing she'll miss, and she can still teach again someday, can't she? As a lay person? No, the priests weren't particularly awful, and the Mother Superior was all right, it's just that she couldn't talk to them, most of them were elderly and they'd grown up in another time, another world, she hadn't anyone to *talk* to, really, no one her own age. "Although," she says, faltering, "there was someone, to be honest . . ." Then Ruthie's head slumps forward, her white shoulders are trembling, and as Janice watches in horror her cousin begins to sob.

"Ruthie, what is it, can you tell me?" Janice says, alarmed, but the sobs are soul-deep, heaving, it's clear she won't be stopping for a while. For half an hour, as it turns out, and all that time Janice tries to console her, gives her cookies and hot tea, brings Kleenex for the tears and smeared makeup; and as the tears subside she urges Ruthie gently to talk, *talk*. And finally the story comes out. Piecemeal. In fits and starts. Rubbing her bruised-looking eyes Ruthie talks about a friend of hers in the convent, Sister Beatrice, whom everyone called "Bea," a cheerful and carefree woman—or so Ruthie had thought—whom everybody loved. In her mid-forties, Bea taught girls' P.E. at the school, she organized the annual field day, she played vigorously on the auditorium piano and conducted uproarious sing-alongs with the students and the other nuns; she was a tall brisk outgoing ruddy-complected woman, always smiling, liked by everyone. Especially by Ruthie, it seemed, for the two had become fast friends. "Particular friends," as the Church used to call it, frowning on anything that took attention away from Christ, but this was a relatively liberal order, and there'd even been a room change so that Ruthie's and Bea's were adjoining. And this wonderful friendship, which began shortly after Ruthie arrived in San Antonio four years ago, had truly changed Ruthie's life.

Bea took an interest in her, Ruthie said, in a way nobody else ever had. Every day they walked the half-mile from school to the convent together, they spent their Saturday "free time" having long talks about their past lives, their families, their childhood dreams, and how Bea had poked and prodded, wanting to hear everything, everything!—as if each tiniest detail were fascinating, even though Ruthie knew otherwise, she knew what a boring life she'd led. "And she heard all about you," Ruthie says, "she took quite an interest in *you,*" but before Janice can respond Ruthie adds, "For some reason Bea *cared,* you know?" (And does Ruthie give her a quick resentful look, or is Janice just imagining this?) "Naturally," Ruthie says, "when I started thinking about—about the decision, the big decision—well, naturally I wanted her advice, wanted to know if *she'd* ever considered—"

Again Ruthie's eyes fill with tears.

"Tell me, honey," Janice says gently. "Come on."

"Well, I—I wasn't prepared for her reaction, not at all," Ruthie says, gulping, patting her eyes and cheeks with the wadded Kleenex. "It was late one night when the others were asleep, and I'd gone into her room on some pretext or other. She was already in her nightgown and I think she'd been kneeling beside the bed, I think she'd been praying . . . for all her high spirits, you know, Bea was one of the most devout nuns, one of the truly pious. It was easy to forget that about her, and I guess that's why she—why she reacted the way she did. Anyway, I tried to tell her as honestly as I could what I'd been thinking, that somehow this life didn't make sense anymore, had lost its meaning, especially since I found myself disagreeing with the Church about so many things. I remember how my heart was pounding, since I'd never dared to say such things out loud before. But I knew I could trust Bea. . . . And she did listen,

for a while. She heard me out. But then—then she got up from
where she'd been sitting, on the side of the bed, got up in that
abrupt way she had and began pacing around the room. Her face
had flushed and her hands were jerking around, like they were being
worked by strings. And Janice, she—she—"

"Yes, baby? Go on." (Though Janice is wishing, by now, that
she would stop. Is wishing she'd never lifted the receiver at the
sound of Ruthie's voice.)

"She lost her temper, Janice. Became completely furious and
enraged, and started screeching at me, at the top of her voice. 'You
little ingrate!' she said. 'You simpering little coward!' And there were
other names, Janice, awful names, and for all I know they're accurate,
for all I know she's right, absolutely *right*. . . . She said she'd always
known about me, deep down inside. That my vocation wasn't really
strong, that I wasn't serious about Christ, that I wasn't a serious
person—she'd wanted to believe that demure little façade of mine,
that I was really as sweet and kind as I looked, but of course she'd
known the truth all along. And then, all at once, she started screaming—her voice was so loud, like a man's voice, the one she uses to
scold the kids out on the playground. She said, 'Well, are you just
going to stand there? Don't you have anything to *say* for yourself?'
I didn't know what to do, so I just backed away, I backed into the
hall and heard several other doors closing softly, and I knew I was
lost then, I knew I was doomed, and so . . . and so that very night
I packed my bags and left, Janice. Just walked out, without a word
to Mother Superior or anyone. Fortunately the school term had just
ended, so maybe none of the parishioners will have to know, maybe
they'll hush it up . . . but I just keep thinking about Bea, Janice,
wondering how she could have spoken to me that way, why she
couldn't understand. . . ."

Coolly Janice gazes at Ruthie's frizzed hair, at the soiled little
face contorted in grief and wonder.

"Because she was crazy," Janice says softly. "Because she was
a crazy repressed lesbian bitch, Ruthie honey, can't you see that?"

Now Ruthie stands, abruptly. The blood has drained from her
face, so that her smeared eyes and crimson lips make her look faintly
ghoulish, faintly monstrous.

"Where's the bathroom?" she says in a tiny, dignified voice. "Please show me the bathroom *now*."

Ruthie stays gone a long time, and while she waits Janice sifts through the box of photographs, idly. For some reason she isn't surprised by Ruthie's story, nor does she feel angry or afraid. She lifts the photographs out of the box, one by one. She sees Janice in the late sixties, a flowered dress, the blond hair long and straight, her arms held out wide as though to embrace the photographer, her lips spread in a bright mindless grin. Crucify me! she thinks, snorting. Impossible to reenter that girl's head, or even to remember the boyfriend's name (Ronnie? Randy?—she recalls a hooded gaze, a dark-toned murmuring along her throat). She sees Janice years ago, home for Thanksgiving, sitting next to her mother in the breakfast nook, their smiles beleaguered and strained; she supposes her father had stopped to fiddle with the camera setting, he never takes pictures when people are ready and so the smiles he gets are always beleaguered and strained. She sees Janice and Jack at the beach, that summer of their first bright passion, Janice's hair bleached the whitish blond of her childhood years, her smile truly radiant, her body terrific, her arm wrapped possessively around Jack's waist, Jack's body also terrific, nothing in the background but water and a whitish-blue sky and a whitish light covering everything. She can't remember who took the picture because, just then, no one else mattered.

She lets the picture drop from her fingers and abruptly starts plowing through the photographs. *No one else mattered. . . .* That wasn't true, of course, but for the first time in her life she realizes that she has no picture of Clifford Bannon, either by himself or with her; she supposes he's in those old yearbooks from Pius and St. John Bosco, but those are still in her room back home, boxed away. She remembers asking Clifford in high school about his family, didn't he have any pictures of his mother, his baby brother who died so soon after being born . . . ? He hadn't seemed to resent the questions but had said, "No, definitely not," and she remembers some stray remark, too, that he'd made not long ago about his father's new family, how awkward he felt going over there at Thanksgiving or Christmas, how he always tried to "duck out before the picture taking starts." Janice feels that stabbing sensation in her belly that has tormented her, on and off, throughout her life, most recently when she watched her friend Laurel and her little boy. She supposes it's sentimental if not downright foolish that she still longs for a baby, that she can imagine Janice Rungren pregnant, giving birth, being a mother ... even an unwed mother, she really wouldn't mind. It would make up for everything, she likes to imagine, even for the emptiness she feels when she allows herself to remember that time with Jack, those thirty-one months that flew by so quickly, or to consider that despite her checkered but ongoing friendship with Clifford there isn't a single snapshot of them together, not the tiniest keepsake or memento. Or to feel certain that he wanted it that way, and that he had detached Janice from himself, off and on, as resolutely as he'd removed all signs of his mother and baby brother from his life. Thinking this, Janice feels a chill down her arms and legs. She rubs her arms, briskly; she recrosses her legs and turns back to the photographs.

She sees herself and Ruthie as teenagers, a snapshot taken at school with Janice dressed wildly, looking bored, and Ruthie dressed plainly, looking thrilled. Behind them, that familiar redbrick wall of the Pius XII school building. Janice bends closely to peer into her own teenaged eyes, which are narrowed almost to slits, knowing, shrewd, angry, pathetic. *Impossible to reenter* ... She sees her parents on their wedding day, anonymous and happy and doomed as they stand behind a wedding cake bearing a miniature replica of themselves on the top layer. For the rest of their lives, Janice thinks, they will stand perched on top of that cake, smiling pointlessly, but where is Janice at the moment this picture is taken, exactly where? Now Janice looks down at her own flat stomach. Will I have another chance? she'd asked the doctor, a catch in her voice, but what had the doctor said? Anyway Janice hadn't trusted him, and she vows to seek out a new gynecologist, find out once and for all; she's thirty-six now, so there aren't that many years left. And why should the resolve strike her now, of all times? Sitting here looking at these pictures, waiting for her cousin to stop being sick and come out of the bathroom and tell Janice all about her new plans, her new life? But it's so simple, really. *A baby* ... Yes, she thinks, amazed at her own calm certainty. Yes, definitely a baby.

She stares at a blurry Polaroid of herself and Ted Golden, with Ted Golden looking bearish, smiling, while Janice looks skinny and drained. She sees a picture of her mother as a little girl, clutching a porcelain doll, her eyes filled with hurt. She sees Janice six months ago, snapped unawares by Laurel as Janice stood frying eggs one Sunday morning, wearing her old pink housecoat with the fingernail polish stains down the front. My God, Janice thinks, these pictures are so mixed up! Mixed hopelessly together! . . . She sees Janice on the morning of her First Holy Communion, long silky hair brushed lovingly by her mother and cousin, matching patent leather purse in one hand, white leather missal clutched in the other, a little girl smiling in bliss just before the ceremony, her soul bright as a new coin.

Janice Rungren, have you heard what she . . . is it true that she . . . how could she possibly, how dare she . . .

Janice Rungren, whatever became of . . .

Janice thinks, Good question!—and she goes back to see about Ruthie.

Things aren't, Ruthie insists, quite as bad as they seem. The worst part, she insists, is practically over. It's been nearly three months, after all, and she has spent most of the summer at her parents' lake house, just resting and recuperating, and her parents have been really wonderful throughout the whole ordeal. The three of them had sat down and decided to tell no one, not even Janice's parents, they would wait . . . wait until Ruthie had decided what to "do" with her life, exactly . . . wait for this awful "transition period" to be over. Wait for her "new life," whatever that might be, to begin.

They are sitting in Janice's bedroom, cross-legged on the bed with a bag of walnut chocolate-chip cookies beside them, and a quart of milk, just like the old days when they would stay up talking after one of Janice's dates. And Ruthie looks so much better!—she has washed her face, put on a nightgown (her few possessions, it turned out, were stuffed in the back of a rented car outside of Janice's building: there were only a couple of small bags and some books and a sackful of the garish new clothes and makeup Ruthie had purchased just yesterday, right here in Atlanta), and she is wearing her old rimless spectacles again. Yesterday she'd gotten fitted for contact lenses and had worn them today, but evidently the weeping had irritated her eyes, or the makeup had, anyway it felt so good to have them *out*.

"But I do love the new contacts," Ruthie adds. "They're blue-tinted, did you notice how *blue* my eyes were?"

"Yes," Janice says, amused. "I noticed."

Now Ruthie seems entirely recovered, she stuffs one cookie after another in her mouth and tells Janice about her plans. She has been driving for several days, she says, and is on her way to Florida. "In fact," Ruthie says, "I almost didn't call, I've been in Atlanta for two days, staying in a little motel not far from here. . . . I'd pick up the phone, put it down. Pick it up, put it down. But the truth is, I'm going down to Florida. I'm planning to live down there for a while."

"Florida?" Janice says blankly. Her cousin might have said "Mars." "But why Florida?"

"A friend of mine, who left the order some time ago, two years ago in fact—she lives down there, right in Miami Beach. She was working in a souvenir shop, where they sell shells and things, and now she's a part-owner and said I could have a job if I ever decided to leave. I mean, it's only minimum wage, but it's more than I've *been* getting, right?"

Ruthie giggles.

"That sounds—it sounds wonderful," Janice says feebly.

"Oh Janice!" Ruthie cries in a pleased voice, "you sound just like your mother!"

This strikes Janice like a blow; she has just been thinking, with some alarm, that Ruthie sounded like Janice herself, or the way Janice still thinks of herself. Carefree, flippant, jokey. The old Janice.

"All right," Janice says. "Your plan sounds a little goofy, Sister Barbara."

"There, that's more like it!" Ruthie cries. She seems elated.

"But Ruthie, have you thought about—"

"I'm tired of thinking," Ruthie says, her voice edgy but determined, "and I'm tired of talking about poor little me. What about you, Janice? How is *your* life going?"

And for another hour, they talk about Janice. For a brief peril-ous moment Janice thinks of truly confiding in Ruthie, telling her of the thoughts she's been having lately about a baby, even about the vow she made earlier this evening, as she pored over those old photographs; but she catches herself in time and claims that her life is ordinary, just like her job and her apartment, that she dates ordinary men, usually men she meets at work, that sometimes she fears that she's stalled, getting nowhere, but at others she's grateful for the lazy formless calm of her life. She doesn't feel the need to prove anything, she's no longer particularly rebellious, so why not enjoy this peculiar state of affairs for as long as it lasts? They laugh, shaking their heads. "I guess you think I'm a bit foolish," Ruthie says, coloring, "to have worn those clothes and makeup, this hairdo I got just this morning. . . . But I—I wanted you to like me," she says shyly, "and I guess I thought you'd still be—well, kind of wild. I guess I've always wanted to be like you."

Janice nods, mock-thoughtful. "Maybe Sister Beatrice wasn't so crazy," she says. "Maybe you *have* gone to the devil."

Ruthie laughs, giddily. And stuffs another cookie in her mouth.

Janice insists that Ruthie take the bedroom, and Janice will stretch out on the living room couch. Ruthie is too exhausted to argue, and soon the apartment is dark, and Janice drifts into a light, patchy sleep. She has a brief dream about her mother, who is holding her black miniature poodle, Sheba, and screeching at Janice for neglecting her, for failing to write, for not visiting, does Janice know the heartache she and her father have endured all these years, silently, and never once complaining? Janice wakes, confused. Her heart pounding. Yes, of course she must call her mother. Yes, of course the dream was outrageous and her mother would never behave that way, she hasn't raised her voice in twenty years, but still Janice must place that call. . . . She has another dream, also brief, in which she is walking down the aisle in a wedding dress, the same dress her mother wore. They are walking toward a familiar-looking man in vestments—is it Father Culhane?—and Janice feels happy, very happy. This is the happiest day of her life. She reaches the altar and turns to the figure next to her, who is wearing a black tuxedo, also happy, smiling happily, and Janice sees that her bridegroom is . . . her bridegroom is her friend Laurel, her short dark tomboy's hair neatly parted, her eyes tawny-bright as she gazes at Janice. Behind them the organ music swells and Father Culhane steps forward and Janice wakes, startled. Sweating. This always happens, she thinks, when she sleeps in an unfamiliar place, she doesn't sleep well and has bizarre dreams and then drags herself through the next day. Doesn't she have a dusty old container of Valium in the medicine cabinet, shouldn't she get up and— Yet a moment later, she's dreaming again. She sees a sky full of cherubs, small infants, looking down upon a field of smoke and fire, dancing flames that make Janice's eyelids twitch. She's trying to keep her gaze trained upward, she's entranced by all the beautiful infants, fluttering, so pink and fat and dainty, but she can't ignore the sound of human voices down below, groaning, crying out, she hears teeth grinding together in consummate agony and so she looks back into that darksome sphere of smoke, flame, writhing shadows. . . . Again Janice wakes. Her eyes opened wide, blinking. God, she's getting tired of this. Perhaps she should take something, after all— But now she waits, cocking her head. What is that sound? What *is* she hearing?

A moment later she's off the sofa, hurrying back toward the bedroom. That low, persistent groaning—it's Ruthie, her cousin, not some stray voice from her dream. When she reaches the door, she hears Ruthie crying out, clearly in great distress.

Janice flips on the light.

"No!" Ruthie cries. "Turn it off!"

So she turns it off, after a glimpse of Ruthie lying with a cloth over her eyes, propped against pillows, her face dead-white.

"Ruthie, what is it?" Janice whispers fiercely. She feels her way toward the bed, bangs her knee against the dresser, then the bedframe. Finally she sits down, finding Ruthie's hands.

"Honey? Did you have a bad dream . . . ?"

Ruthie is moaning. "It's my—my eyes," she says, "something happened to my eyes, it's like they're on fire, like someone is sticking needles into my eyes, oh my God, my *God* . . ."

Janice winces. She says softly, "Oh dear," for at once she understands. The contact lenses.

"Ruthie, how long did you wear your contacts? How long?"

"What? Well, all day, I guess. Since about ten this morning."

"And you just got them today?" Janice cries. "This is your first day? Honey, didn't they tell you to break them in slowly? Ruthie?"

"What?—oh my God, Janice, it hurts so much—no, they didn't tell me, it was a discount place, I think the optician was in a hurry, I don't know—God, Janice, am I going to be blind? Have my eyes been—"

"No, honey, you won't be blind, we'll get you to a doctor in the morning.... I think you've just scratched your eyes a bit, on the surface ... the pain won't last, honey, just try to rest."

"This is my punishment, isn't it," Ruthie sobs, "for being so vain, for leaving the order, for being such a bad person ... isn't it, Janice. *Isn't it!*"

"Don't be ridiculous," Janice says, her heart sinking. "Don't even think such a ridiculous thing. Here, honey, give me that cloth, I'll get some warm water—and stop crying, Ruthie, the tears just make it worse."

"The tears?" Ruthie moans.

"The tears," Janice says, sharply. "The salt inside the tears."

She takes the cloth and goes into the bathroom, not turning on the light until she has the door closed. It's then she understands that she's crying, too. She stares into the mirror and sees that her eyes are brimming. She twists the faucet, wringing the cloth harder than she needs to. Goddamn it, she thinks. Goddamn it to hell....

When she gets back to the bedroom, Ruthie has quieted some. Janice opens the drape a few inches, just enough to see what she is doing, and a cool ribbon of moonlight falls along the night table and the lower half of the bed. Ruthie does not complain. "Thank you," she whispers slowly, "thank you for—for helping me—" and in her broken syllables Janice can hear how much she's suffering. But Janice isn't watching her cousin. She is looking away from the bed—her own vision very sharp, very clear—to where Ruthie's spectacles are perched on the night table, illuminated in the silver fall of moonlight, glittering coldly. They are turned directly toward Janice, as if trying to stare her down. Little rimless octagons, winking in the cold light, bringing a shiver to Janice's shoulders and down the smooth length of her back. . . . "Try to get some rest," she says vaguely, "I promise you'll feel better tomorrow, things always look better in the morning. . . ."

But she doesn't say, not quite yet: Save yourself, honey, get through the pain and then save yourself—nobody else will.

It becomes amusing, after a while, the way she stares at the glinting spectacles, it's only a game she's playing, isn't it, while her cousin sleeps? Yes, but it's a serious game, and if she has to sit here until dawn, she thinks, staring down that glitter of cold knowledge, that absence of mercy—then she certainly will.

Clifford

"Sir? May I help you?" the woman says. She's a small black woman, very young, with glasses.

"I'm here for the test," Clifford says. "I'm concerned about—"

"Here you are, just fill out this form," the woman tells him. "When you hear your number"—she hands him a white plastic card, number 32—"just go back through those curtains to your left."

Numbly Clifford stands there, holding the form and his number; the woman's attention has shifted to the man in line behind him, so why doesn't Clifford move along? Had he intended to blurt out the truth to the first person he encountered? After standing there for several seconds, feeling dazed, he shuffles back to the waiting area.

A small paneled room with scuffed tables heaped with magazines, a coffee machine in one corner, ordinary folding chairs lining the walls. Almost all the chairs are taken, mostly by men in their twenties and thirties. A few look up, briefly, as Clifford walks in. After a quick glance around the room Clifford understands that he recognizes none of them and takes a deep breath, relieved. He has put off coming here, to a place called the Atlanta Gay Center, for several weeks now. He hadn't known what to expect, but it wasn't this routine atmosphere of a crowded waiting room, where men paged idly through magazines and waited their turn.

He sits. The guy next to him, a kid in his early twenties, says, "How's it going?" but Clifford doesn't look over. He mumbles a brief response. He doesn't want conversation and isn't completely sure he wants to be here. From behind the curtained doorway a male voice calls, "Number eighteen," and a man near Clifford, a small-framed guy in his fifties who looks very frightened, crosses the room and disappears behind the curtains. Clifford notices a certain tension in the room after the number is called—most of the men look up from their magazines, or shift their weight inside their chairs. One of them coughs, a few others say a word to their companions. But the moment passes and the men continue reading or just sitting, staring into space. Everything is just as before.

Clifford looks again at his number. He has a while to wait, then. He could change his mind, if he wanted to; simply get up, return the card wordlessly to the woman at the front desk, and walk out. He could do that.

He keeps sitting there. A few months ago, on a Saturday night, Clifford experienced something that he supposed could be called, technically at least, rape. Not that the situation wasn't partly his fault, but nonetheless he would call it rape. (Of course, he wouldn't use that word if he told anyone about the incident; in fact, he hasn't told anyone, nor does he plan to.) But that night was simply the culmination, he supposes, of almost a year's frenetic sexual activity, beginning shortly after his affair with Jack Lassiter ended but not, Clifford supposes, really precipitated by that, since the breakup had been long overdue and the men had said good-bye with a sense of mutual relief.

For a while, it had seemed to Clifford that his ordinary life would resume. He'd gotten back to work, finding somewhat to his surprise that he could still paint and that several local galleries, at least, still responded enthusiastically to his work; he socialized with other artists he knew, and with old friends from the university, and of course with Janice Rungren, who seemed to bear him no ill will about either the distant or recent past. He had occasional dinners with Pete, and with his father and Miriam; he'd begun to get more involved with his family, in fact, now that his half-sisters were getting older and had begun inviting him to birthday parties and school plays. He'd also accepted an offer from a local community college to teach one art course each semester, and had been surprised to discover that he was a good teacher, able to involve himself intuitively in a student's work and give criticism in tactful but precise detail. So his life had been proceeding normally, or so he'd thought; although he hadn't become involved romantically with anyone after Jack, he found himself enjoying his sense of privacy and self-sufficiency, hoping his passions were now being channeled into his work. Although his apartment building had converted to condominiums and the new management had made numerous "improvements" that distressed him, he'd decided to buy his apartment, after all, and thought it possible that he would live there for the rest of his life.

He wanted for nothing, really; he found that the grief and strife and confusion of recent years had passed out of him. One day, walking down Peachtree, he'd stopped into Christ the King Cathedral and had crossed himself with holy water. He took a seat in the back pew. This was a weekday afternoon and no one else was around. Outside was a bright April morning but the interior of the church was dark and cool. He'd sat there for a long time, feeling thankful.

Shortly after that Clifford went to a bar, a new place off Seventh Street, and picked up a man within half an hour. This was the late 1980s, a time when publicity about AIDS was at its height, and he was surprised that anyone would agree to go home with a stranger. The disease had virtually stopped spreading, he'd read, in the gay community; the men now dying were those who had contracted their infection years before. By now, Clifford felt numbed by all the warnings, the statistics, the ongoing deaths. He told himself that he couldn't think about it, that whatever happened, happened, and when the men he brought home wanted to fuck him, Clifford let them, saying nothing about a condom, asking no questions. When one of them asked him a question, as they often did, Clifford would say honestly that he hadn't been tested and really had no idea. At that point, his partner would usually insist on "safe sex," and Clifford gladly went along with that. It was Clifford's habit, during this time, to go along with just about anything. During those first weeks of his immersion in unfashionable promiscuity, it never occurred to him that his behavior was self-destructive, perhaps even a form of suicide.

Nor did he link his activity to a need for punishment, or to some desperate wish to change his life at whatever cost. All that came later. At the time, he simply began seeking out men, in bars, in parks, even in a certain infamous men's room at the university, as though this were merely part of his routine. This behavior went on for eight or nine months. None of his friends or relatives could have thought anything had changed, for Clifford himself was not exactly conscious of a change, mainly because he never thought about it. His behavior was obsessive but blind: instinctive in the purest sense.

He sits holding his white plastic card, reading the posters on the wall. One is a huge map of Georgia, with a "demographic break-down" of all reported AIDS cases in the state. Each case is represented by a tiny red dot, and in the rural areas—the northern mountains, the farm country to the south—there is only a pointillist smattering of dots that Clifford could count on both hands. But in the north central section, roughly where the heart would be if the poster depicted a man, the red spots gradually thicken in all directions as they near Atlanta, and the city itself is one large undifferentiated blob of red. Clifford stares at this red area, which is perhaps four inches in diameter, for several long seconds. Into his mind's eye floats the face of Will Prather, the young boy he'd known and loved but who hadn't, perhaps, really known Clifford. When thinking of that lively mischievous kid, whom he'd loved almost at once and with such reasonless passion, Clifford no longer feels acute pain or grief but a sense of great vacancy, as though the true loss were not his lover but some essential part of himself. Clifford is fortunate, he supposes, that he has lost only one close friend to this epidemic. Not long ago he bluntly asked a couple of his friends, and his Uncle Pete, whether they'd been tested, and they answered without hesitation, as though the question was not unusual. They had tested negative. All negative. For several days he'd felt buoyed by relief. He would lose no one else, then. They were safe, all safe. It was the next weekend that he'd gone to that notorious leather bar in midtown and drank several dry Manhattans and allowed himself to be half coaxed, half dragged out of the bar.

He lets his gaze drift to the next poster, which illustrates various sexual activities and places them into categories. The safe, the possibly safe, the unsafe. Touching, mutual masturbation, and fantasy are definitely safe, the poster says. This good news, printed in pale pink letters, is accompanied by an awkward line drawing of two men lying in bed, each with one hand on the other, each smiling blissfully. As for fellatio, *but not to the point of climax,* this is possibly safe. As is anal sex, *provided a condom is used.* Even with a condom, *withdrawal before the point of climax is strongly recommended.* Printed in letters of deep pink, this advice is accompanied by a three-part drawing which illustrates how to put on a condom.

At the bottom of the poster, in bold red letters, is a list of unsafe practices. Fucking without a condom, swallowing semen, fist-fucking, rimming. S&M activity which involves the drawing of blood. These proscribed activities are not illustrated, but the bright scarlet lettering, the word UNSAFE printed in all caps, says it all.

The kid next to him, who has been fidgeting in his chair ever since Clifford arrived, sees him reading the poster. "Pretty grim, huh?" he says, smiling. The kid is cracking his knuckles, methodically, one after the other. Clifford doesn't know how to answer, so he merely shrugs and smiles. Glancing at the kid, Clifford sees that he's very attractive—longish blond hair, a swimmer's build. He can't be more than nineteen. Again Clifford thinks of Will. When the voice behind the curtain calls out, "Number nineteen, please," the kid stands up and says, "See ya." Clifford smiles again, barely able to hide his relief.

The guy he'd met at that leather bar had also been blond, and had seemed quite young. At least, he'd seemed young when they were still inside. Clifford had been sitting at the bar, nursing his third Manhattan, when he'd sensed somebody's body heat beside him; the guy stood very close, as though deliberately violating Clifford's private space, and when Clifford edged away, the guy came closer still. Clifford finally looked at him: about six feet, very light blond hair, a square-cut face with the mean expression that was standard in this place. He wore jeans, a black leather vest with no shirt, a leather string tied around one bicep. Clifford heard the guy mutter something and so Clifford leaned toward him—feeling at that moment how drunk he was, fearing that he might even fall off the bar stool—and heard the guy say, "Drink up, bud." Another Manhattan had appeared in front of Clifford, though he hadn't ordered it. "Drink up," the guy said again. Clifford drank, and the moment he put down his glass he felt a strong grip under his arm, lifting him off the stool, and the next thing he knew they were outside, stumbling into a battered Chevy pickup. The guy hadn't said anything else, and Clifford tried to think of how to protest, how to get out of this, but somehow the words didn't come. His will not to accompany this guy was weaker, evidently, than the guy's desire for Clifford, so that by the time they were in the truck, driving down Piedmont Avenue, Clifford had resigned himself. Why else had he come to the bar, after all? Wasn't this what he'd wanted?

Only when they got to the guy's apartment did Clifford's doubts get stronger. Inside the small messy kitchen, under a harsh overhead light, he saw that the man was no kid, but might be in his late thirties or even older. It had been a long time since Clifford had slept with anyone older than himself, and now he noticed a pair of deep scars along the man's throat. He stood awkwardly while the guy turned away and opened a bottle of bourbon and poured two large drinks, straight. "Here's to ya," the man said, downing his drink in one swallow. Clifford saw that his eyes were blue but very small, and that they never looked directly at Clifford. "Hey, what's your name, anyway?" Clifford said, smiling, wanting to make light of this. The man rinsed out his glass, took a quart of milk out of the refrigerator, filled the glass and drank down the milk. Briefly he closed his eyes as though in pain.

"Reckon that don't matter," he said, then came forward and again gripped Clifford's arm.

The next half an hour passed in a blur, and in the past few months Clifford has thought and dreamed about the incident so obsessively that he is no longer sure what really happened. He found himself in the guy's bed, face down, naked and spread-eagled, his wrists and ankles tied to the bed's four posts. By the time they'd reached the bedroom Clifford had felt more than drunk: he was light-headed, woozy, and had a sudden image of the guy making those two drinks, his back to Clifford. Had he put something in Clifford's drink, then? Clifford felt vaguely that he should do something, say something, but he could not put his thoughts together.

He lay on the bed and watched as the guy, also naked, approached him. He held something to Clifford's lips—something round and white—and said roughly, "Open your mouth. Come on." Clifford opened his mouth, docile as a communicant, and the guy stuffed the object inside it. A ball of white cloth. A gag. The guy took a roll of bandage tape from the bedside table and wound it twice across Clifford's mouth and around his head. "There ya go," the guy said, "that should do the trick." He stood for a moment, looking down, stroking his large but flaccid penis only inches from Clifford's face. The guy's eyes looked dreamy and almost gentle. "Okay, then," he said, slapping Clifford's buttocks. "Now the fun begins."

At that point Clifford gave himself over to the effects of the drug. He wanted sleep. He wanted to sleep long and deeply and to wake only when this was over. But when the guy lit a candle and began dropping bits of hot wax along Clifford's back and buttocks, his eyes opened wide in pain. As each drop of wax fell, the guy said, "Yeah? Eh?" Clifford began struggling but the ropes were carefully tied and very strong.

His heart pounding, he stared at the small knife, still opened on the night table, that the guy had used to cut the ropes and the bandage tape. He kept craning his neck, as though to make eye contact, a mute appeal, but the guy was ignoring him. He sat on the bed behind Clifford, where he'd begun running the tip of a large dildo along the backs of Clifford's legs. As though trying to arouse him, Clifford thought. The guy had also begun slapping Clifford's buttocks, but lightly, almost playfully, so that Clifford began to breathe easier. Evidently this was all, he thought; what was called "light S&M," just a way for the guy to arouse himself and establish his dominance. Clifford winced as he felt the guy's fingers, covered with ice-cold lubricant, begin probing his buttocks. Glancing back, he saw the guy begin positioning the dildo and he also saw that the guy's penis still hung limply between his legs and now he understood. He thought he understood. The guy was impotent, probably. The macho behavior, the dominance, the kinky stuff—all because the guy couldn't get it up. To Clifford's surprise the guy employed the dildo with the gentle finesse of a doctor performing some intricate procedure. Despite the size of the dildo, there was little pain. There was even pleasure of a sort. Clifford's eyes closed; he gave his mind back over to the tranquilizer and let his muscles relax and the next thing he knew, the guy was untying him. "Look, call a cab or something," he said, going into the bathroom. When the cab arrived, the guy was still in the shower.

In subsequent days it had struck Clifford forcibly that the "rapist," if he could be called that, had been potentially in more danger from Clifford than the other way around. Given his sexual habits, it was doubtful that the guy had ever contracted anything, whereas Clifford had slept with perhaps fifty different men in the past nine months. Glancing around this waiting room, he cannot help wondering what the lives of these men are like, whether they have landed here through simple ignorance or some need for self-destruction or whether they, like the infected babies Clifford saw on TV, are "innocent victims" who are worried about something they might have done five years ago, or ten years ago, before they knew any better. He has been both amused and angered by the media reports, dividing the AIDS population into innocent and presumably "guilty" victims. For some reason Clifford recalls the absurd question-and-answer sessions held by Sister Mary Joseph back in grade school, and how tirelessly the children would persist in their tinny-voiced questions about sin, and guilt, and punishment: If you told a lie but the lie helped somebody, was it still a sin? they would ask. Yes, Sister said. If you stole a bicycle but brought it back the next day and apologized, did you still have to confess the theft to a priest? Yes, Sister said, otherwise you'll have the venial sin on your soul and you'll have to spend time in purgatory—maybe a hundred years, maybe ten thousand years, it all depends. Depends on what? the children asked. It just depends, Sister had said.

Clifford remembers that one day Janice Rungren, who normally spent theology class fidgeting or whispering or defacing her book covers, boldly raised her hand.

"Yes, Janice?" Sister said.

"What about honoring your father and mother?" Janice asked. "What if your father slaps your mother and calls the Pope a bad name and then goes down to the playroom and drinks beer? Do you *still* have to honor him? What if—"

"Janice, that's enough!" Sister had said, very displeased. She began pacing around the room. When the echo of Janice's shrill question had died away, Sister said quietly, "Children should always honor their parents, no matter what," and at that moment the bell rang and Sister's eyes lifted to the ceiling in relief.

Often during these sessions Clifford would feel impelled to ask something, though like Janice he seldom asked questions in this class. When they would talk about the Holy Innocents or pagan babies or limbo, where little babies went who had not been baptized, Clifford would think about his baby brother, Dennis, who had died of brain fever, and how upset his mother had been that he hadn't been christened. This had been one of her obsessive topics of conversation during her last days, Clifford remembers, though by then he'd shut his mother out of his awareness, stopped listening to her shrill demands and tearful questions. But years before, in fourth or fifth grade, he'd wanted to ask: What about Dennis? Will I see him when I die, or not? You mean he's got to stay in limbo, he can't *ever* see God, just because nobody baptized him before he died? And how was that his fault, exactly? Why would God be so unfair, so mean to a little baby? Could you answer me that?

Even back then, the phrase "innocent victim" had made his lip curl.

Even back then, he'd known the futility of asking such questions.

Now Clifford senses commotion, the shifting of feet and chairs, and he hears something: that voice from behind the curtain. Is it Father Milliken calling him forward, ready to hear his confession? Ready to cleanse Clifford's soul for him, render him spotless as a lamb? Feeling groggy, Clifford tries to shake himself awake, and staring at the piece of white plastic he understands at last that they're calling his number.

The efficient young woman who drew Clifford's blood asked him if he'd had "unprotected sex" in the past year, and Clifford said yes. She asked him if he'd had "questionable partners," and Clifford said yes. She asked if he understood the way HIV infection was spread, and Clifford said yes, he read the newsmagazines, he watched the television specials, he knew it all. The woman hesitated, evidently perplexed by the flat uninflected tone of Clifford's voice. He could hear another question fully formed in her mind, *Are you trying to kill yourself, then?* but instead she gave Clifford a small square of paper with his identification number printed on it—this was an anonymous test—and told him the results would be back in two weeks. *Go in peace,* Clifford thought. He thanked the woman and left.

During that two weeks Clifford enters a state of mind unfamiliar to him. He's giddy and tense, charged with a prickly energy that won't let him sit still. He spends long hours in his studio, trying to work, but finds that his half-completed canvases no longer interest him. Half-heartedly he has been preparing for a one-man show slated for the fall at a Buckhead gallery, and he has been doing his usual still lifes, with their elongated shapes and muted colors, executed in Clifford's technically proficient and deliberately passionate style; but his fingers, normally under such exquisite control, will no longer obey his will. They quiver foolishly when Clifford lifts his brush, as though taunting him. After several days of this he decides that the stress of awaiting the test results is affecting him, and that he ought to spend the time in other ways. He puts on running clothes and jogs in the park, though avoiding the area where he'd gone to pick up men. He enlists Janice Rungren's help for some long overdue shopping, holding in the back of his mind the idea that if he does become ill, he won't be strong enough to go looking for sheets and towels, blue jeans and shirts. Janice notices his manic energy as they rush through the mall, from one store to another, and says to him, laughing, "Hey, kid, where's the fire?" For the first time he thinks that he'll have to tell her, at some point; and he'll have to tell Pete, and his father, and everyone else. When he replies to Janice, "Just hyper today, I guess," he can tell from her hesitation that she sees something in his eyes, probably that old guilty, deceitful look, but instead of getting angry she just says, smiling, "Well *relax,* okay? It's a beautiful Saturday, we've got all afternoon."

And he does relax; and they meet for dinner that evening at Partners; and the entire day turns out to be the most pleasant they've ever spent together. For there's no pressure, no hidden agenda. No lingering grudges. Clifford had always known that he could like

Janice, really like her, if the circumstances would ever allow it, and as he leaves that evening he bends close, abruptly, and gives her a quick dry kiss on the cheek. Janice stands there for a moment, her lips parted in surprise, but then she steps back and rolls her eyes. "Well, honey, I guess I can live on that all week," she says, and Clifford drives home feeling absurdly happy.

He begins calling people. Steve and Joan Farley, a couple of old friends from his grad school days, who seem delighted to hear from him. Steve and Joan had gone to Woodstock, and still had their minds in the sixties; they grew little marijuana plants out on their sun deck. They invite him to dinner for the very next night, and Clifford accepts gladly. . . . Several days later he calls his father and they talk for a long while, his father evidently sensing this new openness in Clifford, and the moment they hang up Clifford calls Rita and Larry McCord, back in Texas, with whom he hasn't spoken in years, and they seem overjoyed to hear from him. . . . On the day before he's scheduled to get his test results, Clifford even calls Will's mother up in Boston, though they haven't communicated since the night before Will's death, and though Clifford had been upset that she hadn't invited him to the funeral. On the phone Mrs. Prather seems befuddled, and it takes a moment before she remembers him; after she does, she's a bit guarded but, Clifford supposes, friendly enough. She asks about his work and he asks how the rest of Will's family is doing. As they talk Clifford tells himself that Mrs. Prather doesn't seem to blame Clifford for her son's death. Nor does she seem resentful that Clifford is still alive while her son is not. Perhaps, in her mind, that absolves him of any blame. But he's only fantasizing, of course. Mrs. Prather's rather nasal Bostonian voice gives away very little. Yet when Clifford hangs up the phone, he feels again that abrupt surge of unreasoning joy.

His appointment at the Atlanta Gay Center is for 11:00 A.M., and at 10:15 he sits in his apartment with his hand on the phone. One more call, he is thinking. He doesn't quite understand why, but he has felt the need to call everyone significant in his past or present life, as though urgently bringing his life up to date, placing himself back among the living . . . and so he snatches up the phone and dials Jack's office number.

He tells the secretary, "Jack Lassiter, please."

"Mr. Lassiter is in a meeting. May I have him call you?"

"Get him out of the meeting, please. This is an urgent call."

"Sir, I really can't—"

"This is a personal call," Clifford says shortly. "An emergency. Please get him *now*."

The secretary hesitates, then puts him on hold. A few moments later Jack's voice comes on the line.

"Hello? Yes?"

"Jack, it's me. Listen, I'm calling to say—" He stops, perplexed.

"Clifford? Are you all right?" Jack says, his voice falling to a whisper.

"Listen, I didn't know what I was doing," Clifford says, groping, "I don't think either of us did. I mean, did you feel that? Did you know what you were doing?"

A long pause. Then Jack says, subdued, "No. I guess not."

"I was closed up, and so were you," Clifford says. "We were going through the motions. It was safe, very safe. Do you know what I mean?"

Another pause. Jack says, warily, "Yes . . ."

"I know this sounds corny, Jack, but I really wish you the best, and I—I guess I just wanted to apologize. To say that I'm through using people like that, whether it's you, or Janice—"

"Please," Jack interrupts him. "This isn't necessary."

"It is," Clifford says. "There might not have been another chance. I'm sure there wouldn't have been."

"All right, then. Good luck, Clifford. And thanks."

"May I tell Janice hello?" Clifford says. "I've gotten to be friends with her again, and I—"

"Sure. Tell her hello."

They say good-bye at the same moment.

Clifford sits for another few minutes, catching his breath, staring at the telephone. There's a sweaty mark on the receiver where he'd been holding it. After another minute the telephone rings, but Clifford doesn't answer. He drives to the Atlanta Gay Center and again takes a white plastic card and after half an hour is called back behind the curtain. The same brisk young woman in her white lab coat is awaiting him. She asks him to sit down, and tells him in a mechanical singsong voice that his test results are negative.

"Negative?" Clifford says blankly. "That means . . ."

"That means that there are no HIV antibodies in your blood. A false negative is quite rare," she says, seeing the look of disbelief in his eyes. She pauses. "How long has it been," she says, "since your last questionable partner?"

Clifford is staring at the woman's abdomen, which protrudes slightly; on his last visit, he hadn't noticed that she was pregnant.

"Several months," he says. "Three or four."

"Then it's probably not necessary to repeat the test," she says. "Although you may, of course, if you wish. For your own peace of mind."

"No, it's all right," Clifford says. He sits there a few moments longer, stunned.

"Sir?" the woman says. "Is there anything else?"

"No," he says, and manages to get to his feet.

Driving home, he feels besieged by a sense of unreality. The traffic, the city noises, the bright wintry sky—all seem to be receding from him, rapidly. The lightheartedness of the past two weeks has fled, and walking around his apartment, disoriented, he senses the sudden change in his body, which has begun to feel leaden, inert. He stares out the large curving window of his living room, looking down upon the city; tears start to his eyes. *Whatever happens, happens* . . . He lies down on the sofa and closes his eyes and almost at once his mind is aswarm with dreams. He is walking down the sidewalk in front of his studio, but he's being led by the hand, like a blind man. Will Prather is leading him, a smiling blond-haired Will, his body shimmering like an angel's. Will leads him inside the studio and stands at the door, watching benignly, as Clifford systematically destroys all the canvases he has painted since coming to this city. The attenuated landscapes and buildings, the dozens of muted still lifes, the handful of melancholy self-portraits. . . . Very carefully he slashes each of the canvases into several pieces and within minutes the work of his adult life is packed into a white plastic garbage bag, tied neatly at the top. Will smiles at him. He walks forward, as though to kiss him. . . . Clifford wakes, panicked. He glances at his watch, thinking that it must be late, very late, but it's only a little past noon. Scarcely more than five minutes have passed.

He gets up from the sofa and crosses the room to the telephone. Perhaps he dreamed that conversation with his father, as well? . . . and his lively talk with the McCords, and his rushing half-desperate call to Jack Lassiter? But no, he thinks soberly. He isn't dreaming, not anymore. . . . He lifts the receiver and dials. Janice answers on the first ring.

"Hello?" she says breathlessly. "Hello?"

"I didn't think you'd be home," he says.

"What? Oh, I took the day off. I had a doctor's appointment this morning, and so . . . Clifford, are you all right?"

"Listen, are you busy right now?" Clifford says.

"Now? No, I'm not busy. Clifford, is something—"

"Meet me at Country Place—at the bar," he says. "In just a little while. I need you, all right? Is that all right?"

She pauses, then says in her jokey voice, "Sure thing, kid. I'll be there. I'm never too busy for *you*."

10

Clifford

Clifford bounds up the cement stairway, two steps at a time. Navy blue suit, white dress shirt crisply starched, a tie with diagonal stripes. Clutched in one hand, a bunch of daisies: homely yellow-and-white.

Knocking on Janice's door, he feels like a teenager on his first date. He notes that his palms are clammy. He smiles. It's a bright cool morning in early October, a Sunday.

Janice flings the door wide, smiling. Her eyes brighten when she sees the flowers.

"Terrific, they're my favorite!" she says, reaching for the daisies before Clifford can offer them. Janice steps back, motioning him inside with a facetious, sweeping gesture. "Welcome," she says, "to my humble abode. You've never seen this apartment, have you? And I've lived here more than a year. . . ."

Is there a subtle tone of reproach in her voice? Clifford doesn't think so. They've continued to see each other regularly, but usually they meet at a restaurant in midtown, or Buckhead, or else Janice will stop by Clifford's place. The other evening, when they'd planned this morning's outing over the phone—this "sentimental journey," as Janice had called it, laughing—Janice had insisted that Clifford stop here first. "I want to be escorted," she'd said in a mock-imperious tone. "That's not too much to ask, is it?"

It isn't. Inside, Clifford squints back toward the dimmed apartment. It seems meagerly furnished; even the plain beige sofa and chair in the living room are different from the ones in Janice's house in Morningside. Following his gaze, Janice says offhandedly, "How do you like it? It's called Contemporary Rental. The very latest, you know."

"But what happened to—to your other stuff?"

Janice shrugs. "Got rid of it," she says. "Didn't want any reminders."

Clifford says nothing; he wonders if this morning's plans are a mistake.

"Now don't just stand there like an embarrassed schoolboy," Janice says, taking him by the hand. "Come on back to the kitchen, and I'll make you a mimosa."

"But shouldn't we—I mean, what time is it?"

"Mass doesn't start till ten," Janice says. "We've got almost an hour."

Clifford follows her back to a sunny kitchen filled with ivy plants and knickknacks of white porcelain. There's a tiny breakfast nook with a round white table, two cane-bottomed chairs. Clifford sits while Janice makes the mimosas, talking cheerfully. She's wearing a yellow silk blouse, a white pleated skirt, white pumps. At her wrists and throat are several gold chains, very delicate; there are small diamond studs in her ears. Janice's makeup is subdued, very flattering, and her hair is several inches shorter, curved along her jaw on each side. It seems shinier, less coarse . . . perhaps she has lightened it? Clifford thinks that she has never looked more attractive. Even her movements seem fastidious and graceful, traits he'd never before associated with Janice. As she approaches the table, she catches him smiling.

"Well," she says, pulling her chair close to his, "don't *you* look pleased with yourself."

Clifford sips the mimosa. "I'm glad I'm here," he says. "I'm glad we're doing this."

"Me, too," Janice says. "Like I told you, I thought it would be fun . . . but you know what? Getting ready this morning, I actually started feeling a bit nervous. I mean, how long's it been? Ten years, or twelve? I remember going to midnight mass with my parents one Christmas Eve, it must have been the late seventies . . ." Janice laughs, abruptly. "Gosh, if only my mother could see this. Wouldn't it set her heart to fluttering."

Clifford laughs, too. "But they've always been devout, haven't they?" he asks.

"I guess so," Janice says thoughtfully. "Not when I was little, but after that . . . well, I can't blame them. It's all they've got, you know? After a certain point in your life, you've got to have something, don't you?"

Clifford looks down; with Janice, ordinary conversation can take the strangest turns.

"I guess you do," he says.

Janice touches his knee. "Well, how about you?" she says. "How's the work going?"

"Not bad, I guess. I had a fallow period there for a while—some sort of depression. But I've been pulling out, and the work seems to be changing. I've started painting outside, which I never did before. There's a bit more color in the work now, I've noticed. More light."

"But you're glad now, aren't you?" Janice says, leaning forward. Her blue eyes have an earnest, almost desperate look, forcing Clifford to glance away.

"Glad? Glad about what?"

"You know, about taking that test. Finding out that you're okay."

"Of course," Clifford says uneasily. "Who wouldn't be? . . . I don't know, it was just that I'd gotten accustomed to the idea that I *was* infected, so I had to readjust my thinking. It didn't take long, really. Just a few weeks."

Again she touches his knee; again she is smiling. "Well, I'm glad you're back," she says. "Back among the living."

Following some stray impulse Clifford takes her hand from his knee and in a single movement raises it to his lips; he kisses one side of the hand, then the other, holding it gently in both his own. Then he takes her other hand and repeats the gesture. When he looks up, Janice's face wears a stricken look. Her eyes are moist.

"You look nice," Clifford says.

Janice has withdrawn her hands, cupping them in her lap. Her face has turned a girlish pink. "Thanks," she says softly. "So do you. In fact, I can't remember seeing you in a suit before. Not one that wasn't black, anyway."

"It's new," Clifford says. "Not long ago, Uncle Pete dragged me out to Lenox Square. He said we weren't leaving until I bought a complete new wardrobe, so I did."

Janice laughs. "You always wore black, even in school. Black jeans, those awful black shirts . . ."

Clifford feels a twinge of nostalgia, hearing this; he'd always liked the black clothes.

"I was wondering, Clifford," Janice says, leaning forward again, her blue eyes peering into his, "I wondered if that was your way of mourning, sort of. You know, for the loss of your mother? I always hoped you'd talk to me about that, about how you felt—but you never did."

Clifford sits there a long moment, stymied. He says, "I guess I still can't. Not yet, anyway."

"Sure," Janice says quickly. "I understand."

At the same moment, they glance at their watches.

"Twenty till," Janice says.

"Okay, then," Clifford says. "Let's go."

They sit near the back of the church, not far from the center aisle. Following Janice's lead, Clifford had touched his fingertips to the marble font of holy water in the vestibule, and had genuflected briefly before entering the pew. They're a few minutes early, and they spend the time looking around them, amazed by the vaulting Gothic spaces above their heads, dwarfing the packed congregation and making Clifford feel that he and Janice are children once again, sitting quietly in their Sunday finest, hands folded in their laps. It might be the early 1960s, he supposes, as there are few changes: the same marble altar with its crisp white cloth, the same candelabra and statues of St. Joseph and the Blessed Virgin. This church, like the one Clifford and Janice had known as children, has stained-glass windows depicting the Stations of the Cross. The only difference, he supposes, is the congregation itself. There isn't the hushed pre-mass quiet he remembers from childhood: most of the people are talking among themselves, not even bothering to whisper. And very few of the women have covered their heads, which somehow unsettles Clifford. One of the exceptions is a young dark-haired woman in a pink suit, sitting almost directly in front of Clifford and Janice: she wears a white lace mantilla reaching past her shoulders. Between the woman and her husband are their small children, a boy and two girls, all under age eight. The children are exquisite replicas of the parents, their hair dark and shining, pink faces glowing with health. Every few seconds the mother bends down, smiling, her own face pink and glowing, to answer one of their questions, or to straighten a hair bow or collar. Clifford scrutinizes this attractive family for several long minutes, and he's aware that next to him, Janice is watching them, too. But Janice has been hungrily watching everything; her intense curiosity is almost palpable as she sits fidgeting, craning her neck, taking everything in. When he glances at his watch—it's one minute before ten—she clutches at his forearm.

"Oh Clifford, look over there," she whispers.

He follows her gaze to the side aisle, where a pair of nuns are gliding slowly toward the front of the church. They're wearing old-fashioned habits—veils and floor-length robes of deep blue, starched white wimples—and appear to be quite elderly. One of the nuns is holding the other's arm; they move very slowly, stepping sideways in identical movements when they reach a half-empty pew. Several people have scooted down the pew to make room for them, smiling and gesturing.

Clifford glances at Janice, who is still clutching his arm; her face wears a dazed, almost beatific expression.

"Maybe we know them," Clifford says dryly. "They look old enough."

Janice doesn't seem to hear. "My God, Cliff, I didn't think

we'd see . . . and still wearing the old habits, can you believe it? Isn't that something?"

Clifford smiles. He bends close to Janice and lightly kisses her cheek. "Thrilling," he says. "I wouldn't have missed it."

Janice scowls in mock reproof. "Don't be sarcastic, Cliff," she whispers. "Not today, of all days."

He's about to ask what she means, but just then the organ music sounds: the rich deep chords vibrate in his rib cage and, at first, he feels startled and apprehensive. But after a minute, he allows the music to enter him. Looking toward the altar, he sees the priest in glittering satin vestments begin ascending the marble steps toward the tabernacle. The altar is decked extravagantly with flowers: irises, lilies, white carnations, white roses. Perhaps there was a wedding in the church, last evening; Clifford remembers that wedding leftovers were often used the next morning at Sunday mass. . . . Two altar boys have followed the priest and now stand attentively near the bottom of the steps. Their black-and-white vestments aren't much different from the ones Clifford wore as an altar boy. Abruptly the organ music stops and the priest begins speaking, echoed by the altar boys' high-pitched responses.

Although Clifford knew that most masses nowadays are conducted in English, the words have an alien sound. The English translation sounds cheap, ordinary, and the corresponding Latin phrases come with amazing speed to his mind's ear. *Dominus vobiscum* . . . *Et cum spiritu tuo* . . . He continues watching the priest and altar boys for a minute or two, lulled by his mental repetition of the Latin phrases; but then, as always happened when he was young, his mind starts to wander.

He feels detached from what is happening, as usual, but also has a pleasant sense of destiny. There's a vicarious pleasure in sitting next to Janice, sharing her excitement, sensing that she's achieved a kind of wholeness and integrity in her life that he might not have predicted for her, even a few years ago. Perhaps she thinks the same about him? They've both reached, he supposes, some sort of plateau, perhaps a vague recognition that they're merely part of the world: that it's large enough to include them, after all. He can imagine Janice's bright shrill laughter if he were to express such a thought, but he doubts that she would really disagree. Despite all the turbulence they've endured—the terrible fights, the long estrangements—he understands that their lives have run a parallel course, have formed a sort of pattern, almost as if he and Janice had known that as long as one of them was alive, then the other could never be entirely alone.

Clifford's thoughts drift in this way through most of the mass. He pays little attention to the sermon: some vague words on the subject of "free will," which the plump middle-aged priest delivers in a dull monotone. When the collection plate comes around, he watches Janice drop an envelope into the basket, but feels not a twinge of guilt that he has nothing to offer. When large groups of people begin rising for the communion service, there is no question of Clifford and Janice joining them, but their pleasure in the spectacle is apparently mutual; he senses, for instance, that Janice is also watching the young couple sitting in front of them, instructing their three small children to sit quietly while the parents leave their pew for communion. Now the young mother stands, and is escorted into the aisle by her husband. Both are in their late twenties, dark-haired, beautifully groomed and dressed. Like Clifford and Janice, the three children watch their handsome parents as they proceed up the aisle. Only when the young woman stops and turns halfway back, to smile and wink briefly at her children, does Clifford notice that the woman is pregnant. Her pink linen suit bells outward unmistakably at the abdomen, and again Clifford marvels that her face is also a fine lovely pink, as though radiant with health and well-being as she smiles back toward the pew. One of the children—the smallest one, a boy aged three or four—can't resist lifting his hand in a little wave.

Watching this storybook family, Clifford cannot help thinking of his own family, and as the organ music swells to accompany the communicants surging toward the altar, he's flooded by waves of an aching and limitless sorrow. He closes his eyes, thinking that he'll have to root inside his pockets for a Kleenex, when he feels that his hand is no longer free. Without his quite knowing it, Janice's hand has found his: her fingers have closed quietly around his own.

Janice

When the mass is over, Janice and Clifford file out into the brilliant autumn morning with everyone else. A flood of cheerful, chatting parishioners!—and it seems that she and Clifford are among them. They stand out on the steps for a few moments, looking around, as if waiting to see someone they know. Just as they're turning away, Janice notices that lovely dark-haired woman in the pink suit and white lace mantilla, each of her hands clutching one of her children's hands. The small boy looks up at Janice for a brief moment, aware that she's staring at him intently, hungrily: he gives her a shy smile.

In the car, she and Clifford talk idly about going to a restaurant for brunch, or perhaps stopping at a delicatessen and taking their food into Piedmont Park—it's such a beautiful day, the temperature in the high sixties—but Janice knows that he's still thinking of the church service, too. During the communion period, in particular, Janice had felt her throat tightening, the deep-toned organ music helping to swell the emotion in her chest. Seeing that the pink-dressed woman in front of them was pregnant, Janice had felt that she might lose control entirely and had grasped Clifford's hand, in mingled desperation and joy. But he hadn't reacted, and she hadn't dared to look at him. Nor had he released her hand for several long minutes.

They're driving along Peachtree toward midtown, but aimlessly, for they haven't yet decided what to do. There's still a confused emotional atmosphere in the car, heady and pleasant, but unpredictable. As always, she cannot really imagine what Clifford might be thinking.

"So, do you think you'll go back?" she says to him, smiling.

He looks over, with his little half-smirk. "Sure thing," he says. "But I suppose you will, now that you're supporting the Vatican. . . ."

So he'd seen her drop that envelope into the basket. Now something unusual happens: she blushes. Early that morning, the offering had seemed a clever idea, something the prankish Janice Rungren might be expected to do; she'd enjoyed imagining the priest's expression when he opened the envelope. But the gesture had been serious, after all. And one that would please the priest, perhaps, once he recovered from the shock.

"Just this once," Janice says, slyly. She wants to tell Clifford about the envelope, but she doesn't want to frighten him.

They drive silently for a while. Sunlight streams into the car, across their laps; Janice imagines that she is warmed to her very marrow. For several days the question she wants to ask Clifford has been rising in her, half-voiced, timorous, but she can hardly imagine that she will find the words. In church, when Clifford had sat holding her hand, she'd almost leaned aside and whispered the question then, her emotion had been so strong; but abruptly the music had ended and she saw the priest turning away from the front railing. The communion service was over.

Now she sits feeling the blood coursing in her veins, beating strongly, the blood itself warmed by the sun and her own strange happiness. She understands that Clifford is turning the car into a lot across from his building, though they hadn't discussed going to his place; but she doesn't question him, she doesn't care where they're going. All at once she no longer cares how he will react, either, or how that priest might have reacted, opening an ordinary envelope to find no money, only a small white plastic coil that vaguely resembled a money clip. Would a priest even recognize an IUD when he saw one? Janice wonders. But she supposes it doesn't matter.

And perhaps it doesn't matter how Clifford will respond when she finally manages to frame her stupendous question. Though her obsessive thoughts about a child, a baby, have been with her only for a few months, it seems like many years, like the great dream of her life, appearing to her only recently in the way the saints of legend had received their visions. If not Clifford, she thinks fervently, then someone else; but, on the other hand, surely it must be Clifford.

In the graveled lot, he has parked the car but he keeps the engine running and they both keep sitting there. His face is grave, thoughtful; it might be that he is reading her mind, Janice thinks, that the parallel tracks of their lives have converged at last. This is a fanciful notion but somehow she believes it, has faith in it. Perhaps it's her faith that puts the happy, reasonless smile on her face as she turns her body toward him.

At that moment he takes her hands, both of them, and lifts them to his lips, just as he had done at her apartment. Again he kisses the fingers one by one, his face still very grave, unsmiling.

"Clifford," she says, trying for a light mocking tone despite the scalding lump in her chest, her throat, "just why have you brought me here, exactly? You don't expect a good Catholic girl to spend time in a grown man's apartment, do you? Without a chaperone?"

He has put down her hands, but he keeps holding them. He smiles patiently, or is it wearily.

"I didn't know where to go," he says, "so I brought us here."

"It's all right," she says, then pauses. "I thought you knew"— that bright reasonless smile won't leave her face—"I thought you knew what I wanted to ask you."

"Ask me?" he says, faintly. "You wanted to ask me—?"

"A favor," she says. "A small favor, or a big one, depending on your point of view."

He looks bewildered but docile: like a schoolboy, she thinks.

"Yes, Clifford Bannon," she says, "I need a favor from you. I really do."

And now he smiles, too; yes, Janice thinks, surely he has read her thoughts all along.

With a quick, decisive movement, he shuts off the ignition.

"You name it," he says.